The Sixth Family
Seeds Of Power

Anthony Felicette

The Sixth Family

Table Of Contents

Acknowledgements

First and foremost I would like to thank the Lord my God. Without Him nothing is possible. He is the source of all that is good. He provides the inspiration and the talent that goes into something like this.

To my beautiful wife Pamela. You have supported me one hundred percent though out this entire process. You looked beyond your issues with it and helped me to bring it to life. You helped with the Spanish text and gave your time to bring your amazing cooking for the photo shoot. Thank you, I love you!

To my friends Javier, Ñero, Carlos and Jessie, for the help you provided with the casting call and the photo shoot. Without you it would have been chaos! You kept order and endured long days of work. You helped ensure that we had the very best cast. Your pictures came out awesome and added so much to this project! Thank you so much.

To the amazing cast that helped to bring these characters to life. I am truly blessed to have you all on this project and I am looking forward not only to working on the entire series with you, but to also bring this to other media. Thank you Ceazar, Charles, Diana, Frank, Haley, Jennifer, Jessica, Jesus, Joan, Linda, Lizette, Marcos, Sara, Vincent C., and Vincent D. Let's make a movie!

To our truly talented hair and makeup artist, Lisette. You did incredible work and I can only imagine what you're going to do when we bring this into a movie. I look forward to a long working relationship with you!

To Peter, thank you for your advice, much needed criticism, and hard work proofreading this. You did a great job! I couldn't have done it without you.

Last, but not least to my friend, Lysa Walker from Runaway Publications. What started as a passing conversation turned into you inspiring me to take a project that was collecting dust for the last twenty five years and actually do something with it. Not only that, but you are now also a friend. You helped me to make a dream come true. Thank you!

Chapter 1
A Fateful Phone Call

A nthony Farrell laid in bed in a sound sleep. It was just past eight o'clock, on a spring Monday morning, in 1988. He had a rough night before. He and a few friends had gone on a mission for the club. A local gambler had owed 'Joey Numbers' a couple of thousand dollars from last week's bets and he didn't want to pay up. So Anthony and the boys went to collect.

Anthony was a tall slim man, very quiet but with a temper like dynamite. You didn't want to get him started. He often did a lot of work for the club, as the neighborhood guys liked him a lot. Seventeen years old and he was already part of the club. He was in tight with a lot of the soldiers and knew a lot of the Capo-Regimes. The one fact that stood out the most about him was that he was in tight with all five of the New York Families, although he did most of his work with the Garbaci's. That made a lot of people nervous because no one knew what to say around him, so no one really ever talked around him about anyone else. They just gave him his work and he went off and did it. What he didn't know was today his work was going to change his life forever.

The phone rang two, maybe three times before he jumped out of his sleep to answer it. "Hello," he replied in a groggy voice. "Who's this? Enzo, what's up?"

He sat up and looked over at his clock. "Do you know what time it is, Enzo?"

Anthony didn't usually get mad at his friends calling him so early in the morning, but today he was in no mood to talk on the phone. He knew that if it was Enzo calling him it must be important.

Enzo was one of his best friends. They had known each other for only a few years but they got very close. Anthony had only two other people that were just as close to him: his girlfriend Debbie and his other friend, Mike Maffasio.

Debbie and Mike were close friends as well. Mike was the reason Anthony met Debbie, and Anthony was happy about that.

On the other hand Mike and Enzo weren't close friends. They got along with each other but only when it was convenient for one of them. Only if one needed something from the other. Anthony kept the peace between the two of them, which was usually very hard to do. There was a time when the two of them almost came to blows and Anthony had to step between them. That wasn't entirely smart on Anthony's part considering that Enzo is around five feet ten inches tall and about one hundred and eighty five pounds. Mike being about an inch shorter and ten pounds lighter. Anthony loved his friends though. It was hard for him with Enzo and Mike always being at each other's throats. He felt like he was caught in the middle.

"What can I do for you Enzo?" He sat there in silence for a second as he listened to Enzo on the phone. "You had another fight with her?"

Enzo was rambling on about his girlfriend Joanne and all the problems he had with her. Anthony wasn't particularly crazy about her. She was the immature type and if she didn't have things her way they weren't going any other way. But other than that he really had no problems with her.

"All right Enzo. Listen, meet me at my house." There was a moment of silence. "What do you mean no? Come on En I'm fucking tired. I was up all night kicking the shit out of some asshole. I don't want to go out now. Just come here." Again there was a moment of silence and by this time Anthony was starting to get annoyed. "You know En you're a pain in the ass. What time do you want me to meet you?" Anthony looked over at his clock again. "Fine. I'll meet you outside the club on 77th in two hours. Right. I'll talk to you later. Bye." Anthony reached over and hung the phone up with disgust. He sat up in bed for a minute and then decided to finally get up. He stood up and felt a load of pain down his back. "Oh shit" he moaned to himself. It was days like this that he hated working for the club. His whole body felt sore from the fight he had the night before.

He stumbled into the kitchen and poured himself a glass of juice. Then walked to the bathroom and ran his shower while he picked out what he was going to wear for the day.

He sat on the bed for a second and looked up at a picture of Debbie he had on his dresser. He looked at it like he was in a daze. He really cared for her and he knew she cared for him. That's why she fought with him so much about the kind of life he was leading. Always going out to the club, hanging out with everyone till all hours of the night. She always told him look for a job and try to straighten out his life, but he never really listened to her. She worried about him like crazy when he went off on his missions for the club. They usually ended up fighting the night before, he would storm out of the house and by the time he got back from the job he was on she would usually be so happy to see that he was all right that she'd forget about being mad at him.

He stood up and walked over to the picture, picked it up and kissed it. "I love you Sweetheart," he mumbled to himself. He picked up his clothes and went to the bathroom to take his shower. Once he was done with that it was on to his date with destiny.

Chapter 2
A Friend in Need

Enzo Crescenti stood outside the 77th Street social club waiting for Anthony to meet him. He paced back and forth nervously while he smoked a cigarette.

Enzo was a year older than Anthony. He looked older but he didn't act it. He and Joanne were always going at it and today it came to a head. The two of them finally decided to call it quits and go their separate ways. Enzo was really upset about the decision. You could look at him and see it on his face. When you looked at his eyes you could see tears starting to form. Enzo was a strong person though and he wouldn't let his emotions get the best of him.

He continued to pace back and forth nervously. He looked at his watch, "Come on Ant, I got things to do," he mumbled to himself. Enzo reached into his pocket to take out a quarter. He was getting ready to beep Anthony again when he noticed him crossing the street.

Anthony walked up to Enzo and smiled, Enzo started to laugh. "Fuck you," said Enzo, "I'm standing here an hour waiting for you."

"I'm sorry En," replied Anthony, "I got tied up on my way out the door. Teresa called me."

"Teresa?" asked Enzo.

"Teresa, Mike's girlfriend."

"Oh yeah now I remember. How is she?" asked Enzo

Anthony replied, "She's doing good. Really, I'm sorry I'm late."

Enzo felt bad, but Anthony really knew he wasn't angry with him. Enzo couldn't stay mad at Anthony, they were too good of friends to stay mad at each other. They were so close they treated each other like brothers. The two of them had a bond between them that no one could break. Anthony was like that with Mike as well.

"It's okay Ant, really, I'm not mad" replied Enzo.

"So what's up? What's so important?"

Enzo and Anthony stared at each other. Anthony could tell that he was really upset and Anthony didn't like to see his friends like that. "I'm feeling really depressed." Enzo started to pace back and forth again. "I don't know what's wrong with me."

"I do," Anthony replied, "It's Joanne."

Enzo looked at him and then looked away really fast. He could feel himself holding back tears. Tears of pain from losing Joanne.

Anthony read him like a book. "When are you gonna cut this shit out? I'm tired of seeing you like this. If you and her can't come to some kind of a compromise then it's better if you break up."

"We did." Enzo was silent for a long minute. So was Anthony. "We broke up this morning."

Anthony began feeling bad for the way he just went off on him. "I'm sorry En. I didn't know. Maybe it's better this way. I know just how you feel. I've gone through it. We all go through it."

"I'm just trying to put it out of my mind, but I need a little something to help me."

Anthony studied Enzo's face for a minute. "What are you talking about?" he asked seriously.

Enzo tried to word what he wanted to say but there was just no way to say it except to just come out with it. "Maybe I can get some drugs. Cocaine, pot."

Anthony was shocked with what he just heard come out of Enzo's mouth. "Are you serious or just crazy?"

"I'm serious," he replied. "I've got to do something to get my spirit up."

Now Anthony began to pace. He had never taken drugs or anything like that. He saw friends of his take drugs and it sickened him. "I don't know En. Pot's one thing but you're not gonna do cocaine."

"Ant really, I'm serious, I want pot and cocaine. I don't want crack or anything like that. Just pot and cocaine. Do you know where I can get it?"

"Oh Enzo I don't know about this." Anthony knew he couldn't talk him out of this. "How about Mike? Mike knows a lot of people who handles that shit."

Enzo looked at Anthony. "I don't like Mike. I don't get along with Mike."

Anthony replied, "I know him good, Debbie knows him good. I get along with him. If you want I'll deal with him and then after a while I'll set you up to deal with him."

"I don't know Ant. I don't want to get garbage, I want to get good stuff."

Anthony couldn't believe what was coming out of his own mouth. "He gets good stuff. Trust me."

Enzo smiled. He knew he got Anthony to support him and with Anthony's backing that meant he now had the club behind him even more than before.

Anthony's mind raced a mile a minute. He couldn't believe what he was getting himself into. When Debbie found out there was going to be a huge brawl and this one wasn't going to end overnight. "You know how to get me into these businesses. This is serious shit."

"I know, but I need something to pick myself up. Think about it. The club has been trying to raise you in the ranks anyway. This might be your boost. If they see you do this you'll be noticed more and you'll rise up quickly." Enzo paused for a second and then said "I can also pass you on to more than a few people that I know. It can be a good business for you."

Anthony thought about what Enzo was saying to him and it made a lot of sense and began to appeal to him. For the longest time he'd been trying to rise up the ranks. This might be his big chance. "Alright don't worry about it. The only thing to do is go to Mike."

Enzo could feel the aggravation inside him when he heard Mike's name. Enzo thought for a minute and if he had to deal with Mike then that's all that he could do. For Anthony's sake he would keep the peace with Mike and not start anything. Enzo looked at Anthony dead in the eyes and Anthony knew he wasn't playing around. Anthony knew he had gotten himself involved with something that might be too much to handle.

"Let me tell you something," spoke Enzo; "if Mike gives me one hair of trouble I'll waste him."

Enzo's words rang through Anthony's ears like a loud bell. Anthony knew the kind of temper that Enzo had and he knew he was one hundred percent serious about what he was saying.

"All right Enzo I'll take care of it," Anthony replied. "Don't worry about anything."

"Believe me, I'm not worried."

Anthony felt uneasy around Enzo for some strange reason. Perhaps it was because of this new business that they were about to get involved in, or it could have been the intensity that was coming from Enzo. Never the less the fact remained that Anthony had a lot of business to take care of and if he was going to get anything done he had better get going.

"Listen En, I have to go to the club and see if I can find Mike and try to get things going. I also have to talk to some people in the club and find out if we can have backing for this."

"Alright," replied Enzo. "Just give me a call tonight and let me know what's up."

"No problem En. I'll talk to you later."

"Alright, talk to you later."

The two of them shook hands and walked their separate ways. It was all racing through Anthony's head too fast. He got about a half a block away and turned around to look at Enzo. He felt bad for his friend. He knew what it was like to be in a situation like that. He knew how Enzo felt for Joanne but he still couldn't believe that Enzo had turned to drugs. But what prayed on his mind the most was the fact that he was helping him to do it.

Anthony stared at his friend off in the distance walking away and he felt a cold chill run down his back. He almost felt empty and alone. He stood there staring and said to himself "My God, what am I doing?"

Chapter 3
A Business Dinner

D ebbie moved around the kitchen like she was in a race. She was a short girl only five foot three inches tall, but she had a heart the size of the world. She had a slim but voluptuous body. She had long, curly brown hair and dark brown eyes. She had a pretty face that looked like it belonged to an angel. She was nineteen years old and not too far off from twenty, a few years older than Anthony. She was the second of three children having two half-sisters. She was very smart and had graduated high school a year early and landed a good job with an accounting agency. She agreed to go to college part time to get her accounting degree and her mother agreed to let her get her own apartment. Her mother wasn't that happy with the situation but if it made Debbie happy then that's all that mattered to her.

Anthony and Debbie had been together for a year and they were happy together. The only time a problem came up between the two of them was when Anthony went on a mission for the club; and he goes on a lot of them. Debbie was not happy about the work he does. She argues with him and even pleads with him not to go on his missions but he never seems to listen.

Anthony had asked Debbie to make dinner for him tonight as a favor. Mike and his girlfriend Teresa were coming over and Anthony wanted to speak to Mike about Enzo and his plans. If Anthony needed to get drugs for Enzo, Mike was the person to speak to. Mike was just as involved with the club as Anthony. Anthony was in the numbers and loan sharking end and Mike was in the drug end.

Anthony knew he had to get Mike alone to talk to him about the deal and that was going to be hard with the girls around. He had hoped for a chance in the evening when the girls would go in another room and leave the two to their business. Anthony would really be in hot water if Debbie found out about what he was about to do. He knew he couldn't hide it from her forever, but the longer the better.

Debbie was hurrying around trying to finish dinner. She ran late at work and everyone was going to be there any minute. She was just taking the pot of water with the macaroni off the stove when the bell rang. Her dog started barking like a mad man when he heard the bell.

"One minute," Debbie called out. She put the pot down, dried off her hands and answered the door.

Anthony walked in and threw his arms around his girlfriend and hugged her like he hadn't see her in years. She held him tight and kissed him long. "What was that for?" she asked.

"That was because I love you," he replied.

Debbie loved to hear things like that. It made her feel special. "I love you to." She kissed him again. "Come in, dinner's almost ready."

"It smells great."

"Thank you." Anthony walked into the kitchen and looked around.   "What's wrong?" Debbie asked.

"How much food did you make sweetheart?" he replied.

Debbie started to laugh. "Oh come on, you know how Mike eats. I was afraid I wasn't going to have enough so I made a lot extra."

"Well," Anthony started, "I'm sure during the week I'll find room to eat it. I love your cooking."

"You really like it that much?"

"Almost as much as I like you."

Debbie smiled at Anthony and then went back to her cooking. She was silent for a minute and then she started thinking. "Anthony?"

"Yeah Sweetheart?"

"How come all of a sudden you wanted to have Teresa and Mike over for dinner?"

Anthony started to get nervous. He turned his back to Debbie and went into the refrigerator to get something to drink. "No special reason."

"It seemed awfully funny the way the invitation came out of the blue," she replied.

Anthony was thinking for a way out of this conversation. He knew if he kept along he was in for it. "Well, you don't mind, do you?" Before she could reply he knew he said the wrong thing. That question would only drag out the conversation longer.

"No, of course not," she replied. "It's just you're not usually one for dinners with friends. You usually prefer to hang out in the club with them."

"Well, I figured you haven't seen Teresa in a while and I know how you feel about the club so this is a chance for us to hang out without the pressures of my other friends being around," Anthony replied.

Debbie looked at him, daring herself to ask him what she wanted to. "So you mean no discussing business tonight?" Anthony began to feel trapped again and was searching for a way out. He turned towards her and put his arm around her. "Be careful, I'm near knives," she said.

Anthony smiled, "We both know Mike better than that," he started, "business is bound to come up tonight. That's why I figured Teresa was a good idea."

Debbie looked up at him and stared for a moment. She could never stay mad at him and it was hard to even get mad at him. She loved him very much. "Well, me and Teresa haven't hung out in a while so I guess we could use the time together. Just promise me one thing."

"What's that?" he asked.

"Talk about business in a different room then me and Teresa's."

Anthony smiled. He now knew inside he could pull off his little caper tonight. His plan was in motion. "Sure Sweetheart," he replied, "for you, anything."

Anthony reached down and kissed Debbie softly on her lips. She replied back with a stronger one. She felt completely safe when she was in his arms. Almost like no one could get near her and hurt her. He too felt the same when he was around her. All the business on his mind was shifted to the back of his head and all he could do was think about being with her. He kissed her again, this time much longer. At that instant the doorbell rang.

"Oh man, right now they had to come," Anthony said.

"You invited them," she replied. "You get the door while I finish dinner."

Anthony moved to the door to let his friends in. Once again racing through his mind was the meeting he had with Enzo earlier that day. He still could not believe what his friend was doing, or about to do with his life. But what shocked him more was that he was going to help him do it. The doorbell rang once again with Anthony still standing in the same spot he was the first time it rang.

Debbie looked at him puzzled. "Hello. Are you going to answer the door or are they going to eat outside?"

"What?" Anthony asked puzzled.

"What's wrong?" she asked. "You all right?"

"Yeah, I'm fine." He started towards the door again this time answering it. He greeted Teresa with a kiss hello and Mike with the usually ceremonious handshake and kiss cheek to cheek.

Teresa was a pretty young lady eighteen years old. She stood about three inches shorter then Debbie. She had long brown frizzy hair and brown eyes. Her and Mike were a match made in heaven. All the two of them ever do is fight. The only difference between them and Enzo and Joanne is they make up quicker. Also, Teresa wasn't as childish as Joanne was. Teresa's second love was going to dance clubs. That's where her main arguments with Mike come into play. Mike wanted to go to the social clubs, whether it was the Borden or the Trinity, and Teresa wanted either Ascension's or Aveo's. Teresa wasn't as hard on Mike with his involvement with the club like Debbie was with Anthony. That's not really due to a lack of love but more to her being used to it. She had the attitude if you can't beat them, join them.

Anthony and Teresa were very close friends. Anthony and Mike meet the two girls the same time on a skiing trip and they all hit it off and became close. Anthony has a special friendship with Teresa, more like a brother and sister relationship. Teresa would come to Anthony for advice when she had problems with Mike, and Anthony would usually patch things up between the two of them. At times they would even refer to each other as Bro and Sis. Anthony would also turn to Teresa for advice when he had problems with Debbie, or even problems that he couldn't talk about with Debbie.

Mike stood at the same height as Anthony with short, dark brown hair and dark brown eyes. He was around the same weight range as Anthony, only about five pounds heavier than him and was well built also. He had a strong bond with Anthony and Debbie. He and Anthony often referred to each other as brothers. The two of them went through a lot together. They both entered the club together, and both were well liked by all the families. Mike always stayed on the drug end on the business. He often tried to get Anthony into that part, but he mostly stayed to loan sharking and running numbers. Mike always told Anthony 'You want to make money and rise up, you gotta sell smack.' Anthony never really listened to Mike's arguments about selling drugs. He had enough of a hard time getting past Debbie with what he did now and he didn't want to make it any harder. But now tonight Mike was about to get his wish, he was going to get Anthony into selling and dealing. A new kind of game was about to be played tonight and it was going to change the lives of all the players forever. Even the lives of people who weren't playing yet.

Dinner went by rather fast. They started by eating a salad and then moving to the macaroni and chicken. Anthony was pretty quiet during dinner, mostly thinking about his meeting with Enzo. The thought kept hitting him of Enzo taking drugs and Anthony supplying them to him. The only thought that kept Anthony positive about it was moving up in the ranks and becoming a made member to a family. Then what would he say to Debbie? That was another thought that kept crossing his mind. Who was Anthony kidding by entertaining a thought like that? To be made you had to be one hundred percent Italian, and they had to be able to trace your roots back to Italy or you would never be made. Whacked would be more like it.

Conversation mostly stayed between Teresa and Debbie. They talked about the usual female talk: clothes, make up, cars. That was one of Debbie's biggest necessities, a car. She was tired of relying on public transportation for work and school.

Debbie sensed Anthony's quietness during dinner and he knew she could tell something was on his mind. She asked him several times what was wrong and he just replied with a 'nothing,' or that he was 'just tired'.

Dinner was over and Debbie had started to clean off the table with Teresa helping her. Anthony and Mike moved into the living room. Anthony knew this would be his chance to talk to Mike without the girls around. They sat down and Anthony moved closer to him.

"Hey pal you know I'm not like that."

"Get serious," Anthony replied whispering. "I have important business to talk to you about."

"Why the whispering?"

"I can't let Debbie hear about this," he replied. "I need to get my hands on some drugs. Pot and cocaine."

"For you?" Mike replied raising his voice. "What are you fucking crazy?"

"Shhhh. Lower you fucking voice. They're not for me." Anthony stood up and walked over to the doorway to check on Debbie and then sat back down.

"Well who are they for?" asked Mike.

"Enzo Crescenti."

"What the hell does Enzo Crescenti want drugs for?"

"He's having a lot of problems right now. He dropped out of school, he's got problems with his family and he just broke up with his girlfriend," replied Anthony.

Debbie walked into the room quiet without Anthony spotting her. "Do you guys want any cake?"

Anthony jumped from being startled by Debbie. "No sweetheart, I'm fine."

"You Mike?"

"No thanks," he replied.

Debbie walked over to the front window to look out, thinking and wondering what was going on between Anthony and Mike. "You know Ant, if you didn't sit so close to Mike while talking you wouldn't get so startled when I walk into the room." Debbie smiled at him and walked back into the kitchen.

"I feel like I'm walking on eggs when it comes to her and business," said Anthony.

Mike replied, "Just tell her straight out not to get into your business."

"Yeah, maybe some other time. Anyway can you hook me up?" asked Anthony.

"Yeah, tell Enzo to come to me and we'll talk."

"Enzo doesn't want to go that way."

"Well what way does he want to go?" asked Mike.

Anthony began to feel uneasy about this situation again and he couldn't believe what he was about to ask Mike. "Give me the stuff, I'll sell it to him and bring you back the money."

Now Mike began to feel uneasy. "I don't know Ant."

"What don't you know? You don't trust me?"

Mike looked up at Anthony. "Don't even say something like that. You know I trust you. It's Enzo I don't trust."

"That's why it's better for me to play middle man," replied Anthony. "I know you and Enzo don't get along that good. We'll do it like this for a little while and then I'll set the two of you up together for a deal of your own." Mike sat there thinking for a little while. Anthony thought as well. "Besides, you've been trying to get me into this for ages anyway, so now here's your chance. It could be a big thing for both of us. He said he's got other people he can send our way as well."

"All right," replied Mike. "We'll give it a shot. Don't you have to talk to the club before you do this?"

Anthony replied, "Yeah, tomorrow morning we'll go and work everything out. Remember not a word to Teresa or Debbie about this."

"You got it," replied Mike.

Anthony got up and moved over to another chair. Debbie walked into the room with Teresa behind her, they each had two glasses of wine. Debbie handed one over to Anthony and Teresa gave one to Mike and everyone sat down. Teresa sat next to Mike and Debbie sat across from Anthony. Debbie stared at Anthony and he stared back at her. Anthony's heart began to race because he knew Debbie knew something was going on between him and Mike.

"A toast," started Mike. "To the future."

Anthony gave Mike a bit of a dirty look and Mike just shrugged it away. Anthony looked back at Debbie staring at him. He reached over and held out his hand and she took it. They all raised their glasses and toasted, "To the future."

Chapter 4
The Big Morning

Teresa moved around a kitchen just as well as Debbie did. It was eight 'o clock in the morning and she had woken up early to make Mike breakfast. Mike often came over in the morning to have breakfast with her. Sometimes it was the only peace they had with each other after all the fighting. Teresa was just as dedicated and as loyal to Mike as Debbie was to Anthony. Teresa went through more with Mike then Debbie did with Anthony. Both relationships had their ups and downs, but Teresa's was more of a roller coaster. Mike and Anthony both had bad tempers, but Anthony knew who to take his out on. There was no doubt that Mike loved Teresa just as much as Anthony loved Debbie, but Mike didn't always act like it. There were plenty of times when the two of them went at it and Mike really lost it with her. He would sometimes get to the point of grabbing her by the arm and pulling her around, pointing at her right in her face and on several occasions raising his hands to her. Anthony was there several times when their fighting got out of hand and he had to put a stop to it. That's why Anthony and Teresa had become such close friends. He would usually talk to her after her brawls with Mike. She would pour her heart out and cry to him. He would in turn go back and talk to Mike and usually in a day or so things would be patched back up.

Mike was on his way over to stop and have breakfast before his meeting with Anthony. The two of them were going to the 101st Avenue club, or better known as The Borden Club, to speak to a Capo from the Garbaci family about some drug investments. Anthony wanted to get clearance from his friends on the loan sharking and numbers end to go ahead and get involved with Mike on the drug end. What Anthony and Mike were about to propose to the Garbaci's would make a lot of money, not only for the two of them, but for all five of the New York families as well. Anthony and Mike were already liked very much by the families, but if this deal went through the way they expected it to, they might be able to move up a bit and work for a Capo of a selected family. Whether it may be the Genoso, Garbaci, Protecca, Bonetti or the Luigita family, it would be a huge step up for the both of them. Well not actually made, but they would be working for a real crew. Mike was fully Italian, so someday he had a shot at being a real made man, but not Anthony. They would propose the deal to a Capo of the Garbaci's and he in turn would relay it to his Don. The Don would then discuss it with the others Dons at a sit down with the Commission. If all went fine, Mike and Anthony would be rolling in a load of money. So much money the two of them wouldn't know what to do with it all.

Teresa rushed to get the table set when she looked out the window to see Mike walking up the front walk to her door. He looked up and saw her in the window. She smiled and waved to him. He smiled back. He was dressed in a dark blue suit with black leather shoes and a black silk tie. When Mike got dressed up he looked good. He was a very good-looking guy as it is, but put a suit on him and it's like the frosting on the cake.

Teresa was very confused. She knew all about his involvement with the club. She knew he sold drugs. She didn't approve of it but she lived with it. She knew when Mike went on missions for the club he didn't usually get dressed up. Mike didn't like to get dressed up to take care of business, but today he looked like a businessman going to Wall Street. She looked at his hands to see if he had his bag, but didn't see one. He usually carried a small black duffel bag with the drugs he was going to unload. She knew from there it wasn't an ordinary day at the office for him.

"The door's open. Just come in," she yelled out to him through the window. He in turn just nodded his head and came in.

"What's up?" he asked her in a groggy voice.

"Nothing much. Breakfast's almost ready. Take a seat."

He sat down and Teresa went to the refrigerator to pour him a glass of juice. He sat there looking tired and she tried to study his face and wonder what was on his mind. Now was when she wished Debbie were around. She was good at reading peoples thoughts. That's where Anthony ran into a lot of trouble with Debbie. She could always sense something going on with him. "What's wrong Baby?"

Mike looked up at her, half asleep. "I'm really tired. We should have never stayed up that late last night."

Teresa smiled and laughed to herself. "Well we had to say goodbye to each other, didn't we?"

Mike stared and then smiled at her for a minute. "Saying goodbye is a long kiss. We acted like we were on our honeymoon."

"Well, it was worth it. Right?" she asked. He smiled and nodded his head. "What did your mom say when you got home?"

"Oh please," he started in a disgusted voice. "I'm tired of hearing her bullshit. That's all I ever hear from her. Where were you? What were you doing? Who were you out with?"

"Well Mike what do you expect? You are her son. She cares about you. She knows the shit you do and the people you hang around with. She's worried about you. You can't blame her."

Mike stared at her and began to get aggravated. At that point Teresa knew she said the wrong thing. "If you're so worried about how she feels why don't you go fuckin' live with her?"

Teresa just went back to cooking her eggs. Mike sat there and drank his juice. There was a moment of silence between the two of them and he looked back at her. She caught the look out of the corner of her eye and looked back at him. He stared at her and she stared back quietly. She knew he didn't mean to yell at her. He had a sad look in his eyes. He looked back out the window. She reached down and kissed him on the side of his neck. She then reached over and whispered in his ear "I love you." Mike turned towards her and smiled. From that moment on the two of them knew that argument was over. Teresa handed Mike a plate with eggs and bacon. She took her plate and sat on the other side of the table. "You look nice today. Why all decked out?"

"I have an important meeting at the club today, along with Anthony," Mike replied trying to keep it short and sweet. He remembered what Anthony told him about telling Teresa about his plans. "Anthony's going to meet me here."

"What time's he coming?" she asked.

"He should have been here by now," Mike replied.

Teresa still continued to wonder what was going on with Mike and the club, she knew it must be big now if Anthony was involved. The suit was the first clue, and hearing about Anthony's involvement was the second one. She began to wonder if this big meeting had anything to do with the secrecy of the two of them last night. She too could sense something was going on between Anthony and Mike, not only Debbie. Mike wasn't usually secretive about his business with the club when it came to her but today he was. "You and Anthony have something big cooking?"

Mike began to get a little nervous. He didn't know what Teresa knew and he didn't want to let something out that shouldn't be out. "What do you mean?" he asked.

"Well, you and Anthony were pretty secretive last night."

"So what? We always are, you know that."

"Yeah but last night it was a little bit more."

Mike began to get angry now, he wasn't in the mood for her probing, mostly because of Anthony's warning about not saying anything. "Listen, I'm not in the mood to talk about this. It's my business with Anthony, so stay out of it."

Teresa knew that this must be big if he wouldn't talk to her about it. "But Mike, you always tell me about business. Why can't you tell me about this?"

Mike began to get angrier. He stood up and walked towards the sink to get a glass of water. "Are you going to stop breaking my fucking balls?" he asked. "I'm not in the fucking mood, now mind your own fucking business," he yelled.

Teresa had tears in her eyes. She knew she stepped over the line and she was sorry. She just looked away and started eating her eggs again. Mike stared at her with fire in his eyes for a minute. He was about to start yelling at her again, but then the doorbell rang. "That must be Anthony," she said.

Mike stared back at her for a moment. "So what the fuck you want me to do? Get up and answer it."

Teresa just looked away from him, then got up and answered the door. Anthony was standing at the doorway in a black double-breasted suit and a red silk tie on. When Teresa saw that she was sure something big was going down, but at this point her curiosity had begun to fade. Mike had once again ruined a nice morning for her and she was tired of arguing with him. "Hi Sis, how are you?" asked Anthony.

"How do I look?" she replied in an aggravated tone as Anthony walked into the house and into the kitchen. "Are you hungry?"

Anthony just shook his head no. Teresa turned away and walked into the living room. Anthony looked over to Mike and the two greeted each other with their usual handshake, hug and kiss. "What's wrong with her this morning?" asked Anthony.

Mike replied "The same shit. I don't want to talk about it now. Let's get the fuck out of here before I start to really get pissed off with her." Mike walked towards the door and Anthony followed. He looked in at Teresa sitting on the couch with tears starting to form in her eyes. She looked up at him and he stared at her for a minute. He waved good-bye to her and she smiled and then looked away. He looked at her for a moment wondering what went on between her and Mike. He never saw her look quite like that. He walked out of the house wondering if it had to do with his deal with Mike.

Mike and Anthony were both quiet on the ride to the club. Anthony sat there wondering what had gone down between Mike and Teresa. He himself had a tough enough time with Debbie the night before. After Mike and Teresa left, she too had started her arguing with him.

Mike himself was in a daze as well. He hated to fight with Teresa, but sometimes she had made things difficult. This wasn't the first time the two of them had an argument, but it was the first time they argued about business. Teresa had always stuck behind Mike with his business with the club, but because of his loyalty to Anthony he had to keep his mouth shut to her this time.

"Why are you so silent?" asked Anthony.

"No reason."

"What was up between you and Teresa this morning?"

"The same shit," he replied.

"She looking to go partying again?" asked Anthony.

Mike was beginning to feel uneasy about his fight with her again. "She started asking me a whole load of stupid questions."

"Questions about what?"

"Why was I all dressed up today? Then she started to get ideas about today."

"What kind of ideas?" asked Anthony nervously.

Mike could tell Anthony was starting to get nervous just by his tone of voice. Mike knew Anthony just as well as Anthony knew him. "Relax Ant, I didn't tell her anything. That's why we had the fight."

"Well you usually tell her everything about the club, right?"

"Yeah," Mike replied. "That's why she got pissed off. She started nagging me and breaking my balls, so I blew up at her."

"You have to learn to calm down your temper with her."

"It was the only way I could get her off my back. She just keeps nagging and nagging, I just couldn't take it anymore." Mike started thinking about the fight again and started to get pissed off even more. "How about you? You have any trouble with Debbie?"

Anthony started thinking himself now about the night before. "A little. After you guys left she started her usual shit with me."

"How did you handle it?" Mike asked.

"Sweet talked her. Like usual," replied Anthony. He sat there still thinking about Teresa. "So does Teresa have any idea about what's going on with us today?"

"I don't think so," replied Mike. "She knows it's something big but she doesn't have an idea of how big."

"So how big do you think this is going to be?" asked Anthony.

Mike replied, "This can be really big if we make it happen right." Anthony stayed quiet and Mike asked, "What's the matter?"

"I'm just thinking about this whole thing, that's all. You know how I feel about drugs and that whole thing. I feel like shit doing this for Enzo."

"Look at it this way, you're helping a friend in need."

"Some help," replied Anthony. "Some friend and some need."

"Ant, if you don't help him someone else will."

Anthony thought about that for a moment. "What are you trying to say?"

"If you don't get him these drugs, someone else will. God only knows who it would be and what kind of shit they will give him. I know it bothers you to give one of your best friend's drugs, but you have to look at it in a different light."

Anthony sat there thinking about what his friend was telling him, and on one hand it made a lot of sense to him, but he still couldn't stop thinking that he was helping his friend to actually kill himself. Debbie kept racing through his mind as well. If she found out about Anthony dealing drugs that would definitely be the end of their relationship. He couldn't think about losing her. The two of them came to close too many times over stupid shit like the club and his work.

"What are you thinking about now?" asked Mike.

"Debbie."

"You're worried she's going to kick your ass if she finds out, right?"

Anthony started to laugh a little bit. "Kick my ass isn't the words to describe what she will do if she finds out about it." Mike started laughing out loud. "What the fuck is so funny?"

"You."

"What about me?"

"You let her control you too much. You have to learn to put your foot down with her when it comes to business."

"Mike," started Anthony, "I have enough of a time dealing with her when it comes to running numbers or loan sharking and collecting. She feels more strongly about drugs then I do. If she finds out about this she'll leave me and I can't deal with that. I don't want to go through with her what Enzo went through with Joanne."

"Joanne is a fucking bitch from the word go, and Enzo is just as much an asshole as her to put up with it."

"I can see this is going to be a fun business deal."

"What do you mean?" asked Mike.

"You and Enzo can't stand each other as it is, but once you start going on about Joanne it's going to cause a war."

"You don't think I'm that stupid do you?" Anthony looked over to him and started to laugh. "Don't even fucking answer that. I wouldn't even mention Joanne to him."

The two of them were silent again for the rest of the ride to the club. They were about two blocks away from the club when the two of them started to get more nervous. "You scared?" asked Anthony.

"A little bit," replied Mike. "We're meeting with the big boys today. You?"

"Do bears shit in the woods?"

Mike started to laugh and Anthony began to laugh as well.

Their car pulled up to the club on 101st Avenue and 102nd Street. The street was lined with men, all dressed in five hundred-dollar suits all standing around talking to each other. One man in a brown suit walked up to the car and opened the door on the passenger side. Anthony stepped out and greeted the man. Mike came out on his side and walked over to a few friends of his and greeted them the usual way. After a few moments of conversation on their own, Mike walked over to Anthony and began a conversation with him.

A minute or two went by and Frankie the Hand approached the two of them. He shook Mike's hand and kissed him cheek to cheek. He then turned to Anthony and did the same. "Anthony, you don't know how happy I am to see you make this decision." He spoke to him in a low deep voice with a little bit of broken English with Italian in it. Frankie was a Capo of the Garbaci family and he controlled most of the drug activity.

"I'm happy to be here Frankie," replied Anthony. He himself was trying to fight off just walking away, but he knew he had to do this. He had to do it, not only for Mike and Enzo, but now he had to do it for himself. If he ever wanted to get anywhere in the club this was the key, and now it was his calling. His time was about to come and he was going to make the most of it. He looked around at the people in the street and liked what he saw. All of these men were well respected and he knew that he too would one day be just as respected as all of them. He too would also be as feared as them. When he said yes to Enzo he said yes to a new life, a life he really knew nothing about.

"Come on Anthony, Mike. Let's go inside and start this meeting."

Mike and Anthony looked at each other. The three of them started walking into the club and Frankie put his arms around both of them and the two did the same. Anthony's chill started going away and his body started to warm. He was beginning to know what a cold-blooded person felt inside and for some, strange, sick reason he liked it.

Chapter 5
A Night At The Club

Ascension's was jumping tonight. Ascension was a club in Mineola, Long Island that Anthony and all of his friends hung out in. Not a social club either, it was a normal nightclub that seventeen year olds shouldn't be hanging out in. See, Ascension only let females twenty-one years of age and males of twenty-three and over in. With Teresa's cousin being the bouncer, seventeen year olds had no problem getting in. Certain seventeen year olds like Anthony and his friends.

That's how it started anyway. Once Anthony was introduced to the owner, the real owner of the club, he had it made. See the real owner is Louie the Bones. He got that name by breaking a lot of bones of the people who owed him money. He usually started with their hands and then progressed to their legs. Louie was not a nice person, but to Anthony he was. He treated Anthony like a brother and Anthony had a lot of respect for him. Louie gave Anthony and the rest of his friends Saturday night VIP cards and they were constantly getting parties thrown there for them. After a while Anthony and Mike had a name made for them there. If someone needed money, they went to one of them. If someone needed to make a bet just before the books were closed, they knew Anthony was the person to see. He never turned anyone away. That's why people respected him. That's why people liked him. They also knew not to squelch on a bet with him either. Many a night Louie had emptied the club so Mike and Anthony and a few of the boys could work over an asshole or two that didn't feel like paying. People kept coming back though.

Tonight was a special night at Ascension though, it was a Freestyle Party night. The club was packed with people all trying to get in. On the card were some of the biggest Freestyle artists of the time, and headlining the night was Luisa Menendez. You know Mike and Anthony were not going to be absent for this. By the time they had pulled up, the people were mobbed in the street to get in.

Bouncers were all over the place trying to keep order and calm the people down.

"Mike, we're never going to get in tonight. Look at this mess," said Teresa.

"Relax Sis," replied Anthony. "Who's going to turn us away?"

Debbie shook her head and looked at Teresa who was smiling back at her. "You guys are so stuck on yourselves."

"Give us a reason why we shouldn't be," replied Mike quickly. "Teresa pull over to the valet."

"Mike we're never going to get a spot in there. Look at the sign. It say's lot closed."

"Teresa pull over to the fucking valet."

"Yes sir." Teresa pulled her car down to the end of the block and already the parking attendant was waving his hand for her to go away. "See what did I tell you?"

"I'm sorry Miss, but the lot is full. There are no spots here."

Debbie looked to the back seat towards Mike and Anthony. "Okay professors where do we go now?"

Mike slightly stuck his head out the window. "Excuse me."

The attendant, already walking away, looked back at Mike. "I said there's no spot available." Then he continued to walk away.

"He didn't even give me a chance to say what I was going to say. That fucking bastard. I'll kick the shit out of him."

"Oh, oh, oh, Mike calm down" replied Anthony. "Let me see if I can talk to him."

"Guys, the club is shot tonight. Let's just go do something else," said Debbie.

"Sweetheart, I'm not missing Luisa tonight, and have you ever known me not getting into this place, ever?" questioned Anthony.

"Oh I forgot the Latin Lady is here."

"No, my Latin Lady."

"Oh I'm sorry, your Latin Lady."

"That's better," said Anthony turning towards the window to the parking attendant, "excuse me sir."

"That's a good one, sir," mocked Debbie.

"You get more bees with honey then you do with vinegar" replied Anthony.

"Hey don't you people hear? I said there's no spots now move this fucking car."

"You got a lot of bees there," replied Debbie.

Anthony gazed towards Mike, who was nodding his head quickly.

"What the fuck you nodding about?"

"He didn't even give you a chance to speak." Mike started to laugh.

"I'm glad you find me so amusing. Maybe you'll find this amusing. Open the door."

"For what?" asked Debbie. "There are no spots."

"Just open the door and everyone get out of the car."

"Here we go," said Debbie. The girls opened the doors and everyone got out of the car.

"Teresa give me the keys."

Teresa tossed the keys across the car to Anthony. Anthony caught them and turned towards the parking lot attendant who was across the lot. Debbie moved towards Anthony and grabbed him by the arm. "Anthony don't start anything here tonight, I'm not in the mood."

"Neither am I," he replied.

By that time Mike was already behind Anthony and they were moving towards the parking lot attendant. Anthony instructed the girls, "Walk down to the club, we'll meet you outside."

"Anthony!" Debbie said aggravated.

"Just go," he yelled back.

Mike and Anthony got within about twenty feet of the attendant when he turned towards them. He was looking at some papers and didn't look up at them. Anthony handed out his key to the guy and said, "Park my car."

"I already told you there are no spots here and I can still see that you can't hear."

"And in another minute you won't be able to see asshole," replied Anthony. Anthony quickly pushed the papers out of the attendant's hands. Just as the guy looked up Anthony laid two smacks across the guys face and head. Mike grabbed the guy's hands and Anthony started laying into him with punches to the stomach and face. The guy struggled to get away from them, but Mike made it around behind him and held him tighter. Anthony laid several more punches to his stomach.

The guy finally saw Anthony's face. "Alright, alright, I'll find a spot. I didn't realize it was you guys, I'm sorry."

"You better be asshole." Mike let him go and he fell to the floor.

Anthony dropped the keys into the guys lap as he winched in pain. The two walked away from the attendant and noticed the girls were still standing there watching. Debbie was shaking her head and had a pissed off look on her face. Anthony locked eyes with her and she finally looked away and walked towards the club pissed off.

Now came the usual fun of passing the crowd up and just walking into the club. Also not paying. That usually pissed off the normal paying customer. By this time the two girls were ahead of the line and at the front talking to Teresa's cousin. Mike and Anthony were taking their time as Mike was examining Anthony's bruised knuckles. "I can tell this is going to be a fun night with the girls."

"Why do you say that?" asked Anthony.

"You see the look Debbie gave you when she saw you lay that asshole out?"

"Yeah, how could I miss it?" Anthony's hand was really starting to swell up at this point. He would have to wait to get inside the club to put ice on it to make it go down. He wasn't so pissed off that he had to lay the guy to waste five minutes earlier, he wasn't even pissed that Debbie was pissed at him for laying the asshole to waste. He was pissed that every time Debbie caught a glimpse of his bruised hand she'd give him a nasty look about what had went on earlier. "Well I don't know what you want me to do about it Mike. I can't argue with her the way you do with Teresa."

"We're certainly different in that aspect. It's just tonight there is going to be a lot of business going on here, and I don't want to get into any fight with the girls. You know that Teresa accepts what we do, but Debbie gets mad in front of the people we deal with and that is not good for business."

"Well", replied Anthony, "tonight any business we have to do we do it out of sight of the girls. Debbie is pissed enough, I don't need her starting shit in front of me making book tonight." Anthony had to think about that situation for a minute. Teresa had really learned to accept the part of life that Anthony and Mike had made for themselves. Debbie was another story indeed. She was always harping and horning on what Anthony was doing and whom he was with. Debbie didn't like many of his friends, not many at all. Sometimes he had to wonder if she liked Mike as much as she pretended that she did.

Pretended? That was a new thought in his head. Was it possible for her to pretend that she liked him, or did she really like him? Debbie usually made herself vocal on who she approved of Anthony hanging out with. Anthony knew she wasn't too crazy about Enzo, but she did deal with him to.

Debbie had a ton of patience, more than Anthony in that aspect. Anthony hated a lot of Debbie's friends, but not for the reasons that Debbie disliked Anthony's associates. Anthony friends were just plain dangerous, life didn't mean anything to most of them. Yes, they mostly had families, but like the movies always said about Wise guys, Friday was the wife's night and Saturday was reserved for the girlfriend. Every made man that Anthony and Mike had known had a wife and a girlfriend. Anthony was different in that aspect, Debbie was his and he was Debbie's and that was it. Yeah they both looked, but never touched.

Debbie's friends sometimes were a different story, and that's why Anthony hated them so much. Anthony had labeled nine out of every ten a slut, and he was right. I guess in a sense like that friends living like that could be just as dangerous.

Anthony had to wonder how much longer Debbie's patience was going to last. Sometimes he thought she was just about at her breaking point with him and his friends. Maybe tonight was the night.

The crowd was extra hard to maneuver through tonight. People had lined the entire street trying to make it into the club. And why not, some of the biggest Freestyle artists were coming to the club tonight. But most of these assholes were never going to get a look at them. But Anthony, Mike and their ladies would have a front row seat to the entire night and then more after. Usually Anthony and Mike cleaned the ashtrays at Ascension when they went. Unless they had a late night mission to fulfill by throwing an idiot through a glass window looking for someone's money, they would close the club weekend after weekend.

This night every guido asshole and his dizzy guidette girlfriend were outside Ascension looking to see a superstar. Anthony and Mike had finally made their way to the front of the line and caught up to the girls. Debbie gave Anthony a piercing gaze that could shatter glass. That was how Anthony and Debbie usually kicked off a lot of their fights.

Anthony was not particularly in the mood to brawl with her tonight though. He only wanted to enjoy his evening with his lady, his best friends and Freestyle.

After the usual exchange of greetings between Anthony, Mike and the bouncers, everyone was ready to head into the club. The usual exchange included a few 'How you doins?' Along with the customary hugs and kisses that went along with the lifestyle.

A lot of respect was shown to Anthony and Mike at Ascension, for a lot of reasons too. One, they brought a lot of business to the club. If someone needed money, they came to Ascension. If someone needed to place a bet, they came to Ascension. If someone needed to collect money, they came to Ascension. If someone needed a fix, they came to Ascension. All of those people coming to the club generated business. It cost them at least twenty dollars to get into the club and then a good six dollars for a drink before they even saw Anthony or Mike.

Another reason they were so respected was the fact that Anthony and Mike had generated a lot of protection for the club. It was no secret that once the boys started hanging out at the club it had become a mob hang out. And with it becoming a mob hang out sometimes the wrong mob started to hang out there. Well, at least try to hang out there. If an undesirable was there the owners knew who to come to too remove them.

You also got the occasional out of town yahoo who felt this was the place he was going to rob that night. Yeah, you can guess that he ended up in a dumpster with a face full of shit for all of his effort. If he was lucky that's all he was going to get.

Very quickly the word got out that Ascension was not the place to fuck around at. You were playing with the wrong people and you didn't want to test their patience. Patience was not the thing that Anthony had tonight. Between the asshole in the parking lot and this look that Debbie was giving him, he could tell it was a young night and it wasn't going to get old fast.

Ascension was laid out very weird for a club. It was a beautiful club and it sparked awe in a person, especially the first time someone walked into the place, but its whole layout was just odd as far as clubs go. You see, when you walk into the building you have to walk up a flight of steps on the outside of the building. As soon as you got into the building you were looking down into the club. The lobby that you walked into was a lobby for a financial building. The building consisted mostly of a few banks and some stockbroker's offices. To get to the club you had to walk to the midway point of the building, till you reached a glass front elevator that went down to the level of the club. Right there was where the bouncers were staged, as well as the cashier's box and the line ropes.

Anthony, Mike and the girls had proceeded to the elevator, well ahead of anyone that was waiting on the line for a good two hours. Inside the elevator was the usually beautiful attendant dressed in the sluttiest outfit that you can imagine. That was usually another fight that ensued between Anthony and Debbie, but you could see that after the parking lot incident Debbie didn't even have the slut on her mind.

Anthony and Mike did though. It was a hard ride down to the next level watching this girl push all the right buttons. She knew she had looked good and was going to make sure everyone in the club noticed her.

Trying to avoid her look, Anthony turned towards the glass front and looked out into the club as they descended in it. The club was packed to the brim, and the music was so loud Anthony could hardly hear himself think. Everyone was slamming to the beat, it looked like there wasn't one person in the club that wasn't having a good time. Well, that was about to change when they stepped foot in there.

The elevator had come to its gentle stop and Anthony waited for the doors to open. Debbie already had her back to Anthony, so the operator had taken full advantage of the situation to make eye contact with Anthony. As the doors opened Teresa and Debbie both stepped out of the car. Mike had slowly followed and Anthony began to walk out as well. He took one more glance up towards her and she had winked at him. Anthony, feeling kind of shocked, had begun to turn red and allowed a smile to acknowledge her back as he got almost past her.

She smiled back towards him and said, "Come back and ride me again whenever you like."

That had taken Anthony by total surprise. Usually the girls that were in the elevator were not as forward as this one was, but yet it made Anthony smile. Anthony continued to walk out of the elevator when Debbie had quickly moved past him and prevented the door from closing. She got the door fully opened and was clearly pissed off. Teresa rushed in quickly behind her but was too late as Debbie hauled back and landed a punch right into the young girls face, knocking her completely off the stool and onto the floor. Teresa had quickly grabbed Debbie and began pulling her out of the elevator.

"Get your own man you fucking slut," screamed Debbie.

Everyone that was in the area of the elevator was clearly stunned at what had happened, and even a few of the younger people that were standing there had gotten a good laugh out of the mishap. Everyone except the elevator girl, who was still flat on her ass and holding a quickly swelling face. She knew that is was not wise to get up and go after Debbie after she had seen the look in her eyes, as well as the look on Teresa's face.

The two girls completely left the elevator and turned the corner of the hallway to enter the club. Anthony caught sight of Debbie and she glared back at him. "You tell me I have a temper?"

"Don't start in with me," replied Debbie.

"Don't give me shit about fighting then either," countered Anthony. "Why did you have to hit her like that? Did you think I was really interested in that?"

"No, but I didn't want her to get away with the comment that she made to you. How would you have reacted if some guy said something like that to me?" questioned Debbie.

"Probably would have put him in the hospital," chimed in Mike. Teresa quickly reacted and pulled Mike by the arm into the club and away from the fighting lovebirds. "What are you doing?" questioned Mike.

"Minding our own business," replied Teresa. "Move inside."

Anthony began to smile at Teresa breaking Mike's balls about his interfering in the situation. Slowly shaking his head Anthony looked back at Debbie who was trying her best to keep a straight face through it all, but not managing very well. "Listen, I didn't come here to fight the world tonight."

"Well you should have thought about that before you laid out a guy who was just doing his job."

"You had your round tonight and I had mine. For the rest of the night I want to have a good time, have a few drinks, smoke a few cigars and dance to the music of the artists with my girlfriend. I don't want to fight with you, I just want to have a good time. Okay?"

Debbie wanted so bad to continue on about the fight outside, but she had already realized by her own actions in the elevator she could not win this argument. By her standards all she could achieve was a tie in this fight. She had to concede and let it pass due to Anthony's willingness to let it slide about her knocking the elevator girl flat on her beautiful ass. After a moment of silence, except for the thumping bass that was filling the club, Debbie smiled at Anthony and agreed with him.

"Good," replied Anthony. "Now let's get on with the night." The two of them headed further into the club and stopped at the coat check area. Debbie had removed her ankle length jacket only to reveal an outfit that would rival the elevator girls get up. Her skirt was just as short and just as tight, as well as her top. The only thing that let Debbie carry it off better than her enemies was that she brought class to an outfit like that, whereas the bimbo in the elevator made it look sleazy. Well, sleazy to another woman but hot to most men.

Debbie was extremely beautiful. She was short but well-proportioned for her height. The extremely high heels she had on that night had added four inches to her height and it still made her seem tiny. She was only about five feet three inches tall and the teased out hair added some height, but around most people she was dwarfed. She made her way past several people and to the coat check girl who was also another of the clubs bimbos, but knew Debbie and spoke to her from time to time. The girl had accepted her coat and handed Debbie back a ticket for it. "Nice way to make an entrance guys," snapped the girl.

"Teach her to mess around with my man," replied Debbie.

"You go girl."

Anthony and Debbie proceeded into the club. The place truly was packed beyond belief this night. The club had announced weeks earlier that it was a Freestyle extravaganza and from then on this was going to be the place to be. Anthony had wanted to be here so bad that he would have done anything to go. To Debbie it was just another night to kill her feet, but for Anthony she would do anything.

The club was laid out in a giant square. After you actually entered the club by passing the coat check you were faced with it all. Directly in front of you was a giant square bar that housed twelve bartenders, three on each side. Directly behind the bar on the far side of the entrance was a small dance floor, and right above the dance floor was the D.J. booth. To the right of the entrance was a temporary stage set up for the night's concert acts that were scheduled to perform. All around the bar on the left side of the entrance were booths and tables and all along the right side of the bar were standing tables only. Above those tables were suspended dancing cages that housed some of the most beautiful woman you could picture, and once again all dressed like it was the set of a porn movie.

Anthony had quickly begun to scan the club to see if he was in for a long night of business that seemed it would never end. The only problem was that the club was so packed he couldn't tell. From his right side though Mike had quickly moved up next to him and grabbed him by his arm. "Table is waiting for us."

"Cool, I'm tired already," replied Anthony.

"Well," said Teresa, "get ready cause the night is only beginning."

"You're tired?" questioned Debbie. "I thought you were all set for your Latin Lady."

"Oh I am. Believe me, I am."

The four of them weeded their way through the club and made it to a sectioned off private table that was reserved for them since before the club had opened their doors that night. The table was roped off with red ropes and donned a reserved sign on it. Anyone that was a regular at the club had known whom the table was reserved for and knew not to sit there.

A waitress had arrived at the table at the same time as everyone else had and began clearing away the ropes and laying out drinks and food for everyone. After a few minutes of preparation the table was set and everyone was seated at it. Mike had begun to pour the girls some wine and Anthony had lit a cigar. Once Mike was done Anthony handed him the lit cigar and lit another one.

"Do you guys really need to smoke that crap here?" asked Teresa.

"Don't even bother," replied Debbie, "it doesn't do any good."

"That's right," exclaimed Mike. "Leave us to our vices."

Another waitress had approached the table with a bottle of champagne. "Louie sent this over to you guys."

"Tell Louie thank you very much," replied Anthony.

Anthony sat back and for a moment enjoyed himself. Well he always enjoyed being at the club, but for some reason tonight especially.

Mike had felt good about himself too. The two of them caught each other's glance and just smiled at each other. "You know something Mike," started Anthony.

"What's that Bro?" replied Mike.

Anthony smiled and surveyed the club, the Kingdom. "I'm gonna own this fucking place someday."

Mike laughed and held up his glass to Anthony for a toast. Anthony held up his glass back to him and toasted to Mike. "I'm gonna be right there with you Bro. Right there with you."

The D.J. started to kick the smoke machine and the club had started to get very misty. It was rapidly approaching midnight and it would be another hour before the show had kicked off and the girls were already getting fidgety and wanted to dance. After a few unsuccessful attempts at getting Anthony and Mike on their feet they just gave in and went up on their own.

Anthony and Mike had begun to settle in on their night at the club in their own way as well. The bottle of wine was almost gone, the empty beer bottles were beginning to line up along the table and they were already on their second set of cigars. Anthony had been scooping out the people in the club since he got there and was only waiting for the people to start approaching to begin business as usual. One particular guy had stuck out in his mind, mostly because he kept hanging around the table waiting to be called over. Anthony had labeled him Larry the Loser. Mainly cause he would do nothing but borrow money from Anthony, claiming that he had to pay the rent or turn back on the electric, but every time Anthony had saw him he was blowing the money at the race track or in a poker game at the club. Anthony could really give a shit what he did with the money, but when it came time to put the food on the table he never did and that was what pissed Anthony off.

"You know," started Mike, "Larry is ready to break balls."

"Yea I see him." Anthony had gestured to Larry to come over, but naturally Larry reacted like 'you mean me?'

"Stupid mother fucker."

"Get the fuck over here you degenerate gambler," yelled Anthony.

"You gonna give this prick more money?"

"Why not? He always pays back."

Larry had approached the table with that somber look, like he was always looking for a handout. "Hi guys. How are you doing tonight?"

"Cut the shit Larry. What do you want?" snapped Anthony.

"Well, ah, I was wondering if you could spot me a couple of hundred until next week."

"How the fuck did we ever guess that?"

Anthony started to laugh at Mike's ball breaking and shunned him off with his hand. Mike quickly spotted someone that he had to do business with of his own and tapped Anthony on the shoulder. Anthony looked at him and Mike began to whisper in his ear. Clearly

Larry was unnerved and began to think that the boys were going to work him over. Anthony noticed that Larry was beginning to slip away and become scared. "Where are you going?"

"You guys look busy, I'll talk to you some other time."

"Sit the fuck down asshole, we're not gonna hurt you," Mike replied as he got up to approach his own business associate who was clearly waiting for his own opening.

Mike and his newfound friend begin walking around the club slowly, talking and admiring the pretty ladies and getting reactions back from them all. Mike was a big time player. He no doubt loved Teresa very much, but he loved to play with other woman all the time. That was the big difference between him and Anthony. Anthony was more of a family person, dedicated to one person at a time. So was Debbie. That's why they got along so well. What had brought him together with Mike though, no one could answer.

Mikes friend was not looking for money tonight. This guy never was. The only thing on his mind was scoring some drugs so he could get lucky with a tramp from the club.

Everyone that came to the club to do business with Mike and Anthony knew who to go to for what each person wanted. If you needed money you went to Anthony. If you wanted to make a bet you went to Anthony. If you needed a car stolen or parts from a car you went to Enzo. If you needed drugs you went to Mike. But after the meeting that Anthony had at the club with Mike, all that was going to change. If you needed drugs, soon you'd be able to go to Anthony as well. That had unnerved Anthony at first thinking about it, now he was beginning to feel a little easier. Enzo had started him down this path. It was a path that would change his life forever.

From the distance Anthony was watching Mike deal his drugs. He did it so quietly and unnoticed that it was very smooth. Mike quickly pulled a dime bag out of his pocket and slipped it into a pack of cigarettes. After a minute he would hand the guy the pack of cigarettes. The guy would take out one and lite it up like nothing and put the pack into his pocket. After another minute of casual conversation he would reach into his other pocket and pull out an identical pack of cigarettes. Only this one had a wad of cash tucked inside along with a few cigarettes. He would hand them over to Mike who would in turn pull out a cigarette only to check inside for the cash, lit up the cigarette and pocket the pack. It was all a very smooth operation, and that's how Mike had dealt with all of his customers. A quick trip to the bathroom to remove the money from the pack of cigarettes and reload with another dime bag and he would be ready for his next customer. That was how business was done in Ascension with the drug trade.

Anthony sat in amazement and watched how smooth Mike was when he was dealing. He was also trying to ignore this pain in the ass bullshit story that Larry was telling. His patience was beginning to wear thin with the shit Larry was spreading when Teresa had begun to approach the table to pick up her cigarettes and a drink to take back to the dance floor with her. "What happened Larry? Lose the rent money again?"

Being a little drunk from waiting so long to talk to Anthony about his money situation, naturally he was going to mouth off to Teresa, but it was going to end up being a mistake. "Go fuck yourself Teresa."

Anthony immediately reacted with a swift backhand that caught Larry completely by surprise and knocked him clear off the stool that he was sitting on. Before Larry could get up Anthony was already ushering Teresa back to the dance floor to keep Debbie there and occupied so she wouldn't see this asshole get the beating of his life.

After Teresa was quickly on her way back to the dance floor with her orders to keep Debbie busy dancing, Anthony had already had Larry picked up by the neck and was herding him towards the men's bathroom. "What the fuck is wrong with you Larry? Why'd you talk to Teresa like that?"

"I'm sorry Anthony! I didn't mean it!" Larry had begun to plead and by that point he knew he was out of luck. The two of them had reached the bathroom and Anthony pushed him head first through the door and into a stall.

Mike had caught a glance of what went on and quickly followed them to the bathroom figuring Anthony was going to need a hand with this jerk-off. "Anthony, everything alright?"

"Yeah, nothing I can't handle. Hang out outside the door"

Anyone that was in the bathroom at that point had quickly emptied out when they saw the look on Anthony's face. Larry had begun to get up from the toss down that Anthony had gave him, but he only met a sharp kick to his ribs that laid him right back on the floor. "Larry, you know someday your mouth is going to get you in a lot of fucking trouble. Today is that day."

"Anthony, please, I'm sorry!" Larry was beginning to feel the pain now and the alcohol was not helping him in the slightest bit.

"You don't think I'm still going to give you any fucking money do you?"

Larry had tried to get up again and this time Anthony grabbed him by the back of his neck and dragged him to a urinal that someone hadn't felt like flushing. Anthony pushed Larry's face down into the urinal and repeatedly kicked him in his back until Larry was almost at the point of not moving. After a minute Anthony pulled him by the back of the hair and tossed him onto the floor where Larry remained.

"Larry, I don't want you to talk to my sister like that again. You understand me you fucking idiot?"

After a slow and painful nod Anthony stepped over him and walked out of the bathroom only to be greeted by a pissed off Mike. "What's the matter with you?"

"What did he say to Teresa?"

"Mike, it's over. The guy is lying in a puddle of about ten guys' piss. Just drop it."

Mike had begun to shake his head and they walked back into the club. "You know one of these days I'm gonna kill that son of a bitch with his stupid mouth."

"That's why I took care of it. Now come on, let's have some fun."

Mike quickly agreed and they went back to their partying. They headed out to the dance floor to join the girls and unwind from the excitement that had already taken over most of their evening.

Most of the rest of the evening went off without a hitch. The boys managed to conduct all of their remaining business without any more incidents. The girls had settled in to their own fun and really began to have a good time. There were a few moments when they got to their usually mushy, girly selves and managed to drench the guys in lipstick, but all of it was a nice time.

The Sixth Family

The concert had finally come, and that was the height of their good time. The four of them couldn't get any closer unless they were on the stage, and they had that spot for all of the acts. The final act to come on was Luisa Menendez, and that was Anthony's favorite. Anthony had seen her perform in the club many times and they always had fun together. Anthony and Debbie had gotten to know her and hung out with her whenever she was in New York. Anthony had teased Debbie and Debbie had teased Anthony about how he felt for Luisa, but they knew it was nothing. It was more like a school kid crush, and at times Debbie had actually found it kind of cute.

Naturally when she had taken the stage and saw her favorite fan there she was going to dedicate her most sexual song to him, just to make him get red. Naturally the oooh's and ahhh's from the rest of the people in the club didn't help Anthony's blushing situation and made him more embarrassed.

At the end of the act Anthony had reached by the side of the stage and handed Luisa a load of roses like he usually did, and she greeted him with the usual hug and kiss that made him blush more. After the concert had ended all the Freestyle stars had ended up back at Anthony and Mikes table for drinks and partying that would last for hours more.

By the end of the night the girls were completely wiped out, Mike's pockets were full of money that he made selling his drugs and Anthony's pockets were emptied from the money he had lent out to everyone.

It had to be closing in on six in the morning when the four of them had finally left the club to head home. That was a typical weekend at Ascension. It was like that week in and week out. A lot of times it was more than just the four of them. Sometimes it was only Mike and Anthony and the girls went their own way for the night. That was Ascension. And little did Anthony know how much more he would come out of this lifestyle with by the time he was finished.

Chapter 6
Refill And Drop Off

Enzo Crescenti was coming down off another high. It had been over a week since Anthony had begun supplying Enzo with the drugs he requested and things for Enzo did not look any better. At least in his own eyes.

Enzo was not taking this last breakup with Joanne well at all. They had their fights, much like Teresa and Mike did, but Joanne was a different person then Teresa was. Joanne was just a plain out child. She had never grown up, and probably never will either. Her family was screwed up from the get go and that didn't help the situation either. Enzo had come from a good family. They owned their own limo business, had a beautiful house and it was filled with a lot of love. Where Enzo had started to go off the track had stemmed from Joanne. Joanne liked hanging out with Anthony and Mike, although they didn't have to much use for her. Mike just didn't like her because he didn't like Enzo. Enzo had no love at all for Mike either, so that was an even feeling. Anthony just dealt with Joanne for Enzo's sake. If Anthony was closer to anyone else besides Mike, it was Enzo.

Debbie had a like for Enzo as well. They seemed to relate to each other much the same way that Anthony and Teresa did. When Debbie had a problem with Anthony she could talk to Enzo and he would smooth everything over for them. Much the same was when Teresa had a problem with Mike, Anthony was there to fix it. The only misfortune of the situation was that no one could talk to Joanne like an adult to smooth over problems with Enzo, and that's where Enzo lost out in the friendship. Yes all his friends were there for him through thick and thin, but unless he dated a more mature person, nothing could be done to salvage that relationship.

Everyone around Enzo, including his family, had told him to get rid of her from the get go. But when you're in love you don't listen to anyone, not even yourself.

Enzo himself had his hands in the club too. He was good for stripping cars and reselling the parts and he was in tight with a lot of the chop shops all around Queens and Brooklyn. He supplied a lot of business to the families. Car theft was a very big and very profitable business. Now that Enzo was going to combine drugs with the mix, no one really knew what the outcome would be. Enzo had a bad temper as it was. Once you started to mix drugs with his temper he would most likely become very unstable.

This morning was not going to be a load of fun for Enzo. First he had to meet Anthony and pick up his next fix. After that then both Enzo and Anthony were going to drop off some car parts that Enzo had grabbed several nights ago, to a chop shop in Brooklyn. From there the two were going to go to a social club and drop off the money from the parts, plus the week's numbers that Anthony had collected. Then it was on to separate ways for the both of them for the remainder of the day. For Anthony it was going to consist of spending the rest of the day with Debbie. For Enzo it meant another day of being alone.

Enzo marched out to his car, a Buick Regal that was really hooked up. It had chrome rims, bigger tires, booming system and was freshly painted. It should be hooked up like that. What went around came back around and slapped Enzo right in his face. You see, Enzo's car was just recovered from being stolen. It was missing for almost a month, and when they found it, it was almost a total loss. A lot of people viewed it as a form of justice with what Enzo was causing around the neighborhood with all his antics regarding cars.

Anthony was working on finding some leads through the club to locate who might have done the job, but so far all was coming up empty. Enzo had his ideas on who had done it. Anthony had his ideas as well but no one had any proof. Anthony was leaning towards it being a random job due to how beautiful the car was and all of its extra added features. Enzo was leaning towards the possibility that someone had a hard on for him personally, or it was revenge for all the jobs he was pulling in the neighborhood.

Either way everyone was coming up empty on who did the job. Once the guy was out in the open though, it was over. About the only thing that could save him was if he was a made member of another family and he was acting upon orders from a boss. The one problem with the theory that he was a made man was the fact that most of the time made men don't usually run around stealing cars. So if that's not the case, the guy better never hope he is found out.

Enzo pulled out of his drive and headed to Anthony's house. It was a futile drive being that Anthony only lived a block and a half away. Leave it to Enzo to go on a cruise for not even two blocks, but that was Enzo Crescenti. Just plain lazy. He wouldn't exert himself if he didn't have to.

Enzo reached his destination within a few minutes. Anthony was already outside waiting for him. Enzo flashed Anthony a quick smile and Anthony smiled back at him. Once Enzo got fully in front of Anthony's waiting spot, Anthony slowly proceeded to go to the car and get in. The usual hand shake and cheek to cheek kiss took place and Enzo quickly pulled out of the spot like they were being chased.

"So what's up Ant?"

"Nothing much En, just tired."

"Debbie keeping you up late at night?"

Anthony laughed at the question. "Nah, just been working like crazy."

"I didn't know you got a job."

Anthony ventured a look at a wiseass smile that belonged to Enzo. "Now what makes you think I got a real job?"

"Well, since when does lending out money take energy out of you?"

"It's not the lending out part that is tiring. It's trying to collect it that is exhausting."

"Someone is giving you a problem paying?"

"Everyone. It's like the word is out not to pay me or something. For the life of me I can't figure out why either. This last week has sucked."

"That's because everyone knows you are a sucker," laughed Enzo.

"Fuck you."

"Ant, you have to get tough with these assholes."

"Enzo, you don't have to tell me that. Last night me and Mike dropped this asshole into a garbage compactor to get the fucking money out of him." Enzo laughed. "That's funny to you?"

"No, the fact that you are collecting the shit with Mike is. That guy is a fucking putz."

"He gets you your shit doesn't he?"

"Yea that's about all he's worth."

"That's nice."

Enzo looked over to Anthony getting more serious with the conversation. "You gonna start taking sides now?"

Anthony looked back at Enzo with a little pissed off stare on his face. "We gonna start this shit again?"

Enzo just waved off Anthony and let him be. He knew that he was starting to cross the line. Enzo and Anthony were best friends, there was no doubt about that. Enzo knew that if he needed Anthony, Anthony would be there in a heartbeat. But what he also realized was that Anthony was also best friends with Mike, and Mike was someone that Enzo just did not like.

No matter how hard Enzo had tried, he just could not take to Mike and it was clear that Mike really had no use for Enzo either. The two of them did not spend much time together. They had seen each other around the club and it always consisted of the usual nod and dirty look towards one another but that was it. There was no hanging out, no chit chatting, no nothing.

It was no secret to everyone at the clubs either that the two did not like each other. For the most part peace and quiet were kept and they avoided each other, but by no means did either of them back down from the other. With the attitude on the both of them it was surprising that they had not gotten into it by this point in time.

Then there was Anthony. He was stuck in between his two best friends, two people that he loved like brothers. Two brothers that thought of each other like Cain and Able did. Anthony knew he was stuck between a rock and a hard place with Enzo and Mike, and he hoped that he would never have to choose between the two friends. That was a decision that he was not prepared to make, and probably never would be.

Anthony shook Enzo off and they remained quiet for much of the ride. Anthony started to let his mind wonder about the new business he was getting himself into, drugs. Who would have thought that Anthony was getting into dealing drugs? Anthony had tried to make himself think that it wasn't that bad, and it wasn't going to get that bad either. Enzo was his only customer, and if it stayed with just Enzo being his only customer then it couldn't be that bad right? WRONG. There was no way Enzo was going to be his only customer. The families would never allow it, Enzo wouldn't allow it. He already had people lined up to send Anthony's way.

Anthony's situation was this: He was a good earner, good for all of the New York based families. He lent out money and he collected money, he ran numbers for all of the families, and when he got his cut he always kicked some of it up to the local Capo that he was collecting it for. He always knew how to make the powers that were above him happy, and that's what kept him in such good standings with all of the five families of New York. Whenever he went somewhere he was always introduced as a friend of someone's in the family, that always brought him respect.

Anthony was a good earner, and all the five families profited from his earnings. That's why everyone had jumped for joy, Mike included, when Anthony decided to go down the drug road with Enzo. It's no secret that the families had frowned upon the handling of drugs in New York, so it was always a secret thing. Some of the older bosses still lived by the cardinal rule, 'you deal you die,' case closed. But a lot of that was just a front. Times were changing, the 1950's and 1960's were long gone. It was now the 80's closing in on the 90's and a lot of the old bosses were starting to find themselves out numbered on the deal and die rule.

Eventually Anthony would have to branch out with his newfound business and Mike was just waiting to help set him up with his own shop and become partners with him. A lot of people didn't like to deal with Mike cause of his mood and attitude, so he saw a golden opportunity to make a fortune with Anthony. With the respect Anthony carried with everyone he dealt with they would make a fortune. And once that started happening the next thing would be to kick up the take to a Capo, and then up to the bosses. And so on goes this thing of ours, or more commonly known as La Cosa Nostra. What Anthony didn't know or realize though, was down the long road, once things started to come apart in the future, this thing of ours wouldn't be known as La Cosa Nostra anymore, it would become La Cosa Nuestra.

"What are you thinking about Ant?" questioned Enzo.

Anthony stayed shut for a minute and just looked around at the streets as they drove then towards Enzo. "You ever wonder where our lives are going to take us En?"

Enzo laughed and lit up a cigarette and passed it to Anthony, then lit one up for himself. "What are you getting cold feet about Ant?"

"It's not that En. I just wonder where we are all going to end up living like we do sometimes."

"Well, you are not as bad as me. You don't take drugs, you only sell them now."

Anthony rolled his eyes at Enzo. "You know I'm not a drug lord from some movie. You asked me to get you some stuff and I got it for you."

"Yet," snapped back Enzo.

Anthony cocked his head back and gazed at his friend. "Yet?" he questioned somewhat surprised.

"Yet, just what I said. Yet. And I'll tell you why before you ask me again."

Anthony began to laugh. "Oh I have got to hear this."

"Everything you do, you're the best at it. You get into a situation, even a hard situation, and you twist it to your advantage and you come out on top. Look at what you have done with the numbers business in this city. You took a very small time operation and you have it down to a science. Yes, you have trouble collecting sometimes, but that's cause you have not capped someone yet."

"What?"

"You heard me."

"Capped someone?"

"You want me to fucking spell it out? You haven't clipped anyone."

"I haven't had reason to."

"Oh no?" asked Enzo surprised?

"No," replied Anthony.

Enzo sat shaking his head and then he began laughing once again. "What about this jerk off you mentioned from last night?"

"What about him?"

"You said you had to throw him into a dumpster right?"

"Yeah," replied Anthony.

"Ok tell me you didn't want to pull the lever and squash him like a bug?"

"No, I didn't. I threw him in there cause he was giving me a hard time."

"So you scared him into giving you the money by throwing him into the dumpster, right?"

"It worked, I got the money."

"But what if it didn't? What if he didn't give you the money? Would you have pulled the lever?" Anthony stayed looking at Enzo for a second and then looked out the window and stayed quiet. "My answers right there. Eventually someone is not going to pay, and there will be another asshole in the dumpster, or hanging out the window, or on the other end of the 1911 that's under your shirt, and that night you will be out of patience and the asshole is going to be out of a lot more." Anthony never turned and just kept looking out the window at the passing cars. "Just like the numbers and the sharking, the drugs will come to be under your control, and when drugs are in the mix someone gets clipped. There are a lot more assholes to deal with when it comes to drugs than with sharking and numbers."

Anthony weighed Enzo's words and then smiled at him and slapped his friend on his shoulder. "That is the truth."

"Fuck you," replied a laughing Enzo as he realized Anthony was referring to him.

They drove a little further on and Anthony reached into the bag that he brought with him. Enzo watched him from the corner of his eye, anticipating his every move. Enzo had already begun to get hooked on his fixes from Anthony. He tried very hard not to let anyone begin to realize that he was getting hooked, but it was not easy. He woke up in the morning dying to get high. He could not fall asleep at night unless he was high. Midday while working for his father in the limo business he would sneak off to the bathroom and snort a few lines of coke just to keep him going till it was time to head out of work and with his friends and get high. Then on to steal some car parts and once again get high. That was what he was beginning to live for, to get high. In his mindset there wasn't much else to live for anymore. Joanne was gone, that was it, their relationship was over. If you could ever really call what they had a relationship. No one really did call it that, certainly not Anthony or much of his other friends.

Enzo envied Anthony's relationship with Debbie, most of the friends in the circle did. What they had was only seen in movies. Oh yes, they fought, and when they fought watch out, but when they made up they were actually much closer to each other than before the fight. That's what kept them going, always getting closer and closer to each other.

Not Joanne though. No one at all knew what made that child tick, and child is an understatement when using a word to describe Joanne. She was just a spoiled brat that always had to have her way. That's what sparked off this recent falling out between her and Enzo. She wanted to go away and Enzo couldn't get away from work and she went into one of her temper tantrums and stormed off pissed at Enzo. Enzo couldn't give in to her and she broke up with him. Anyone that was around to witness the argument though had said the same thing. This looked like the last fight that the two would have as a couple. A little that Enzo was also sick and tired of her being a child, and her tired of Enzo working so hard. The two were just like oil and water, they just don't mix well.

It wasn't easy for Enzo to just let Joanne go. He loved her, and love was a strong bond. It was clear to everyone around that Enzo loved Joanne a lot more then Joanne loved him. Enzo kind of knew it too, but he was so blind about her with his feelings that he didn't want to let her go.

The night after she broke up with Enzo, Anthony stayed up all night with him talking and trying to console his friend. Anthony had brought over some beers and they decided to drown away Enzo's sorrows. The only problem was in the morning the sorrows were still there and Joanne had not come back.

Somehow Anthony was trying to figure out how to get his best friend out of his sorrows and not let him sink deeper and deeper into drugs. One option was to stop getting Enzo the drugs. That might work, but chances were that it would not work and Enzo would just move on and get his fix elsewhere. That was something Anthony had wanted to avoid since he felt that he was giving Enzo good stuff and he knew it was not junk. He didn't want to trust some yahoo from the street to give his best friend a hot dose of something and in the morning he wouldn't wake up. No, so Anthony had decided to run the course and give his friend what he had wanted until a better solution had come along and he could help him out of the hole he was in and digging himself deeper into.

Anthony handed over a kilo of coke and several dime bags of pot to his friend. Enzo looked around since they were at a red light and then closed up the windows of the car to conceal them behind the limo tinted glass. "Why didn't you wait for a cop to pull next to me to hand me that shit?"

"Oh there's no one around," replied Anthony. "I think all this shit is starting to get to your brain already and it's making you paranoid."

Enzo tasted his coke and then put everything into a black duffel bag that he had under his seat. The light had changed to green and they pulled away and began moving again. Enzo reached into his upper shirt pocket and handed Anthony a wad of hundred dollar bills. Anthony began counting it and then put it away when he was done.

They drove a little more on till they were almost at the club, mostly in silence and just listening to music.

They had arrived at the club and the rest of their day together went pretty much as they had planned. They hung out at the club for a few hours, Enzo had unloaded his radios from the jobs the night before and Anthony had turned in his take from the night's numbers receipts and sharking.

Anthony kept pretty much to himself at the club, occasionally joking with a few of his friends but not really saying too much. What Enzo had laid on him about having to eventually clip someone over money or drugs had begun to weigh on his mind. What also weighed on his mind was the fact that it was coming closer to the line when he would have to tell Debbie what was going on between him and Enzo and his new responsibilities in the club now. Could he get away without telling her everything? Probably so if Enzo wasn't the one taking the drugs but having Enzo in the mix certainly made things a lot harder. Right now he was going to play it by ear and see where this new road would take him.

Chapter 7
Confession

Anthony tossed and turned in bed for most of the night. He chose to sleep by Debbie's house and he usually slept very well when he stayed over there, but this night he just could not sleep. The rain poured on and on outside and the thunder kept rolling, but for some reason he just could not sleep tonight.

He threw his feet over the side of the bed and took a deep breath. After a moment he knew he had awakened Debbie when she placed her hand onto his back. He looked over his shoulder and saw her looking up at him. "What's the matter?" she asked.

Anthony replied, "Nothing Babe, just go back to sleep."

After a second he rose from the bed and headed downstairs to get something to drink. Debbie watched him stroll out of the room and at this point she was fully awake. It didn't take much to wake her, but she felt Anthony rolling back and forth and never really got into a good sleep herself. She knew her boyfriend better then he thought and she wanted to know what was bothering him. After a second she pulled herself up out of bed, grabbed her robe and followed Anthony downstairs only to find him in the kitchen drinking some soda.

"You know you will never fall asleep downing coke like that." Anthony cracked a smile when he heard her say that. Downing coke. It brought his mind to Enzo and him with his brand of coke. "Well," Debbie said, "you can't be in too bad of a mood if you cracked a smile."

Anthony replied, "I'm not in a bad mood Babe."

"So why are we in the kitchen at 2AM instead of in bed?"

Anthony took another sip of his soda and put his glass down and looked past Debbie out into the night air. He took a deep breath and looked at her. "I don't know. I just can't sleep tonight."

Debbie stroked his hair and then sat down next to him. "Well I felt you toss and turn since we went to bed. Something has got to be on you mind."

Anthony managed to glance at her. Oh boy, what was on his mind? Enzo, the club, drugs, money. Everything that he knew he could not talk to her about, but wanted to so much. They were always able to talk to each other, but lately they couldn't talk anymore and the last thing he wanted to do was to fight with her about his other life.

Debbie stroked his hair again. "I know that something is wrong, and I know that we don't talk the way we used to and I guess that is partially my fault if, not mostly my fault."

Anthony looked at her fully now. "Well, sometimes I am beginning to feel like I can't talk to you anymore. I know that you don't like some of the things that I am into, and it creates a lot of tension between us."

"I'm sorry if you feel that you can't talk to me anymore. Believe me, I don't want to drive you away like that. Is that what is bothering you? Are you not happy with me anymore?"

Anthony shook his head so quickly that he made himself dizzy and reached for her hand and squeezed it tight. "Don't ever think like that. There is nothing in this world that would take me away from you or anything that I would let take you away from me. I am very happy with you. Don't ever think like that again."

Debbie continued to stare at Anthony, she actually felt better at that moment and took comfort in his words. He always knew how to settle her fears and calm her when she was worried about something. Here the tables were reversed. Debbie had come to speak to Anthony about what was bothering him, and here he was consoling her and calming her of her fears. She took a deep breath, and let out a sigh of relief and smiled at him and received a warm smile back. She reached over and took a sip of his soda. "Okay," she started, "if I promise not to fight with you will you talk to me about what's bothering you?"

Anthony stared at her and thought for a moment. Maybe he could unburden himself at this very moment without having a fight with her. It sounded a little cruel but maybe take advantage of her fears that he would want to break up with her a moment ago and use it to break the news to her about his new business, as well as Enzo's situation. After a minute of thinking he asked, "You promise no fighting?"

Debbie thought about it for a minute and then replied, "Yeah."

Anthony took a deep breath and tried to figure out how to start telling her what was on his mind. "Well, Enzo has some problems. A lot of problems."

"Is he in any trouble?"

"Well that depends on what you consider trouble?"

Debbie sat back with a scared look on her face as she started to think the worst. Anthony looked at her out of the corner of his eyes and held her hand to calm her again. "Hold on Babe, calm down. It's not the trouble that you are thinking, like he's in trouble with the club or anything like that." Debbie let out a sigh of relief and took another sip of soda. "You want something stronger? You look pale."

Debbie finished the soda and then poured another glass. "No, it's just, I know the life you guys are living and I'm nervous for all of you."

"I know," said Anthony.

"Go on Babe."

"Well you know how hard he is taking this Joanne shit, it's ripping him apart."

"I know," said Debbie, "he's taking it hard."

"I have to tell you I really don't see this cunt coming back."

Debbie slapped Anthony across the arm. "Don't use that word, I hate that word."

"I'm sorry, but I can't think of anything else to call her at this point."

"Well how about bitch? That fits her pretty good."

"OKAY, BITCH! Can I please go on before I don't want to talk about this anymore?"

Debbie laughed a little. "Okay, I'm sorry, go on."

Anthony then continued on, "Well, with all the problems that Joanne brought on to him you know he quit school?"

That really took her by surprise. If she thought anyone was going to finish school it was Enzo. In a sense it didn't surprise her. Enzo was spoiled by his parents. They had money and they gave Enzo anything he wanted. They owned a very good limo business, so Enzo figured he could just sit back and coast with the family money.

He was right. "Yeah, Teresa told me, and I saw his mom in the store a few days ago and she told me too."

"Yeah, he is going down a dark path Deb, and taking a few of us with him too." Debbie remained silent and just listened to Anthony. For once they were talking about dark topics and Debbie wasn't getting mad and Anthony felt okay talking to her about it, this was weird.

"I'm assuming," Debbie started, "that you and Mike are who you are talking about?"

Anthony got up and took a beer out of the fridge and pointed it towards Debbie and she accepted. He opened up the cap and handed it to her. He then took another one out, opened it and took a sip. He motioned towards the living room and then headed to the other room. He reached out and held her hand as they walked through the dark house. No other lights were on and for some reason they kept it that way. Maybe the darkness was going to hide the looks on their faces as they went through with this conversation. By this point in time Anthony made a conscious decision that he was going to be straight with Debbie on the subject of Enzo and Anthony's new life.

They moved to an oversized chair, Anthony sat down and then Debbie sat in front of him and laid back into him. He put an arm around her and they sat in silence. She laid her head onto his chest and listened to his heartbeat. She felt secure, like no one in the world could touch her at that point. She dreaded the words that were to come from his mouth, as if she already knew. "Tell me about this dark path that we are all on."

Anthony laughed a little. "You're not on this path Sweetheart."

"Well the way I look at it, Sweetheart, whatever path you are on, I'm on the same."

Anthony stayed silent and thought about that. Would she go along with this madness? Would she stand beside him while he fed a mutual friend drugs? That is something he would soon find out. He let out a very long breath. "Enzo has started taking drugs."

Debbie's eyes were long shut, so when that flash of lightning came she thought it was her consciousness slipping out of her from the words that rang into her ears. Enzo is taking drugs. Why did that surprise her so much? There was a long silence between them, neither one of them knowing what else to say. It would be Debbie to make the next move. "Are you going to tell me that you are taking them as well?"

"No!"

"That was a very quick no."

"It wasn't something that I had to think about."

Debbie let out her own long breath now, a breath of relief. "If you're not taking drugs, then what is your role on this dark path?"

"Well that's where it gets complicated now, doesn't it?"

"You tell me?" She asked again, "What is your role on this dark path?"

"He came to me for the drugs."

"And you got them for him?"

"Yes." Back to silence they went. Then it was Anthony's turn to break it. "There wasn't much at that point that I could have done."

"Did it ever occur to you to say no?" she asked.

"My first reaction was to say no. My reply was yes." In his mind he knew that was a shitty answer.

Debbie shifted her position but never moved her head from his chest. She still listened to his steady heartbeat and quiet breathing. Why was he so calm in telling her this explosive information, what was wrong here? Neither of them were getting the reaction from each other that they were expecting. THIS WAS GOOD. "Anthony, I'm not going to pretend that I like this. You know my feelings about your lifestyle, now you've added drugs to the mix."

"I know," he replied.

"You are right, this is a dark path that you are walking down. Drugs are a very dangerous thing in this world and I have no reservations about telling you this. If you ever take a drug that is not a prescription or an over the counter drug, I will leave you."

Anthony stroked her hair. "I am not a drug addict, I will never take drugs. That is a promise." Debbie let out another sigh, and that was it, Anthony unburdened his soul. The guilt that was keeping him from sleep was now off his chest. He shared another part of his life with the woman that he had fallen in love with. "Deb?"

A minute of silence and she answered him, "Yes?"

"I'm not going to do this for the rest of my life, I can't." She nodded her head in what he believed to be agreement with him. "Do you hate me?" he asked.

"No, I love you," she replied.

"That was a quick no," he stated.

"I didn't have to think about it." She pushed in tighter to him and he held her closer to him. For the rest of the night they laid there, not sleeping but not talking, just existing as one. They never shifted position, never moved, they just held each other. Glad to be in each others arms, not wanting the moment to end.

Chapter 8
Car Shopping

Several months had passed and business was moving along as planned. Mike had gotten Anthony fully involved in his drug business and the money was coming in quick; in many instances too quick. Anthony didn't know what to do with it all. It's not that he was cheap, but he wasn't looking to spend it. He always felt like people were watching him and he just didn't want to attract attention to himself or his friends.

Enzo was in on the sale of it now as well. He was taking it and he was selling it, he still wasn't dealing with Mike though. Anthony was still the middle man for that situation. Sometimes it wore on him, but he knew what he had to do to keep the peace. Enzo wasn't budging from his stance that he wasn't crazy about Mike, Mike wasn't budging either.

What was getting hard to figure out was the pecking order of their little crew. Anthony was still deeply involved with his numbers and loan sharking business. Enzo was still in deep with his car part business; and Mike was making a fortune on his drugs. But since Anthony got involved in the sales now, Enzo was involved as well. They all had their own customers, but since this was just a business that was mostly controlled by Mike now there were three people all trying to call the shots. Well Anthony really wasn't looking to call shots, but he could see Mike and Enzo eventually bumping heads, and there was only so long Anthony felt he could keep the peace between the two of them.

By no means did Anthony want to start calling shots. After all who was he really? He wasn't fully Italian, so it's not like the club would ever make him or bump him up to Capo. Mike and Enzo were the only two that ever had that shot, and if they kept the money coming in the way they were it would only be a small amount of time until the books were opened and one or both of them were made.

That would be another bridge to cross if they were both made part of a crew. Anthony could be a part of that crew, but not made, and who would end up being the boss of that crew? All he could hope for was that it wouldn't be either Mike or Enzo. He couldn't imagine either of them giving the other orders. It would never work, no matter how hard either of them tried.

He needed to put some of those thoughts out of his head for now. Today he was going car shopping for Debbie. She was really starting to get tired of public transportation. Maybe if he spent some of the money he was making it would actually make him feel better. So far all he really bought was a very expensive gold chain and a diamond cross. Since the day he bought it he never took off.

He was walking towards a car lot that Enzo knew of and wanted to make sure there were no hot cars here. The last thing he wanted to do was to put his girlfriend into a stolen car and then have her get stopped. He didn't even want to think about that argument.

He walked a little further and there was Mike standing at the lot talking to one of the owners. Just as he promised, he was there to help Anthony pick out a car for Debbie. Mike greeted Anthony with their usual hello and then they went into the lot to look around.

"Do you have an idea of what you're looking to get for her Ant?"

"Not a piece of shit, that's for sure."

The lot owner walking behind the two chimed in with his response, "Oh there are no pieces of shit here that's for sure. I sell very clean vehicles."

Mike looked over his shoulder and responded back, "Clean is one thing, running is something else. I wouldn't want my friend here to get stuck with a lemon."

Anthony shifted his gaze from the cars they were slowly walking past towards Mike and tried to reel him in a bit. "Mike, I'm sure this nice gentlemen wouldn't sell me a lemon. He would have to deal with Enzo if he did. I'm sure he doesn't want to deal with Enzo."

"How about this one Ant?" Mike pointed over to a blue Cutlass. Anthony shifted his path and walked over to it and looked inside. After a second he opened the door and sat inside of it.

"This has a lot of miles on it," said Anthony.

"One hundred thousand or so," responded the salesmen.

Mike began walking away towards a Regal. Anthony got out of the Cutlass and shut the door and kept moving in his own direction as the salesmen followed slowly behind. Anthony reached into his jacket and pulled out a cigar and started to light it up. After he got it lit he kept moving on. His eye was caught by a Lincoln, but then he talked himself out of it, Lincolns were pieces of shit. That wasn't what he wanted to do.

After a few more passes of nothing that interested him he ran back into Mike down another row of cars. These cars seemed to be a lot more expensive. There were a few Cadillac's down this row and that's what was calling to him. At that moment he and Mike locked eyes on the same car, a blue 1987 Cadillac Fleetwood sedan. This car was fully loaded; all leather, moon roof, and sound system. There was nothing that was missing from this car. Anthony and Mike both eyed the car for a moment until they looked at each other. "It's a nice car Ant."

"Yeah, it is." Anthony walked over to it and got in. Low mileage and very clean. You couldn't tell this car was a year old, it looked right off the line. Mike came around the passenger side laughing really hard. "What's so funny?" asked Anthony.

"I'm picturing tiny Debbie driving this boat."

Anthony thought about that and then he had to start laughing. "Don't let her hear you, she's very self-conscious about her height."

"And Teresa isn't?"

"This is true. How much is this car?"

"I could do it for twenty thousand."

Mike had a puzzled look on his face. "20K?"

"Yes sir."

Anthony began to chime in, "Brand new is not even twenty two. I'm sure it's not worth twenty." Anthony started the car to listen to the engine. More important than that, what does the radio sound like. Before he could even turn it up Mike told him to.

Mike walked around the driver's side to hear the sound system. "It's got no balls."

"None of the stock systems do," replied Anthony.

"I'm sure Enzo can fix that with his stock of radios."

"Oh yeah, I'm not paying twenty grand for this car though."

Mike said, "I don't blame you, what do you want to pay for it?"

Anthony thought about it for a minute. Actually, if he made a few calls he probably didn't have to pay anything for it, but he didn't want to go down that road. It was about time he started spending money. Hell, he should even buy himself a car. Then it dawned on him that he would buy himself a car. It was about time he started treating himself a little. He was making a fortune now and he hadn't spent a dime on anything else other than a new gun and a gold chain with a diamond crucifix, and the gun wasn't even a legal purchase. "I think I want a car for myself at this point, I'm tired of bumming rides off you and Enzo."

"Okay, maybe we can get this douche to give you a break on two rides. Did you see anything you liked?"

Anthony sat quietly staring straight ahead. It took about a minute before Anthony started to smile and Mike caught the direction Anthony was looking in and then turned his head. Anthony was staring at what looked like an almost new Buick Grand National. Mike turned his head back to Anthony. "NO WAY!"

Anthony laughing asked, "Why?"

"You're going to buy a Grand National? You know how much that car must cost? Even from this place?"

It was already too late to talk Anthony down. He had that look in his eye when he set his sights on something, it was going to be his. In a moment he went from not wanting to attract attention, to buying two very flashy cars at the same time. He stepped out of the Cadillac and motioned for the salesmen to come over. "Do you like the Cadillac?"

"Yeah but I'm not paying you twenty for it."

The salesmen made a slight face and Anthony tried to let it go, but still managed to get a wise crack in. "Before you put a stupid look on your face that my friend and I have to smack off, I want you to hear something out."

The salesman figured out by that point that maybe he should keep his mouth shut by the comment and the seriousness of the look on Mikes face as he exited the Cadillac and walked over to them. "What is your offer?"

"How much is the GNX and how much is the Cadillac if I took both?"

The salesmen began to laugh and Anthony and Mike just stared at him. After a few seconds of laughing and Anthony and Mike just looking he stopped laughing. "Come on, let's be serious. You want the GNX and the Cadillac?"

Anthony slowly nodded his head.

"What's so fucking funny?" asked Mike.

"You kids are wasting my time. I entertained the idea of you possibly buying a Cadillac, but figuring its most likely going to be a Cutlass or a Regal. But really, a GNX?"

Anthony let out a long breath and then looked over to the salesman. "I'm not joking around." Anthony took the bag that Mike had been carrying around and opened it up. The salesmen looked into it and saw that it was filled with money. "Still think I'm joking?"

The salesman's smile quickly faded away and he began to look surprised. "How much is in the bag?"

"How much are the two cars?"

The salesman thought about it for a minute. "That GNX brand new is thirty thousand. That one there has less than a thousand miles on it. Some guy bought it for his kid and he racked up two grand in tickets and lost his license in less than a month. That car hasn't even been broken in yet so for all intent and purpose it's brand new."

"I understand, but it's not brand new."

The salesman thought about it again. "I can do the two for forty five K." Anthony shot Mike a glance and they strolled over to the GNX. Mike looked at him and shook his head as if to say no.

Anthony glanced over the GNX but already has his mind made up. He was leaving with this GNX and the Cadillac. Quietly he asked Mike, "how much is in the bag?"

"Fifty," responded Mike.

Anthony smiled at the salesman while taking a long drag on his cigar. After a second he locked eyes with him and kept the lock until the salesman was completely uncomfortable. "I'll give you forty for both." He put the cigar back in his mouth and waited.

The salesman walked back and forth thinking about the offer. Anthony could tell he was not going to take it, so before he could refuse him he added, "And I will let the comment slide where you called us a couple of kids wasting your time." The salesman stopped pacing and looked at them.

Mike added, "He's working on his temper."

The sales man asked "You have that much cash on you?" Anthony nodded his head. The salesman thought again for a minute and then said, "Okay, let's go fill out some paperwork." The salesman walked towards his office. Mike looked over to Anthony and put his arm on his shoulder and they began to walk towards the office.

"What do you think Debbie is going to say?" asked Mike. Anthony just shrugged his shoulders and took another long drag from his cigar before he tossed it and made his way into the office.

Chapter 9
Surprise!

Mike had helped Anthony get the Cadillac back home and then he headed off to the club to do his thing. Mike had several deals going on that day and Anthony didn't want to think about work anymore. He was now focused on getting the GNX and the Cadillac tinted and he wanted them to be back home before Debbie got home so he could surprise her with the car.

He wasn't too worried about her reaction. He figured she would be happy since starting tomorrow she wouldn't have to take the bus any more.

Driving around the GNX was a dream. The salesman was right, that car wasn't even broken in yet. It still had the new car smell, the carpet, the leather, the whole car was flawless.

He cruised around the neighborhood before he headed to the tint place and he got the reaction he was looking for. Heads turned to watch the sleek black Buick glide by. The throaty sound of her dual mufflers made people stop and look at him, and that's what he wanted. Everyone in the neighborhood already knew him, so all he was doing was nodding and saying hello back to the people saying hi to him.

He also had a few bags of stuff on him that he knew he could unload between the tint jobs, start to make some of his money back. In this business it would be a month and he would be even again on both of the cars, maybe even in two weeks. For his age he had more money than he knew what to do with.

He looked around at the suckers that had real jobs. Not him. You wouldn't catch him working a nine to five job. He thought about what he told Debbie a few months ago. He didn't want to do this his whole life, but he quickly saw this turning into a long term career. What if he did give this up? What would he do after it? Not get a real job! Fuck that. What was he going to do, go work at TSS? Yeah right, do what stock shelves in the automotive department or something? He was going to start being smart with the money, invest it, do something with it where it would start making more money.

Between what he was doing with numbers and sharking and now drugs, he literally had bags of money. Mike and Enzo did to. They couldn't put it in a normal bank account, they didn't have jobs. That would raise a red flag for sure. Enzo had mentioned some kind of a business they could start at least to have a front to show some kind of income. He wasn't sure how that would go. Mike had one idea and Enzo had another idea and then came the arguments.

Anthony pulled into the tint shop and everyone there stopped what they were doing to look at the car.

One of the guys that worked there came over and shook Anthony's hand as he got out of the car. "Is this yours?"

"Yep. Can you tint her up for me?"

"Shit yeah, what percent?"

Anthony looked over at the samples on the wall. "Limo."

"You got it." The tech got into the car and pulled her into the shop further back. Anthony slipped his sun glasses on and then went to sit outside the shop.

Anthony knew the shop pretty well, Enzo did a lot of business there. When he had radios and car parts he usually stopped there to see if anyone needed something. They paid pretty well, especially for radios. He sat outside for a few minutes and then the owner of the shop came out and sat next to him. "Hey Anthony, how you doin'?"

Anthony reached over and shook his hand. "Good Barry, how you doin'?"

"Apparently not as good as you. I'm not driving around a GNX."

Anthony laughed a little. "Come on Barry, this shop is a goldmine. You're always busy."

"Well that's what I wanted to talk to you about."

Anthony looked over the rim of his glasses at Barry. "What's up?"

"I was wondering if you can loan me some money."

Anthony looked around the street. He never liked talking business on the street but at least this was the least risky of his business to be talking about on the street. Anthony looked to his right and saw two ladies that he knew walking up the block. They said hi to him and he said hi back and then they went about on their way. After a minute he turned his attention back to Barry. "How much are you looking for Barry?"

Barry looked around now himself and then trained his attention back to Anthony. "Five or ten grand."

"Which is it, five or ten?"

"I would like ten, but I would be happy with five."

Anthony sat and thought for a minute. "I'll give you five now and five when I come back with the other car after the GNX is done. Does that work?"

Barry had a huge look of relief come over his face. "Yeah that's great."

"I have to charge you three points though."

Barry thought about it for a minute. "That's the best you can do?"

"I have to kick up to someone else, so yeah that's the best I can do. Is three points going to be a problem?"

Barry thought about it for a moment, "No, that will work."

"Good," started Anthony, "cause if you fuck me with paying this back I'm gonna hurt you Barry." Anthony stared over his glasses at Barry and Barry very nervously nodded his head.

"You won't have a problem with me Anthony, I promise."

"Good." Anthony got up and walked back into the shop and Barry followed him. Anthony walked back to the GNX and went into the trunk and pulled out the money. He looked around the shop to see if anyone was paying attention and then closed the trunk and followed Barry into the office where he gave him the money. When he was done he left the office and went back to his seat outside.

After about an hour of sitting there he could hear the roar of the GNX fire up and come out of the shop. Barry walked back out to thank him again. Anthony told him he would be back with the Cadillac and the rest of the money and he would square up with him for the two tint jobs then, to which Barry informed him that the tint jobs were on the house. That made Anthony smile, not because he was saving five hundred dollars on tint. The five hundred didn't mean anything to him. It made him feel respected, that's why he loved this life so much. That's why he could see himself not keeping the promise to Debbie about getting out of this.

He got in the GNX and roared out of there. The second part of the tint job went just as smooth. He brought Barry the balance of the money back and now Barry's clock was ticking. One week and his first payment was due, but Anthony didn't think he would have a problem with Barry.

After about another hour the Cadillac was done and Anthony was bringing that car back home. He was beeped several times by a few of his new contacts looking for their weekly fixes. He met up with them along his ride back home and made a little bit of money. Things couldn't get any easier than this.

Anthony got home, got cleaned up and ordered food for Debbie and himself so she didn't have to cook when she got home. He wanted to surprise her with the car. She would be home soon and the food should be there any minute.

Anthony was looking forward to a night at home, he was tired from running around all day. He was hoping Debbie wanted to stay home to. Someone mentioned to them that Ascension was now opening on Thursday nights. He didn't think he had much to worry about with Debbie wanting to go there on a weeknight. If it was Teresa, that would have been a different story, not Debbie.

He just about had the dishes out when his beeper started going off and the doorbell rang both at the same time. He let out an annoyed sigh when he looked down at the beeper. Before he even had it clipped back onto his belt it went off again, it was Enzo. What was it this time? He already gave him his stuff. Anthony made his way to the front door with a handful of cash to pay the delivery guy. On the way to the door he picked up the cordless phone and was about to dial Enzo when the beeper went off for a very annoying third time. "What the fuck?" he let out. He dialed the number and then answered the door as he put the phone to his ear.

"Sixteen dollar," said the Chinese delivery guy. Anthony handed him a twenty and took the two bags of food and closed the door as the delivery guy was already making his way back down the steps towards his bike.

Anthony made his way back to the table with the food when Enzo finally answered the phone. "What the hell? You beep me three times, on top of each other, and then you take like 20 rings to answer the phone." Anthony listened intently to Enzo raging on the other end of the phone. He was taking the food out of the bags and opening the containers while Enzo was jabbering in his ear. "Enzo calm down you're not making sense. Who did they find?" Anthony stopped in his tracks when he heard what Enzo said next. "Are you fucking kidding me? How good is this information?" Anthony continued listening to him.

Enzo just revealed to him that someone gave him a tip on who took his car a few months back. Enzo had so many feelers out to find out who took the car, but after a while everyone just thought there was no information about it and they weren't going to find out. Even Mike had reached out to people trying to see what he could find out. Anthony was surprised as hell when Mike tried to lend a hand. But now someone else came through for Enzo, if the information was reliable. Many times people gave false information either to get ahead or to get someone else in trouble for something they didn't do. Either way, Anthony needed more information before anyone acted on anything. "Enzo calm down, you don't even know if it's the right guy." Anthony listened to more of Enzo ranting on. "En." Anthony heard a key in the front door and turned around to see Debbie coming in from work. He met her look and smiled at her and she smiled back. "En."

Debbie walked in and closed her front door. She removed her coat and made her way into the dining room. She reached up and kissed Anthony on his cheek as she passed by and went into the kitchen to grab drinks for dinner. "Oh Chinese food!"

Anthony looked and her, covered the phone, and in an accented voice he said, "Sixteen dollar worth!"

Debbie busted out laughing and tried to contain herself. "That's not nice."

Anthony stopped laughing and tried to go back to reeling Enzo in. "En listen to me, I know you're pissed. Please, take a day to gather some more info on it and we can discuss it tomorrow. Let's see what else we can find out about it, okay?" Anthony went into silence listening to him but this time a little calmer. "Okay, I will catch up with you sometime tomorrow, bye."

"Do I even want to know what that was about?"

"Hmm, probably not." Anthony ventured a look towards her, but she didn't make eye contact with him. He continued on with putting the food on the plates while she brought in the drinks. "How was work today?"

"Don't change the subject," Debbie said as she flashed a smile.

Anthony finished loading the plates and then he said to her, "I'm not changing the subject. That was Enzo, he thinks he found out who might have taken his car."

"He thinks or he knows?"

"Well," replied Anthony, "if you ask him he knows, but to me it sounds more like thinks."

"Why do you say that?"

"Unless there is really strong evidence, this could just be someone looking to get someone else into trouble and I am in no mood to get involved with his antics tonight, I'm tired. I had a long day, and the last thing I wanted to hear about was his car."

Debbie said, "Yeah, I think he is out of hand with his drugs. He is becoming paranoid, you have to keep an eye on him with that stuff."

"Yeah, I know. So a little off topic because I don't want to talk about Enzo anymore tonight."

Debbie looked at him curiously. "Okay." Anthony took her by the hand and they headed out of the house through the side entrance. "Anthony the food is going to get cold."

"It will be okay, we'll only be a minute."

They walked thru the yard towards the driveway and then out of the yard. Debbie looked at the Cadillac and the GNX in the driveway, but it didn't click to her. "Whose cars are these?" she asked.

"Well, what would you say if you didn't have to take the bus or the trains tomorrow?"

Before Debbie could answer him Anthony dangled the keys in front of her face. She looked at them and then it made sense to her. She had a smile on her face from ear to ear. "Oh my God! ANTHONY!" Debbie threw her arms around him and they hugged tight. Anthony picked her off the floor and spun her around. "I can't believe you bought this for me."

"It's all yours Baby, go and check it out."

Debbie let go of Anthony and ran to the Cadillac all excited. As she was looking over it her eyes caught a glimpse of the GNX. She stared at it and then turned around and looked at a smiling Anthony. "Whose car is that?"

"That would be mine."

"You bought two cars?" she asked.

Anthony replied, "Well, it was a very good deal."

"Oh yeah I bet. I swear I don't know what I would do without you."

Anthony moved over close to her and put his arms around her. "Well, you're never going to have to find that out now, are you?"

Debbie replied, "Nope," and reached up and kissed Anthony.

Chapter 10
Making Plans

It was several weeks now since Enzo got his tip about his car, but no one was moving on it. Everyone deemed it non-credible. It took Anthony to talk down Enzo as usual. Even Enzo was convinced at this point that the tip was false, and even if it wasn't false there was not enough evidence to move on it.

At this point the most important thing in everyone's life was bringing in more money, and that's what they were all doing. It was coming in by the bags and everyone was starting to run out of places to hide it.

Anthony was on to something at this point, and naturally he was including his two closest friends in it. Offshore accounts were the way to go. Anthony had made a new friend recently, a lawyer named Mickey Maldonado, or as he liked to be called, Mickey Maldo. He was a short guy, with blondish brown hair and he wore glasses. Everyone at the club referred to him as Mickey the Mouse, due to his short height and as a play on his name. He was fresh out of law school, but he knew his way around a court room like a veteran.

Mickey and Anthony got along from the start, and when Anthony explained to Mickey he had a cash storage problem, Mickey turned him on to the idea of off shore accounts. They were completely untraceable by the IRS and the Federal Government. Since Anthony and the rest of his friends didn't have jobs on the books, storing their money in a traditional bank account would spell trouble for everyone involved. Some of the higher ups in the families had already embraced the idea of off shore accounts, and everything was working out wonderfully for them.

Anthony had discussed with both Enzo and Mike this idea and they both seemed to be interested in it as well, Mike especially. He was making more money than Anthony and Enzo combined. He was in the drug end from the beginning. Anthony had just gotten into it, but he already tripled his profits from day one, so you can imagine how much Mike had stocked away.

Enzo was a different story. He sold here and there, but he was more interested in getting high, then making a profit. Enzo was also becoming more and more unstable as each day passed. He was always on edge and the slightest thing would set him off. Anthony was trying to keep Mike away from him as much as possible, but Anthony had his own responsibilities and he wasn't always around to play babysitter. Anthony was also getting tired of playing middleman between the two of them with their drug deals with each other. What could he do though? He was afraid they would kill one another. Somewhere along the line they needed to begin dealing with themselves so Anthony could concentrate on his other businesses.

The growing problem of storing the cash was now pretty much off everyone's mind. They were all opening accounts in the Grand Cayman Islands and Switzerland. Mickey was handling the opening of the accounts as well as the wire transfers. Everything that needed to be done, Mickey would take care of, for a small fee of course and Anthony as well as Mike were more than glad to pay it.

They were all still talking about opening some kind of a business together, not only as a front for the cash they were making, but also a place that they could centrally deal out of and hang out at the same time. If anyone was nosy enough to see what they were doing, it looked like they were working. It was a good plan and everyone was actually on board.

Mike and Anthony had more than enough money to start this up, but Enzo didn't, and he was looking for a way to get it. He started getting more brazen with his car thefts, now doing it in broad day light. That was not good, it was only a matter of time before Anthony felt it was going to catch up with him.

The three also argued about what kind of business it would be. All three of them were interested in cars, so the idea of a custom shop was out there. A place similar to Barry's, where you could go to get your windows tinted, but they wanted it on a larger scale. They wanted to sell rims, tires, radios, ground effects, neon lighting, you name it they wanted to sell and install it.

Anthony and Mike were also looking at a dance club, but that would be a much more expensive venture. Enzo didn't have any interest in clubs, so the idea didn't call to him. He was pushing for the custom shop, but for his own agenda. He wanted to turn it into a chop shop where he could take the cars he was stealing, strip them, and sell the parts for profit. Mike was against that idea because he felt it would really attract too much attention. The drugs were enough to be going in and out of there, but stolen cars would have put it over the edge.

Anthony started to hang around Mickey a lot the past few weeks and the two were becoming fast friends. Mickey tried his hand at lending out some money and it didn't go so well, so Anthony made sure he collected for him. When the idiot that didn't want to pay Mickey saw who he brought to collect, Mickey didn't have another problem with him.

Anthony's reputation was starting to build up around the New York area when it came to collecting on bets and loaned out money. Every now and then there was the usual asshole who was late with paying, but in the end they always paid.

This is what was troubling to Anthony when it came to Barry. He really didn't think he was going to have a problem with Barry, but for the past few weeks it was one story after another when it came time to pay up. There were a few instances when Anthony went there at a scheduled time and Barry wasn't even around. Part of him started to feel as though he was being made a fool of.

Anthony looked out the bedroom window at Debbie as she pruned her roses. Things were going good between the two of them and Anthony was now pretty much at her house full time. The fighting was still there, but they were both working on it. Anthony was also giving things to Debbie a lot more often now. That wasn't really keeping her quiet though, in fact she was fighting with him more over it. She just felt what he was giving her was wrong.

The phone was ringing as Anthony was looking for something not that nice to wear. He was planning on paying a visit to Barry that was unannounced and he didn't want to ruin good clothes. He reached over and picked up the phone and answered it, it was one of Debbie's sisters, Lourdes.

Lourdes was the youngest of the three sisters at eighteen years old. There was an older sister, Cristina who was twenty five and Debbie was the middle child who just turned twenty.

For Debbie's birthday Anthony graced her with a diamond necklace, but that almost turned into a usual fight.

Lourdes still lived with their mother while Cristina was out on her own, if you could consider Lourdes actually living at home. Lourdes had begun to pursue a modeling career that immediately took off. She already appeared in several magazines and was flying all around the country at a dizzying pace.

Cristina worked for a women's clothing retail store in central Queens. She had worked there for several years and was satisfied with her life as were the other two sisters. She also had a boyfriend, but Anthony hadn't heard too much about him.

Anthony had yet to meet Debbie's two sisters, no one's schedule could line up and make it happen. Debbie had talked about setting up a dinner, but it just never seemed to work out. Deep inside Anthony began to think Debbie didn't want to expose her sisters to his life. Somewhere along the line they would have to meet him. It's not like Anthony and Debbie weren't serious about each other. In time Anthony had hoped it would all work itself out.

"How are you doing Lourdes?" asked Anthony. Anthony listened to her for a minute while he was still searching for his shirt. "I saw the magazine layout, it came out really nice."

Anthony looked out the window again while listening to Lourdes on the phone. He picked up a shirt that he really didn't want to wear and put it on. He then reached into a safe that was in the closet and pulled out a 1911 pistol. "So when am I going to meet you and your sister?" He continued to check the gun to see if it was loaded. Once he saw it was he slipped it into his waistband and then covered it with his shirt. "If you like dance clubs you should come and check out the one that we go to." He listened for a minute. "You don't have to worry about getting in, that will be taken care of."

Anthony moved out of the bedroom and into the hallway when he heard a car horn blow outside. He looked out another window and saw it was Mike. Anthony motioned to him from the window that he would be down in a minute and Mike acknowledged.

"Don't worry about it, I'm younger then you and I get in every time I go, we run the place. Do you want to talk to your sister? She's outside in the garden." Anthony waited for a minute while she gave him her message. "Okay, I will let her know. It was nice to finally talk to you. Hope to meet you guys soon, bye." Anthony put the phone down and then headed out of the house and into the garden area. Teresa was there talking to Debbie while she was finishing up with the garden. Anthony walked over to Teresa and gave her a kiss. "Hey Sis."

"Hey Bro," she replied.

Anthony reached down and picked up the bag of garden tools that Debbie was finishing up with and asked Debbie, "Are you done with these Hun?" Debbie replied with a nod and Anthony moved to put them in the garage.

"Wow," said Teresa, "you have such a thoughtful boyfriend. He puts the things away for you when you are done."

Anthony laughed as he went into the garage. Once he was out of sight he reached into the bag and took out the rose sheers that Debbie was using to cut the roses. He looked to make sure Debbie wasn't in there with him and then he slipped them into his back pocket and pulled his shirt back over to cover them. He laid the bag down on a shelf and then went back out to the yard. "What are you two ladies doing tonight?"

"Thinking about grabbing something to eat and then catching a movie," replied Debbie.

"Cool. Oh before I forget, right before I came out your sister called."

Debbie picked up her head from her flowers and looked towards Anthony. "Cristina? What did she say?"

Anthony replied, "No, Lourdes"

Debbie rolled her eyes. "Ugh, what did she want?"

Anthony looked at her with a bit of confusion. "Why do you always react like that when you hear her name?"

"I'm not really looking to have this conversation right now."

Mike's horn blew once again. "Let's go!"

"You never want to have that conversation."

Ignoring Anthony's comment she asked, "What did Miss Prissy want?"

Anthony decided to also ignore the fact that she was ignoring his question and he just decided to answer her question. "She said she will be in town soon and she wanted to get together, finally meet me. I suggested Ascension if her and Cristina were interested. She said to call them when you had a chance."

"Oh joy, I can't wait. I'll make sure I get right on it."

Anthony looked over at Teresa who just had a smirk on her face. Anthony had a confused look on his face. He reached over and kissed Teresa on the cheek. "Have fun tonight and be careful." Teresa smiled at him.

Anthony took Debbie by the hand and they walked out of the yard. Anthony was clearly annoyed. "You know I love you right?"

"Of course I do," replied Debbie.

"Don't talk to me like that again in front of anyone, I wouldn't do that to you."

Debbie was clearly taken aback by Anthony's quick and sharp comment. After a second she realized that she embarrassed him in front of Teresa. "This is not about you, it's about me and my sister."

"Then don't take it out on me. I'm beginning to think you don't want them to meet me because of the living I make."

Debbie thought about it for a second while she was looking at Mike who was clearly waiting for Anthony, very impatiently. After a second she looked back up at him. "While I might not be too crazy about your lifestyle, this is not about what you do or who you associate with."

"Then what is it about?"

'It's about them, or more so it's about her."

"Lourdes?" asked Anthony.

"Yeah, I haven't gotten along with her since as long as I can remember, it's a really long story. I promise you, I will tell you about it when we both have more time, but believe me, it's not about you."

Anthony looked towards Mike and signaled to him that he would be there in a minute. "Okay, we will talk about it later then."

Debbie smiled at him and then reached up and kissed him. "I'm sorry for being nasty."

Anthony smiled back as if to say it was okay. He kissed her again. "Be careful tonight, I will see you later."

Debbie kissed him back. "You be careful to."

"I will." Anthony walked away and got into the car. He waved to her as Mike sped the car off and she waved back at both of them. She watched the car peel down the block and then went back into the yard to Teresa.

"Are you two okay?"

Debbie smiled at her. "Yeah, we're fine. Just a stupid spat. Me being stupid."

"Anthony looked pissed."

"I think more embarrassed that I spoke to him like that in front of you."

"Well, you really weren't talking to him personally. It was about your sister."

Debbie picked up some more of the gardening tools and moved them to the garage while Teresa followed. "It was shitty, so I get him. My sister just pisses me off and I'm not in the mood to see her. The problem is Anthony is beginning to think it's about him and his job."

"Is it?"

Debbie stared at Teresa for a moment. "I never thought about it like that, but really, it's not about Anthony or his work. Now that the bug is there that could be another factor, but not really. It's more about her."

Teresa thought for a minute. "Are you jealous of her?"

Debbie shot Teresa a weird look. "Jealous of her? I don't think so. Why would you think that?"

The two of them walked out of the garage and back towards the house. "Well," started Teresa, "she's a model, she is very pretty and her career is taking off pretty quick."

"Are you saying I'm not attractive?"

Teresa laughed a little and Debbie smiled at her. "Not at all. I meant jealous of her lifestyle, the glamour and glitz of it. Shit I don't know her and I'm jealous of her."

Debbie laughed at her comment. "No, I don't give a shit about her modeling. This goes so further back than that. I'm not going to go into it now, maybe some other time."

"No problem," replied Teresa and they went into the house.

Chapter 11
Final Collection Notice

Mike pulled up slowly down the block from Barry's tint shop and parked on the corner. Anthony and Mike both sat in silence for a few minutes while staring down the block at the shop. After a minute Mike asked Anthony, "Have you figured out what to do with this asshole yet?"

Anthony kept his eyes trained on the shop. "Barry?"

"Yeah."

"I guess I will figure it out when I get in there."

"That's not really the smartest approach."

Anthony thought about that for a second, all the while not taking his eyes off the shop. He truly didn't know himself what he wanted to do at this point. He never thought he was going to have a problem with Barry, but by this point he really felt he was being made a fool out of and he was pissed about it. All it took was for word to get around that Barry was jerking his chain about paying, then everyone else in the neighborhood that was borrowing from him would get the same idea and it would be open season on not paying back. No, Anthony wasn't going to let that happen. An example had to be made and Barry was going to be the example.

Anthony liked Barry up until he gave him the run around. There was nothing here to do with personality, this was purely about money and about image. Anthony now had an image to upkeep. At that moment of Anthony's deep thought Enzo pulled up the block from the opposite direction. His car pulled parallel to Mike's until their driver windows were next to each other. Enzo rolled down his window and Mike did the same.

"What's up losers?"

"Looking in a mirror Enzo?" asked Mike

Enzo clearly didn't like the comment, but he let it slide. He looked over to Anthony who still had his eyes trained on the shop. "What's the plan Ant?"

"That's the problem," replied Mike, "there isn't one."

Anthony looked back and forth between his two friends. "There is one forming now. Enzo drive around the block, park and walk down the alley behind Barry's shop to the back entrance that he has. Wait at that entrance, I don't want him to slip away from there."

"When do you want me to come into the shop?"

"When Barry tries to run past you."

Enzo nodded his head and then pulled away and rounded the corner. He drove to the next corner and parked his car. After a minute he got out and made his way down towards the alleyway and waited by the back door.

"What are we going to do?" asked Mike.

Anthony smiled at him and said, "Walk in the front door."

Mike smiled and they proceeded to get out of the car and walk down the block. Anthony noticed that the shop was pretty empty and they looked like they were getting ready to close up. Anthony reached towards his back pocket and touched the area to make sure the rose clippers were still there, they were. Then he patted the 1911 under his shirt. The two walked across the street and kept an eye along the block. It was pretty empty, no one walking by.

Mike and Anthony entered the shop and looked around. A worker looked at them and he could tell that he was going to be in the wrong place at the wrong time. Anthony looked at the worker, "Where's Barry?"

The worker pointed to the office and Anthony motioned for him to get out of the shop. The worker dropped what he was doing and walked out. Anthony motioned to Mike to move over to the pull chains that close the bay doors and wait for Anthony's signal. There were still several other workers in the shop. Anthony thought for a second on how to get their attention. Anthony reached over to a table and picked up a wrench and banged it on a metal garbage can. Everyone stopped what they were doing and looked over at Anthony. Anthony raised his voice and said, "Everyone get the fuck out." The workers stood there, looking at him. He reached under his shirt and pulled out the 1911 and that sent everyone running out of the shop. Anthony motioned to Mike and Mike already knew to start closing the doors.

Everyone got out the bay doors just as Mike finished pulling them down. At that same moment Barry came out of the office. "What the fuck is going on out here?"

Anthony locked eyes with Barry and Barry took off like a bat towards the back door. Mike moved first and went after him and then Anthony followed. Barry reached the back door and pulled it open. As he stepped thru it he was met by a crushing blow to his face from Enzo. Barry fell backwards thru the doorway and back into the shop only to be met by more blows and kicks from Mike.

Anthony stopped his sprint and walked towards the scuffle while putting his pistol back into his waistband. Enzo had stepped back into the shop and closed the door behind him and locked it. Mike had picked Barry up by this point and now Enzo was laying into him with punches to the body and the face, all while Barry was squirming and pleading with them to stop.

Anthony watched the beating for a minute. Mike turned Barry around to face Anthony. "Stop fucking squirming asshole."

Anthony walked over to Barry with the wrench still in his hand and he didn't hesitate to swing the wrench and connect it to the side of Barry's face. The blow caused Mike to let him go and Barry hit the floor. Enzo stepped back and blocked the door in case Barry got the energy or the idea to try and make a break for it.

Anthony raised the wrench and started raining down on Barry's ribs and side. "What the fuck Barry? You don't return my calls and you keep dodging me for my money."

Barry laid there and tried to plead his way out of it but Anthony wasn't in the mood to hear his bullshit stories. "You have to give me some more time Anthony."

"I don't have to give you shit Barry. I gave you ten grand and it's been a complete run around from you. I'm tired of this shit." Anthony reached down and grabbed Barry by the shirt and pulled him up to his knees. When he got him to his knees Barry reached out and took a swing that narrowly missed Anthony. That sent Mike into a frenzy who started to lay punches back into Barry's face.

"Are you out of your fucking mind?" asked Mike

Anthony motioned to Enzo, who moved over to the scuffle and used his bulk to pick up Barry. They moved him over to a table and tossed him up against it. Enzo smacked him around for a minute, while Barry struggled to get away from him. Mike was right next to them and he also restrained Barry and got a few more hits in on him.

Anthony watched the fight for a minute while still trying to process where this was going to go. He looked at Enzo and the conversation they had a while back rang in his ears. He was wondering if Barry was going to be the asshole that Anthony was going to have to shoot.

Anthony wasn't sure if he was ready to go down that road, but the way Barry was acting he might have to; especially after he tried to swing at him.

"Hold him down," instructed Anthony.

Enzo got Barry situated on the table and Mike joined in on keeping him down. Anthony moved over to the table and looked down at Barry who was now crying. Anthony could tell he was in pain. "Why are you making me do this Barry? Why can't you just pay me what you fucking owe me?"

"Anthony please, what are you going to do?"

Anthony watched Barry laying there in pain. He wasn't struggling to get away anymore, he just laid there crying. Anthony walked around the table and Barry laid there with his eyes closed crying like a baby. Enzo and Mike watched Anthony for any sign that he would give them, but he was totally concentrating on Barry.

"You a righty or a lefty Barry?"

Barry began to cry harder now. "Anthony please! What are you going to do?"

Enzo twisted Barry's arm. "Fucking answer him."

"Righty!" Barry screamed out.

Anthony moved to the table where Barry's left arm was, the arm that Mike was holding down.

"You want me to break it Ant?" asked Mike.

"Noooooooo," cried Barry.

Anthony shook his head and stared at Barry for a second. Barry's face was full of blood from a clearly broken nose and cut lip, his eye now began to swell from the beating he just received. Tears streamed all down his face. He opened his eyes to meet Anthony's gaze. "Please Anthony, please."

Anthony reached into his back pocket and pulled out the rose clippers and grabbed Barry by the wrist. Barry tried to pull away, but was just met by Mike exerting more pressure on his arm.

Enzo looked up and caught Mike's gaze, both with a look that silently spoke 'What the fuck?'

Anthony opened the rose clippers and locked them onto Barry's pinky and before he could try to struggle to get it away, Anthony closed the clippers and began shearing off Barry's left pinky finger. Blood squirted in the air and all over Anthony's shirt, face and hair. Barry writhed in pain and screamed for all he was worth. The crying was now replaced with screaming and cursing.

Anthony opened the clippers and locked down on Barry's ring finger and tried to sever off that finger as well. This finger was a little tougher and Anthony had to exert more pressure onto the finger. You could hear bone cracking and splitting over Barry's screams. Finally Barry's wedding ring went flying off in the opposite direction of the severed finger and once again blood filled the air along with Barry's screaming and cries.

Anthony unlocked the sheers, stepped back and motioned to Enzo and Mike to let him go. Barry pulled his wounded hand into his chest and laid there crying.

"Barry take this as a warning. The next time I come back here and you don't have the full amount of money, I'm going to cut the rest of your fingers off. If I have to come back again after that and you still don't have the money, I'm gonna cut your hand off. After that it's on to your right hand, and then you're not going to be able to tint windows anymore. After that you won't want to know what I'm going to cut off." Barry nodded his head slowly. Anthony reached behind him and grabbed a rag off the shelf and tossed it to Barry who immediately put it over his bleeding hand.

There was blood everywhere. The rag quickly turned red, you could have wrung it out like a sponge. Anthony put the clippers back into his back pocket and headed towards the back door. Enzo and Mike looked at each other, still with the same look on their faces and then followed Anthony to the door.

"Remember what I said Barry, this is your last warning."

Anthony walked out the door with his friends close behind him while Barry laid on the table continuing to cry and bleed.

The ride home from Barry's shop was pretty much quiet. Anthony didn't really speak and Mike wasn't sure what he wanted to say to him. Mike dropped Anthony off and they said they would speak the next day.

Anthony walked up the walk and looked to see if Debbie's car was there and it wasn't. He proceeded to go into the house and called out to her, just to be sure, but there was just silence. He moved further into the house and made his way upstairs while he took off his blood soaked shirt. He moved over to the washing machine and tossed the shirt in. He looked at his pants and they had blood in a few spots as well. He pulled them off and put them in the machine as well. He threw detergent in and started the wash.

He made his way into the bathroom, looked up at the mirror and stared at himself for a minute. He had blood all over his face and hair. As he looked at himself he could hear Barry's screams and cries in his head. He turned the water on and rinsed off his face, but the dried blood was still there. He shook his head and thought for a minute as he tried to get the image of Barry out of his mind. As he was thinking he reached over and turned the shower on. He looked back at himself in the mirror. What was he becoming? He just cut off someone's fingers. He tried to rationalize what he just did by thinking that it could have been worse. He could have shot Barry.

He finished getting undressed and moved towards the shower, but stopped and looked at himself again. Once again he heard Barry pleading for him to stop. He closed his eyes for a minute then opened them and looked at himself once more. "Fuck you Barry," he said to himself, "pay your fucking debts." He moved into the shower to wash Barry's blood off, and hopefully the memory of what he just did.

Chapter 12
Therapy And Delivery

Several days had passed since Anthony had served Barry with a collection notice and all was quiet. Mike had swung by there and Barry had a payment ready for him, it was even more than the minimum. During the week Mike had dropped it off at the house, along with Enzo's weekly fix. The weekly fix that was now turning into a semi-weekly fix because the weekly just wasn't cutting it anymore. Enzo was going through the stuff too fast.

It was Saturday and Debbie and Anthony had decided to spend the day together. The problem was Enzo wanted his drugs and Anthony had to drop them off to him. The last thing he wanted to do was have Debbie with him for that. She never took part in his business, but what was he going to do with her? Maybe she would wait in the car.

Anthony came down the stairs dressed and Debbie was already in the kitchen ready to go. "Do you want something to drink?"

"Yeah," replied Anthony as he looked around for the bag Mike dropped off with Enzo's stuff. "You see the bag Mike dropped off the other day?"

"You mean with Enzo's drugs?" she asked as she poured Anthony a soda.

Anthony shot her a look from the corner of his eye. "I'm guessing you looked inside?"

Debbie cocked her head to the side and said, "You should know me better than that."

"So how do you know what's in the bag?"

"When Mike handed me the bag he said, 'Here are Enzo's drugs'."

Anthony just laughed and then drank his soda. "What do you want to do today?"

"I need to get some clothes for work and you said you wanted some nicer clothes for the clubs, so I figured we could spend some time today doing that."

"Okay," replied Anthony, as he drank his soda while trying to figure out what he was going to do with Enzo's delivery. "I hope you are going to drop that crap off on the way to shopping. I don't think it should stay in the car all day and I already don't want to drive around with it."

It was as if she read his mind. "Yeah I need to get rid of it. You don't seem too mad about it."

"Do you want me to be?"

Anthony smiled at her and replied, "No, of course not."

"Anthony, it is what it is at this point with Enzo. I'm not happy with it, but what can I do? I'm not going to argue about it and I just don't want to talk about it, so let's just drop it."

Anthony finished his soda and replied, "Sounds like a plan to me." He put his glass in the sink and grabbed his keys.

"We taking your car or mine?" asked Debbie.

"What do you think?"

Debbie smiled and followed him out of the house. "Never miss an opportunity to drive the GNX huh?"

"Nope."

They left the house and headed to the GNX. Anthony got in and popped the locks and Debbie got in. "Can I drive it?" she asked.

Anthony started the car and looked over at her. "Really?"

"Please?"

Anthony thought about it for a minute and then said, "On one condition."

Debbie had a curious look on her face. "What?"

"I'm still waiting for you to tell me the story of what is up with you and your sister. Tell me the story while we drive over there and you can drive there."

She thought about it for a minute. "Enzo's house is five minutes away, the story will take too long."

Anthony said, "No, Enzo is at the office today for his family's limo business, that's over in Woodhaven. We have to go there and then I figured we could go to Queens center."

Debbie thought about it for a minute. "Okay."

Anthony smiled and they traded places in the car. Anthony sat looking at her as she messed up all his seat and mirror settings.

After a minute of her getting adjusted they pulled out of the driveway. "This car is very fast, please don't wreck it."

"Relax, it will be fine. So where do you want me to begin?"

Anthony tried to get himself used to someone else driving his car. He hated being a passenger in someone else's car, so he hated it even more being a passenger in his own car. After a minute he said, "Start at the beginning. There has to be something that triggered this war between the two of you."

Debbie thought about it for a minute. "That would be the day she was born then."

Anthony had a confused look on his face. "What? You have to be kidding me." Debbie didn't answer him. "Come on now, how could she being born make you hate her so much?"

"I told you this is complicated."

"Let's be real, birth?"

Debbie slowly replied, "Actually, conception."

"I don't understand how that is possible."

Debbie thought about it for a minute while Anthony nervously watched the road. "You know that we have different fathers, right?"

Anthony asked, "Lourdes and Cristina are from the same father right?"

"Yep," replied Debbie.

"But Cristina is the oldest and Lourdes is the youngest. If you're the middle child what did your mom do, just go back and forth between husbands?"

Debbie thought about it for a second. "I guess you can say that. You see my mom was married to Cristina's dad and they had Cristina. Things didn't work out between them and they got a divorce. A few years later she met my dad and they got married and they had me. A few months after I was born Cristina's dad started showing up and somewhere along the line my mom slept with him and she came out pregnant with Lourdes. The rest is history."

Anthony continued to look at her and process what she just told him. He turned away and looked out the window as they drove down Woodhaven Blvd. After a second he asked her, "That's why you don't get along with her?"

"Uh huh," replied Debbie.

"Debbie, that doesn't make much sense."

Debbie glanced over at him for a second before looking back at the road. "Why?"

"Deb you were less than a year old when that took place. How can you hold her responsible for that?"

"If it wasn't for her my parents would still be together."

"You don't know that for sure. She's not with their dad now either. What if after a few years they didn't get along and they split up like her first marriage?" Debbie didn't answer him. "Come on Deb, it's got to be more than that."

"Why can't two people just not get along? Look at Mike and Enzo, they don't get along."

Anthony thought about it for a minute. "I guess, but you are basing it on something that happened between your mom and two other guys. She was young when she had Cristina, she still had growing up to do. Besides, you and Lourdes are family, Mike and Enzo aren't."

"Growing up with them wasn't easy. It wasn't that bad with Cristina, but she was a little older. What made it a little harder with Cristina was she was a full sister to Lourdes, I felt like the outcast."

"Well I can understand that, plus you are the middle child."

"What does the middle child have to do with it?"

"It has a lot to do with it," explained Anthony. "Cristina was the oldest and Lourdes was the baby. They both probably got away with things that you couldn't because of that. The middle child is always the outcast of a family, or the forgotten one might be a better way to put it."

Debbie thought about it for a minute. "I never really looked at it like that. It didn't help that I am Italian and they are both Puerto Rican."

"Why didn't that help? Are you a racist now?"

Debbie gave Anthony a dirty look and said, "I'm not a racist."

"Then what does that have to do with anything?"

"I'm just saying it was another thing that made me different from them. They would talk to each other in Spanish and I would feel like it was about me, even when I knew for sure it wasn't."

"I get that. How did they learn Spanish? You're mom doesn't speak it."

"Their father was around for a while during their younger years. Mine left after my mother cheated on him. He divorced her and took off, but their father would come around a lot. He would take them for weekends and the summer. He taught it mostly to Cristina and she taught it to Lourdes. After a while he took off as well." Debbie went quiet for a long minute as she thought about it. "I know I am being difficult, but we just clash. We always argue. We can argue about anything. If Lourdes says something is blue, I say its red and vice versa. Our personalities just bang into one another and it has always been like this for as long as I can remember."

Anthony understood but remained silent. After a minute he asked, "Are you sure you don't have an issue with them meeting me?"

"No, it's got nothing to do with you."

"How about what I do?"

Debbie thought about that question. "I can't say I am proud of that, but it has no bearing on them meeting you. Actually they would probably like it, especially Lourdes."

"Why do you say that?"

"If I don't like something you can bet she will."

Anthony smiled and started to laugh. Debbie laughed back with him. "You know Deb, this sounds like you have more issues with your mom then you sister."

Debbie glanced at him out of the corner of her eye. "I don't think so."

"I do. When you really break it down Lourdes had nothing to do with the choices your mom made. She didn't ask to be born. This pretty much all comes down to your mom making some pretty bad choices." Debbie stayed quiet and just concentrated on driving. Anthony looked over to her and she did not return the look. After a second he knew he struck a nerve with her. She was close with her mother and she probably didn't want to hear that, who would? Who would want to hear that their parent was wrong and she was holding the anger towards the wrong person. After a minute he looked back at her. "I didn't mean to insult your mom."

Debbie turned the car into the driveway where Enzo's limo business was located, stopped the car and looked at Anthony. "It's okay, but this conversation is over. I don't want to talk about my mother or my sisters anymore today."

Anthony heard her tone and replied, "Okay," and with that they got out of the car. Anthony reached under his seat and took out the bag with Enzo's drugs and they moved inside the building. He looked around and there were a few people hanging around, but all were workers from the limo business. Two guys were cleaning the cars and there were a few drivers standing around talking amongst themselves. Anthony asked one of the drivers if Enzo was around and the driver pointed him towards the office. Anthony started to make his way towards the office and then it dawned on him that Debbie was coming with him. He turned to her and stopped walking. "Do you want to wait in the car?"

Debbie looked back at him, she was clearly annoyed from the conversation about her family so he already saw the spark of fire in her eyes. "It's not like I don't know what you're going in there for. Let's just get this over with." She started to head towards the office and Anthony slowly followed along behind her. They reached the office and Enzo looked up from some paperwork and waved them in."

"Hi En," said Debbie. She moved into the office and gave him a kiss and a hug.

"Hey Deb, how are you doing?"

"I'm doing good and you?"

"I can't complain."

Anthony moved into the office behind her and closed the door behind him. Enzo shifted his gaze from Debbie to Anthony, as if to wonder why the door was being closed. Anthony caught the look and patted the bag. Enzo smiled in agreement. Anthony moved over to Enzo and shook his hand and kissed cheek to cheek.

Debbie looked on and started laughing. "Really? Cheek to cheek?"

"Would you prefer if we kissed on the lips?" asked Anthony.

"Maybe Anthony would prefer that, but not me," chimed in Enzo. All three of them laughed for a minute and then Anthony popped the bag on top of the desk. Enzo looked over to the bag and then at Debbie and then at Anthony. "Debbie working with you now?"

Debbie moved away from the desk and took a seat across the room. Anthony looked over at Enzo. "No, we're just on our way to the mall and you were on the way. It's not really a secret to her what is going on here."

"Okay," said Enzo as he sat back down in his chair. Anthony pulled the stuff out of the bag and handed it to Enzo. There was several kilos of coke and several dime bags of pot. Enzo reached over and took the bag of coke and opened it. He put his index finger in the bag and dipped it into the coke and then tasted it. After a second he smiled.

Debbie looked on at the two of them conducting their business. She wasn't sure if she was still annoyed from talking about her sister or if what she was seeing in front of her. She knew Anthony did the things that he did and it started to make her wonder what she didn't know he did. It was one thing to know about what he did, but it was another thing to see him do it. Yeah, she saw him lend out money in the club and she also saw him take bets, collect on bets and pay out on winning bets. Drugs were a little bit different. They were dirty to her and she knew that most of the people that took them were not the type of people she wanted to associate with.

Enzo reached over and took the bags of pot and started inspecting them. He reached into one and pulled out an already prepared joint. He examined it and then lit it up. Debbie had a disgusted look on her face and looked away. Enzo took a drag of the joint and then reached into his pocket. He pulled out a wad of cash and tossed it to Anthony.

Anthony picked the money up off the desk and started counting it. "I know this isn't all of it En."

"No that's just for the weed, I have the coke money here." Enzo reached under the desk and pulled out a briefcase and handed it to Anthony. Anthony took the briefcase and moved over to a table and popped it open. There were stacks of cash inside bundled in one thousand dollar stacks. Debbie looked over at the briefcase and her eyes opened wide at the sight of all the money. Anthony looked through the stacks to make sure it all looked legit. He took two stacks of money out of the briefcase and put them in his jacket pocket then he closed the briefcase.

"Where are you going with the money you put in your pocket?" asked Debbie.

Anthony winked at her and replied, "Shopping."

Debbie had a slight smirk on her face and shook her head. She moved towards the desk and kissed Enzo goodbye and then went towards the door. Anthony picked up his briefcase, shook Enzo's hand and then headed out the door behind Debbie to head to the mall.

Enzo sat back and continued getting high.

Chapter 13
Making A Deposit

Mike and Anthony arrived at the club on 101st Ave. When Anthony's GNX pulled up a few guys standing around turned to look at it. It was the hottest car in the neighborhood and Anthony knew it. It made him feel good when people turned to look at his car.

He and Mike jumped out of the car and went into the trunk to grab their packages and head inside. They were both carrying two large duffle bags full of money. Anthony also had a briefcase full of money. The duffle bags were set to go over to an offshore account and the briefcase was the kick up to the higher ups from the club. Once a week Anthony always brought a briefcase full of money to send on to the powers that be. It's how he stayed in everyone's favor.

One of the guys standing outside the club yelled over to Anthony, "There he is, Tony Two Fingers."

Anthony shot a look over to who yelled that at him, a puzzled look, and replied "Tony Two Fingers?" Mike began to laugh and Anthony shot him a look. "What's that about?"

Mike looked back at him, "You haven't heard that yet?"

Anthony replied, "No, what's that about?"

"Think about it."

Mickey Maldonado was waiting at the entrance to the club, Anthony waved to him and he waved back. They said hello to a few of the guys outside and then headed into the club.

"Mickey the Mouse," said Mike in a squeaky voice.

"How you doin' Mike?" asked Mickey.

Mike patted the duffle bag full of cash and smiled from ear to ear. "Pretty good I think, Mickey."

Mickey smiled and said, "Looks like it."

They moved to a back room and Mike handed Anthony his bag and he handed Mike the briefcase. "I'll take care of the big boys," said Mike.

Anthony said, "Okay," and Mike walked out of the room.

Anthony placed the two large bags on top of the table and Mickey looked inside. His eyes opened wide. "All hundreds?"

"Some fifties but mostly hundreds."

"How much is here?"

"Fifty thousand in each bag."

"Wow, you guys are doing pretty good for yourselves huh?"

Anthony motioned to Mickey, "Yeah, I wanted to talk to you about something."

"Sure, what's on your mind?"

Anthony motioned for Mickey to sit and they both did. He looked around the room to be sure they were alone and then leaned in close to Mickey. "I'm looking to invest some money in some people."

Mickey had a confused look on his face, "I'm not sure I understand."

Anthony tried to figure a way to explain it better. "I want to start having people on a payroll, I guess that's the best way to put it. Kinda like you are, on a retainer I guess."

"You want people to work for you?"

Anthony made a motion that wasn't a yes or a no. He looked around again, "I want people in my corner, in case I ever need them, like you are. If I get into trouble with the law I know I can call you and you will be my lawyer, but I want more than that. Do you know any judges that can be persuaded by money to rule in my favor, or cops that will look the other way when I need them to, if I need them to? People like that."

Mickey sat back and thought for a minute. "I think I know where you're going with this. You expecting any trouble?"

Anthony answered, "No, but you never know. We do a lot of dangerous things and you never know when I might need people like that in my corner. Also, down the road, it could never hurt to have people with influence in my corner."

"Sure I understand, and it's probably very smart." He thought for a minute, "I do know someone that just became a judge, and I actually know a few local district politicians that are always looking to make some money on the side. Politicians are always a good thing to have in your back pocket. They're just starting out, but I see these people wielding a lot of power in the future. Congressmen and senators, just for starts."

Anthony agreed, "Now you're thinking on the same level as me."

Mickey took a drag from his cigarette. "I'll take care of it."

Anthony smiled and patted Mickey on his back, he was glad he became friends with him. He was proving to be a very useful contact, and thru him Anthony was going to start making a lot more friends and contacts. "Keep this between the two of us, okay?"

Mickey smiled and said, "Anything for Tony Two Fingers."

There is was again, Tony Two Fingers, Anthony thought to himself. "You to?" he asked Mickey.

Mickey laughed at Anthony, "Hey that's not an insult. It's kinda catchy, I like it!"

Mike walked back into the room and handed Anthony a bottle of beer, then handed one to Mickey. Anthony and Mickey got up and the three headed out of the room. Mickey had the two duffle bags with him and headed towards another room, "I'll take care of these guys."

Mike and Anthony nodded in Mickey's direction and he disappeared into another room. "Everything all right in there?" asked Mike.

Anthony replied, "Yeah we were just talking shit, nothing important." Mike motioned and they headed over to a pool table to shoot a game. "Hey, let me ask you something."

Mike replied, "Sure, what's up?"

Anthony thought for a second and then asked Mike, "You've heard this Tony Two Fingers thing before?"

Mike smiled at Anthony. "Of course I have. I'm surprised you haven't. You still don't know what everyone is talking about?"

Anthony stared at the pool table thinking hard about Mike's question. He scratched his head for a second and then it hit him. He looked up at Mike who still had a smile on his face, "The shit with Barry?"

Mike laughed out loud, "I'm surprised you just got wind of that." Anthony shrugged his shoulders and then laughed out loud. Mike held up his beer to Anthony and Anthony tapped it with his. "You have to admit Ant, it's a fucking good name." Anthony thought about it for a minute, it really was a good name. It had a certain ring to it. Now after Anthony knew what it meant it made a lot of sense. After a minute of thinking about it Anthony nodded his head in agreement. "You made a name for yourself out there. The word is out on the street: If you don't pay your bills, Two Fingers is going to collect, and it's not going to be pleasant."

Anthony smiled and sized up a shot that he missed. "How did that whole thing sit with you? We never really talked about it."

Mike lined up a shot that he sunk perfectly, then studied the table for his next shot while thinking about what Anthony just asked him. "Well, I guess it could have been worse for Barry."

"How so?"

Mike stopped looking at the pool table and right at Anthony. "You were thinking about shooting him, I'm pretty sure that would have turned out a lot worse for Barry then just losing two fingers. Possibly would have turned out worse for both of you."

A few other guys came and went in the club and stopped to talk to Mike and some stopped to talk to Anthony. That's pretty much how the rest of their day went. A few guys stopped in to see Anthony for their weekly payments and some stopped to see Mike for their weekly fixes. They stayed for a few hours, drank a few beers, played a few games of pool and then went on their way. This was their life, and they were loving it.

Chapter 14
Sisters Of Destiny

Ascension was off the hook again. When wasn't it? That club didn't know what it was to have a slow night. Tonight Anthony was working with the resident DJ there. On the side, for fun, Anthony would spin there. When he had free time in the past he would spin for a living, block parties mostly, but that was almost a thing of the past. He had no time for it any more. Tonight he decided to make just a little time for it, he missed it. It was always a lot of fun to be the person keeping the club dancing. Combined with his love of Freestyle he was a natural DJ.

Tonight was going to be a special night as well; he was going to meet Debbie's two sisters, Cristina and Lourdes, for the first time. Lourdes was back in town after being on a grueling modeling tour that pulled her all over the country and she was looking to unwind. Anthony was looking forward to meeting both of them. He had heard a lot about them, and from what he heard he thought they would get along great with him.

A waitress came over and brought Anthony a drink. He reached over and handed her a twenty and told her to keep it, not because he had a tab to pay, but because he wanted to tip her. She responded with a cute smile and went on her way. Anthony surveyed the club as he worked on his next mix. He started cutting some Luisa Menendez in and the crowd went wild. He looked out around the club and saw Mike in one corner doing his usual dealing, then he looked at the other end of the club and saw Enzo sitting in a booth with a few guys from the social club. They were having a few drinks and talking what looked like important business, Enzo never looked up at him.

Anthony felt a tug on his pants, looked down behind him and saw it was Debbie. "Hi Baby," he said.

Debbie smiled at him and he motioned to the other DJ he would be back in a few. He removed his head phones and made his way out of the DJ booth and down to Debbie. He was met by a kiss and a hug. "How's the DJ'ing going?"

"Agh, it's okay. I haven't done it in a while so it takes time getting back into it."

"Yeah, I bet."

"I forgot how much work it actually is. I would rather hang out."

Debbie laughed and replied, "I know you would."

The same waitress came by and handed Debbie her usual drink and walked off. Anthony looked around and then asked "Where are your sisters?"

Debbie took a sip from her drink and then cautiously motioned her head towards the coat check area, "They're over there." Anthony looked over her shoulder and saw the two of them at the coat check area getting their tickets, with Cristina's back facing them. He recognized them from the pictures Debbie had recently shown him, and from Lourdes's pictorials. Cristina was about 5'4" with dark brown hair that stopped at her mid back and dark eyes. She stood about 5'7" now in heels and club wear. She was a pretty girl at age twenty five who worked as a cashier in a woman's clothing store in Queens.

Lourdes stood normally at 5'7", but on this occasion she was about 5'11" in her club wear, four inch heels and a tight one piece black lace dress. She had near waist length straight dark brown hair and dark brown eyes. She was eighteen, closing in on nineteen. Anthony could see why she was a model, she was a beautiful girl. All three of them were. He could see the resemblance between Cristina and Lourdes from them both having the same parents. He could see the Latin in them the same way he could see the Italian in Debbie. Neither of the two fathers were in the picture and Anthony wasn't going down that road with Debbie again. After the talk they had about her relationship with her sisters, he didn't want to have that talk again, neither did Debbie. Anthony looked over at the guy that was standing behind them. "Who's that with them?"

Debbie looked over and then rolled her eyes when she looked back to Anthony. "That, is Cristina's wonderful boyfriend."

Anthony shifted his look from the guy to Debbie, "Why the eye roll?"

Debbie locked eyes with Anthony. "He's a fucking asshole. I have no use for him at all."

Anthony said, "Oh, I guess he fits in with that whole Spanish dynamic?"

Debbie cracked a smile at Anthony's sarcastic remark. "Not for the same reasons."

"Puerto Rican has nothing to do with it?"

"Ha, ha," replied Debbie. "He's Dominican, not Puerto Rican, and that has nothing to do with it."

"So why is he an asshole?"

Debbie looked over to them still getting their tickets and talking amongst themselves. Lourdes looked over and shed a slight smile to Debbie who just annoyingly turned her head away and back towards Anthony. "Well for one thing, he hits my sister."

Anthony's look changed and he turned his head a bit to the side, "Excuse me?"

Debbie locked eyes with Anthony and said, "Yeah," then she looked towards Cristina and caught her attention. Debbie pointed to the roped off table they had reserved for them and motioned to Cristina that's where they would be sitting. Cristina nodded her head and Debbie took Anthony by the hand and pulled them away from the table, towards the center bar before he could train his vision on Cristina. Once they got to the other side of the bar she stopped and said to Anthony, "Listen I don't want any shit with this asshole tonight, please?"

Anthony looked at her and then across the bar towards her sisters making their way to the table and then back to Debbie. Anthony squinted towards their direction but it was hard for him to make out what he thought he saw on Cristina's face. Once Debbie caught his look she squeezed his hand to snap him out of the stare. "Okay, I get that, but what do you mean he hits her?" asked Anthony.

Debbie looked away like she was sorry she brought it up, but she had no choice. Anthony would see Cristina's face when she made the introductions so she had to tell him. "He has been known, from time to time, to put his hands on her. She doesn't talk about it much and from what I got out of Lourdes about it, it happens more often than not." Debbie paused for a second and then hesitantly added, "As a matter of fact, she is bruised up right now."

Anthony took a deep breath and shook his head in disbelief. "WHAT?" Before Debbie could answer, Anthony asked, "Why is he here tonight then?"

Debbie laughed for a second, "Did you think he would actually let Cristina come to a club like this without him?"

Anthony let out his annoyed sigh and shook his head yet again. He looked over thru the crowd at Cristina and confirmed what he thought he saw briefly a moment ago. A really bad blackened left eye and a bruised fat lip on the right. He felt his blood begin to boil and then he started to dial it back. The only thing that went through his mind at that moment was to round up a few of his friends, take this asshole around back and give him some of what was given to Cristina.

As if Debbie could read his mind and his facial expressions she said, "Listen, this is none of our business. That is between them and I don't want any part of it and I don't want you or any of your friends getting involved in it. Do you understand?" Debbie could tell by the look on Anthony's face he wasn't happy about this.

After a second Anthony replied, "Okay."

Debbie was a bit taken back by his quick response, but she was ready to accept it. She wasn't sure if he was placating her, or if he was really serious about not starting anything.

Anthony reached over to the pretty waitress that gave them their drinks and pulled her over to them. He pointed out the table that Cristina and Lourdes were sitting at and told her to give them whatever they wanted with no tab and no charge. The waitress nodded and went about her way.

Debbie took Anthony's hand and they made their way through the crowded club and back to the table. Once they got there Debbie began to make the introductions. "Anthony, these are my sisters, Cristina and Lourdes." Anthony reached over and extended his hand to Lourdes first.

She reached out took his hand and smiled at him "Hi Anthony, it's nice to meet you."

Anthony smiled back at her and said, "It's nice to meet you too."

Cristina stood up and Anthony extended his hand towards her as he looked closer at her bruises, they were terrible. Her left eye was badly blackened, so bad that parts of her face were purple. Her lip looked the same way, blackened, purple and swollen. He tried to put it out of his head for a minute as he said, "Hi Cristina, it's nice to meet you."

Cristina smiled shyly and took Anthony's hand, "It's nice to meet you too Anthony."

Anthony turned towards Cristina's boyfriend and locked into a stare with him. After a moment he pushed himself to extend his hand towards him. Debbie noticed and said, "Anthony this is Cristina's boyfriend, Carlos."

Carlos looked down at Anthony's hand and after a second he shook it. "How are you?" he asked with a heavy Spanish accent.

Anthony locked onto Carlos' eyes and shook his hand tight. Carlos gazed back at him while shaking his hand. "I'm good," Anthony replied while staring at him. After a second Carlos looked away and Anthony let his hand go. Anthony continued to size Carlos up. He was six feet tall and a little over one eighty. He had a light complexion, dark eyes and dark, tight curly hair. He had a dark, shadowy, sporadic beard. He was wearing a white shirt and black pants. Anthony wasn't sure if he was already tainted by what Debbie told him, or if Anthony just got the notion that this guy was a piece of shit. Anthony thought about it for a second, and then came to the conclusion that he was a piece of shit.

At that awkward moment the waitress came over and broke the silence by asking what everyone wanted to drink. Anthony noticed Lourdes reaching for her purse and he motioned for her to stop. "This is all on the club tonight. Order whatever you want to drink and don't worry about it."

Cristina smiled at Anthony and Carlos noticed. "What the fuck are you smiling at?" asked Carlos in a nasty tone.

Cristina got nervous and tried to show she didn't mean anything by it. Stuttering, she replied "I, I just thought that was really nice of him for that." She couldn't get her words out fast enough.

Carlos stared at her, "You think I don't have money on me or something?"

Before a very nervous Cristina could answer him Anthony interrupted with a somewhat raised voice, "That's not the point!"

Carlos quickly turned his blazing gaze from Cristina towards Anthony and Debbie began to get nervous about the situation that was already brewing.

Anthony locked his blue eyes with Carlos' black eyes and continued, "My friends run this club, amongst other things. These ladies are my girlfriend's sisters. We drink in here for free, so that means you all do as well." Anthony shifted his gaze away from Carlos and directed his next comment towards the sisters and not to Carlos. "You're family." Anthony motioned to two other waitresses and they brought over champagne and glasses and set it up for the table. Anthony then turned back towards Carlos and said somewhat sternly, "Case closed." Carlos continued to stare at Anthony, but he was un-wavered by the black stare that Carlos was giving to him. Anthony reached into his pocket and pulled out a cigar case and offered one to Carlos. Carlos looked at the cigars and then back to Anthony. Anthony pushed the cigars closer to Carlos, "Cubans."

Carlos looked at them for another second and then replied, "Nah, I only smoke Dominican cigars."

Anthony looked at him and let out a little laugh, but more of a snicker. "Cuban cigars are the best. You ever have one?"

Carlos looked at him in disbelief and said, "I just told you I only smoke Dominicans."

Anthony pulled the cigars back and began to lite one up for himself. Through the flame he caught Cristina's scared look. He tried to convey to her to relax by his look, but he wasn't sure if she was getting it. The girl looked terrified. He shifted his gaze to Lourdes and cracked a smirk at her and she smiled back.

Carlos looked back at him, "You ever smoke a Dominican?"

Anthony continued lighting his cigar and never met Carlos' gaze. He took his time lighting the cigar and wasn't really in a rush to answer this asshole, but he did leave himself open for a wiseass comment with that question. Did this stupid fuck just ask Anthony an open ended question like that? After a second Anthony locked eyes with him and gave him a very cold stare of his own now. "Stick around, the night is young; maybe tonight." Anthony pulled a long drag out of his cigar and continued to stare at Carlos thru the cigar smoke that he just blew in his direction.

After a second Carlos understood the remark, and he didn't like it. "I'm going to the bathroom," he said as he walked off visibly annoyed.

Anthony pulled another long drag out of the cigar and caught the gaze of the three women. He cracked a slight smile and looked at Lourdes and winked at her. Cristina was visibly calmer once Carlos walked away and smiled at Anthony who smiled back at her. "Drink up ladies, we're here to have fun tonight. I'm already having fun." Anthony made his way back to the DJ booth to tell them he was probably done spinning for the night.

Debbie looked at her sisters and the three of them laughed. "That, is my boyfriend!" Debbie made her way to sit between the two of them.

"He's got a way about him," pointed out Cristina.

Debbie agreed, "That he does."

"He doesn't back down huh?" asked Lourdes.

Debbie looked at her and replied, "No and sometimes that's a problem."

Lourdes took a sip of her drink and then looked at Cristina, "He shut Carlos up." Cristina smiled and Lourdes continued, "I like him." Cristina laughed and then agreed with Lourdes.

"Great!" laughed Debbie. "Everyone likes him."

Lourdes chimed in, "Everyone except Carlos."

The three sisters looked at one another and laughed out loud for a minute.

Debbie looked at Cristina, who was still laughing. "I'm sorry Cristina, I don't mean to make fun of him."

"It's okay Debbie, everyone knows he is an asshole; myself included."

Debbie looked around to see if Carlos was anywhere in earshot before she continued with the conversation. "I see he is still hitting you."

Cristina took a long sip out of her drink and then nodded her head somewhat embarrassed. Lourdes unbelievingly shook her head and asked, "Why do you put up with that shit Cristina?"

Cristina thought about it for a second but didn't really answer. Lourdes looked at her again. "He better not ever do that shit in front of me."

Debbie rolled her eyes at Lourdes and said, "Yeah, like you can do something about it." Lourdes looked at Debbie and rolled her eyes as well, but didn't reply to the sarcastic comment. One brewing argument tonight was enough. Everyone was silent for a minute and then Debbie broke the silence. "You better hope he doesn't do it in front of Anthony."

"Really?" asked Cristina sounding somewhat intrigued.

Debbie shot Cristina a dumb look, "Really, Cristina?"

Lourdes asked, "Didn't you just get that whole thing about smoking a Dominican? Did you really think Anthony meant a cigar?" The three laughed again as Cristina realized what Anthony meant. Lourdes looked over to Debbie, "And you think I'm the ditzy one?"

Ignoring Lourdes, Debbie said, "I will try my best to keep Anthony on a leash but if Carlos puts his hands on you tonight, no one in this club will be able to contain him."

Cristina thought about that for a minute and it didn't seem to bother her. "What is Anthony capable of?"

Debbie looked at Cristina out of the corner of her eye and then motioned in Anthony's direction for her sisters to observe him. Anthony was working the entire club, walking around, shaking people's hands, kissing girls hello. Every now and then guys handing him envelopes obviously loaded with cash that was owed to him. Guys twice his size paid him respect like he was the larger one. "Look at the people that he knows and associates with. Is there any illusion what he does, who he knows and what he is capable of? What his friends are capable of? Sometimes it scares me."

Lourdes asked, "Why?"

Debbie looked at Lourdes somewhat annoyed, "The entire neighborhood is calling him Tony Two Fingers. Isn't that enough to unnerve someone?"

Lourdes thought about it for a second, "What does it mean?"

"Is he missing two fingers?" asked Cristina.

"No!" replied Debbie.

Cristina thought about it some more, "Is he missing eight fingers?" asked Cristina again.

"Cristina, NO! Wouldn't you have noticed that when you shook his hand?"

Lourdes began to laugh and Debbie looked over to her and asked her somewhat annoyed, "What's so funny?"

"Maybe," began Lourdes giggling, "he's good with two fingers." Both Debbie and Cristina continued to just stare at Lourdes, not knowing what she meant. Lourdes, still giggling, did a motion of two fingers going into a hole, "Get it?"

"Really Lourdes?" asked Debbie visibly annoyed and not trying to hide it. Lourdes finished laughing when she saw Debbie wasn't amused. "I think it means something a little darker then finger fucking someone." Debbie went quiet for a minute and then added, "Anyway, if it was that, I would know about it."

Not able to pass the opportunity up Lourdes quickly asked her, "Would you really?"

Debbie gazed at her sister with a look that could kill. Before she could fire back Cristina asked, "What did you have in mind?"

Debbie calmed herself down from Lourdes's comment and thought about it for a minute before she replied. "I don't know, maybe he broke someone's fingers who owed him money or something."

After a moment Anthony made his way back to the table with a tray of chocolate covered strawberries to go along with the champagne. He placed the tray down and sat across from the girls. "What's up girls, having fun yet?"

Without hesitation Lourdes asked, "What's Tony Two Fingers mean?"

Both Debbie and Cristina quickly turned their heads towards her and at the same time yelled, "LOURDES!" Cristina was trying to contain a laugh while Debbie tried to contain her anger. She didn't want Anthony to know they were talking about this.

Lourdes looked back at both of them and Anthony stayed quiet, clearly taken back by her question. "What? Come on, you want to know and apparently it's not a secret if everyone in the neighborhood is calling him that." Anthony continued to remain quiet and then the three sisters slowly turned and looked at him.

"Well?" asked Debbie, none too amused by her boyfriend's street name.

Lourdes could see there was uncomfortableness and she decided to make it even worse. "Well, Cristina thinks you are missing either two or eight fingers."

Anthony looked over to Cristina who tried to hold back a laugh, but she was already cracking up. Anthony held up both of his hands to show he had all ten of his fingers. After a second he looked towards Lourdes, "And your idea Miss Model?"

Debbie started to laugh and then said, "Oh, you don't even want to know her idea." The girls all busted out laughing and then looked at Lourdes. Lourdes clearly began to turn red, not willing to reveal what her notion of his nickname was and then Debbie finally gave it up. "My little sister thinks you finger fuck with two fingers."

Anthony stared at her for a second before he busted out laughing and somewhat red himself now. After a minute he shook his head implying no. At that moment Carlos made his way back to the table and everyone began calming back down. Carlos sat and grabbed a glass of champagne and Lourdes tried to further the conversation along hoping to once again get under Carlos' skin, as well as Debbie's. "My older sister Debbie thinks it means you broke someone's fingers or something."

Anthony took a drag out of his cigar and let out a long puff of smoke towards the table, mostly towards Carlos' direction. He looked at Debbie who didn't look too amused at the conversation, or Anthony's antics towards Carlos anymore. Anthony's eyes danced back and forth between the three sisters, but not towards Carlos. After a second he looked at Lourdes, since she was the one who asked the question and they stared at each other for what seemed to be a long minute. "Or something," he replied nodding his head. He placed his cigar back into his mouth and took a long drag. After a second he looked at Debbie who took his remark and let it annoy her even more. At this point everyone returned to silence and just listened to the music and surveyed the club.

After a minute or so Mike, Teresa and Enzo made their way to the table to say their hellos. Debbie made the introductions for everyone and Mike and Teresa joined the party as Enzo made his way back into the crowd. Much of the evening went without incident. Anthony kept his conducting of business to a minimum, as well as his drinking. Debbie had noticed that and questioned him and

128

he said he needed to stay alert, in case of any trouble. She knew he was referring to Carlos, but she didn't argue with him. She let the comment about Tony Two Fingers go and managed to have fun the rest of the night.

Anthony and Carlos traded wise cracks back and forth for most of the night, but it never really led up to a confrontation. It always seemed to defuse before it got past the point of no return. Anthony wouldn't have minded a confrontation with Carlos in the club. It was his territory, and before even he knew it Carlos would have had more than several pairs of hands on him before Anthony could even get into it with him. It just never came. Anthony could tell that there would be one though, just not tonight and not here. This would come down to just the two of them sometime in the future, He could feel it. Anthony did manage to get out of Carlos that he was a barber and ran a shop on Knickerbocker. As far as that, Anthony really didn't want to know any more about him.

Anthony had as much conversation as he could with Cristina and Lourdes. He noticed he had to talk more to Cristina when Carlos wasn't around. She would just shut down when he was there and really wouldn't carry on a conversation. The girl looked scared. She trembled when Carlos was near her. When he moved, even to get his drink, she would flinch. Anthony knew that was a sign of her being afraid she was going to get hit. That annoyed him, but he kept himself in check, for Debbie's sake.

Anthony did manage to have a long conversation with Lourdes. She told him all about her modeling trips, he could tell she was enjoying her career. She was young, eighteen years old, traveling the world and making money in the process. Who wouldn't be enjoying that? He was surprised to hear that she was single and didn't have a boyfriend. He hoped for her sake that when it did come time for her to choose a guy she would be wiser than Cristina in that department. It would be a shame for a girl with her looks and potential to get mixed up with a guy like Carlos, who could put his hands on her and possibly put an end to her modeling career.

Anthony could tell that Debbie wasn't too happy about him spending time with Lourdes. Not that she didn't trust him in that respect, but he could really see on display Debbie's dislike towards her younger sister. Many times throughout the night Lourdes had tried to engage Debbie in conversation, but Debbie would either reply back with one word answers or just had a very obvious annoyed look on her face when she had to answer her back. Lourdes was the better of the two by just letting it go. Anthony wondered how long that would last before Lourdes lashed out at Debbie. He knew Debbie's temper at times, and he could tell that when that volcano blew the two of them were going to go over the point of no return.

Anthony made his way back from the DJ booth thru a crowded dance floor to find only Teresa and Mike sitting at the table. He asked where everyone was and apparently Carlos and Cristina were dancing while Debbie went to the bathroom and Lourdes was trying to get a drink at the bar. Anthony watched her waiting patiently. He made his way there and approached her. "Hi Miss."

Lourdes smiled at him and gave him back a, "Hi." He noticed that no one was paying attention to her waiting for a drink, so he made his way behind the bar. One of the bartenders saw him coming over and went to stop him, until he saw who it was. Anthony waved him off and then he approached her from the other side of the bar. She saw him and started to laugh, "Now you're a bartender?"

"What can I get for you Miss?"

Lourdes thought about it for a minute, "Vodka and cranberry."

"Do you have ID?" Lourdes shot him a somewhat sly and flirty look. "How old are you?"

"I'm legal," she giggled.

He thought about that for a second, he knew she wasn't twenty one, "Legal for what?"

Lourdes thought for a second and with the same sly look she replied, "Certain things."

Anthony cracked a smile and said, "That works for me." He began making her a drink. "So what do you think of the place?"

Lourdes looked around and replied, "I like it. I can see myself hanging out here more often." She thought for a minute and then decided to ask him, "Do you own it?"

Anthony replied, "No. I wish I did though. This place is a cash cow."

"You certainly walk around here like you own it, and the people here treat you like you do."

Anthony looked up at her and caught her gaze as he made her a drink. "Yeah, I know a lot of people here."

"Apparently you know a lot of people everywhere. How old are you?"

Anthony moved closer to her so people around them wouldn't hear him. "I'm going to be eighteen."

Lourdes said, "So, you're not legal yet." She laughed and he smiled at her and then she continued, "See that's not normal. A seventeen year old pretty much running a club that you need to be twenty one and over to get into? You got your hands in this place."

"Actually, guys have to be twenty three and older to get in here." Anthony finished pouring her the drink and handed it to her. He smiled at her. "The owners are connected to people that I'm connected to."

Lourdes smiled and kept staring at him when she said, "That's cool."

Anthony grabbed a beer and leaned on the bar and tapped it to her glass. "Stuff like that doesn't bother you?"

"Stuff like what?"

"Being connected."

Lourdes replied, "Not at all. I like it."

Debbie was right when she told Anthony that Lourdes would be intrigued by his work. "Well you are very different from your sister, that's for sure."

"That's the truth."

They both laughed a little and kept drinking. Lourdes caught Anthony's gaze and kept it for a minute. "Can I ask you something?"

Anthony smiled at her and then said, "Sure."

"Would you tell me what Tony Two Fingers means?"

Anthony cracked a smile and then grabbed a rag and cleaned up some spilled drink near her arm. After a second he put the rag down and said, "You know, I feel comfortable around you."

Lourdes looked into his eyes and replied, "I feel comfortable around you too. It's almost like a natural friendship."

"If you promise not to tell your sisters I'll tell you."

Lourdes took a sip out of her drink and replied, "Okay."

"Someone owed me some money and he thought I was a fool, so I went to his shop with a couple of guys and we beat him and I cut two of his fingers off." Lourdes continued to sip out of her drink and remained locked in a stare with Anthony. "How does that sit with you?"

Lourdes put her empty drink down and Anthony gave her a refill. She waited for him to finish the drink and then said, "It sits fine with me. If he borrowed that money then he should have paid you back."

"You sure you don't think any differently of me now?"

Lourdes shook her head quickly to dismiss any idea that what he just told her bothered her. "Not at all, we're cool. Like I said, I like that stuff. You are respected and I like that. He got what was coming to him, probably got off easy." Lourdes picked up her drink and sipped out of it and smiled at Anthony.

Anthony leaned over the bar again and said, "Let me ask you a question now."

Lourdes said, "Okay, your turn."

"What's up with this asshole Carlos?"

Lourdes laughed and put her drink down. "Well you got it right that he's an asshole." She went quiet for a minute and then caught Anthony's gaze again. "He is physically and emotionally abusive to her." Anthony nodded his head. "You know?" Anthony took a sip from his beer. "Debbie told you?"

Anthony replied, "Yeah and the bruises on her face. I could tell by the way she is acting as well."

"You mean the quietness?"

"Yeah, among other things."

"Meaning?" asked Lourdes.

"I see the way she flinches when he moves. It's a reaction to getting hit. Sometimes children do that when they are used to getting hit by their parents."

"I never thought about that."

"Why does she put up with it?"

Lourdes shrugged her shoulders, "I don't know. If I had to guess it's certainly not because she loves him."

"What makes you say that?"

"She's afraid Anthony, deathly afraid of him. I know my sister, and being with this guy is not her. She mentioned one time that she would love to be rid of him."

That intrigued Anthony. "Rid of him how?"

Lourdes took a sip of her drink. "Not with him anymore. He won't take no for an answer though. I heard a fight they had one time and she literally begged him to go and he said he wasn't going anywhere. They would be together until one of them died."

Anthony thought about that for a second. He didn't like the sound of that. "You ever talk to her about it?"

"Yes, all the time."

"You know, I don't like getting involved in people's relationships, but if someone is in danger I can't see myself not getting involved. Your sister asked me not to start anything with this guy and I'm trying my best not to, but you're family. I feel horrible standing by and seeing family being treated like that. I just don't know if this is my place to get involved in this, at least not now."

Lourdes replied, "I understand."

"I would like it if you talked to her again when he's not around. Try to find out if she is really serious about getting away from him. If so, I can see what I can do to help her."

"Okay," replied Lourdes.

Anthony grabbed a pen and a napkin from the bar and wrote down his pager number and then handed it to Lourdes. "That's my pager number. You can reach me there if you or your sister ever need anything." Anthony took another sip of beer and leaned closer to her. "Don't mention any of this conversation to Debbie okay?"

Lourdes smiled at him, "You don't have to worry about that, Tony Two Fingers." Lourdes smiled and winked at him and made her way back to the table. Anthony watched her walk back there. After a second he grabbed his beer and made his way out and away from the bar before some asshole thought he was a bartender and asked him for a drink. He walked slowly around the club and found a dark corner where he thought no one would see him. He lit up another cigar and looked out on the dance floor. He found Cristina dancing with Carlos, who had his back towards Anthony. He watched them for a few minutes and there was simply no joy on her face at all. She looked like a prisoner without chains. Anthony took a long drag from the cigar and after a second he noticed Cristina was locked onto his eyes. He tried to convey to her that she would be alright, but her blank look spoke that she didn't believe him. After a minute he just moved on his way. It was starting to get late and by the time he got back to the table Mike and Teresa had left the club and Anthony was just about done as well. By that point everyone said their goodbyes and Debbie and Anthony headed home.

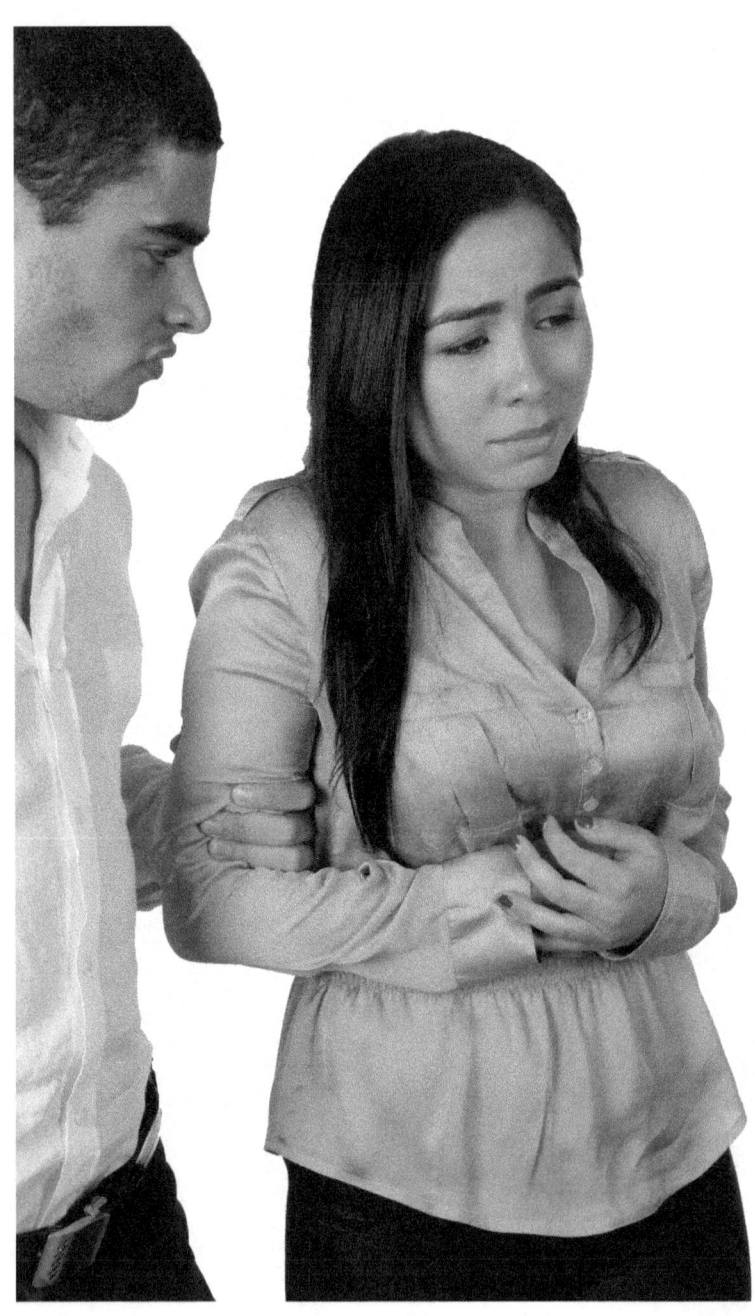

Chapter 15
Mike's Opinion

Anthony was making his rounds in the neighborhood, he had already made most of his stops and now he was pretty much just taking the GNX for a cruise. It relaxed him after a day of collections.

It was a few days after meeting Debbie's sisters and he was still processing what he found out about Cristina's boyfriend abusing her. He hadn't had a conversation with Debbie about it, and he could tell that she didn't want to get involved in it. The extension of that was that she didn't want him involved with it either. He thought about it a lot the past few days and he really didn't want to be involved in it either. He had his hands full with his work. That took a toll on him having to lay into the people that owed him money. To have to do it to someone that he really wasn't connected to was going to make it harder. To be honest with himself, it's not like Carlos was a small guy either. Anthony had no illusions that it wouldn't be a tough fight. Carlos had about fifteen pounds on him and he could tell he was in shape. He looked like he worked out a lot more then Anthony did and he was well defined, more than Anthony was, in the muscle department. With the people Anthony had to deal with they all knew who he was with, who was behind him and they feared him because of that. This asshole didn't seem to know anything about Anthony and who Anthony's friends were. If he did, it didn't look like it bothered him.

Anthony pushed Carlos from his mind and cruised down one of the blocks leading to the club. Even with the radio loud he could hear his cars exhaust system rumbling. As he raced the engine everyone on the street looked at him. He pulled up in front of the club and a few of the guys turned and looked at him. They waved and he checked out the block, looking for Mike. After a second Mike must have heard the rumble from the GNX and he came outside to greet Anthony. Anthony waved him over to the car and to get in. Mike did and Anthony took off down the block hard, sending the turbo in the GNX into overdrive.

"Hello to you to Ant," Mike said as he held on tight as Anthony raced down the block and took a hard left off 101st Ave, heading towards Atlantic Ave. Anthony smiled as he watched his friend shit himself. "You angry at me about something?"

Anthony laughed and then slowed the car down. "I'm just opening her up. She feels like she wants to race today."

"What's up?"

The GNX reached Atlantic Ave and Anthony made a right and resumed normal driving. "What did you think of the girls at the club the other night?"

Mike asked, "Which girls? The club was packed."

"Debbie's sisters, Numbnuts."

Mike laughed, "They were okay. That douche bag that was with them is another story."

Anthony laughed and looked at Mike from the corner of his eye. "You didn't have much use for him either, huh?"

Mike laughed, "No and it's not like you could carry a conversation with him either. He would give you one word answers and he just looked like he had a chip on his shoulder."

"I have to tell you something about him."

Mike looked over to him and waited while Anthony remained silent. "Well?"

"I don't want you to talk to Teresa about this okay? If she takes it back to Debbie I'll have my hands full."

"No problem," replied Mike.

"This scumbag beats Cristina."

Mike looked away and shook his head to himself. "That's where those bruises came from?"

"Yeah," replied Anthony.

After a minute Mike said to Anthony, "And let me guess, you want to do something about it."

Anthony had a look of shock. "You saw her face. You wouldn't?"

"I don't know Ant. You really want to get involved with that shit?"

Anthony couldn't believe what he was hearing. "Put yourself in that situation for a minute. What if Teresa had a sister that was getting beaten like that? Wouldn't you want to get involved?"

Mike thought about it for a second. "Honestly I don't know. Maybe I would, but I can't say for sure. That is tricky shit to get involved in."

"What do you mean?"

"Well," started Mike, "let's say you do get involved and Cristina really doesn't want you to. Now you are in a really bad situation with your girlfriend's family." Anthony looked back out the window. He knew Cristina wanted help, she was just afraid to ask. "You know how woman are. They talk all this shit about not letting a guy treat them like that and then when some guy does treat them like that, what do they do? They stay with them." Anthony had nothing to say because he knew Mike was right. "Before you get involved with that shit you have to be one thousand percent sure she is ready for you to get involved, and even more then that you have to make sure Debbie is on that same page."

Anthony couldn't argue there, Mike was right about that. Debbie was very clear that she wanted nothing to do with that whole situation. "I guess you're right."

Mike said, "I know what's going through your mind Ant. Leave it alone until things are a little clearer. You just met these girls, give it some time to get to know them. I know how you get."

Anthony asked Mike, "What does that mean?"

Mike replied, "Ant, you get close to people very quickly. I know you feel like you want to rescue this girl and be her hero, but take it slow. Get to know her and maybe you will see this is who she is, and quite possibly she likes being treated like that."

"Who in their right mind likes being treated like that?"

"That's what I mean. Who knows if she is in her right mind?" Anthony stayed looking at Mike for a second and then back out the windshield. Mike had a point, Anthony did rush into friendships and relationships. Before he knew it he always had a new best friend. He was always like that, got close to people fast and would usually end up getting hurt. "Not to mention that motherfucker is big."

"Yeah he is, but that don't mean shit. I've had at it with guys just as big."

"Yeah? How did that turn out for you? Oh wait, don't answer that yet. Were you with back up?"

Anthony made a frown, "You saying I can't handle him?"

"I don't know, but he looks like he would be a handful."

Mike was right on point today, maybe Anthony wasn't thinking straight. "Maybe you're right, I don't know where my head is today."

"I do."

Anthony asked, "What do you mean?"

"You sure your mind isn't on Debbie's sister?"

Anthony thought for a second. "Of course it's on her sister, I'm worried about her."

Mike said, "I'm not talking about Cristina."

Anthony caught Mike's gaze, "What are you getting at?"

"I'm talking about the other sister, the model, what's her name?" asked Mike.

"Lourdes."

"Yeah, Lourdes. Are you sure she's not on your mind?"

"Why would she be on my mind?"

"Really?"

Anthony continued to stare at Mike. "Yeah, why?"

"I know you pretty good my friend. Just as good as Debbie does. It seemed like the two of you spent a lot of time together at the club."

"So?"

"So? Look at her. Oh wait, all you did was look at her."

"Get the fuck out of here, you're crazy."

"Am I?" asked Mike.

"I would never do anything like that to Debbie. That's her sister."

"I didn't say you would do that to Debbie."

"So what are you saying?" asked Anthony

"I'm saying that you noticed that girl, and if I noticed that you noticed that girl, you can bet damn sure Debbie noticed to."

Anthony looked quickly at Mike, "Did Teresa say anything?"

Mike replied, "Nah, nothing like that. I'm just saying as your friend, it was very obvious to see that girl caught your eye. Rightfully so Ant, don't get me wrong. She's a fucking model, she turned everyone's head in that club, mine included and she knew it."

"She's a looker."

"Uh huh, and your girlfriends sister, which even for looking purposes puts her on the no-no list."

"I know that jerkoff, that's not me."

Mike shot Anthony a really sarcastic look and Anthony returned the same look. "Don't look at me like that, you know what I mean."

"Actually I don't," said Anthony.

"What kind of conversations did you have with that girl?"

"We talked about everything. About her modeling and traveling. We discussed Cristina and that scumbag. We talked about a lot of shit."

"Maybe you want to impress her by helping Cristina?"

Anthony shook his head in shock and headed back to the club. "I don't know why I reached out to you."

"I'm just bring up possible points."

"No, you're really not."

After a minute they pulled back up to the club and Anthony put the car in park. Mike looked over at him and Anthony stared back. "This is us talking as friends now."

Anthony said, "Go on."

"I know you would never ever do anything to hurt Debbie, let alone with her sister."

Anthony asked, "But?"

"But, you have to admit something, if not to me, at least to yourself."

"Go on."

"Something got into your head the other night about that girl."

Anthony sat there quiet for a second, after a minute he looked back into Mikes eyes. "We had a conversation about being connected."

"Connected to each other?" asked Mike.

"No," answered Anthony shaking his head, "about being connected in the lifestyle."

"Oh, you didn't get into details with her right?"

"No, not at all, but it was so easy to talk to her about these things. A lot easier to talk to her then to Debbie. She admitted she liked what I told her. I did, now that you mention it, feel a connection to her."

"A connection?"

"Yeah, it was weird and hard to explain."

"What did you tell her about that she liked?" asked Mike.

Anthony paused for a minute and swallowed hard, "I told her where Tony Two Fingers came from."

Mike looked surprised, "Oh Ant!"

Anthony looked away a bit embarrassed, "I know, I know. I probably should have kept that quiet."

"You don't want Debbie to find out where that came from and you tell her sister. Real smart."

Anthony replied, "You see that's where I think you might be wrong. I asked her not to tell her or Cristina and she said she wouldn't and at that moment I really felt like she would keep that between her and I. I can't explain how or why, but I just know she'll keep that quiet."

"Well," started Mike, "I hope so, for your sake. If Debbie gets her hands on that story you're going to be in for it on two levels."

"Two levels?" asked Anthony.

"Well, one: for cutting off someone's fingers and two: for telling her sister the story and not her."

"That's the fucking truth!" After a second he looked back at Mike who was getting ready to get out of the car.

"As far as this scum bag her sister is seeing, I know two guys from a Staten Island club. If the time comes and something needs to be done about him, let me know and I can put you in contact with them. I think it would be better if guys like them dealt with him instead of you and I."

Anthony asked, "Who are the two guys?"

"You ever hear of the Double R Boys?"

Anthony thought about it for a minute, the name sounded familiar to him but he wasn't sure. "I think I've heard of them."

Mike said, "Think about it, you've heard of them. They are two really big guys, one of them is fucking crazy."

"Why do they call them the Double R Boys?"

"It's short for Rocco and Roy. When the Capo here has an issue that is really tough, they send these two guys to handle it. They are no joke and they don't fuck around. Rocco is bigger than Cristina's boyfriend, much bigger, and Roy is just fucking crazy. If they get their hands on him, there won't be anything left to identify."

"How do you know these two?"

Mike thought about it for a second. "You remember when Teresa had that fender bender last summer with that guy who was connected in Brooklyn and he started a load of shit over it and there was going to be a sit down?"

"Yeah, now that you mention it, what ever happened to that asshat?"

"These two took care of it for me."

Anthony stayed quiet and then after a minute said, "Okay, if it comes to that I will let you know."

"You got it Bro." Mike reached over and shook Anthony's hand and then kissed him cheek to cheek. "Oh, before I forget, I have Enzo's shit. Do you want it?"

Anthony was in no mood to go to Enzo's house and drop that off now. "Is there any way you can give it to him? Don't you think you guys can get along long enough to make a deal on your own?"

"Yeah, that's not a problem. I can get it to him."

"Cool, thanks Mike. I'll talk to you over the weekend."

Mike said his goodbyes and got out of the car. Anthony sat there for a second, messing with the radio, looking for something to listen to. After a minute he found something, Luisa Melendez. He revved his engine up and took off.

Chapter 16
Birthday Barbeque

It had been just shy of two months since Anthony had met Debbie's sisters. They managed to get together more than a few times and, as expected, Anthony had begun to become good friends with them. Debbie even began to lighten up a bit with her attitude towards Lourdes, not a lot, but enough for them to get along civilly. She didn't even seem to mind Anthony having a friendship with her. It was, after all, her sister and she knew Anthony had no interest in her any more than a friendship. She knew how Anthony was when it came to friendships: he got close to people fast and people got close to him fast. It was his nature. He pulled people into his circle without that being his intention. Sometimes his personality was bigger than life and people liked being a part of that, especially Cristina and Lourdes. They didn't have a lot of friends, so when the opportunity came to befriend Anthony, it was natural. They hit it off great.

Carlos was not hanging around as much, he was working a lot. There were a few barbeques and he came to them, but a lot of the hanging out that was taking place he was absent from. Cristina made it seem to him that she was spending time with her sisters and Anthony wasn't included in that, but he really was. Anthony didn't mind Carlos' absence, no one did, Cristina included. He wasn't talkative, and when he was he was a wise ass. That put Anthony into wise ass mode as well, then it was nothing but back and forth, trading comments between the two of them.

On a few occasions the three sisters talked alone and Debbie and Lourdes tried to persuade Cristina to open her eyes, but she would always change the conversation. To everyone it was apparent that Cristina was ready to try and move on from him, but something kept her there and it was probably fear. Carlos was very intimidating, he was a big guy who was dominant and overbearing. Cristina knew first-hand what he was capable of and she didn't want to incur his wrath, so she just lived with it. When she wasn't working she was spending time with her sisters and she kept close watch on the time because she knew she needed to get home before Carlos to at least start dinner or there would be another argument.

Anthony was also not around as much as he was before he met the sisters. He hung out with them when he could, but his work was taking him in different directions now, and that was keeping him busy. He always made time for the girls, but he had other responsibilities now.

Anthony wasn't street dealing as much anymore, he was now going on buys and deliveries. The Capo's for the clubs would give him a packet of information and a suitcase of buy money and he would be on his way. He would usually have to go to some shit part of town, meet with people he really didn't want to meet with and pick up packages of drugs from them, usually kilos of uncut cocaine, give them money in exchange and then head out of there and back to the club. They in turn would give him his cut of money and he would be on his way to do it for another family from another club. The money kept rolling in and it was double from what he was making while street dealing.

It was tiring work, and it was also too easy. He was wondering when the hammer would fall and he would come across someone that wanted the money without giving over the drugs. He wondered how, or if, he would get out of that situation.

On the bright side of it, if it was a bright side, he was making a lot of connections. He wouldn't classify them as friends, that was for sure, but he was networking and making business contacts. Many times he was offered jobs working for the other people he was dealing with, but at this point it didn't interest him. He was busy enough with the Italian clubs, he didn't have time for getting mixed up with Spanish cartels. Even so, they were still good to have in his back pocket. He never knew when he would need them.

Also, by this point, Mike and Enzo were pretty much dealing with each other on their own. He really wasn't the middle man any longer. They weren't getting along any better, but they weren't killing each other either. With all this new work and Enzo and Mike dealing with each other, Anthony wasn't seeing Enzo as much as he used to, let alone talk to him much. When they did see each other at the clubs it was a two minute conversation and then Enzo was on his way to get high. Anthony wanted to talk to his friend about it, but he just left it alone. Enzo wasn't in any place to talk to rationally and Anthony knew it. When the time was right it would come up. Until then he would leave it alone.

Anthony noticed that Enzo was hanging around with people at the clubs that Anthony didn't really talk to either. Maybe that's what Enzo needed though, some more friends. By the look of them though Anthony didn't get the feeling it was friends Enzo was making, it always looked like business and it was the type of business that started taking place behind closed doors. Anthony wasn't going to think about it, he had enough on his plate and the last thing he needed was more business.

This weekend he didn't have any work to do though. They were having a barbeque for his eighteenth birthday. It wasn't going to be a big thing, some friends and that was it. On the list was Mike and Teresa and Enzo was supposed to come, but Anthony wasn't a hundred percent sure he was going to see him. Mickey the Mouse was supposed to come with his girlfriend as well. Lourdes said she would be there, but she had a photo shoot in the morning. Once that was over she promised she would head right over there. Cristina was off from work, so she said she would be there to help Debbie cook and get things set up. Unfortunately Carlos was also going to come, however he had to work, so he was coming when he was done. Debbie's mother had also expressed interest in coming over. Anthony had met her a few times and she seemed like a nice enough lady, but he had his reservations about her since Debbie told him the story of her sisters and husbands. He got the impression that she also knew a little more about his business then he would have wanted her to know, and she seemed to shy away from him because of it. Anthony wasn't sure about anyone else. He was sure people would be stopping by all thru the day and night, as well as some of Debbie's friends and co-workers that he got to know. Whenever they had a barbeque that was how it went.

Anthony had gone out to get fuel for the grill and to pick up a few last minute things that they needed. Debbie went in her car to also pick up a few things, as well as a few gifts for Anthony. The both of them had been in and out of the house all morning. Back and forth from the house to the store to the house and back out again.

Now they bumped into each other in the house. Anthony was just getting back from the supermarket and Debbie from the liquor store.

Debbie began pulling the bottles of liquor out from the bags and Anthony was putting the stuff from the supermarket in the refrigerator as he watched her. She pulled out an odd looking bottle that had a yellow net around it. He tried to read the label from across the room and then he had to ask, "What is that bottle?"

Debbie smiled and looked over at him, "It's called Brugal."

"Bru what?"

Debbie laughed and repeated, "Brugal."

"What made you buy that? What is it anyway?" Anthony came over to look at it and before Debbie could answer him he started to realize who it was for.

"It's Dominican rum."

Anthony looked at her out of the corner of his eye. "You bought this for that asshole?"

Debbie shrugged her shoulders a bit, "Cristina mentioned that he drinks that."

"The rum we have isn't good enough for him? Wait! Don't answer that, I forgot he only smokes Dominican cigars since Cubans aren't good enough either, so I guess I can see him wanting Bru-whatever."

Debbie continued to stare at him and tried to suppress a smile, but she wasn't very successful. "You only drink Coors Light right?"

"I drink whatever people give me. If Bud light is there, I drink Bud Light. I don't make people go out and buy Coors Light."

"No one made me go out and buy anything. Cristina mentioned it so I just decided to pick it up. He's a guest here and that's what we do, take care of our guests."

"Yeah, I'll take care of him."

Debbie cocked her head to the side and saw that Anthony was annoyed with the subject of Carlos. "I know you would, but not tonight."

Anthony continued putting the groceries away. "Why is he even coming here anyway? It's clear we don't like one another, so why would he come?"

Debbie began helping him put away the groceries. "Did you want Cristina to come?"

"Yeah, of course!" replied Anthony.

"Well you knew he was going to come too. He doesn't let her go anywhere without him. I'll be surprised to see if she actually comes early to help me cook."

Anthony just shook his head in annoyance, "I really don't know how she lives like that."

"Do you think I would go to a cookout without you?"

"That's different. You're not afraid to go without me and I wouldn't stop you from going without me. You just wouldn't go without me the same way I wouldn't go without you. That poor girl is a prisoner."

Debbie agreed, "I can't argue with you there."

"Have you spoken to her much about getting away from him?"

"More then I usually do."

"And?"

"And, she doesn't respond back about it. My guess is she feels she has nowhere to go."

Anthony opened up a beer and took a sip out of it. He stared at Debbie until she made a face. "Does she really have nowhere to go?"

"It's not easy moving back to your mother's house once you move out. She is too old to go there anyway. Cristina needs to be on her own, not back with Mama." Anthony continued drinking his beer and staring at his girlfriend. Debbie tried to push the thought off, but she knew where he was going with this. "Let me guess, for some reason why do I think you are not talking about her going to my mother's house?"

"Cause I'm not."

"How did I know? Anthony, she is not coming here."

"Really? That is your sister. You wouldn't let her come here if she needed to?"

Debbie began putting more groceries away. She did not want to have this conversation right now. She didn't want to have it later either, but she knew Anthony was not going to give up on this subject. "Anthony, I would never turn my sister away, either one of them." Debbie thought about that for a minute, "Well, maybe Lourdes, but not Cristina."

Anthony had a mix of annoyance and shock on his face. "Are you kidding me?"

"I told you, I don't like her." Anthony shook his head to himself as he started putting burgers onto a plate to take outside to put on the grill. He then grabbed the fuel tank and headed outside. After a second Debbie followed him. "You're just going to walk away from me like that?"

Anthony turned to look at her as he put the fuel tank down. "I really can't believe you just said that about your sister." Anthony went towards the barbeque and started unhooking the tank, but it wouldn't budge. The wing-nut was locked too tight and he couldn't release it. Debbie watched him fiddle with it for a minute as he started to get annoyed. No doubt part of his annoyance was the nut, and the other part was her no care attitude about her sisters, especially Lourdes. Debbie walked over to where Anthony had some tools and took out a pair of pliers and then handed them to him. He took them and then went back to messing with the wing-nut.

"Anthony."

He didn't pay her any mind as he loosened the nut and pulled the tank out. Once the tank was out he laid the pliers down on the grill rack. After a second he looked over to her and she just stared at him. "Yes?"

Debbie let out a long sigh, "I don't want to argue with you okay? It's your birthday and I want you to have a nice day. Enjoy your friends, enjoy your presents and have a nice time. Please, let's not fight about my sisters or Cristina's asshole boyfriend."

Anthony continued staring at her, after a minute he agreed, "I don't want to argue with you either, but I just don't get it."

Debbie put her hand onto his leg and he held it. "Don't get what Babe?"

"I know what you said about your sisters, and maybe it's because I don't have a real brother or sister, but I just don't get your burning hatred towards them, more so towards Lourdes."

Debbie thought about what he said for a minute and then kind of gave in to him with her look. "I don't hate them the way you think I do."

Anthony arched an eyebrow at her comment, "Really?"

Debbie tried to hold back a smirk. "I know what I said, and yes I have my issues with them, especially Lourdes, but I don't really hate them. They are my sisters and yes, as much as I hate to admit it, I do love them. Both of them." Anthony continued to stare at her. "I would never turn my back on either of them if they ever needed a place to stay, especially Cristina with what she is going through with Carlos. But, I don't want to invite that issue. I told you before I don't want to get involved in her private life. I don't really want to talk to her about it, but I am."

Anthony replied as he stood up, "Okay."

They walked slowly back toward the house to start bringing more food and decorations out. Debbie looked over to him and he put his arm around her and she put her arm around him. "You really like my sisters, don't you?"

Anthony replied, "Yeah, like I said, I don't have a real brother or sister, so it's almost like they are my sisters too."

Debbie smiled at him and hugged him tighter. "That's sweet, I am glad that you like them and get along with them."

"Do they like me?"

Debbie laughed and asked, "Do you really need to ask that?" Anthony smiled down at her. "Of course they like you, they love you. I told you that you would all hit it off." Debbie went silent for a minute and then said, "Just make sure it remains a friendship."

Anthony looked down at her again and she was smiling at him. "What does that mean?"

"I see the way Lourdes flirts with you, and you back with her. Keep it friendly Mister."

Anthony started laughing and then Debbie did as well. After a second she could she him turn a shade of red. "You don't have to worry about that."

"I know, I'm just teasing," said Debbie laughing, "but I'm serious."

Anthony laughed harder and they headed inside to grab the food. Anthony examined the bottle of Brugal that Debbie bought. Debbie put more burgers onto a plate and then grabbed some hot dogs and started doing the same. "Any chance we can open this before he comes and I can dunk my balls in there?"

Debbie stopped what she was doing and looked at him with an annoyed look on her face. "Really?" Anthony stared at her trying to hold back a smile and Debbie began laughing. "I swear, I don't know what I am going to do with you."

"You would be lost without me Sweetheart." Anthony then grabbed the plate of burgers and headed outside. Debbie shook her head in amazement and laughed to herself as she looked at the bottle of Brugal. After a second she grabbed another plate of food and took it outside.

When Debbie got outside Cristina was coming into the yard with their mom Brenda. "Hey! You actually made it," said Debbie laughing.

"What does that mean?"

Debbie looked at her sister out of the corner of her eye with a look that spoke 'Oh come on, you know what I mean,' as she kissed her mother and hugged her sister. "I am just surprised you actually came early. I didn't think you could actually get away."

"I promised I would, and if you are referring to Carlos he actually didn't say anything once he saw Mama pick me up."

"Oh, that makes sense now," said Debbie smiling.

Anthony walked over and said hi to Cristina and her mom. Their mother was nothing like Cristina and Lourdes, she looked more like Debbie. She was in her early forties and she had reddish brown hair, but closer to brown, and not a lot of make up on. She kissed Anthony hello and wished him a happy birthday. Cristina hugged Anthony and he hugged her back, "Thanks for coming Cristina, it means a lot to me."

Cristina remained with her arm around Anthony and his around her waist. "I wouldn't miss your birthday."

"Oh sure," said Debbie, "miss mine but not his."

Cristina smiled as Debbie tossed a dish cloth at her that she grabbed mid-air. "I don't remember you having a party Sis!"

"She didn't want anything," replied Anthony.

Cristina tossed the towel back to Debbie who took it and started heading inside.

"Tell me, what can I do to help you?" asked Debbie's mom as she followed Debbie into the house.

Anthony and Cristina walked towards a swing that was in the yard and they sat on it together. Anthony looked over to Cristina who smiled at him. "It's good to see you smile." Cristina smiled at him again and then looked down. "I don't see you smile enough. How are you doing?" he asked.

After a second Cristina looked up at him. "I'm doing okay."

"Are you really?"

She thought about it for a minute and then replied, "About as good as I can be doing."

Anthony looked away and then back at her. "I know your sister's have had a few conversations with you."

Cristina smiled and said, "More than a few."

Anthony laughed and continued to look around the yard and then back to his friend. "Cristina, you always have options in your life." Anthony paused. "More options than you might think."

She looked down and suddenly looked sad. Anthony continued to stare at her and he reached over and held her hand. She held it back, grasping his hand tight. He held her hand tighter and he knew her thoughts through the silence. She looked up at him with glassy eyes. She had beautiful eyes, beautiful but sad. He reached over and put his arm around her and she leaned into him and started to cry. He stroked her long hair and rocked the swing back and forth slowly. He could feel her crying as she leaned into his chest. "I'm sorry," she said.

Anthony continued holding and soothing her like a child. "There is nothing that you need to be sorry for Cristina, nothing at all."

After a second she had tears streaming down her pretty face. Anthony reached over and wiped them away and she smiled. "I didn't come here to ruin your birthday, Anthony, with my crying and problems."

Anthony shook his head to her to calm her fears of ruining his day. "You didn't ruin my day. Don't think like that at all. You made my day by coming. I know what you are going through Cristina. You are not alone in this. You need to know that. You have a family that loves you very much."

Cristina said, "I know." She tried to compose herself and then started again, "I'm...I'm scared."

153

Anthony asked, "Of Carlos?"

"Yeah," replied Cristina, "I can't do this anymore. He is so mean and abusive. I don't know why I've stayed there this long. I've created something by staying there so long and I don't think it can be un-done anymore."

"It's never easy getting out of a relationship. I'm sure that even with everything that he has put you through, somewhere there is love on your part."

Cristina shook her head quickly to dispel what Anthony just said. "That part of it died a long time ago, if it ever really existed."

"So why are you still there then?"

Cristina continued to stare down at the ground and she shook a little. After a minute of silence she looked up to Anthony, "I'm afraid he's going to kill me."

Anthony locked eyes with her and stared at her. "Why do you think that? Did he ever say that to you?"

She continued staring at him and through tears said, "He told me if I ever tried to leave him, he would kill me." Cristina began to cry harder again and Anthony held her hand. He looked towards the house and he noticed Debbie and Brenda watching them through the kitchen window. He stared at Debbie and she just stared back motionless. "I looked him in the eyes the other night and there is nothing there anymore."

"What do you mean?" asked Anthony. Cristina looked towards the house and noticed her family watching them. She started to let Anthony's hand go and he stopped her. "Don't pay them any mind, it's okay." Cristina looked back at him and then relaxed a bit. He instantly soothed her. He calmed her in a way that she hasn't been calmed in a very long time. She felt safe when he held her. She felt like Carlos couldn't get near her or hurt her ever again. "Go on."

She swallowed hard and continued, "There is nothing left inside of him. He has soulless eyes. He has no remorse for anything or anyone."

"I've seen people like that."

"You can see it in him?" After a second he nodded his head. "Anthony, he is dangerous. He's evil, pure evil. I am afraid he is going to kill me. I'm so scared. It's not only me I am worried about."

Anthony cocked his head to the side just a bit. "What do you mean?"

Cristina looked back towards the house and then after a second back towards Anthony. "He told me that if I ever cheated on him or left him that not only would he kill me, but he would kill my family as well."

Anthony remained looking at Cristina. Anger began to spark up inside of him but he tried not to show it to her. He took a deep breath in and held it for a long minute and then finally let it out. He looked towards the window and the mother and daughter were gone, no longer watching them. "What do you mean he threatened your family?"

Cristina looked away, almost afraid to tell him. She began to tremble and he softly stroked her hand. "He said if I left and tried to stay with someone from my family he would kill them and everyone else. He would kill Lourdes, my mother, even my uncle." She sat quiet for a second and then added, "And Debbie. He said he would hunt them down, one by one, and when he was finished with them, then he would come after me. I have nowhere to go, even if I did leave him."

Anthony let that sink in for a minute. "Cristina, are you really ready to be out of this situation?"

"How can I go after what I just told you?"

"If that wasn't a factor, or if he couldn't hurt you anymore, would you really consider being rid of him?"

Cristina put her head down and thought about it for a long minute and then replied, "Yes, there is nothing left with him for me. I have no feelings for him except for hatred. Hatred for what he's turned me into. Ask my sisters, this is not me!"

"Okay, listen to me." Cristina stared at him intently, hanging on his every word. "This is not something that can happen in an instant. You might have to live with this a little longer until I can figure out how to get you out of there safely and protect you and your family, but I promise you as sure as I am sitting here holding your hand, I will help you and I will take care of this for you."

Cristina remained staring at him and she allowed a slight smile to come across her lips. She knew he was telling her the truth, that he would help her in any way that was possible. "Okay." She knew she could depend on him.

"Do you trust me?"

Cristina stared into his blue eyes. "I trusted you the first time I met you. When you stared at me in the shadows of the club, I knew you were a friend to me and that I could lean on you."

Anthony smiled at her and reached over and hugged her. She hugged him back and they rocked back and forth on the swing. She felt safe again, safe in his arms. Safe, until Carlos would come later and all the safety would flee her as quickly as possible and be replaced with fear. Fear for her life. "Don't worry, okay?"

Cristina nodded her head and got up. She started to turn towards the house to help her family get ready for the day, but then turned back and looked at Anthony sitting on the swing looking up at her. She reached down and kissed him softly on his cheek and whispered to him, "Thank you."

Anthony smiled and watched her head back into the house. He sat back in the swing and closed his eyes. He needed to control his anger. When Cristina told him about Carlos' threats to her and her family it enraged him. It was all he could do to keep from just grabbing him when he walked in tonight, but he knew that wasn't going to be the right thing to do. He knew by the look on his face that anyone, especially Debbie, would be able to tell that this or something heavy was on his mind. How he was going to mask this was beyond his thoughts.

After a few minutes with his thoughts he was about to get up and Debbie came out of the house. She looked towards him as she made her way over to a table to put some plates and utensils down. After a second she smiled at him. He gave her a smile back and then she headed over to the swing to sit next to him. "Are you okay?" she asked.

"Yes."

Before the conversation could go any further Mike and Teresa came through the yard gate. Mike carrying beer and Teresa carrying trays of food.

"There's the birthday boy!" yelled Teresa loudly across the yard.

Anthony smiled at her, "Hey Sis."

"Hey Bro, happy birthday!"

Anthony turned to Debbie and kissed her on the cheek. "We can talk about this later?"

Debbie smiled and asked, "Promise?"

"I promise."

Debbie smiled at him. Anthony headed towards his friends to say hello. Debbie now sat back in the swing to think. She watched her boyfriend with his friends from across the yard. She didn't really need to talk to him later about what went on. Deep inside her she already knew that Cristina had opened up to him and now he was on a path to help her. No matter what, she was now going to be a priority to him. After a second Debbie shook off her annoyance and decided that she would wait to hear what he was going to tell her and then take it from there. She got off the swing and went back into the house. After a few minutes Teresa made her way into the house to lend a hand and Anthony had the grill lit with Mike standing by his side, talking what looked like guy talk. In the back of everyone's head was, 'How would this day end?'

A few hours had gone by and the party was in full swing. The yard, as usual, was packed with people. There were people from all walks there. More people from the clubs were there than anticipated. Several of Debbie's co-workers were there, and a few of her friends too. The food and the booze were flowing, the music was pumping, and the people were dancing. Everyone was having a good time. Cristina was laughing and she seemed to get past the conversation that she had with Anthony. It seemed to be out of her head and she was allowing herself to have a good time. She even had a few drinks and that lightened up the mood, not only for her, but for Debbie as well. Debbie also had a few drinks and she was feeling good. She was cooking and having fun. The yard smelled of barbequed food, it was intoxicating.

Anthony was making his rounds through the yard seeing and talking to as many of his guests as he could. He would spend a few minutes with each of them and then move on. Enzo actually showed and was with a few of the guys from the club and they were playing poker.

Mike was at another table with Mickey the Mouse and a few of the other guys from the club, talking business and also playing cards.

Teresa was off with friends of Debbie that she got to know at a few of these parties, all was good.

Anthony walked through the yard while smoking a cigar, when a Corvette came screaming down the block and screeched to a stop. It was Carlos. He drove the car towards a spot and parked it. Anthony watched him from the yard and as soon as he caught a glimpse of him he could feel the anger come back from the conversation with Cristina. He also noticed Carlos was with a friend. Anthony looked closely at the friend that was with him. He looked oddly familiar to Anthony, but he couldn't put his finger on it. Anthony took a long drag from his cigar and headed towards the house. He looked for Cristina as he made his way through the crowded yard. He found her sitting on the swing talking to a few girls. He didn't want to ruin her fun, but she needed to know he was there. Cristina caught his look and he didn't need to say a word, she could tell by the look on his face. Her whole demeanor changed and she knew she had to become someone that she couldn't stand being, a prisoner. Anthony sadly motioned to her and made his way into the kitchen. As soon as he got in there Debbie was talking to someone on the phone. She told the person to hold on and then handed Anthony the phone. "Who's this?"

"Lourdes. She just got finished with her shoot and is looking for a ride."

Anthony put the phone to his ear, "Hey." He listened to her on the other end of the phone, but his attention was on Carlos through the kitchen window. Debbie continued fussing with the food in the oven while her mother helped her. Cristina had managed to slip away from the swing before Carlos found her and also made her way into the kitchen, not far behind Anthony. He continued to listen to Lourdes. "What station are you at?" Debbie watched him knowing what was coming. He motioned towards Debbie to ask if she would pick her up and she motioned back that she drank just a bit too much. Debbie noticed that Anthony didn't really seem to be paying any mind to her or Lourdes. She saw what his attention was on and maybe it wouldn't be such a bad idea if he did leave for a few minutes to pick her sister up; maybe diffuse the situation. Anthony put the phone back to his ear. "Carlos just got here. Do you want him to pick you up?" Everyone in the room laughed hard and Anthony pulled the phone away from his ear as Lourdes gave him a mouthful. After he stopped laughing he told her he would be there in a few minutes and then hung up.

"Are you okay to drive?" Debbie asked him.

Anthony went into the living room to grab his keys and Debbie followed him. "Yeah, I'm fine. I haven't drank that much."

Debbie followed him back out of the living room and towards the yard. Anthony put his cigar back into his mouth and made his way through the yard towards Mike. Debbie stopped short when Anthony waved her back. Anthony put his arm around Mike and began talking quietly in his ear. Mike's eyes opened wide as he surveyed the yard. Anthony continued talking to his friend quietly as Debbie watched in the distance. Mike kept nodding his head and seemed to be hanging on Anthony's every word. After a minute, Anthony finished talking to Mike and walked away from him and back towards her. A few of the guys huddled around Mike and he began talking to them, much the same as Anthony was talking to him. When Anthony got back to her she asked him, "What was that all about?"

Anthony took a drag from his cigar and replied, "Club business."

"Where is my sister?"

"Jamaica."

"Jamaica Avenue and Woodhaven?"

Anthony shook his head and made a frown, "Jamaica station."

"Ugh, be careful over there."

"I will." He kissed her and then turned quick, just to bump into Carlos head on. His friend standing behind him.

"Leaving so soon?" asked Carlos.

Anthony backed up a bit and locked into a stare with him. Mike saw it and stood up, as well as the three guys from the table. Debbie saw that and motioned to Mike to sit back down, but he didn't pay her any mind. Debbie watched the exchange with her heart in her mouth. She knew these two had no use for each other, and she really wasn't in the mood for a brawl. Now there were friends involved, from both sides.

Anthony smirked at Carlos and replied, "Don't worry, I'll be right back." Anthony let a puff of smoke out of his mouth and right into Carlos' face. After a second he held up the cigar for Carlos to see. "Cuban?" Anthony offered. He knew that would get under his skin.

Debbie just shook her head at the complete wise ass that her boyfriend was. She couldn't believe that he just offered Carlos a Cuban cigar, again. That was Anthony. When he didn't like someone he would antagonize them.

Carlos took a deep breath and just stared at him, never giving him an answer. Anthony made his way past him and his friend, who he didn't even bother to acknowledge, then turned back and looked at Carlos. "Debbie bought you some Brugal. It's over there by the bar. Help yourself."

"Brugal huh?" Carlos actually allowed himself to smile. "Now you're talking. That's good rum. You try it?"

Anthony puffed on his cigar and replied, "Nah, I only drink Puerto Rican rum. It's the best." He walked out of the yard and into the GNX smirking and laughing to himself. Carlos watched him rev the engine up and back out of the drive way. After a second he straightened out the car on Pitkin Avenue and sped away. Carlos watched him till he couldn't see the car anymore.

Debbie quickly moved towards the house. Mike and his friends then sat back down. Carlos headed through the yard with his friend towards the bar. He picked up the bottle of Brugal and poured himself a cup with some ice and then his friend did the same. He took a drink and said, "Puerto Rican rum my ass. This is the best shit." His friend smiled in agreement.

The GNX sped along Woodhaven Boulevard towards Atlantic Avenue. Anthony was pushing the speed limit and the timing of yellow to red lights. He didn't want to be away from the party for long. Not with that asshole there; and he had a friend to boot. The cutoff for Atlantic quickly approached and he made his way to the right. He just had a powerful stereo system put in and he was cranking "Paul Revere" by the Beastie Boys as loud as it could go. At the red light not only was his car shaking from the bass, but so was the car in front of him, behind him and the car on his left as well. He looked over to his left and noticed an agitated old man, very annoyed that his car was bouncing to Anthony's radio. The light turned green and he was on his way again.

Carlos moved through the yard, scoping out a spot to sit. He was also looking for Cristina. His friend was right in tow behind him. His friend wasn't quite as big as he was, but he still had some build to him. He had dark hair and a light complexion. He had the same scruffy, shadowy beard as Carlos and wore the same style of clothes as he did. He had lighter color eyes then Carlos did though. His name was Luis and he looked like he was a piece of shit as well. They both found a spot on the far side of the yard, but near the grill. They sat, lit up their own cigars and drank their Brugal. They decided to take the bottle with them since no one else seemed to be interested in it. Carlos looked around at all the people. He turned to his friend and asked, "You ever see so many stupid people in one spot?"

Luis shook his head and looked around himself. "The guy that left in the Grand National, I've seen him before."

Carlos looked at him very surprised. "¿Oh, si?"

Luis replied, "Si, in Brooklyn, doing a buy."

"No!"

"Si, si."

"A street deal?"

Luis took a long drag out of his cigar and then replied, "No, this was a big buy."

"He was buying or selling?"

"Buying. Ten keys of yeyo."

Carlos was very surprised. "¿A quién?"

Luis leaned closer to Carlos and said, "The Perez Brothers."

"How do you know this?" asked Carlos sounding shocked.

"I was there. You know I hang with the Perez brothers."

Carlos replied, "Si." He thought about it for a minute and said, "I wonder how this cabrón knows them."

Luis took a long sip from his cup and emptied it. He reached over and filled it up again and drank some more. "This guy is conectado Papi. If he was dealing with the Perez brothers he's with the greaseballs."

Carlos stopped drinking and looked at Luis. "Nah. Él no!"

"Oh si! Probably the Garbaci's."

Carlos shook his head to himself, he couldn't believe it. Then it hit him. He wondered if Cristina knew, or if the rest of the girls knew. Debbie would have to know. She was driving a Cadillac and he was driving a Grand National. He noticed Debbie coming over to the grill near where they were sitting. She opened the grill and added some burgers. "Debbie."

Debbie looked at Carlos out of the corner of her eye. She hated talking to him and wondered to herself why out of the whole yard he needed to sit next to the grill. She didn't notice that he was there or she would have sent her mother out to the grill. "Yes Carlos," she replied somewhat annoyed.

"Where is Cristina?"

"She is in the kitchen, cooking with our mother."

Carlos got up and motioned to Luis that he would be back. "Gracias Mami," he said to Debbie and then headed into the house. Debbie rolled her eyes, she hated being called that. She closed the grill and then went to talk to some friends so she could avoid being in the kitchen with him.

Anthony pulled up at the Jamaica train station and Lourdes was waiting right where she said she would be. He brought the GNX to a halt right next to her and she opened the door and got in. "Hi Miss Model."

"Hi Birthday Boy!" Lourdes said all excited. Anthony smiled at her and she smiled back. She reached over and hugged him tight and then kissed him on his cheek. "So you are finally legal!"

Anthony giggled at her as he raced the GNX out of the spot. She leaned back in her seat from the thrust of the car and tried to get herself situated in the seat. "What's the matter there?"

"I forgot how fast this fucking car is. What's the rush?"

"Carlos is at the house and I don't want him out of my sight."

"Oh, I thought you wanted to be rid of me that quick," she said in a sly voice.

Anthony looked at her out of the corner of his eye. "I think you know better than that Sweetheart."

Lourdes smiled and blushed a little. "Be careful, my sister tends to be jealous."

"You're telling me? She mentioned that to me earlier today."

Lourdes looked at him quickly. "Get out!" Anthony laughed and nodded his head. "What did she say?"

"We were talking about Cristina's issues with Carlos and she said to me you really like my sisters and I said yes and she said that you guys liked me to. Then she said she was glad we all hit it off and to make sure we keep it just friendly, especially with you."

"She said that about me? That bitch," Lourdes said laughing.

"She said she was joking, but she was serious. She said she noticed us flirting with each other. Then the conversation changed to something else."

Lourdes laughed and said, "Yes, that's Debbie." Lourdes began playing with her long hair. Some of it was wrapped in the shoulder belt. She pulled it loose and threw it over the headrest of the seat. Anthony looked at her and shook his head. She noticed and asked, "What?"

Anthony laughed and replied, "Now your hair is going to be all over the seats when you get out."

Lourdes giggled a little and said, "I can always cut it all off." Anthony looked at her out of the corner of his eyes and gave her a look that said, 'I don't think so.' Lourdes caught the look, smiled at him and said, "Okay then, don't complain Mister."

Anthony smiled and then he decided to change the subject. "Well I had a long talk with Cristina today."

Lourdes asked, "Oh yeah?"

He replied, "Yeah," and continued, "She really broke down to me."

"Wow."

"I was surprised, but it was kind of a defining moment between us."

Lourdes stayed looking at him, "really?"

"Yeah, I felt very close to her. She cried in my arms. I felt her shaking."

"Really?" asked Lourdes sounding very surprised.

"Yep." Anthony went silent for a minute trying to figure out how to ask her what was on his mind. He didn't want to reveal anything Cristina said to him if she didn't reveal it first.

"What are you trying to figure out how to ask me?"

Anthony looked over to her and she was staring at him with a cute smile. How did she do that? How did she know he was struggling to ask her something? "What makes you think I am trying to figure out how to ask you something?"

"Maybe I am getting to know you better than you think."

Anthony had a look on his face that said he didn't buy it. "Try again. We don't know each other that long."

"That's not nice. I think we've gotten to know each other very well in such a short time, but actually it was your eyes."

"I'm sorry, I didn't mean anything bad by that." Lourdes smiled at him and then he asked, "My eyes? What do you mean?"

They approached a red light, stopped, looked at each other and locked eyes. "Well," she started, "other than the fact that you have the most beautiful blue eyes that I have ever seen, they also speak very loudly."

Anthony, who now began to blush, didn't take his gaze off of her, so he didn't notice the light turn green. The guy behind him did and couldn't wait to blow his horn. Anthony looked in the rear view mirror and then very annoyingly hit the gas and sped off. "Go on," he said to her.

"That's it my dear. Your eyes say there is something on your mind, so just spit it out and ask me."

Anthony smiled to himself and then asked, "Did Cristina mention to you that Carlos threatened to kill her?"

"Oh yeah, a few times. That's not a secret."

"Did she ever mention that he threatened to kill everyone else in the family if she left him?"

Lourdes thought about it for a minute. "She mentioned it the last time Debbie and I talked to her about getting away from him."

Anthony was in shock. Debbie knew about this and didn't mention it to him? "Really? Debbie knew about this?"

Lourdes stated, "You seem surprised."

"I am! Why didn't Debbie mention this to me?" They approached another red light and stopped. Anthony looked over to Lourdes.

Lourdes began laughing and asked him, "Do you really need to ask that?"

"Apparently."

Lourdes laughed harder. "Don't you know Debbie? You know she doesn't…" Lourdes cut short her sentence due to a blazing car horn behind them.

The guy in the car behind them let off on the horn and yelled out the window at the top of his lungs, "PAY ATTENTION TO THE FUCKING LIGHT. IT"S GREEN ASSHOLE."

Anthony kept his gaze on a somewhat surprised Lourdes. He slowly turned his eyes from her to the rear view mirror and this idiot behind them started laying on the horn again. After a second Anthony shifted the GNX into park. "Hold that thought for a minute." Anthony opened his car door and stepped out of the GNX and looked at the guy in the car behind them. The guy held the horn for another second and then Anthony started walking slowly towards the car. After a second the guy let off the horn. As Anthony approached the car the guy looked at him. Anthony was in no mood at this point. Anthony stopped next to the car and stared at the guy. "You got a fucking problem?" The guy was clearly shocked that Anthony approached the car and he could tell that he might have started something that he wasn't ready to finish. "You in a hurry or something?"

The guy swallowed hard and pointed to the traffic light. "The light is green and you're just sitting there."

Anthony calmly looked at the light. By now other cars were piling up behind them and the light changed to yellow and then back to red. "It looks red to me."

The guy had a stupid look on his face and shook his head. "Are you fucking kidding me? That light was…."

Before the guy could finish his sentence Anthony laid a slap into the guys face. Within a second Anthony had him by the back of his hair and started banging his head into the steering wheel and horn. "You like playing with the horn you fucking jerk off?" Two times, three times, four times. Anthony just kept banging the guy's face into the steering wheel and then pulling it back and then banging it again, each time making the horn go off. Five, six, seven. "CALL ME AN ASSHOLE?" yelled Anthony. Eight, nine, ten and then Anthony let him go. The guy had blood coming out of his nose and face and was moaning from the beating that he just received. His nose was clearly broken in more than one place. Anthony stopped and looked at the cars lined up behind them watching the situation unfold, but all remained quiet. "Next time think twice before you blow a horn and call someone an asshole. You never know who the fuck you could be talking to dickhead!"

Anthony walked back towards his car. He got in, threw the car into drive and burned out from the red light. About a block away he ventured a look to Lourdes who was trying to hold back a laugh. "Sorry about that."

"It's okay," she said laughing, "that asshole had it coming. It was kind of funny."

"Good, cause if I was with Debbie I would be hearing about this till Christmas."

"Your secret is safe with me Darling. You're always safe with me." Lourdes winked at him.

Anthony smiled and said, "So you were saying?"

Lourdes laughed and then continued. "You know Debbie, she doesn't really want you involved with this whole thing so it doesn't surprise me that she didn't tell you what Carlos said."

Anthony thought about that for a second and that did make sense to him. Lourdes was right and he could see why Debbie didn't tell him what was said. Still, she could have shared that information with him. He needed to put that out of his head for now. "Well, Cristina said she is pretty much looking for a way out. I just have to see how I can help her achieve that."

Lourdes asked, "What about Carlos?"

"I don't know. That's what I have to figure out. Do you think he can make good on his threats?"

Lourdes looked over to Anthony, who was already glancing at her. "I honestly don't know. I have thought about asking my agency for personal protection, but I don't know if I want to let my sister's personal life bleed into my professional life."

Anthony asked, "Are you that worried that you are looking for protection?"

Lourdes thought about that for a minute. "I don't know. He's a big guy and he has crazy friends. I think he's crazy himself."

Carlos walked into the kitchen and looked around. He stood quietly in the doorway and watched Cristina and her mother preparing food. After a second he cleared his throat and they both turned around startled. Cristina's mom looked at him for a second and then turned back towards the food. Cristina turned completely pale, but managed a slight smile. "Hi Carlos," she said.

Carlos stayed staring at her and cocked his head to the side. "What are you doing?"

"I'm helping my sister cook for the barbeque."

Carlos motioned his head to look out the kitchen window. He observed Debbie outside with a few of her friends having drinks and laughing. He motioned for Cristina to look out the window. Cristina looked at her sister. "It looks to me like you are doing all the work for this cabrón's birthday while his girlfriend is having fun with her friends." Cristina began to get nervous. She caught her mother's look and her mother just turned away. She looked like she didn't want to get involved. Cristina went back to messing around with the food and Carlos walked over to her. He pressed himself up against her and in turn that pressed her into the counter. He put his head closer to hers and in a low voice said, "You didn't even come outside to say hello to me?"

Cristina began to shiver a little bit. She looked towards her mother again, but her mother never looked in her direction, she just kept her attention aimed at the food. "I… I'm sorry Carlos I've just been busy in here. I didn't know you were here yet," she lied.

Carlos clearly began to get more annoyed with her. He put his hand on her wrist and began applying pressure on it. "Busy? ¿Ocupado con la fiesta de cumpleaños de esta culo blanco?"

Cristina was clearly uncomfortable and starting to feel pain in her wrist and hand. She also wasn´t sure when Anthony was going to get back. She didn't want him to walk in here for this. She looked up at Carlos with tears starting to form in her eyes. "Carlos, I'm helping my sister, that's all."

At that moment Debbie walked into the kitchen with Teresa and a few of her friends. Carlos remained looking at Cristina with a look of rage on his face. Debbie stopped in her tracks and began to process what was going on. Debbie looked at her mother, her mother rolled her eyes. Hoping to defuse the situation, Debbie asked, "Is everything alright?"

The GNX moved swiftly down Woodhaven Boulevard and approached Liberty Avenue. Anthony was changing lanes left and right to get back to the house as fast as possible. "You know," started Anthony, "I recognized a friend of his."

"A friend of Carlos'?"

Anthony replied, "Yeah, I think I saw him at least one time on a business thing I went on for the club."

"That's possible. His friends are into some things like you are."

"That complicates things. I am not sure who they know, the same way they don't know who I know. This might take some time for me to do what I can to make sure you and the rest of your family are safe."

Lourdes asked, "What about Debbie?"

Anthony shrugged his shoulders. "I'm sure if your family was in real mortal danger she will get over me getting involved."

The GNX turned off Woodhaven onto Pitkin Avenue.

The standoff in the kitchen continued. Everyone remained still except Teresa. She quietly backed up and out of the house and headed towards Mike's table. She got his attention and told him what appeared to be going on in the kitchen. Mike scoured the yard looking for his friends, but he didn't see them. He walked off quickly trying to find them.

Carlos turned his head towards Debbie and said, "I'm talking to Cristina. Why don't you mind your business Mami and go outside?"

Debbie was clearly taken back by what Carlos just said to her. "Excuse me? This is my house."

Cristina began to shake even harder. Debbie looked over at her. Cristina shook her head a little as if to say please don't argue with him, but at that point Debbie wasn't having it. She had a few drinks and she really wasn't thinking that she was not even half of Carlos' size.

Carlos continued holding onto Cristina's wrist tightly while staring at Debbie. At that moment the GNX could be heard pulling into the driveway. There was no mistaking the rumble from the exhaust system. The sound of it even drowned out the music that was coming from the yard.

At that same moment Mike and two guys from the club walked into the kitchen. "Everything okay in here?" Mike asked as his eyes danced between Debbie and Carlos.

Debbie continued to stare at Carlos unmoving. "Yeah Mike," she replied.

Mike could tell it clearly wasn't. Carlos was still holding onto Cristina's wrist and staring at Debbie. "Anthony just got back with your sister."

Carlos released Cristina's wrist when he heard that and looked towards her. "We'll talk about this later." Cristina looked up at him full of fear and just nodded her head quickly. "Make me and Luis a dish of food and bring it out to us, we're sitting by the grill." Cristina nodded her head again and quickly began to do as she was told.

Carlos made his way out of the kitchen through the group of people that assembled in there, giving dirty looks to each and every one of them as he made his way out of the room and back into the yard. Once he was completely out, Debbie walked over to Cristina to see if she was okay. She was trembling out of control with fear. Debbie turned to Mike and said, "Mike can you please go outside and keep Anthony away from here?"

Mike clearly looked like that was not what he wanted to do. "Deb."

Debbie walked over to him and pleaded with him, "Please, Mike. I don't want this to happen right now. There will be a war here. I have work friends here. I can't have them see this. My boss is here, PLEASE!"

Mike hesitantly replied, "Okay," then he and the guys from the club walked out of the kitchen.

Debbie went back to tending to her sister. "Mama, look after the food, I'm going to take Cristina upstairs to calm her down."

Cristina quickly protested. "I have to get Carlos his food."

Brenda turned around quickly and said to Debbie, "Why don't you let your boyfriend take care of this already?"

"Mama please! That's not helping the situation right now. Please take care of the food and bring him his plate while I tend to her okay? Please?" Debbie looked out the window and saw Anthony and Lourdes making their way through the yard, only to be met by Mike handing him a drink and trying to divert his attention from the house. She turned her head back towards her mother, "Please?"

After a second her mother reluctantly agreed and finished making the dishes while Debbie pulled Cristina out of the kitchen and upstairs.

Lourdes looked throughout the yard at all the people that were there. She was looking for her sisters, but didn't see either one of them. She turned towards Anthony and said she was going into the house and would be back.

Carlos sat with Luis drinking and waiting for his food. Luis looked over towards Lourdes's direction and asked, "¿Quién es la chica caliente?"

Carlos looked towards Lourdes and replied, "Hermana de Cristina."

Luis asked, "¿Oh si?"

"Si," replied Carlos, "she is a model."

Luis eyed Lourdes from top to bottom before she walked off towards the house. "I have to meet her."

Carlos laughed a little and said, "Yeah, good luck. She's a bitch. Coño maldita!"

Luis and Carlos both cracked up laughing. "It's all good, I could teach her."

Brenda came out with two plates of food and walked over to the table where Carlos and Luis were sitting. She approached them and put the plates onto the table and turned around to walk away. Carlos said to her, "Mama, where is Cristina?"

Brenda stopped in her tracks and stayed with her back to them. She closed her eyes and took a deep breath and then turned around to Carlos. "She is upstairs with her sister. Debbie is trying to calm her down." Carlos began to eat his food. He had a smirk on his face, shook his head and mumbled something to Luis in Spanish and they both laughed. After a second she moved closer to the table and said, "Please, leave my daughter alone." Carlos stopped eating his food and looked up at her. "Just get out of her life."

Carlos looked at Luis and then back to her. "When I want your opinion I'll ask, till then, mind your fucking business." Carlos picked his fork back up and went back to eating, not paying any attention to her. She stared at them for a moment and then walked off visibly annoyed and somewhat shaken.

Lourdes walked through the house calling out her sister's names, but there was no answer. Lourdes started to head towards the stairs and was met by Teresa coming down. Lourdes asked if she saw her sisters and she pointed to the bedroom. Lourdes made her way up the stairs and into the bedroom. She saw Cristina hysterical and Debbie trying to comfort her. She closed the door behind her and ran to them. She asked what happened and Debbie filled her in. Lourdes stood shaking her head in disbelief, not knowing herself why she couldn't believe it. This was typical of Carlos and his bullshit. "Cristina you have to do something to get away from this asshole. Let Anthony help you."

Debbie and Lourdes looked at each other. Debbie became agitated and said, "Let's leave Anthony out of this for now."

Lourdes continued to stare at Debbie in disbelief. "Are you kidding me? What do you want to do, wait for this guy to kill her?"

Debbie stood up and went face to face with her sister while Cristina watched, tears streaming down her face. "I am not going to have my boyfriend get into it with this asshole at his birthday party. This is something Cristina has to deal with on her own."

Lourdes stood shaking her head not getting what her sister was saying. Cristina pleaded with her sisters, "Please girls don't fight!"

"I swear, I don't understand you Debbie," said Lourdes.

"It's not your place to understand me Lourdes. Stop trying to make Anthony get involved with this."

"I am not trying to make him do anything. He wants to help her, and at this point I believe he is the only person that can."

Debbie shook her head and went back to tending to Cristina who was starting to calm down a little bit, but was now focused on trying to make her sisters stop fighting. Debbie looked back to Lourdes. "Really? You're not trying to sway him into helping her? I see how you are with him."

"What the hell does that mean?"

"I see how you use your flirty little voice and bat your eye lashes at him, smiling and winking at him. You are trying to wrap him around your finger so you can get him to do whatever you want him to do," yelled Debbie.

Brenda walked into the room and shut the door. "What is going on in here? I can hear you yelling from downstairs."

Lourdes yelled back, "Are you fucking kidding me? You think I do that with him to wrap him around my finger? We are just joking around."

"Knock it off, both of you!" yelled Brenda. "This is about Cristina, let's not make it another argument about the two of you." Lourdes and Debbie both looked at their mother and calmed down. "Debbie, if you don't want your boyfriend to know what is going on, than keep yelling and fighting with your sister like this. I'm sure that will make things better and not lead him on that there is a problem here right now," she said sarcastically.

Debbie looked at her sister with fire in her eyes and received the same look back. Debbie moved over to Cristina and put her arm around her and said, "I'm sorry."

Cristina motioned to her sister and said, "It's okay, go outside and be with your guests."

Debbie shook her head no and then her mother said, "She is right, go outside," she looked at Lourdes, "both of you. I will stay here for a few minutes with Cristina until she feels better. If we are all in here Anthony will wonder why. Go outside and spend time with your friends."

After a second Debbie agreed, stood up and walked towards the door, Lourdes followed and they left the room.

Anthony roamed through the yard, talking to people here and there. He noticed Luis head to where the alcohol was and grabbed the third, and last, bottle of Brugal and head back to the table. Anthony sized him up a bit and he was sure now that he saw him at one of the deals he went on a few weeks back. Anthony made his way to the swing that he sat on earlier with Cristina, sat down and lit up another cigar. He noticed Mike and Teresa were acting funny, almost like they didn't want to talk to him. He chalked it up to an argument that they must have had with each other and they were trying to work it out, like usual. He looked to his right and saw Debbie and Lourdes coming out of the house. He smiled at them and they smiled back, although they didn't look to happy themselves, either one of them. Debbie asked him, "Have you eaten anything yet?" He shook his head no and she went to make him a plate when Lourdes stopped her and said she would go make all of them plates. Debbie sat down and Anthony put his arm around her.

"Is everything okay here?" he asked her.

"Yeah," she said hesitantly.

"Everyone seems to be acting weird. You and Lourdes looked annoyed."

Debbie shrugged it off and admitted, "We had one of our usual sister spats, nothing to worry about."

Anthony stared at her. "She's here two minutes and you two already go at it?"

Debbie looked at him visibly annoyed that he seemed to be keeping on about it. "Let it go please. I'm not in the mood to go into it and it's over, so just drop it."

Anthony agreed and took a drag from of his cigar. He looked around the yard for Cristina. "Where's your other sister?"

Debbie motioned towards the house and replied, "She's inside with my mother, freshening up." Anthony looked away and continued to smoke his cigar. "I'm going to help my sister with the plates. I'll be right back."

"Okay," replied Anthony, as he sat back while Debbie got up and headed to the grill. She got around the corner and made eye contact with Carlos who just stared at her. She looked away in disgust. Lourdes was at the grill to pull some food off for the plates. Debbie approached her and said, "Need a hand?" Lourdes looked at her and didn't really answer while she just continued making the plates. "Silent treatment?"

Lourdes shrugged her shoulders. "I'm not about to argue with you."

"I don't want to argue with you either. Let's put upstairs behind us."

"It's not quite that easy now, is it Debbie? I can't believe what you said to me about Anthony."

Debbie reluctantly agreed and replied, "I know, I didn't mean..."

"Maybe I'll just stop coming around here if that's what you're going to think of my friendship with your boyfriend."

Debbie thought about that for a minute. "If you want to hurt him, then by all means go ahead and stop coming around here. You're only going to hurt him. He thinks of Cristina and you like sisters. He told me that today. You would crush him if you stopped talking to him over me saying something that I said out of anger." Debbie went silent and watched her sister make the plates of food. "I shouldn't have said what I said. I know that's your personality, and that you don't mean anything by it. I'm sorry, but don't punish Anthony for it."

Lourdes finished making the plates and then said, "I'm sorry too. I don't want to hurt Anthony in any way."

Debbie smiled at her and she smiled back. They both picked up the plates and moved to a table and Anthony came over and sat by them and they all began to eat. Lourdes looked over towards Carlos' direction and noticed both of them staring at her. She made eye contact with Luis and he blew her a kiss. After she realized what he just did she looked away feeling very uncomfortable. She noticed the two of them talking and laughing. She took it that they were talking about her. Luis kept trying to make eye contact with her again, but she would just look away every time their eyes met. After a minute Carlos got up and made his way to where they were sitting. "Lourdes."

Lourdes didn't want to look up but she knew if she didn't things could get out of hand quickly. Debbie looked across the yard and noticed that Mike had his eyes trained on what could be unfolding at their table. Mike whispered into a friend's ear and he walked off towards the other guy that was in the kitchen with them. Anthony kept his eyes trained on the food in front of him. "Yes?" she replied.

"My friend Luis wants to meet you."

Lourdes looked over to Anthony who now made eye contact with her. He was wondering what her response would be. She said, "I'm not interested Carlos."

Carlos stared at her for a minute, she didn't make eye contact with him again, but this time concentrated on her food. "Are you sure? He is a nice guy. I think you would like him."

She said, "No."

He continued looking at the table for a minute and then he made his way back to his seat shaking his head. Lourdes looked over and they were laughing once again, then she looked away from them.

As the day turned into night, people still came and went from the party. Some of Debbie's friends left and more came. The same for Anthony's friends. There was a lot of picture taking and Anthony was having a good time. The food was still coming and the booze was still flowing. Anthony had a few drinks, but he was still level headed. Carlos and Luis had finished the third bottle of Brugal and were now on to different liquors. Anthony noticed they didn't go near the Puerto Rican rum, he smiled to himself feeling responsible for that. Debbie caught him smirking to himself and asked what that was about, but he just waved her off.

Anthony also noticed how Luis was looking at Lourdes. Every chance he got he would try talking to her but she would always make herself scarce, or just shoot him down or plant herself next to Anthony and he would back away. The guy wasn't able to get a conversation going with her.

Debbie, Lourdes and Cristina headed inside to clean up a bit while Anthony made his way to the bar and made himself a rum and coke and Carlos moved in behind him. "Let me ask you something?"

Anthony cocked an eyebrow at him, "What's on your mind?"

Carlos pointed over to the GNX. "How fast is that car?"

Anthony thought about it for a second. He knew how fast the car was and he knew Carlos had a Corvette. "Zero to sixty in 4.7 seconds with a stock engine. Faster than the Corvette."

Carlos looked over at the car and then back at Anthony. Then he trained his eyes towards Luis and he winked at him. Luis headed towards the house. It worked, he had Anthony occupied. "No way!"

Anthony replied, "That car does the quarter mile in thirteen and a half seconds at one hundred and two miles per hour. Your car can't match that."

Carlos' laugh stopped and his smile started to fade away. Anthony moved back slowly, deeper into the yard, and Carlos followed him. Anthony was not in a mood to debate how much faster the GNX was than his car. "Maybe you would like to try and find out sometime?"

Anthony sat back down at the table and looked over at Carlos who sat across from him. Anthony took a deep breath and held it for a second. He relit his cigar and blew the smoke across the table right into Carlos' face. "Racing isn't my thing."

"Why?" asked Carlos.

Anthony dragged on his cigar and looked around the yard that had thinned out a bit. Mickey the Mouse came over and patted Anthony on the back. "I'm heading out Ant." Anthony excused himself from Carlos and got up to say his goodbyes to Mickey and talked to him for a few minutes.

Luis stood in the doorway of the kitchen and watched the girls clean off the plates. Lourdes turned away and tried not to make eye contact with him. He walked over to her by the counter, "Hola Mami." Lourdes continued to pay attention to what she was doing and not look at him. "Why don't you want to talk to me?" It was clear that Luis had just a bit too much to drink.

Cristina and Debbie looked at each other and Debbie rolled her eyes. Debbie whispered to Cristina, "Can anymore happen today?"

Cristina shook her head slowly in disgust and responded, "He's not going to let up."

Lourdes finally looked at him and she was completely disgusted. "I have no interest in getting to know you."

Debbie looked out the window and saw Mickey leave and Carlos talking to Anthony. She found it weird that Carlos was actually talking to him, but she found it even weirder that Anthony was engaging him in return.

"Come on Mami."

Lourdes' face said it all. "Don't call me that," she said sickened.

"Why?" he asked. Lourdes stared at him and she tried to calm herself down. "You're very beautiful, you know that?"

Debbie watched them out of the corner of her eye and then back out the window. She saw Anthony start to look up towards the window but Carlos moved to his left and blocked his view. Then it made sense to her. Anthony was keeping Lourdes occupied most of the time she was there so this asshole wouldn't bother her. Now Carlos was keeping Anthony occupied so Luis could talk to her.

Lourdes tried her best to keep her composure, but she was starting to get annoyed. Cristina looked at her and then back to Debbie. "This is going to get out of hand."

Debbie agreed with her and then said, "Lourdes, why don't you go outside? Cristina and I can finish up in here."

Lourdes locked eyes with Debbie and then replied, "Okay." Before she could walk away Luis put his arm on the counter blocking her way out from the left side and his body on the right side. Lourdes was trapped. "Excuse me, please," she said somewhat annoyed. Luis wasn't moving. He was just looking at her with what seemed to be very dirty thoughts on his mind. His eyes dotted up and down her body and it made her sick.

Debbie looked back and forth at Luis, her sisters and the window. She didn't know what to do and the room seemed to be closing in on her. She noticed Lourdes had a face of stone. She couldn't tell if Lourdes was scared, angry or repulsed.

Lourdes tried to move away again and Luis kept blocking her. "I asked you nicely, please move."

"Or what, Mami?" Luis reached over with his free hand and touched Lourdes's arm and stroked his finger up and down on it. Lourdes tried to push him away and he became more aggressive. He held her arm tighter and tried grabbing her face.

"Hey!" yelled Debbie.

That was it. Anthony heard that and looked towards the kitchen window. Carlos moved again and blocked his view. Anthony looked at Carlos who had a smirk on his face. Anthony went to move past him and Carlos blocked him. "Where are you going?"

"You got two seconds to get out of my way."

Carlos' eyes lit up, "Or what?"

Mike was quickly there with the two other guys from the club. Carlos turned and was distracted by them. Anthony took that opportunity to move to his right and get around Carlos and quickly head towards the house. Carlos tried to reach for Anthony, but he missed him. He started to head for the house and the club guys blocked him. This was not what Mike wanted, but at least it was three against one. Carlos looked at Mike and he remembered what Luis told him earlier about Anthony being with the grease balls. He stopped, stared at them and didn't move.

Anthony got into the kitchen and saw that Cristina was huddled in the corner visibly scared. Debbie was trying to pull Luis' hand away from Lourdes's face and she was struggling to get away. Anthony's face turned red and he felt his adrenalin kick in. Without thinking he moved toward the three and pulled Debbie out of the way.

"ANTHONY NO!" yelled Debbie, but he wasn't paying attention to her. He was completely focused on getting this scumbag off of Lourdes. Anthony grabbed Luis by the back of his shirt and pulled him hard off of her. Luis let his grip go, but as he did he scratched Lourdes's face. Anthony used the momentum he had and tossed Luis clear across the kitchen. Luis hit the table back first and tumbled over it and landed on the floor, next to the garbage bags. Debbie moved to Lourdes to see if she was okay.

"Get her inside," he instructed to Debbie and Cristina. Debbie moved towards him to try and calm him down. She grabbed him and looked up at him. She had never seen a look like that in his eyes. She could swear she saw fire. She didn't know how to calm him down. Now she was scared of him. She didn't know what he was capable of at this point. There was no reigning him in.

Luis struggled to get up and Anthony moved around Debbie, shrugging her off of him. Anthony grabbed Luis who was stumbling up and tossed him back through the screen door and out into the yard.

"ANTHONY STOP!" yelled Debbie, but he never heard her. If he did he just ignored her. Debbie went to go after them and Cristina stopped her.

"Debbie don't, you will get hurt. Let's help Lourdes, she's bleeding." Debbie looked at Lourdes who had a gash on her face. The two sisters went to help Lourdes as their mother came in from the living room.

Luis hit the ground in the yard hard. He had been thrown down the three steps from the kitchen by Anthony and within seconds Anthony was there on top of him picking him up again. He was caught completely by surprise by the throw across the table.

Carlos tried to move around Mike and his guys, but they wouldn't let him past them. Mike looked up at him. "Come on now, this is between them. Do you see us getting involved? Stay out of it." Mike's heart was racing, the last thing he wanted to do was to get involved with this; but now Anthony was, and by extension he was now too.

Carlos looked at them and knew he could probably take these three guys, but for now he would sit it out. If anyone else from Anthony's side got involved then he would make his move. He knew Luis could handle himself. It was only a matter of time before he turned it around.

People all around the yard were clearing out of the way as the fight ensued. Anthony was laying into Luis at a furious pace and Luis couldn't mount a defense, let alone an offense. Every time he tried, Anthony was just took quick to either block or attack. Tables were being knocked over while food and drinks were flying all over the place. Anthony tossed him over another table and then met him when he was trying to get to his knees. Anthony hit him with another blow to the face, which knocked him onto his back. Anthony climbed on top of him and started laying into his face. Luis managed to toss him over to the side and Anthony lost his balance and tumbled over to the floor. Luis got up quick and laid a kick to Anthony's ribs as he was trying to get back up.

Mike watched the fight and winced when Anthony got kicked. It was a hard kick and he could tell it knocked the air out of him. Carlos smiled as he watched the tide turn a little.

Debbie came out of the house trying to gauge what was going on. The yard was a mess. She looked to her right and saw Anthony and Luis at it rolling around in the grass. She went to move towards them and Teresa stopped her. "Don't Debbie."

Debbie yelled, "Are you nuts? We have to stop this."

Teresa held her back. "Don't, you can't break that up, you'll get killed!"

Debbie stopped fighting as she came to her senses and watched.

Anthony grabbed Luis' arm and used it to throw him off balance. The two of them rolled back in an entwined struggle towards the other end of the yard, near the grill. Anthony managed to get Luis' arm high enough and then he came up with his left knee into Luis's mid-section. That completely knocked the wind out of Luis. Anthony delivered three more blows like that and Luis was completely hunched over in pain. Anthony stood him up straight and punched him in the face, knocking him back into the grill. Luis hit the grill and collapsed onto the side shelf of it. He managed to reach over and grab a knife that was laying there. Anthony moved closer to him as Luis turned around with the knife swinging. Anthony was too close to him and Luis connected with the swiping motion of the knife and he caught Anthony across the chest with it. The knife sliced open Anthony's shirt and caused a gash across his chest.

Debbie and Teresa looked on in horror as this began to escalate out of hand. Everyone in the yard was stunned and remained silent, but no one dared get involved. The only noise they made was a loud gasp when Anthony was cut with the knife.

Anthony fell back towards the side of the grill and winced in pain. He held his chest and quickly felt the warm blood that was coming out of the stinging wound. Luis moved closer to him and Anthony reached over and grabbed a handful of dirt with his right hand and tossed it towards Luis's face. The dirt hit Luis right where it was intended to, his eyes. That stunned him for the brief second that Anthony needed. Anthony reached over and grabbed the pliers that he used earlier that morning to loosen up the propane tank for the grill. He got to his knees with the pliers and locked them onto Luis' balls. Luis screeched in pain as Anthony tightened the grip on the pliers. Anthony held the pliers with his right hand and grabbed

Luis's arm that had the knife with the other. He then proceeded to bang that arm on a table till he dropped the knife. Anthony twisted the pliers around ninety degrees to the right and Luis howled even louder in pain. He knew he had to end this soon. The knife was out of reach by hand and his only weapon at this point was the pliers, but that wasn't going to get him too far. Anthony reached over with his foot and kicked the knife into the bushes. He couldn't risk having Luis be able to get his hands on that knife again. Anthony squeezed the pliers as tight as he could and he could feel Luis start to get weak. Anthony pulled him towards the grill and he opened the cover to expose the hot surface. Anthony dropped the pliers releasing his grip on Luis's balls and grabbed him by the back of the hair. "You want to fight dirty mother fucker? See how this feels." Anthony pushed Luis's face onto the burning grill. Luis screamed for all he was worth as Anthony held his face there for what seemed to be an eternity. Anthony himself was having a problem from the heat, almost burning his hand as he held Luis' face there. He could only imagine how Luis felt. Everyone screamed when Anthony pushed him onto the grill.

Anthony felt Luis' body go limp and his screaming ceased due to passing out from the pain. Anthony began to pull his face back off the grill, but it was burnt into the grill surface. As he tugged back he felt the resistance from the skin being fused into the grill grating. The smell of charred flesh filled the yard. Now Luis' hair started to singe and burn and that smell joined the smell of the skin. Anthony pulled harder this time and when he did he left most of Luis' skin on the red hot surface. Luis' limp body fell back to the floor.

Anthony leaned back onto the table to get a hold of himself. He looked down at his cut and it was bleeding badly. He looked down to Luis who was motionless as smoke flowed from his face and hair, and then staggered his way back towards the crowd. Debbie was being held by Teresa and they were both crying. He turned to Carlos who had fire in his eyes. Carlos pushed his way past Mike and made his way towards Luis to try and give him a hand. The other guys from the club kept a barrier between Carlos and Anthony the whole time. At this point Anthony didn't have any more energy to tangle with Carlos but he felt like this wasn't over just yet.

Debbie broke free from Teresa and ran to Anthony and hugged him. He winced in pain as she pressed up against his cut chest. "Oh my God, are you okay?"

"Yeah," replied Anthony.

Mike came over to him. "Go inside and clean that up. We'll keep him out here and away from you."

Anthony nodded and turned to go into the house. In front of him was Lourdes crying with a cut on her face. He looked at her and after a second reached for her face with his right hand and gently touched her cheek where she was cut. He still had anger burning in his eyes, especially when he saw her face cut open. They stared at each other for a moment and then he made his way into the house and she followed.

Anthony stumbled to a chair and sat while Debbie and her mother searched the house for antiseptic. Lourdes followed in and went to find her sister. Cristina slowly entered the house and looked at Anthony. She had tears in her eyes. Anthony looked up at her. "Cristina, I'm not sure if you should be in here. I don't know what his reaction is going to be to all this. Maybe try to appease him for now? I don't know. I don't have the answer." Cristina blankly nodded her head and walked out of the house.

Mike walked back and forth in the distance of the yard and watched Carlos try to tend to his friend, but he wasn't able to help him. Luis was unresponsive and literally smoking. His face was completely burnt to a crisp on one side and his hair was still smoldering. Little blood was coming out from his wounds, due to being cauterized by the intense heat, but his face was completely raw. Mike could only imagine the shape his balls were in.

Teresa approached Mike as Cristina was making her way slowly and cautiously towards Carlos and Luis. "Mike, what now?"

Mike looked at Teresa and she could see that he was somewhat nervous, but he really didn't have an answer for her. He just shook his head as if to say, 'I don't know.' People had completely cleared out of the yard now and mostly everyone was gone or in the process of leaving. Mike looked over to make sure the two guys from the club were still standing guard at the doorway and they were. "I'm wondering if I should get a few more guys from the club to come here."

"Do you think that would do any good?"

Mike just shrugged his shoulders. "I don't know about this hurt guy either."

Cristina approached Carlos and he looked up at her. She could see he was fuming with what just took place. Very nervously she said, "Is there anything I can do to help?"

He remained silent and didn't really answer her. After a second he said, "I'm going to take him to the hospital, but I can only fit him in the car."

"It's okay, take him and do what you need to do. I can get my mother to take me back home."

Carlos thought for a second and then said "Okay." He stood up and stared at her. He had something to say, but he just didn't. His eyes spoke everything he needed to say. She too knew this was not over. He reached down and picked up a limp, almost lifeless, Luis and headed towards his car. "Don't make me come looking for you."

Mike watched him put his friend into the car and then he got in and took off. Mike made his way into the kitchen and told the two guys to continue standing guard and to be alert. When Mike got into the kitchen it was almost chaotic. Debbie was nervous while her mother tended to Anthony's wound. Her mother was a nurse, so she knew what she was doing; and it looked like Anthony needed at least a nurse to tackle this wound. Her mother was soaking gauze bandages and then placing them on spots of the wound that were bleeding heavily. "I don't know if I can stop this bleeding. You might need stitches."

Cristina entered the kitchen and went to check on Lourdes's face. She was holding a gauze pad soaked with antiseptic on it as well.

"I can't believe this happened," said Debbie.

Anthony looked at her but didn't say anything. He looked to Cristina and then to Mike. "Where is he?"

"He took his friend to the hospital."

"Did he get up on his own?" asked Anthony.

Mike replied, "No," and Debbie just began shaking her head.

"I told him I would get a ride with my mother," added Cristina.

Anthony asked, "Are the guys still outside?"

"Yeah," said Mike, "I was tempted to get more people here."

"For what?" asked Debbie.

Mike looked at Anthony and then towards Debbie, "Just the look on his face. I have this feeling this isn't over."

Debbie asked Anthony, "Is this what you wanted?"

Anthony was still looking at her, "Did I start this fight?"

"Did you need to cook the guy?"

Anthony sat shaking his head. "Did you see him try to stab me?"

"You knocked the knife out of his hand."

Anthony put his head down and took a deep breath. As he did that he winced in pain and part of his wound gushed out more blood. Brenda had packed parts of the slice with gauze and that seemed to stop a lot of the bleeding but she was still working on a tough area that didn't want to stop.

Lourdes looked over to her sister who gazed back at her. "I suppose this is going to be my fault right?"

"I didn't say that, but he didn't need to get as extreme as he did with him."

"Really?" asked Anthony. Debbie shut up and looked back at Anthony, she could tell he was still fired up. "He came into our fucking house and acted like that?" Anthony began to raise his voice and Debbie's face changed. "He put his hands on your family and you think I didn't need to get that extreme?" Debbie put her head down. "He came at me with a knife and I shouldn't have done whatever I could to put a stop to that fight?" Anthony went quiet for a second and tried to calm down. Debbie now had tears in her eyes. "He's lucky I didn't fucking kill him."

"The way Carlos carried him out of here he might still die," added Mike. Debbie sat shaking her head. After a minute she walked out of the kitchen crying. "Do you want me to go and talk to her?" asked Mike. Anthony shrugged his shoulders as if to convey he really didn't care at that point. He seemed fed up all the way around and she was just adding to his tension. Mike and Teresa walked away to try and defuse the situation with Debbie while Brenda continued to try and close up Anthony's cut.

Anthony looked to Lourdes, "How's your face?"

Lourdes came over to the table and removed her gauze. Anthony examined her face, "It seems to be only a scratch. It's not too deep. I think you'll be okay."

Her mom turned her attention towards her and examined the cut. "You'll be okay. I don't think it will scar at all."

Lourdes sat down. She and Anthony stared at each other. "Are you okay?"

"Yeah," he replied. "Are you?"

"Yes. He could have killed you with that knife." Anthony continued staring at her. Brenda watched them as she worked on Anthony's cut. Anthony reached over and Lourdes took his hand and held it. "I was nervous for you."

"I'm okay."

Lourdes smiled at him and he smiled back at her. "Thank you." He continued staring at her and then winked.

Teresa was sitting on the couch hugging Debbie while Mike was kneeling in front of her. "Deb look at me."

Debbie had tears streaming down her face. "I can't believe this took place here tonight, I really can't."

"I know," said Mike, "but it did and nothing can change that now. You have to understand something."

"What?"

"Anthony did what he needed to do. It was absolutely necessary what he did."

"Mike, you're just saying that because he's your best friend."

Mike shook his head and Teresa added "Deb, he's right."

"You too?" Debbie asked Teresa.

"Debbie I'm serious, Anthony was in a tough spot. When I saw that guy turn around with that knife, I didn't know what to think."

"Trust us," added Mike, "he did what was necessary, and believe me I agree with him. He's lucky Anthony didn't kill him. He would have had that coming."

Debbie sat thinking about it for a minute while Teresa ran her fingers through her hair, trying to soothe her friend. "I just don't know where this is going to lead."

Mike thought for a minute. "Let us worry about that okay?"

"What do you mean?"

"Anthony knows how to take care of himself and I got his back. Hopefully this asshole will see us as people not to fuck with, and back down."

Debbie thought about that for a minute and then looked at Mike. "Hopefully, but I don't think the jerk will get that message."

"I don't know about that Deb," added Teresa. "He really fucked that guy up."

After a second Debbie chuckled, "Come on, I guess I have to make this right with Anthony." Debbie got up and so did Teresa and Mike.

"You don't have to make it right," said Mike, "you just have to let it go."

Debbie reluctantly agreed and they went back into the kitchen. Brenda was finishing up Anthony's cut and putting bandages onto it. She was telling him not to stretch too far or he could open it back up and that he should see a doctor to get stitches. Debbie moved over to the chair and put her arm around him and kissed him on the top of the head. He looked up at her. "Are you okay?" she asked.

"Yeah," replied Anthony and then he went quiet for a minute.

"What's wrong?"

He continued to look at her and then said, "We didn't cut the cake."

As hard as she tried she couldn't hold back the laugh that came bursting out of her mouth. "I think there's a knife in the bushes by the grill that we could use." After a second everyone else started to laugh as hard as they could. She reached over and kissed him and hugged him as tight as she could and he hugged her back.

Chapter 17
Repercussions

Several days had passed since the barbeque and all had been quiet. Anthony took a few days off from the club to try and let his wound heal a bit, and for the most part it was. Lourdes had to call off two photo shoots due to the cut on her face, but it was starting to fade. For the most part Debbie had left the fight alone and didn't bring it up anymore. Neither did Anthony. He wasn't in the mood to fight. Now the club was paging him with a code that meant he needed to come in.

Cristina had called a day earlier, and she let them know that Luis was still unconscious. He had third degree burns on one side of his face and a lot of his hair was gone. He had extensive nerve damage and was going to need more than one surgery and skin graph to repair his face. When Debbie told Anthony he just shrugged and walked away, he didn't care. Why should he? The scumbag put his hands on someone that he shouldn't have and he got what was coming to him, the same way Barry did. Barry didn't pay his debts, so he got what was coming to him. In both cases it was Anthony that gave what was coming to them. Anthony was starting to become dark and unremorseful. Debbie noticed that as well. She noticed it when she told him what Luis' condition was. She could see the uncaring attitude he displayed in his posture and his eyes. What did she want from him? Should he break down crying? Send Luis a box of chocolates and some flowers? Maybe a teddy bear, or a card? Fuck that shit and fuck him.

Anthony was walking down the stairs when the phone began ringing. He made his way to the kitchen and picked it up. It was Lourdes. "How are you?" he asked. He listened to her talk for a minute and then he looked over at the clock on the stove. "What time?" he asked. She was doing a photo shoot modeling shoes today so there would be no face shots, after that she wanted to meet up for lunch. He was silent for a few more seconds and listened to her. He looked at the clock again and then thought for a minute. "I have a stop to make and then I can meet you there around that time. Will that work?" He listened for a minute more and then said, "Okay, I'll see you in a little while." He hung up and then looked around for his keys and found them on the table.

He started to make his way for the door, but then stopped. He felt his waist and then went back upstairs into the bedroom. He went into the closet and opened the gun safe, pulled his 1911 out and checked to see that it was loaded. It was. He placed it in his waist, closed the safe and headed out of the bedroom and out of the house. He reached the GNX, got in and took off. He made his way down Pitkin Avenue towards Crossbay Boulevard. All the while he was thinking to himself about the barbeque. He kept playing it over and over in his head. What he could have done different and what he would have done the same. He always came back to the same conclusion, he did what he needed to do and he would do it all again. No one was putting their hands on those girls.

One thing that kept playing through his mind was that he was expecting to hear from the police, and he didn't. Surely the hospital would have asked how that happened, and he was expecting Carlos to tell them what had happened, but apparently he didn't. There could be several outcomes from that. The one Anthony kept rehearsing was the possibility that they were going to handle it themselves. Anthony would have done the same thing if it was reversed. Anthony would never have talked to the cops. He would wait till he got better and then handle it himself.

Anthony reached Crossbay Boulevard and made a quick left and headed towards 101st Avenue. A song he couldn't stand came on the radio and he changed it to another station. His pager started going off again and he ignored it. He was only a mile away from the club.

He drove for a minute more, turned the corner to the club and saw Mike's car parked right in front. He pulled up behind it and parked. He got out of the car and a couple of the guys came over to talk to him. He asked where Mike was and they told him inside with Frankie the Hand. "Thanks," replied Anthony, and he went inside. He looked around the club and noticed Mike sitting in the back. He didn't look good. They caught each other's glance and headed towards one another. They met mid room and kissed cheek to cheek. "What's wrong with you?" asked Anthony, worried about his friend.

Mike replied, "Frankie wants to talk to us about the barbeque."

Anthony had a look of shock. "It made its way to him?"

"Yeah," replied Mike.

"How?"

"I don't know, but he's not in a good mood about it."

"Why?"

Anthony never got his answer. At that moment a door opened from the back room and Frankie came out. "You two, in here, now!" Frankie motioned for them to come into the room. They did as Frankie shut the door and they all moved to a table and sat. "You two knuckleheads want anything to drink?" They both shook their heads no. Frankie poured himself a glass of wine and then sat across from them. After a second he looked up at Anthony and asked, "Did you barbeque a Dominican guy the other night at your birthday party?"

The question was kind of funny and it reminded Anthony of when he was fighting with Debbie that night right after the fight. She pointed out that he didn't need to cook Luis. Anthony said, "Yeah, why?"

Frankie laughed, looked at Mike and then back to Anthony. "The guy you roasted has ties to the Perez brothers."

Very calmly Anthony asked, "And?"

Frankie smiled a little bit and took a drag from his cigar. "They are beefing about it. They're pretty pissed."

Anthony got up annoyed. "Oh fuck that!"

Mike watched them quietly, kind of shocked that Anthony got up like that.

"This guy is in the hospital in pretty bad shape. Didn't you think there could be repercussions from this?"

Anthony thought about that for a minute and then replied, "Yeah, I know."

"What happened, you didn't have enough food so you started cooking your guests?"

Anthony tried not to laugh, but it did lighten up the tension a bit. He let a smile creep across his face and so did Frankie. "He disrespected people in my house, family."

"What happened?"

Anthony took a deep breath, poured some wine and then sat back down. Frankie handed him a cigar, he took it and lit it. "He made a lot of passes at Debbie's sister. She wasn't interested in him and then he started getting very aggressive with her. Debbie tried to separate them, and it got a little physical. I went in the kitchen and put a stop to it."

"You couldn't stop it without frying him?"

Anthony replied, "We fought our way through the yard and ended up back by the grill. He got his hands on a knife and slashed my chest."

"Oh yeah?"

Anthony replied, "Yeah," and then he pulled up his shirt to show Frankie the cut. Frankie examined it and nodded his head. "I needed to put an end to it."

"So you cooked him?"

"Frankie, it wasn't like that."

"Then make me understand it."

Anthony thought about it for a minute. "There was a pair of pliers laying there and that's all I could get my hands on. I grabbed them and locked onto his balls and started twisting."

Frankie grabbed his crotch and looked at Mike, "OH! MADONNAMEI!"

The three laughed and Anthony continued, "I was able to get him to drop the knife and that was the only way I could put an end to it. The grill was there and I pushed his face onto it."

Frankie took another drag from his cigar as he listened. Then he turned to Mike, "What was your part in this?"

Mike replied, "I just needed to keep his boy out of it while they fought it out. Motherfucker is big."

"What was this guy doing at your barbeque anyway? He a friend of yours?"

"Fuck no! He came with a friend that is dating Debbie's other sister. He's a fucking problem too, especially now."

Frankie asked Anthony, "Why is he a problem?"

Mike shook his head, trying to convey to Anthony not to bring up Cristina's problems, but he wasn't listening. Anthony said, "He abuses Debbie's sister."

Frankie thought about that for a minute. "Why is he a problem, especially now?"

"Cause of this. I was expecting to hear from the cops and I never did, so they must have made up some story like it was an accident or something."

"Why would they do that? Why would they want to protect you?" asked Mike.

"To take care of it themselves," replied Anthony, "not protect me."

Frankie agreed with Anthony. "Yep, that's why they made the beef. Did you know this guy was with the Perez's?"

Anthony though about that for a minute. "I had an idea he was with somebody, but I wasn't sure who. I thought I saw him on a buy, but I do so many I had no idea which one he was at."

"You bought from him directly?" asked Frankie.

Anthony replied, "No, he was in the background. He wasn't even paying attention."

"This guy is out of the hospital already to make the beef to the Perez's?" asked Mike.

"No I spoke to Cristina yesterday and he's still unconscious."

"Really?" laughed Frankie. "You fucked him up pretty good."

Anthony smiled, "He's lucky I didn't kill him."

"Who made the beef then if he's still sleeping?" asked Mike.

Mike and Anthony both looked at Frankie who was shaking his head. "How about the boyfriend?"

Anthony thought about that for a minute. "I don't think he has his hands in anything. The guy's a barber."

Mike thought about that for a second. "Maybe that's where they move their stuff through, the barbershop? Motherfucker drives a Corvette. Hair don't buy you a Corvette."

Anthony thought about it for a minute and it did make sense. "I guess anything is possible."

All three went quiet for a minute. Frankie asked, "So now what?"

"Why are you asking me?" asked Anthony.

"I'm asking you because this is your mess."

Anthony took a drag from his cigar for a minute. "My mess? No backing for me on this?"

Frankie took a sip out of his wine. "Anthony, you're not a made guy."

Anthony got up annoyed and walked around the room again. "What the fuck does that have to do with this Frankie?"

"It has a lot to do with it Anthony."

"With everything I do for you guys? Fuck that. With everything I do for all the fucking families, I can't get backing for this? I can understand if I cooked another made guy, but this is some lowlife that knows a drug dealer tied to a Dominican cartel. How fucking high on the food chain can he be?"

Frankie thought about that for a minute. "Apparently high enough for the Perez's to beef. We make money off the Perez brothers."

"You don't make money off of me?"

Frankie was quiet and thought about it for a minute. "Anthony I'm not saying we're just going to leave you to the wind."

"What are you saying then? It sure seems like it."

"Anthony, I have a boss too. I need to answer to him." Frankie was quiet for a minute, "What did you have in mind?"

Anthony walked back and forth while thinking and then sat back down across from Frankie. "How bad is this beef from the Perez brothers?"

"Pretty bad, I would think. They didn't get into specifics, but you know what you did to this guy. If someone did that to one of ours, I don't have to tell you how we'd respond."

Anthony looked at Mike and Mike just stared at the table, deep in thought. After a second he looked at Frankie, "Take them out?"

Frankie had a surprised look on his face. Mike picked up his head and looked at Anthony with a similar look on his face. "Take out the Perez brothers?" asked Frankie.

"Si," replied Anthony.

"Clip them?" asked Frankie, taken back a bit.

"I don't think a sit down is going to do anything to squash this. They don't think like us."

"If it was a Colombian cartel you would've had a hit squad at your house that same night," added Frankie.

Mike agreed with Frankie.

"I'm in pretty good with the Colombian cartels, like Mariana's," said Anthony, "but I can see that."

"I don't know about taking them out Anthony." Frankie thought about it for a minute. "This really doesn't have anything to do with business." Frankie was quiet for a very long minute. "You know a lot of guys, friends of ours. You guys have a small crew of your own. I can't sanction anything against the Perez brothers, but you do what you have to do and I'll look the other way. Capisce?"

Anthony and Mike just stared back at him. After a minute Anthony looked back at Frankie and replied, "Si, capisce."

"I'll keep them off of you as long as I can, but they don't answer to me. Watch your back, both of you."

Both Anthony and Mike nodded. They all stood up and Frankie came around the table, hugged Anthony and they kissed cheek to cheek. "Understand something though: this is your job, not ours. This is all on you. You're not operating under our flag. You fuck this up, we have to look the other way. This family is not going to war with the Cartels over some skirt getting felt up at a barbeque. Got it?"

Anthony frowned at Frankie. He didn't like hearing that. He thought they would have backed him more then what they were, but he had to live with it. After a minute he nodded, his head but didn't say anything. Frankie reached over and gave him a lite slap on his face. Anthony smiled at him and headed out of the room with Mike following.

Heading through the club Mike trailed behind Anthony and asked, "You want a drink?"

Anthony replied, "No, walk with me."

"Okay," replied Mike. They headed out of the club and they both walked slowly down the block. "What's up?"

"You with me on this?"

Mike was quiet as they slowly moved down the block. "What do you think?"

Anthony smiled at him. "You had me worried for a bit. That took you a while to answer."

Mike smiled back at him. "This is serious though, we have to plan it and be careful. There can't be anyone around to come back and tell this story. The guys won't back us up any more, they're just looking the other way."

"That fucking pisses me off."

"Why? This is business for them. It's got nothing at all to do with their business."

"I don't make them money? I bet if one of their shipments disappeared from the Perez brothers they would act."

"Yeah, they would, cause that's their business; this isn't. Besides, you heard him, you're not made."

Anthony shook his head annoyed. "Another stupid fucking rule."

"There is nothing you can do about that, so just let it go."

"That's easy for you to say. You're on the rise to be made. You and Enzo both. I'm left sitting in the fucking wind. Debbie is right about this lifestyle. There's nothing in it for me."

Mike laughed, "What are you going to do? Get a nine to five?" Anthony was very frustrated. "I know you're pissed, but right now you need to concentrate on the problem at hand."

Anthony agreed with Mike. After a second he asked, "Who else can we bring in on this? Enzo?"

Mike thought about that for a second. "I guess if he can go without getting high for a couple of hours."

"That's true. Who else?"

"Mickey the Mouse is out of the question."

"No fucking way. His heart would be in it, but he is definitely not cut out for something like that. He'll make someone a good Consigliere someday, that's for sure."

Mike laughed and added, "That's for sure."

"However, Mickey might have some connections he can lean on to get us information about what we're going up against."

"Okay, for information he's in."

Anthony thought about it some more. "How about the Double R Boys?"

"For sure. I don't think we're going to need anyone else with those two, but let me think about it."

Anthony stated, "Don't think about it too long. We have to move pretty fast on this. I have no idea what they're planning on their end. The quicker we put an end to this, the quicker we can get back to not looking over our shoulders."

"You have a plan?"

"I'm working on it. Reach out to Mickey and see if he can recommend anyone else. Reach out to the Double R Boys as well. I'll get in touch with Enzo and I will be in touch with you over the next day or so and we can all meet up to come up with a plan."

"You be careful, okay?"

"You to Bro."

They hugged and Anthony headed towards the GNX.

"Where you headed to?"

"Lunch with Lourdes."

Mike smiled at him, "Playing with fire there my friend."

Anthony smiled back at Mike and opened his car door. "It's not like that Mike."

"Okay, be careful. I'll wait for your call."

Anthony winked at him and got in the car. Mike headed back to the club. Anthony started the GNX and Luisa Menendez was on the radio. He was happy.

Chapter 18
Lunch Date

Anthony made his way through Manhattan. He hated driving in Manhattan and he was questioning himself as to why he agreed to meet Lourdes there for lunch. He drove to the restaurant she told him she'd meet him at and there was the lot across the street she told him to park at. He took the GNX into the lot and was met by a parking attendant. The guy was clearly in awe of the car. Anthony stepped out of the car and looked at the guy. "The keys are in it." The guy nodded and approached the car with a smile from ear to ear eager to drive the GNX. Anthony didn't get a warm and fuzzy feeling from the attendant. He looked at him over his sunglasses and then put his hand on the guys shoulder. He glared at him over his glasses as he said, "You fuck this car up or pull some Ferris Bueller's Day Off shit, and they won't find you. Understand me?"

The guy was clearly shaken up a bit. He replied, "Yes."

Anthony smiled at him and rubbed his shoulder. Anthony reached into his pocket, pulled out a twenty and handed it to the guy. The guy handed him a claim ticket and Anthony walked away and headed across the street. The restaurant was on the corner and had outside seating. Across the other street was Central Park. Manhattan was busy as usual for that time of the day. It was just getting a bit past lunch time, so the restaurant was a little emptier than expected. He approached the place and Lourdes was sitting outside. She caught his gaze and he smiled at her. She smiled back and waved to him as he approached. He made his way around the barricade and towards her table. As he got there she stood up and he hugged her. They hugged for a second and she gently kissed him on his cheek. "How are you?" she asked.

Anthony pulled back and they sat down and smiled at each other. "Better, now that I am out of that traffic."

Lourdes giggled, "You should have taken the train. It's much quicker."

"I drive a GNX. I look for any reason to drive it. I'm not getting on a train. Besides, guys like me don't take trains."

"Guys like you? What do you mean guys like you?"

Anthony started to feel uncomfortable for a second as he tried to figure out how to explain to her what he meant. "You know, guys in my line of work."

Lourdes laughed, "Your line of work huh?" Anthony looked towards the street and then back at her. She reached over and whispered, "You mean wise guys?" Anthony laughed and agreed. "Shouldn't you be driving a Cadillac or a Lincoln then?"

"Your sister got the Cadi. I'll stick to my GNX." Lourdes laughed and then held his gaze. Anthony smiled and asked, "What?"

"You know, we've kind of had this conversation and I got bits and pieces of what you do." Anthony stared at her. "But what do you really do?"

Anthony sat back and looked around to see how close other people were to them. By this point most of the restaurant had cleared out. He leaned on the table and she leaned in closer to him, seeing that he didn't want to talk loud. "I do a lot of things. Some of them you know about, like lending out money."

"What else?" she asked.

"I run numbers and I pay out and collect on bets." Anthony sat back. He wasn't sure if he wanted to go on.

"I think there's more to you then loan sharking and book making."

Anthony continued to hold her gaze. He leaned back on the table again. "I deal with drugs." Lourdes didn't look surprised. If she was, she didn't let it show on her face. "You don't look surprised."

She thought about that for a second. "For some reason I'm not."

"Are you bothered by it?"

"No, I'm not."

Anthony thought about her response for a minute. "Are you sure?"

Lourdes smiled and said, "Yes, but tell me more about it."

Anthony thought about that for a second. "Well, I got involved in it because a friend of mine was depressed. He just broke up with his girlfriend and he wanted something to pick him up. One thing led to another and I got deeper involved in it."

"Deeper how?"

"Well, I began to make a lot more money and started selling to other people. I've made a world of connections by doing it. The thing is, and I know this may sound really weird, but I try to keep it respectable."

"Respectable?"

"I know that sounds stupid."

"No, it really doesn't, but explain it."

Anthony looked around again and then back to Lourdes. "I don't sell to kids. I don't sell near schools. I keep it to an area that has only known that stuff. I try not to bring it into other areas that haven't been exposed to it, or try to push it on people. I guess you can say I keep it around low lives."

Lourdes said, "I understand."

"Shortly after I met you and Cristina my role with that stuff has kind of changed though."

"How?" she asked.

"Well, I'm not doing as much street dealing now as I was a few months ago."

"Why?"

"Just the role the families have me playing. They are sending me on buy deals now."

"Buy deals? What are those?"

"They give me a shitload of money and a pickup point to go to, I usually meet with people from the Spanish Cartels and we make a deal, usually for kilos of coke. If it's a good deal I buy it and take it back to the club. They in turn cut it up, mix it, and send it out for distribution on the street."

Lourdes sat back, "Okay, well it sounds like you're moving up there."

"I don't know about that."

"Why?"

"I don't think I'll ever move further up then where I am now."

"What makes you say that?"

Anthony thought about his conversation earlier with Mike. He replied, "Someone like me really can't get too far in this thing."

Lourdes looked confused. "You seem to be pretty successful, and everyone I see you with seems to like you."

"It's not really about liking me."

"What then?" she asked somewhat confused.

Anthony took a deep breath, "I can never really be made." Lourdes continued to look at him. "I'm not one hundred percent Italian, and in order to be a made guy you have to be one hundred percent Italian. They trace your roots all the way back to Italy to confirm."

"Well that sounds pretty stupid."

"That's the rule though, and without being made I can never get any higher. I will forever be stuck as an associate."

Lourdes took a sip of water. "No way of changing that I guess?"

Anthony smiled at her. After a second he laughed. "Not unless I overthrow all the bosses and families and make things the way I want them to be. Change a hundred years of rules and traditions."

Lourdes laughed and said, "I'll give you a hand."

He laughed for a minute and said, "That would be something. You want to rule the underworld with me?"

She smiled and replied, "Sure! My sister would love that. I can only imagine how I would be accepted in your world."

"What do you mean?"

Lourdes laughed and replied, "Well, if they won't fully accept you, and you're half Italian, can you imagine a female Puerto Rican giving orders?"

Anthony laughed hard and then she did as well. He sat back and asked, "Are you sure all this stuff sits okay with you?

Lourdes smiled and laughed again. "It all sits fine with me. I told you, I like that stuff, all of it, except this stupid rule that you're subject to." She went quiet for a second and then said, "I love making you squirm."

"I bet you do." They both sat staring at each other for a minute. "How's the face?"

Lourdes turned the side of her face that had the cut towards Anthony, "How's it look?"

He tried to hold it back, but he couldn't pass up the opportunity to flirt with her just a bit. She left herself completely open for a compliment. "As pretty as always."

Lourdes turned her face back and tilted her head a bit to the side. "Why thank you." She giggled as she blushed a little and he laughed. "How's the chest?"

"It's getting better, your mom did a good job of fixing me up." Anthony paused for a minute and then asked, "So what do I owe the pleasure of receiving a lunch invite from you?"

"Well," she started and then she paused to take a sip of water, "it's my way of saying thank you for the other night."

Anthony didn't understand, "Thank you for what?"

Lourdes cocked her head to the side again. "Really? The barbeque. That asshole all over me and you tossing him a beating."

Anthony smiled slightly and continued looking at her. "Lourdes, you really don't need to take me to lunch for that. If it happened again I would do the same thing."

"I know you would, but I just wanted to say thank you. You have no idea what that meant to me."

Anthony remained quiet, after a second they smiled at each other again. At that same moment a waiter came over and gave them menus and went over the specials. They looked over the menus and put their orders in and the waiter went about his business. "So, any more news about that asshole?"

Lourdes replied, "Just what Cristina called and said yesterday. He's pretty messed up."

"Good, it was all worth it then."

Lourdes asked, "What was?"

Anthony stared at her. He knew he shouldn't say anything to her about the sit down from earlier today, but for some reason he couldn't resist telling her. "I got called to the club that I do most of my work out of today. Apparently this guy has friends that deal with my friends. Remember I told you I recognized him from a job I went on."

"Yeah," replied Lourdes.

"They weren't too happy with me cooking him and they complained to my friends." Lourdes's face changed and Anthony noticed it. "What's wrong?"

Lourdes was quiet for a minute. "I'm sorry. I didn't want you to have issues because of me."

"Hey, don't think or say something like that. You didn't cause this and none of this is your fault. I'm a big boy, I made my bed and I have to lay in it. If it came up again I would do the same thing except next time he wouldn't get up, ever."

Lourdes asked, "What did your job say? They pissed at you?"

"No, once I explained everything to him he understood where I was coming from."

"What about the people this dirt bag works for?"

Anthony looked out to the traffic and the people going by. After a minute he looked back at Lourdes. "Well, that's a little more complicated, but nothing that can't be handled."

Lourdes went quiet. Anthony reached over and touched her hand. "You okay?"

She looked back at him and said, "Yes."

"You sure?"

Lourdes put her other hand over his and they held each other. "I just feel like you are in danger now because of me."

Anthony squeezed her hand and stared at her. "Listen to me, okay? There is nothing here that I can't fix. My job leads me to more dangerous situations then this every day and I always come out of them."

"What if these guys do something to you?"

"They aren't going to get the chance. It's going to be taken care of well before that. I promise."

They sat holding hands for a moment. She caught his gaze and then smiled at him. "Okay," she replied

"Good, now let's enjoy lunch." Feeling better, Lourdes smiled again.

They talked all throughout lunch about everything from Anthony's work to Lourdes's modeling. The lunch went by quickly and they decided to walk for a little while in Central Park. They walked along a trail and talked about Lourdes's family. She told him pretty much the same story that Debbie did about their mother. He didn't understand how Debbie held what she did towards Lourdes. He recognized that there were issues in that family, but he dealt with them the best that he could. He didn't want to come between the two sisters and he was starting to feel like he was stuck in the middle, especially since getting closer to Cristina and Lourdes, more so with Lourdes. He felt that Debbie's dislike was really focused on Lourdes rather than Cristina. It didn't help that he was so close to her. They walked down the path slowly and Lourdes looked at him. "What about Cristina?"

Anthony looked over at her; the Sun was reflecting off her hair and she looked beautiful in the shimmering light. He shifted his mind off of her and back to the conversation. She must have realized his mind was somewhere else and she started to blush a little while she fought a smile. "I'm working on that, along with the rest of the issue."

Lourdes said, "Okay," and they continued their stroll. "Do you think you will be able to tell me when this is all over?"

Anthony thought about that for a minute. "Well, if there was anyone in this world that I would tell, it would probably be you."

Lourdes smiled at him as they walked along. "Really?"

Anthony replied, "I don't know what it is about you, but I feel like I can tell you anything and you're not going to judge me for it. You're not going to make me feel guilty about it and you're not going to give me a speech on how wrong I'm living my life." Lourdes nodded her head and they walked along. "Even what we talked about over lunch; I could never talk to Debbie about the things I told you regarding my work."

"I know. In a way that's sad. You are probably harboring so many things with no one to talk to."

Anthony replied, "Sometimes I am." He went quiet for a second and then said, "I just feel very close to you, sometimes, like you're my own sister."

Lourdes slipped her arm in his and leaned her head onto his arm. "I'm glad you feel like that. I feel like I can tell you anything too."

He thought for a minute on how he wanted to word what he needed to say next. "For now though, and for your own good, I can't tell you everything."

Lourdes nodded her head and Anthony could feel her head rub up and down his arm when she did. He looked over, the wind blew, and as it did he could get the scent from her hair and her perfume, it felt almost intoxicating. Where was his mind going? Why was he having thoughts like that? Why were things like her perfume getting to him? He needed to purge them from his mind. Maybe Mike was right, she was in his head and he was having trouble getting her out of it. "I know," she said.

"You okay with that?"

Lourdes replied, "Yeah, I'm oaky with that. I trust you. I trust you like no one I've ever trusted before. If and when you're ready, you'll tell me, and if you don't, that's okay too."

Anthony and Lourdes both smiled at the same time, but not to each other, just to themselves. Somehow they both knew they were smiling. They continued to walk along the park, arm and arm, slowly down the trail.

Chapter 19
Dinner Arguments

Cristina was busy in the kitchen preparing dinner. She looked at the clock a few times, but each time she just never registered the time in her head. She ran late at work and was exhausted and now dinner was going to be late. She was moving as fast as possible, but she was already too far behind. Carlos was going to be home any minute and she remembered what happened the last time dinner wasn't ready when he got there. She didn't want to go through that again. She had the rice going and the oil was heating in the pan for the pork chops when the phone rang. She didn't want to pick it up, but she felt that might take her mind off of worrying what Carlos would say when he got home and dinner wasn't ready. She picked up the phone, "Hello?" It was Lourdes. Cristina continued cooking dinner and setting the table while listening to her sister. Lourdes was telling her about her photo shoot, but Cristina wasn't paying much attention. She was too nervous about dinner being late. "That's great. How is the scratch on your face?" Cristina moved to the refrigerator and pulled out the drinks. She looked at the clock again and realized Carlos should be walking through the door. "You what? You went out with Anthony for lunch?" Cristina stopped what she was doing and listened to her sister. "Did Debbie go to?" Cristina still remained silent and unmoving while listening to her sister. Once she heard Anthony's name she didn't think about Carlos anymore. She slowly began to come back to realization and began pouring the drinks. "Lourdes, what do you think Debbie would say if she heard you were out alone with him for lunch?" Cristina listened to her some more. "I know you don't really give a shit about what she thinks, but still." Cristina listened some more. "Lourdes, I know it was an innocent lunch, but still you know how Debbie gets." Cristina put the soda back in the fridge and then put the pork chops into the pan. They sizzled out loud and Cristina had to explain to her sister that she was cooking. "No, I haven't heard anything else about his friend except that he is really fucked up. How was Anthony feeling?" Cristina listened to her sister while she looked at the clock again. She was wondering to herself why Carlos wasn't home yet. "Oh well, that asshole got what he deserved, fuck him." Cristina giggled to herself as she asked her sister, "So tell me about your date." She turned around and Carlos was standing in the doorway listening to her conversation.

Anthony and Debbie had a quiet dinner. Debbie talked about her day, but she seemed weird. She wasn't the same since the barbeque. She seemed distant and at times snappy and a bit nasty. Anthony looked over at her while she was putting away the dishes and pushed himself to ask her, "What's wrong with you Deb? You haven't been right since the party."

Debbie continued to put the dishes away and kept her back to him. "Should I be in a good mood after that fiasco?"

Anthony put the soda away and stood staring at her. "What did you want me to do?" He knew he just opened a can of worms.

"I didn't want you to do anything."

Anthony took a deep breath and jumped into what seemed to be an argument. "So I should let some scumbag come into our house and put his hands on family right?"

"I'm not having this argument with you again," replied Debbie.

"This wouldn't be an argument if you just talked to me sometimes."

Debbie slammed down a dish into the cabinet and looked at him. "What the fuck is that supposed to mean? I don't talk to you?" Before Anthony could answer she started again, "When I do talk to you, you don't like what I have to say."

"Everything is a fight with you lately. I say red and you say blue. It seems like you're always looking to disagree with me about something. You're the same way with me that you are with Lourdes."

"Really now?" asked Debbie.

"Yeah, really," replied Anthony very sarcastically.

Debbie laughed to herself and moved to finish putting the dishes away. "Well, I'm sorry I've been so confrontational, but all I asked of you since you met my sisters was to stay out of the shit with Carlos."

"I haven't gotten involved with that at all. This shit with Lourdes was something totally different."

"And you had to be her knight in shining armor. It's all tied together. Do you really think that you and Carlos can be in the same room together at this point?"

Anthony was confused that she actually asked that question. "What makes you think I plan on ever being in the same room with him again?"

Now Debbie was confused. "He is dating and living with my sister. If you want to continue a friendship with her, how do you plan on doing that without him coming around? Do you think after that party he'll ever let her come here again without him, let alone come here at all?"

Anthony laughed, "He's never stepping foot in this house again, even if he wants to, and if he's smart he better never come near Ascension again."

Debbie looked at the floor for a second and then slowly looked up into Anthony's eyes. "Who are you to make that decision?"

Anthony stepped back and held her stare. "Excuse me? Are you sticking up for him?"

Debbie let out a deep breath. "OF COURSE NOT!" she yelled. "But you can't tell him if he can go to Ascension or not. That's not your club, you don't own it."

"I guess you don't know me very well then." Anthony laughed at her and then headed into the living room.

Debbie followed him. "What do you mean, and why are you walking away from me?"

"I'm going to sit in the living room, and do I really have to explain to you how Ascension works? Me and my friends keep that place running. What makes you think if he or any of his friends show their face there that they're going to get in?"

"I understand completely how Ascension works. I don't understand why you can't stay out of this shit with my sisters."

Anthony rolled his eyes, "My God, you don't quit with that shit! I haven't gotten involved with Cristina's issue. Lourdes' was something completely different. That asshole came into this house and disrespected her, you and everyone else here. He got what was coming to him. I did it once, and if I had to I would do it again."

"Oh you would, huh?"

Anthony starred at her and replied, "Yeah I would. Maybe next time he wouldn't get up though." Anthony went quiet for a minute and then said sarcastically, "Well, he didn't get up from this one either though."

Debbie continued to stare at him, taken back by what he said. "Is that what you're turning into? Is that what you're becoming?"

Anthony continued to stare at her as the house phone rang. She jumped slightly and Anthony moved to answer it. "Hello?" he said visibly annoyed. He listened to the person talking on the other end of the line, it was Mike. After a second he asked "Where?" He listened more, "A Colombian cartel or Dominican Cartel?" He went back to listening as he watched Debbie just stare at him and shake her head. "When? Tonight? What time?" He listened some more and then looked at the clock in the kitchen. "Okay, it's not like I have anything better to do here. Pick up the package and come here, we'll take my car." Debbie shook her head again and then moved over to the couch to sit. After a minute Anthony hung the phone up. He went back into the living room and looked at Debbie who sat motionless on a chair and continued staring at the floor. "You were saying?"

After a moment Debbie picked her head up again, "What was that about?"

Nonchalantly, Anthony replied, "Work."

Debbie asked, "Since when does it involve cartels?"

Anthony let out a sigh and walked to the window and looked out. After a minute he closed the blind and the one next to that one. "What does this have to do with the conversation we were just having? Do you want to have two fights?"

"I'm not fighting about your work, all I asked was a question."

"You heard Dominican cartel and you want to tie it to Carlos, so let's move on to the next question, okay?" Debbie began to cry. He hated seeing her cry, but this argument was a few days coming. "What did you mean when you asked me what am I becoming?"

Debbie continued to cry. She reached over to an end table and took a tissue from a box and wiped her eyes. As she did more tears streamed down her face. A million thoughts were running through her mind and she couldn't put them in order. She composed herself as best she could, but tears continued to stream down her face. Anthony waited patiently for her answer. "I don't know you anymore. I don't know what you've become."

"I haven't become anything. I'm the same person you started going out with."

Debbie began shaking her head as she continued to cry. "No, you're not. I can see how different you've become; you've changed."

"Changed how?" asked Anthony visibly annoyed.

"That right there is how. Just the way you answer me. Your whole attitude. You've embraced this wise guy lifestyle and attitude. That was never you, but your work has changed you."

Anthony moved to another window and looked out. "No it hasn't, that's your imagination." After a second he closed the blinds there as well and then made his way back towards Debbie. "I don't know why you think like that."

Debbie dried her tears again and asked, "Why does everyone call you Tony Two Fingers?"

Anthony swallowed and continued to stare at her. He didn't want to tell her the reason. Not now, not while she was on this kick of him turning into a monster. He thought as fast as he could and lied, "That's just what the guys at the club call me. It doesn't mean anything."

Debbie shook her head and looked away from him. "You can't even be honest with me. You have to lie to me about a nickname."

"Debbie, that's all it is, a nickname. You're making too much of it."

"NO I'M NOT!"

Anthony stepped back because of her raised voice and just stared at her. "Why are you yelling?" he asked.

"The entire fucking neighborhood is calling you that. I watched you cook a person on our barbeque grill. I'm not making too much OF IT! This is what I mean. You've turned into a mafia hood."

Anthony moved slowly around the room as he tried to think of a way to diffuse the situation. "I am not a mafia hood. You need to calm down."

Debbie took a deep breath and tried to calm herself down, "Or what? Are you going to cut two of my fingers off?"

Anthony slowly managed to let a smirk come across his face although he really didn't want one to. He moved to a chair and sat across from Debbie. "No," he said calmly, "I'm not going to cut your fingers off. I would never, ever, do anything to hurt you. You should know that."

"I don't know anything anymore."

Anthony looked away and tried to compose himself. "You know about that name?" Debbie slowly nodded her head. "Lourdes told you?"

Debbie was in complete shock. "My sister knew what that meant?" she asked in a very aggravated tone. "You told my fucking sister and you never told me?"

Anthony realized he said the wrong thing at that moment. "If your sister didn't tell you then who did?"

"I overheard Enzo at the barbeque," replied Debbie sounding somewhat sickened.

Anthony replied, "Oh." After a minute of silence he looked back to Debbie who was just staring into space. "I don't know what you want me to say Deb, I really don't."

"Did you really need to cut someone's fingers off?"

Anthony continued to stare at her and then replied, "He owed me money and he was treating me like a jerk off. What did you want me to do? Send him a letter of collections?"

"Don't be a fucking wiseass."

Anthony stood up and yelled, "I'm not being a fucking wiseass! That's my business. That's my lifestyle. He owed me money and he refused to pay. Bottom line, case fucking closed! I'm not gonna stand here and justify what I did and why I did it."

Now Debbie was clearly taken back by Anthony's outburst. After a second she sat back in her seat and started crying again. At that moment Mike's horn began blowing outside. Anthony moved to a window and looked out to make sure it was him. Once he saw him he motioned to him he would be right there. He moved away from the window and looked back at Debbie. She never looked up at him. He moved to the dining room table, took his keys off of it and came back into the living room. Debbie still didn't look up at him, but mumbled, "I guess the conversation is over."

Anthony stood motionless in the living room and stared at her. "We can finish it later. I have to go."

Debbie agreed and then finally looked at him. She didn't say anything else and sat there for a second, tears still streaming down her face. Finally she got up and moved towards his direction. He reached out to her, but she just brushed him aside, moved past him and headed up the stairs. Anthony stood there for another minute in silence before he finally made his way to the front door. He opened it, stepped out and then slammed it shut.

"FUCK HIM?" yelled Carlos.

Cristina began to shake so violently that she dropped the phone. She couldn't believe that Carlos was standing in front of her. When did he come in? She hadn't heard him come in at all. She was so engrossed in her conversation with Lourdes that she never heard the door. "Carlos."

"Are you having a good laugh about Luis being sent to the hospital?"

"No," replied Cristina.

Carlos moved closer to her and pushed all the food off the table and into the wall. He was clearly infuriated. The food, dishes and cups struck the wall and shattered into debris all over the kitchen floor and walls. Cristina reacted with a scream as she cowered into a ball up against the hot stove. Lourdes could be heard on the other end of the phone, yelling for Cristina to answer her if she was all right. Carlos reached out and grabbed her by the hair and pulled her up from the floor. She squirmed and begged for him to stop while she cried. Carlos grabbed Cristina's arm and moved her towards the stove top. "You want an idea of what Luis felt like?"

"NO please!" begged a crying and terrified Cristina.

Carlos threw the food that was on the burner onto the floor and took her arm and forced it down on the hot stove and held it there for a second. Cristina let out a blood curdling scream through her cries and begged him to stop. She tried to pull her arm up and away from the heat but he was too strong for her. The smell of burning flesh filled the kitchen, much like when Luis' face was on the barbeque grill. After a few seconds Carlos pulled her arm off the stove, leaving a layer or two of skin on the surface. Carlos spun her around and smacked her across the face. Cristina fell back across the table. She rolled over it and fell off, hitting the kitchen floor hard, banging her head in the process. She felt like she had been hit with a brick across her face. For a brief second it took her mind off of the pain from her smoldering arm, but only for a second. Before she knew it Carlos was pulling her up again by her hair. He grabbed her and threw her up against the wall hard. He reached out, grabbed her face and made her look at him. The look in his eyes was complete insanity. She had never seen him that mad; had never seen him that out of control. He got close to her and gave her a piercing, burning look. "How does it feel to burn, huh? How does it feel to feel what my friend felt?"

"Carlos, please stop what you're doing."

"You want me to stop? Did your friend stop when he cooked Luis on that grill? All over that tramp sister of yours."

"Carlos please," begged Cristina. "Why are you doing this to me?"

Carlos pulled her away from the wall and out into the hallway. She tried to move away from him, but he had her by the back of her shirt, which was starting to tear. He spun her around to face him. He pulled back and struck her again. This time it wasn't a smack to her face though, it was a punch. He connected a solid hit right in the middle of her face. She started to fall backwards, but he was still holding her by the shirt. He pulled her towards him and as he did he wound back and struck her again with another punch to the face. This shot broke her nose and cut open her lip, sending blood in the air and across the room. He pulled her towards him again and one more time he punched her in the face. This time he let her go as she moved away from him from the momentum of the punch. The last hit sent her clear across the living room and into the coffee table.

Barely being able to speak she said, "Please stop." Her head was clanging like a bell. She had never been hit like that before in her life, not even from Carlos. He had hit her many times before, but his hits usually consisted of smacks, never punches. This time he hit her like he was hitting another man. She wasn't sure how much more of this she could take. Her vision had begun to blur and she couldn't breathe through her nose. She could taste blood in her mouth and it hurt to try and talk.

"You think this is bad? Wait until my friends and I get our hands on your sister's boyfriend. They won't be able to give him an open casket at his funeral when we're finished with him."

"No!" Cristina managed to mumble through her pain and tears. She slowly moved off the coffee table, but couldn't stand on her own. As she moved away from the table she lost her balance and fell to the floor. The entire room was blurry and spinning.

Her 'No' infuriated him more. He moved over to her and kicked her in her side as she laid on the floor. His kick landed in her rib cage and she cried out in pain and terror. He pulled back and kicked her again in the same spot, and again and again, until he heard what could only be her ribs cracking. With that crack he could hear that she was now having trouble breathing. Her crying and begging had also stopped. There was only the sound of her gasping for air with a heavy wheezing. He stepped back and looked down at her. He was clearly tired from the beating he just gave to her. He leaned up against the wall and looked down at her still with fire in his eyes. She was unmoving. The only movement coming from her was her labored and shallow gasping for breath. She was unconscious. Carlos took a deep breath and pushed himself off the wall. He went towards the kitchen and still heard Lourdes yelling into the other end of the phone. He picked up the phone and held it to his ear. After a second he said "Puta! Come and get your sister off the floor before she dies." With that he hung up. He looked around the apartment for a second. He looked back to Cristina who was still unmoving. After a minute of looking at her he made his way out of the apartment and left.

Chapter 20
Vision Of The Future

Anthony's GNX made its way slowly through the streets of Brooklyn. It wasn't a nice part of Brooklyn either. Most of the buildings were decrepit and falling apart. As Anthony drove down the block he could feel people staring at the car. He usually enjoyed it when people admired his car, but these looks were different. These people looked like they wanted to strip it.

Mike looked around the area and shook his head. There were people in numerous alleyways which could only be drug addicts getting high while sitting around a fire in a trash can. It was hardly romantic. "Maybe we should have taken my car."

Anthony was thinking the same thing. Mike had a Cutlass Supreme, it would have stood out much less in this neighborhood than a brand new GNX. After a minute Anthony agreed with Mike. They proceeded down the block and parked in front of a small apartment building. Standing outside were three guys who were obviously on guard duty. Anthony turned off the car and said to Mike, "I need you to stay out here and keep an eye on the car."

Mike looked at Anthony and asked, "Are you out of your mind?"

"Why? What's wrong?"

Mike looked around the neighborhood again and gave Anthony a really sarcastic look. "Do I need to explain it to you?"

Anthony laughed and said, "If something happens to the car while we're in there we'll really be screwed."

Mike thought about it for a minute and replied, "Okay, well how about in there?"

"What about in there?"

"You're going into Mariana's drug den by yourself."

"At least it's not the Perez brothers." Anthony checked for his gun and felt that it was there. "I'm not worried. I know Mariana; she's not going to kill me."

Mike had a frown on his face and Anthony smiled at him. "I hope you know what you're doing."

Anthony opened the car door and stepped out. He stuck his head back in and said, "Me too. Sit over here in case we have to get out of here quickly. I will be back in a little while."

"Okay," replied Mike.

Anthony made his way towards the entrance of the building. He spoke to the three guards outside for a minute. One guy pulled out a walkie talkie and spoke Spanish into it. After a second he came over to Anthony and asked him to open the bag. Anthony did, and once the guy saw it was full of money he sent him upstairs. Anthony made his way up to the third floor and there was an open apartment with two more guys standing outside the doorway. Anthony made his way towards it and one of the guards stopped him and started frisking him. Anthony watched the guard as he was feeling his legs and said, "Let me save you the trouble. There's a 1911 on my belt." The guard stopped searching Anthony and started to reach for the gun but Anthony stopped him. "And you're not taking it."

At that second the other guard made his way towards Anthony to take the gun away but a female voice was heard from the apartment that said "¡OYE PARA! Déjalo entrar aqui, ahora."

The two guards backed off and Anthony stared at both of them. After a second he slowly made his way into the apartment. It was dimly lit with very little electric light, but there were dozens of candles lighting the room. In the corner were several more guards seated at a table playing cards and drinking what looked like clear tequila, but he wasn't sure. Anthony made his way further into the apartment. One of the guards came over to him and pulled out a chair at another table. Anthony looked around and then sat. Anthony put the bag of money on the table and the guard inspected it. Then he laid a bag of his own on the table in front of Anthony. Anthony opened it and there were four kilos of cocaine in it. Anthony inspected each kilo to make sure they were real, they were. Anthony looked at the guard and winked. The guard patted Anthony on the back and then picked up the bag of money and made his way back to his card game. Anthony looked around the apartment. The apartment was dingy and felt eerie. There were numerous statues of Catholic saints all throughout the apartment in what looked like shrines. There were candles lit in front of them. Some statues had what appeared to be offerings in front of them. Some had money, some had alcohol, and some had cigars. It was all very weird to him. He had met with Mariana in the past, but they never met here. It was usually at a house in Queens.

A minute or so went by and Mariana made her way out to where Anthony was seated from another room. She was wearing a long black dress that was low cut on the top which emphasized her round, perky breasts. It also had a long slit up the side that showed almost all of her leg. With a pair of high heels on as well she looked like she was going to a gala or a ball, instead of commanding a drug cartel. She was a beautiful young woman in her early to mid-twenties. She stood about five feet, five inches tall, but her heels put her in the five foot eight range. She had very long, somewhat wavy, dark hair with a single stripe of red in it. She had dark eyes and wore heavy, dark eye shadow and eye liner. She had full red lips and a dark, tanned complexion. She always had a lot of make up on and always looked good, at least the few times that Anthony saw her. He couldn't imagine her ever looking bad. If she wasn't a drug queen she could have been a model. There was something very mysterious about her though. Anthony was captivated by her eyes. He always felt like he was being drawn into her and she was reading his mind. She smiled at him and he smiled back at her. "Hola, Antonio," she said. When she spoke in English she had a broken accent, but her voice was still sweet and as beautiful as she was.

"Hello, Mariana."

Mariana giggled a little and put two glasses down on the table. "We have to teach you Spanish Antonio. I told you that the last time we saw each other."

Anthony laughed and watched her move to the table where the guys were playing cards. "Good luck with that," he replied. She retrieved the bottle of alcohol and made her way back to their table. As she did she brushed Anthony gently along the back of his neck and hairline with her perfectly manicured hands. She sent chills through his body. She poured two glasses and Anthony could smell the power that came out of it. He had tequila before and this was not tequila. "What is that?"

Mariana glanced over at Anthony as she poured the drinks. He locked eyes with her and he felt that reading feeling again. "This, Antonio, is Aguadiente."

He thought about that for a minute and asked, "Fire water?"

Mariana smiled and lit up as she replied, "Si, Antonio. Very good."

Anthony smiled back at her and she sat across from him and crossed her legs. She reached over and picked up her glass, after a second he picked up his. She leaned on the table and held her glass up. Anthony reached over with his and tapped it to hers. He pulled his glass back and smelled it, it was strong. "I can't shot this."

Mariana smiled slowly and replied, "No you don't have to Mi Amor. Just drink it slowly and enjoy it."

Anthony reached over and took a sip from the glass. As soon as it hit his mouth he felt it sting. He winced from the flavor and began to swallow it. It burned going down. He could feel the heat run through his chest. Once it hit his stomach it was also set ablaze. It fully left his mouth and he put the glass down. He gasped for air and made a noise that showed it was hard for him to handle, almost like a gag. He felt like he was on fire. He looked up and Mariana's glass was completely empty. She was having no reaction to the alcohol. Anthony could tell she was used to drinking this stuff. Mariana was smiling at him as he tried to hold the burning alcohol in and not get sick. She began pouring herself another glass. After a second Anthony managed to get out, "Now I know why they call this stuff fire water."

"You don't want to smoke while drinking this. It takes some getting used to, but once you do it's fabulous." Mariana sat back and relaxed in her chair. Anthony took a deep breath and finally recovered from the fire water. He sat back and relaxed for a minute, he was sweating. He noticed Mariana staring at him intently. "Something is on your mind Antonio. What is wrong?"

This is what Anthony always felt around her. She had read him again. It was probably very clear that something was on his mind by the look on his face. He couldn't hide his emotions. He couldn't hide his feelings. The fight with Debbie weighed on him a lot. He bottled it up when he left the house. He didn't vent to Mike and that's why it showed on his face now. "Oh Mariana, I didn't come here to burden you with my problems."

Mariana had a soft smile across her face and reached out and touched Anthony's hand. Her touch was soft and her skin was smooth as silk. Her touch instantly calmed him. He couldn't believe she could have an effect like that. "It's okay my friend. You and your problems are not a burden. I always look forward to seeing you."

"You look forward to trying to read me Mariana."

Mariana laughed and Anthony smiled at her. "This is true Antonio, this is true. Other than your problems at home, I hear you have some problems on the street."

Anthony was taken aback by her comment. How could she know he had problems at home? This was her talent though and he should be used to it. She always did this to him. On top of her intense, un-relentless flirting, she read him like a book and it made him feel uncomfortable. He noticed Lourdes could do the same. She could also read him like a book. The difference was that when Lourdes did it he didn't feel violated. "What have you heard about my problems on the street?"

Mariana let Anthony's hand finally go and she sat back in her chair again. She took another sip of her drink, "I hear the Perez brothers have a price on your head."

"I know they are not happy with me."

"That is to say the least. I heard you fried one of their runners at a barbeque of yours."

"Grilled him actually."

Mariana laughed and Anthony followed right behind her with a laugh of his own. "At least you have a sense of humor about it, but from what I understand it's serious. The runner still hasn't woken up yet and the Perez's are not patient in waiting for your Italian friends to turn you over to them. They're going to take things in their own hands soon."

Anthony's smile faded and he leaned on the table. "You seem to know a lot about this."

"I have a vast intelligence network that works for me."

Anthony said, "That, I'm sure, is useful for you."

"It can be. It can also be useful to you."

"How so?" asked Anthony curiously.

Mariana thought for a minute. "We can discuss that later." She looked over to the group of guy's playing cards and shouted, "Déjanos."

The table full of men stopped playing cards. All of them except one got up and left the room without even looking over to them. The remaining one looked at her concerned and said, "Mariana."

Mariana locked her stare with the man and replied, "Ahora."

After a second he got up and left the room, closing the door behind him. Anthony pointed out, "You command their respect, impressive."

Mariana said, "You can command the same respect from your organization."

Anthony laughed out loud, but Mariana remained serious. "I doubt that greatly. I will never rise any higher than what I am right now. Not with the strict rules that they follow."

Mariana smirked and said, "I know the ways the Italians follow. They are ancient and built upon the Roman Empire. I never cared for that line of thinking."

"That makes two of us, but what can I do?"

"Be patient Antonio, be very patient. The organizations that you work for will not exist in the future. Time is on your side."

Anthony thought about that for a minute and then replied, "Since the turn of the century these families have been in power. I don't see them going anywhere any time soon."

Mariana reached out and took Anthony's hand again. She closed her eyes and mumbled something in Spanish that Anthony couldn't understand. With her eyes still closed she reached out with her other hand and found his immediately, as if she didn't even need to look for it. She grasped both of his hands tightly and remained silent. Every now and then she mumbled something but Anthony couldn't make out what she was saying. He moved slightly and she snapped, "Stay still!" Anthony stopped moving and he stared at her. After a minute or so it began to feel like an eternity, but he didn't want to move again. Mariana usually read him just by looks, this was the first time she engaged in touching him physically. Of course he didn't buy any of it, but he figured he would let it play out. After another minute or so he felt a slight bit of heat radiating from her hands to his. He noticed her expression changed as well. She looked almost uncomfortable at times, then happy and then fearful. This continued on for several more minutes until her eyes popped open.

The only problem was her eyes weren't there. All Anthony saw was white. He could no longer see the beautiful dark brown or black that her eyes consisted of. They were rolled in the back of her head and all he could see was white. As she was doing this he noticed some of the candles in front of the saints started to dim and flicker, as if they were in a breeze, but he could feel no air circulate through the apartment. She leaned her head back and looked towards the ceiling. She gasped for breath and squeezed his hands tighter. As she did the heat intensified and ran up his arms. It was only for a minute, but he felt the heat through his entire body. As this was happening all the candles went dim in the room, as if they were about to blow out. After a minute the heat disappeared and Mariana brought her head back to facing him. Her eyes rolled back to normal and she stared at him. When she did this all the candles came back to their original illumination. After a second she let him go and her look returned fully to normal again. She now looked tired and drained.

"Are you okay? What was that?"

Mariana composed herself and replied, "I saw things. Some things you wouldn't understand and some things that I cannot tell you. You must trust me Antonio."

Anthony thought about that for a minute. He didn't want to insult her, but he didn't believe in any of this. He decided to hear her out though and not make her feel uncomfortable. "Go on."

She took a deep breath. "In your life you will go through many challenges. There will be many joyous times in your life, but you will also face many, many tragedies. You will hurt so much in your lifetime that my heart hurts for you Antonio. You will cry uncontrollably. You will make decisions that will affect thousands and thousands of people in the future. You will walk with a guilt that tortures your soul from a distant point in your life till the end of your life. A guilt you will never be able to hide from. A guilt which you will never be able to let go." Mariana closed her eyes as if she was concentrating and trying to see something in her mind. "I see a city on fire. I see death and destruction all at your hands. Families destroyed. It looks like Hell on Earth. People burning alive. Some tragedies are very far in the future and some are right at hand."

"At hand?" he asked.

"Yes. This issue with the Perez brothers can be a tragedy on your doorstep if not addressed soon. But, you will address it and you will avert it."

Anthony didn't need a mind reader to tell him that this was a serious issue at hand and it needed to be dealt with soon. "This is being looked at soon."

Mariana shook her head quickly. "Your friends in the families are not helping you. Not the way you need them to. Not the way you want them to. I see disagreement over it. I see you are not happy about how you've been treated by your friends."

That caught him off guard. There was no way Mariana could know that the club wasn't providing the support that he wanted against the Perez brothers. That just occurred this morning. It didn't matter how good her intelligence network was, she couldn't know that and he doubted anyone from the club was giving her information.

"The friends that you do have, they won't be able to handle what needs to be done."

Anthony thought about that for a minute. He decided to feed into what she was saying to him. "What needs to be done Mariana?"

"Antonio, I know you don't believe me but I speak from my heart. De mi corazón. In the future, not so far in the future, but in the future you will play an important part in your line of business. You will have great power. You will lead a strong organization that will have influence across the seas."

Anthony's look was skeptical. "How is that possible?"

"With my help this will be possible."

Anthony thought about that for a minute. He knew that Mariana was a powerful person in her organization. She was powerful here in America, as well as in her country of Colombia. He didn't think she was more powerful than the five New York families though. In his mind no one was more powerful than them. He couldn't imagine them ever being unseated from power. He also couldn't imagine himself running a family like she just described. "Mariana, you have to forgive me, but I can't picture that. I can't picture being in charge of something when they won't even make me."

"I understand your confusion, but you have to trust me. Especially with the Perez situation. Without that, none of what I have seen will come to pass, neither the good nor the bad."

"The bad?"

Mariana replied, "That is something that we cannot discuss Antonio. It is forbidden. However, there is no shortage of bad. In the very near future as well as the very distant."

Anthony let out a sigh. He still wasn't buying any of this, but he was intrigued to hear her out about the Perez brothers. "What is your suggestion for the Perez's?"

Mariana looked away for a minute as if she was thinking. "You are going to have a meeting soon with the friends that will help you in your struggle against them, no?"

Anthony was hesitant, but then he admitted, "I have a small group that will help me off the radar. The families will not back me against them."

"I know. Cancel your meeting with your friends. I will help you in your fight against them. Make no mistake about this though, it will not be easy. There will be a lot of bloodshed, but it is the only way to achieve the outcome that is beneficial to both of us."

"What do you mean both of us?"

"Antonio, I have no love for the Perez brothers or anyone in their organization for that matter. It is of no consequence to me to eliminate them and anyone associated with them."

"That will create a power vacuum."

Mariana smiled at him. "I am counting on it."

"A vacuum for your cartel to step right into." Mariana smiled at him. He thought about it for a minute. "What if the families disagree? For the most part they are already against eliminating the Perez brothers. My operation is without their support and backing. There is a good chance I can end up on a slab next to them for what I am planning."

"That is why you need to follow the plan that I will lay out for you. They will resist me stepping into the Perez businesses, but in the end they will live with it. It could look more like my cartel went to war with them over territory. We can make it point away from you. What I am more interested in is the future that I see with you in power. We will control everything. That is why I am backing you. There is a mutual benefit for both of us."

Anthony thought about that for a minute. He still didn't buy any of her future seeing powers, but there was an opportunity here that he couldn't pass up; her organizations effort to help him against the Perez brothers would be invaluable. "Okay, I'm listening."

"Cancel your plans for your meeting with your friends. I will provide support for you in the way of manpower."

"Manpower?" he asked.

"I will give you an army. You will command my army throughout the city and lead an all-out assault on the entire organization of the Perez brothers. From top to bottom, street dealers up to the Perez brothers themselves, everyone will be eliminated."

Anthony thought about that very long. After a minute he caught her gaze. "I was initially thinking of taking out the Perez brothers and two other people, not the entire organization. Innocent people can get caught in the middle of this."

"Innocent people already have." Anthony continued to look at her wondering what she meant. "Your friend from the barbeque was innocent in all this. She was the catalyst that put this in motion." Mariana was referring to Lourdes. Anthony was referring to innocent people on the street that could be caught in the crossfire. "I know your apprehension Antonio, but this is the only way to ensure your survival in this matter. Sometimes there are innocent people during wartime that pay the ultimate price. We will try our best to avoid them."

Anthony thought about it for a minute. After a second he agreed. "I have a question though. If this won't point to me, how can I command your army?"

"My men will do most of the leg work with the smaller dealers. You can lead the assault on the Perez brothers and the others that you want to exact your revenge against."

Anthony said, "Okay," and thought about it some more. This could be a good alliance with Mariana. Anthony heard a lot of stories about how her cartel waged war. He was glad they were on his side and not against him. He looked up and met Mariana's very sexy gaze. After a second he said, "I am putting my trust in you Mariana."

"Good, Antonio, good." Mariana raised her glass and Anthony slowly picked up his. He was not looking forward to drinking the fire water again. "A toast: to the future, Antonio. To the future."

"To the future Mariana." They clinked their glasses and drank. Anthony didn't struggle as much as he did the first time he drank, but it was still a chore to get it down.

"Now, this is what we will do….."

Chapter 21
Massacre In Flushing

A nthony and Mike pulled up at Anthony's house. Anthony parked in the driveway and shut the car off. The ride back had been very quiet. Mike didn't ask any questions and Anthony didn't offer any answers. Mike went to get out of the car and Anthony stopped him. "You okay?" he asked.

Anthony replied, "Yeah, listen, the meeting we're going to have about the problem?"

"The Perez brothers?" asked Mike.

"Yeah," replied Anthony, "stall it or call it off."

Mike shut the car door. "What are you talking about? Everything is in motion. The Double R Boys are coming from Staten Island and everything."

Anthony looked down for a second. "No, stall it or call it off. Mariana said she can put it to bed."

"Mariana? Put it to bed how?"

"She has a lot of connections Mike. She said she would take care of it for me and they wouldn't be an issue again."

Mike looked perplexed and a bit annoyed. "You really trust this woman?"

"Yeah, if she doesn't deal with it the right way then we will. Maybe for now we can use the Double R's for protection until all this blows over."

Mike thought about it for a minute and then reluctantly agreed, "Okay." Mike opened the car door again and they both got out. They said their goodbyes and Mike headed to his car, got in and left while Anthony headed inside.

Anthony walked through the dark, quiet house. It was late and he was tired. He hadn't expected Debbie to be up so he wasn't planning on fighting with her, but at this point anything was possible. Lately that's all she wanted to do was fight. Fight about his work, fight about her sisters or fight about Carlos and Luis.

He flipped on the light in the dining room and looked around. The room looked the same as when he left. He flipped it back off and headed upstairs. He opened the bedroom door and made his way into the dark room. He tried not to make noise. He didn't want to wake Debbie up. He sat on the bed and let out a long breath. He looked over his shoulder and in the dark it didn't look like Debbie was in the bed. He gently slid his hand across the bed to feel if she was there. He realized she wasn't when his hand made it to the other side of the bed. He reached over to the nightstand and flipped on the light. She wasn't there. He looked around the room and then got up and headed out into the hallway. He made his way to the next bedroom and opened the door and looked in. She wasn't in there either. He went back to their bedroom and opened the closet. He let out a sigh of relief, her clothes were still there. "Debbie," he called out but there was no answer.

Crazy thoughts started running through his head. He began roaming through the house calling her name but there was no reply. He went into the back bedroom and looked out the window to the drive way and saw that her car wasn't there. That was something that he missed when he came home. He hadn't even noticed her car wasn't there. He was concentrating on getting Mike off the Perez brothers.

He reached to his waist for his pager, but it wasn't there. He looked around the bedroom and then went back down to the dining room. He flipped the light on and saw it sitting on the dining room table. He ran out of the house after the fight and forgot to grab it and he never even realized it. He picked it up and looked at it. He began cycling through the pager to see if he missed anything. There were six duplicate pages from Lourdes with a 911 code in it. Something was wrong. He reached for the phone and called Lourdes's number, but the phone just rang and rang. After too many rings he hung up.

Anthony headed into the kitchen towards the fridge. There was a small note pad on there that they would usually leave messages on for each other. Anthony flipped on the kitchen light and looked at the pad; his heart sunk. It read 'Cristina's in Flushing hospital. Going there now.'

Anthony flipped back off the lights, grabbed his keys and left the house. He ran to the GNX, got in, burnt out of the driveway, and headed towards the hospital. Anthony sped through the streets of

Queens racing towards the hospital. There was no traffic at this hour and he wasn't paying attention to red lights or stop signs.

It took him about twenty minutes to get there. He pulled up and screeched to a stop in what was clearly a no parking zone, but he didn't care. Standing outside the hospital was Lourdes. Anthony jumped out of the car and headed towards her. She saw him and ran to him. He stopped in front of her and she hugged him tightly while crying. "What the hell is going on?" he asked.

Lourdes pulled away from him and he brushed her long hair from her face. She was a mess. She seemed like she was crying for hours. Her eyes were all swollen and red. Any makeup that she had on was long gone, down her face and all over her shirt. Gone was the beautiful model that he had lunch with earlier that day. All that was in front of him now was an emotional wreck, still beautiful, but an emotional wreck. She tried to contain herself and after a minute she was able to speak. "Carlos beat the hell out of her. We were talking on the phone while she was making dinner and then all of a sudden I heard a noise, I guess the phone dropping. Then I could hear her screaming and begging him to stop. My God, Anthony I heard the whole thing!"

Anthony's face changed to a look of rage. He pulled Lourdes towards him and she hugged him tight again while crying hysterically. After a second he asked, "Is she okay?" Lourdes didn't answer right away. After a second he tried to pull her back, but she wouldn't let go of him. He let her hold him for another minute and then she finally let go. He asked again, "Is she okay?"

Lourdes looked confused. She replied, "I don't know. She's unconscious, has been since she got here. He really beat her. He burned her. HE FUCKING TORTURED HER!" she yelled while crying.

"Okay, calm down." Anthony looked around and then pulled her into the hospital. "Where is she?"

"In the ER."

Anthony looked around to try and find the ER and she pulled him in the direction of where it was. They walked down a long hallway and made a left at the end of it. About twenty feet down, outside the doors of the ER, Debbie and her mother were standing there. Brenda was crying and Debbie was trying to console her.

Debbie watched Anthony as they approached. Anthony reached out and took her hand. Lourdes let him go and grabbed her mother and they cried and hugged. After a second they walked over to a few chairs to sit.

Anthony looked down at Debbie. After a second she looked up at him with tears in her eyes. They walked to a different set of chairs and sat. "What happened?" he asked.

Debbie took a deep breath. "When you left I went upstairs and I tried to lay down for a little while. I fell asleep and I woke up to your pager going off like crazy. Right after that the house phone started ringing. I answered it and Lourdes was hysterical. I couldn't understand her. My mother got on the phone and told me what happened. Apparently he came home while she was cooking dinner and talking to Lourdes. He heard her conversation, something to do with Luis and he snapped and beat the shit out of her."

Anthony thought for a minute. He looked out towards Lourdes and Brenda and then back at Debbie. "He did this over Luis?"

"I don't know the whole story. When Lourdes calms down she can tell you. Maybe she will make more sense when she relaxes. Right now she is too upset to explain everything."

"Are you okay?"

Debbie replied, "Yeah," but didn't look at him. "For now, at this moment, for my families sake let's not talk about our argument, okay?"

"Okay, how bad is Cristina?"

Debbie finally looked at him. "She's bad."

"How bad?" asked Anthony visibly angry.

Debbie took a deep breath. "We haven't spoken to a doctor yet, but she is unconscious. He burned her on her arm and did something to her face."

"Her face? Burned?"

"No, kicked or punched. I think she has a broken nose. Her face was full of blood when they brought her in."

Anthony turned red with anger, he tried to contain himself, but it was apparent that he was having a tough time. Debbie was doing nothing to calm him down either. After a minute Lourdes and her mother came over and sat next to them. Anthony asked Brenda,

"Are you okay?" She nodded her head. Anthony asked Lourdes the same question.

"It was one of the scariest things I have ever heard in my life. You would have thought Carlos was beating a guy by the way she was screaming." Anthony had a sickened look on his face.

Brenda said, "He's hit her in the past, but he has never done anything like this. He took it to a different level this time. It looks like he actually tried to kill her."

Anthony asked, "Lourdes what was said on the phone that set him off? Debbie mentioned something about Luis."

Lourdes looked at Debbie and Debbie just looked away. After a second she looked back at Anthony and replied, "I asked her if there was any word on his condition and she said 'no' and then something like 'that asshole got what he deserved, fuck him.' I guess Carlos came in and heard that and snapped. He burned her on the stove and then beat her." Lourdes started crying again and her mother put her arm around her. "I heard the whole thing over the phone, I never hung up. When he was done he picked the phone up and..."

Anthony asked, "And what?"

Lourdes took a deep breath and continued, "He picked up the phone and said 'Puta, come pick her up off the floor before she dies.' He sounded so fucking cold you can tell her didn't give a shit about what he just did. Maybe he did try to kill her."

Anthony looked at everyone and asked, "What's Puta?"

Lourdes answered, "It's a slut or a whore in Spanish."

Anthony sat back, visibly annoyed by the comment. Debbie looked at him out of the corner of her eye, but didn't say anything. After a minute a doctor emerged from the ER and came over to them. They all stood up. Cristina's mom asked the doctor, "How is she?"

The doctor took a deep breath and motioned for everyone to sit. They all did and then he answered, "Well, she is in serious, but stable condition. We managed to stop the bleeding from her mouth and nose but she has other, more serious issues."

"What kind of issues?" asked Anthony.

The doctor replied, "She has several broken ribs. One of the ribs punctured her lung. When it punctured the lung it caused it to collapse. We have her on a ventilator and that is helping her breathe. I think she will heal and the lung will refill, but we have to wait that out."

"Oh my God," said Brenda. Lourdes reached out and took her mother's hand.

The doctor paused for a minute, and then continued, "She has a broken nose and a serious third degree burn on her left arm. That should heel, but she'll have a bad scar on her arm, and she'll probably need skin grafts in the future."

Anthony sat shaking his head, he couldn't believe what he was hearing. Debbie watched him from the corner of her eye. After a second she finally reached over and held his hand. Through all her anger and fighting with him, she did recognize that he cared for her sisters and he didn't want to see Cristina in this situation. She squeezed his hand and he held hers tightly.

"Is she conscious?" asked Anthony.

The doctor replied, "Barely. We are keeping her heavily sedated due to the breathing tube so she drifts in and out of consciousness. We are also restraining her. When a patient has a breathing tube in its only natural to try and pull it out, so we've got her hands restrained so she can't do that."

Anthony said, "I understand. Can we see her?"

The doctor thought about it for a minute. "You can, but only for a few minutes. After that I have to insist that you leave."

Anthony and the girls agreed and everyone stood up to head into the ER. The doctor led them through the ER towards a section on the other side of the large room. After a minute they reached her bed and she was unrecognizable. She had a breathing tube inserted down her mouth that was connected to a respirator which was helping her breathe. There were numerous machines behind her that were monitoring her vitals, as well as an IV drip plugged into her arm. The arm that was burned was completely bandaged up. Most of her face was bandaged as well, to stop the bleeding from her mouth and nose. Both of her eyes were blackened and even with the bandages, you could tell that her face was swollen.

When her mother saw her she completely broke apart. Lourdes held her, but she was hysterical as well. Anthony noticed Debbie had tears streaming down her face. She was trying to contain herself, but it wasn't working. She was holding it in better than her mother and sister, but it wouldn't be long until she would burst like them.

Anthony looked back at Cristina and a tear streamed down his face when he saw her. He moved to the side of the bed and held the hand that wasn't burned. He could feel her gently squeeze his hand. "Cristina," he said softly. Her eye lids shuttered gently and Anthony moved closer to her ear. "Cristina, can you hear me?" She squeezed his hand and gently opened her eyes as far as she could. She looked around and then made eye contact with him. When she saw him she squeezed his hand tighter. She tried to talk but she was unable to due to the breathing tube. "It's okay, don't try to talk." Anthony looked up across the bed and Debbie was looking down at her sister. She reached down and gently touched her other hand that was bandaged. Debbie looked over at Anthony, and, as if she could tell what he was thinking, she nodded her head. Anthony leaned back down to Cristina's ear and said, "Sweetheart, you need to try and rest okay. Don't worry about anything, you're safe now. No one is going to hurt you in here. No one is going to hurt you anymore. I promise." Anthony looked up again at Debbie and said, "I'm going to take care of it." When he said that Cristina squeezed his hand. He moved back slowly down to her and kissed her gently on her head. Her eyes fluttered again and then she drifted back out. Anthony kissed her again and then stood up straight. He let her hand go and moved away from the bed and headed out of the ER. After a second Debbie followed him. Lourdes and her mother moved over to the bed to be near Cristina.

"Anthony," yelled Debbie.

Anthony looked over his shoulder as he strode out of the ER. "What?"

"Where are you going?"

They went through the doors of the ER and headed back to the lobby. "I needed to get out of that room." They went back to the waiting area and Anthony looked at Debbie. She too had swollen eyes now. From the crying during their argument earlier that night and the crying over her sister, she looked drained and a complete mess. Anthony moved to a chair by the window and sat. Debbie followed and sat next to him.

"What are you going to do?"

Anthony looked down at the floor and put his head in his hands. "Are you going to fight with me about this now?"

Debbie put her hand on his back and rubbed it while he was hunched over. "No, I'm not going to fight with you about this. I know that I can't anymore."

After a minute Anthony sat up straight and asked, "No?"

"No." She went silent for a minute and then started to cry again. "He almost killed my sister. I have never seen her like this. Something has to be done. I know that now."

Anthony looked around and held her hand. "Lower your voice."

Debbie looked around and then asked, "What are you going to do?"

Anthony looked around again. "I don't know yet. I have to talk to some people. Listen I can't get into everything, but this is more complicated then you are aware of."

"What do you mean?" Anthony stood up, walked a few feet away and looked out the window. He stared out the window for a second and then he moved closer and looked outside again. "Hello? Are you listening to me?" Anthony waved her off as if to be quiet as he studied what he was looking at outside the window. Debbie moved closer to him and asked, "What are you looking at?"

Anthony was quiet for a minute as he studied what was going on outside. He was looking at his car. There were two guys near the car. That wasn't out of the ordinary but they were Hispanic looking and on one of them he could see the barrel of what looked like a machine gun sticking out of the bottom of the guys jacket. "That's what I'm looking at."

"Two guys standing near your car?"

"If you look close one of them has a machine gun."

"A what?"

Anthony turned towards her and responded, "A machine gun." Anthony walked towards the other end of the lobby and looked out another window.

Debbie followed him quickly. "Anthony, what's going on?"

Anthony stared out the window and then banged his fist on the window sill. "Damn."

"What? What is it? What the hell is going on?"

Anthony noticed two more guys standing on the street corner. Both looked like they were with the two that were standing guard near his car. "I need you to go back to your sister and mother and tell them not to leave the hospital."

"Tell me what's going on?"

"I can't right now. Go tell them and I'll tell you in a bit. Please, go do what I asked you. Tell them and yourself, stay away from the doors and the windows." Anthony headed for a pay phone.

"Anthony?"

"NOW DAMNIT." Debbie headed back towards the ER at a quick pace and Anthony got to the pay phone. He reached into his pocket and pulled out some change. He fed the phone and then dialed a number. He kept an eye on the door while waiting for someone to answer on the other end. "Hello, let me talk to Mariana." Anthony waited for her to get on the phone. He looked out the window and noticed the two guys from the corner talking to each other and occasionally looking at the hospital. After a minute Mariana got on the phone. "Mariana, its Anthony. Listen I have a problem. I'm at Flushing hospital. Someone very close to me was just put in here as a result of the barbeque. I came here to see her and I just noticed a group of guys outside. Two are by my car and two more are on the corner watching the hospital. I'm pretty sure they are with the Perez brothers. My friends are too far away to be of help. Do you have anyone you can send to get me out of here?" Anthony listened to her instructions for a moment and agreed with her. "I don't know how many there are, but I suspect there are more than four. They can be in here for all I know." He listened to her talk some more. "Okay, I will keep an eye out and wait. Thank you Mariana."

Anthony hung up and he noticed Debbie and her family coming towards them. He went to meet them and he pushed them back into the hallway. Lourdes asked, "What's going on?"

"Stay out of the waiting room. It's too much out in the open." They all moved back into the hallway and Anthony looked back towards the door. "Is there a cafeteria here?"

Brenda pointed to a different hallway. "Yeah it's around this way."

"Good, let's head there and I will explain." They all made their way to the cafeteria in a hurry. Anthony kept turning around and looking over his shoulder towards the entrance of the hospital for anyone coming in that looked suspicious. They made it into the cafeteria and headed for a table that was not near a window and sat.

Debbie and her family looked on nervously. "What is going on? Who are those guys out there?"

Anthony took a deep breath and looked towards the door, then back at the three girls looking at him, waiting for an answer. Now he had to be honest with what was going on. "Okay, this whole situation just got a lot more complicated."

"What do you mean?" asked Lourdes.

Anthony shifted his look to her and then back to Debbie. "The guys outside are with a drug cartel that is run by the Perez brothers."

"Ok, and?" asked Debbie.

"Listen, the guy from the barbeque, Luis, he belongs to this cartel and now that I am starting to think about it, I think Carlos might have some ties to them as well."

"Are these the guys you told me about at lunch today?" asked Lourdes.

Anthony shifted his look to Lourdes and then back to Debbie really quick. She looked at her sister with an inquisitive look on her face. Anthony gazed back towards Lourdes and nodded his head. At that point Lourdes must have realized what she said and her entire expression changed.

Debbie turned and stared at Anthony, "The two of you had lunch today?"

Anthony looked back at her and nodded. After a second he looked at Brenda, who now tried to diffuse this situation. "Not now Debbie. Don't go there, I'm sure it was nothing. We have other things to worry about now. Anthony continue."

Debbie took a deep breath and gave her sister a nasty look. Lourdes said, "Debbie, it's not what you think. It was an innocent lunch."

Debbie looked back at Anthony and asked, "If it was so innocent why didn't you mention it to me?"

Anthony replied, "You didn't speak to me at dinner, and when we did speak after dinner we had an argument. It really was an innocent lunch, nothing went on like you're thinking. Do we really have time for this right now?"

Debbie shrugged her shoulders slowly and then said, "Go on with this story."

Anthony looked at the three and then continued, "Like I said, Luis is a runner for these brothers. The brothers made a beef to the club I do most of my work out of because of the shit that happened at the barbeque. Frankie from the club met with me and Mike this morning to tell me about it."

"So what does all that mean?" asked Debbie nervously.

Anthony knew he had to tell her, "When I left for the meeting tonight during the argument, it was with a cartel based out of Colombia, run by a woman named Mariana, and they seem to know about it as well. Apparently the Perez brothers put a price on my head."

"Oh my God!" yelled Debbie. "Are you kidding me? What the fuck are you involved in?"

"Calm down and lower your voice. I don't need any cops in the hospital getting wind of this."

"Maybe that's exactly what we need. There are men outside with machine guns watching your car and waiting for you to come outside to kill you," replied Debbie.

"I don't need cops involved in this. I already spoke to my contact and they are sending help."

Debbie looked confused, "Why is this cartel sending help? Why are you not going to your club for help?"

Anthony looked away for a minute at the doorway and then back to Debbie. "They don't want to get involved with it. They said it's not about business, and that I'm on my own."

Debbie started shaking her head. After a minute she said, "I told you about this fucking job. All the shit that you do for them, and who knows what else, and now they won't help you."

Anthony agreed with her and said, "I know, you're right, but right now I can't think about that. I have to concentrate on how to get all of you out of here safely."

"Anthony?" asked Lourdes.

Anthony turned and said, "Yes?"

"A minute ago you said you are starting to think Carlos has ties to these guys to?"

Anthony replied, "Yeah, why?"

Lourdes thought for a minute and then responded, "Something I heard on the phone while Carlos was beating Cristina."

"What did you hear Sweetheart?" asked Brenda.

Lourdes thought about it for a minute and then replied, "Carlos said something to Cristina like 'wait till me and my friends get our hands on your sister's boyfriend. They won't be able to give him an open casket.'"

"Oh my God," said Debbie again. This time she was more nervous than the last time she said it. "What the hell are you going to do? These people are going to kill you and us."

Anthony looked at her, but didn't reply to her question. He looked like he was in deep thought, then he turned his attention to Lourdes. "You went to your sister's house after Carlos beat her?"

"Yes, me and my mom went together. We found her on the floor unconscious."

"Was Carlos there?"

"No, we were worried about that; that's why I was paging you. We were scared to go there alone. When you didn't answer I called the house and Debbie said you went to work and you forgot your pager; we knew we had to get over there."

"I'm going to bet he was thinking the same thing," said Anthony.

"What are you talking about?" asked Debbie.

Anthony thought about it for a second. "I think the beating of Cristina was a set up."

"A set up?" asked Brenda. "What do you mean?"

"I think Carlos and his friends wanted me so bad that he sacrificed Cristina to get to me. He figured, like all of you did, if he beat her so bad I would respond and go there. I'm going to bet there were guys like this outside Cristina's house waiting for me to show up and take me out there. Fortunately, I forgot my pager home, so I never knew what was going on. The two of you show up at the house instead of me to help Cristina and take her to the hospital, so they go to plan B and stake out this place in the hopes that I would show up here."

"And you walked right into it," replied Lourdes.

"Yep, I must have gotten here minutes before they did, or else they would have taken me out as soon as I got out of the car."

Debbie put her hand over her forehead and shook it slowly from side to side. "Now what are you going to do? What are we going to do?"

Anthony replied, "I have to wait for Mariana's crew."

"Why didn't you call Mike?"

"Mike's too far away, Mariana's cartel is closer."

"I don't believe this. All over this guy putting his hands on you Lourdes."

"What the fuck is that supposed to mean?" asked Lourdes angrily.

Debbie replied, "This wouldn't be going on now if it wasn't for that shit at the barbeque."

Brenda said, "Debbie this is not your sister's fault. How many times do we have to go over this? She didn't ask for that guy to touch her and she didn't ask Anthony to get involved in it."

Debbie calmed down a little bit. "I know it's not Lourdes's fault. I just feel like this whole thing could have…."

Shots rang out outside the hospital in a rapid fashion, sounding like machine gun fire. Bursts of light could be seen outside the glass, lighting up the street in the night. The girls started screaming and Debbie stood up at the table.

"GET ON THE FLOOR," yelled Anthony. Lourdes and her mother jumped out of their seats while Debbie stood at the side of the table screaming. Anthony jumped out of his seat and pulled Debbie down to the floor while covering her. All three of the girls continued screaming. Anthony looked around and said, "Crawl towards the door. Whatever you do stay away from the windows and don't get up. Go now!"

All four of them started crawling towards the door as more shots rang out in the street. This time it sounded like return fire was also coming from up the block. The girls were hysterical as they got to the doorway and looked out into the hallway. Several people were running down the hallway away from the shots. Anthony got to his knees and pulled the girls out into the hallway. "What are we going to do?" asked Lourdes.

Anthony pointed towards the ER. "Head back to the ER. It should be safe in there." The four turned and headed back down the hallway towards the ER. They made their way to the end of the hallway and made a turn just to walk into a tall, dark Hispanic guy in a leather jacket and a do-rag. He looked like he was part of a gang, but instantly Anthony knew who this guy belonged to. Anthony made eye contact with him and in a split second he pushed the girls back the opposite way while at the same time dodging a swinging punch from the guy. From the momentum of pushing the girls back Anthony slipped and lost his balance and landed on his right knee. Debbie and her mother started screaming in fear as Lourdes was frozen in place.

The guy yelled something in Spanish and Anthony was sure at that point he was not one of Mariana's men. This guy belonged to the Perez brothers. As Anthony was on his right knee he spun on it and with a sweeping motion he brought his left leg around behind the guy's legs and sent him tumbling to the floor backwards smashing his head on the floor. This stunned the guy as Anthony directed the girls back towards the ER. As he did the guy started getting up, dazed from banging his head on the floor from the fall. The girls got past him and headed down the hallway towards the ER as more shots could be heard outside the hospital. Anthony made his way up from the floor and turned to follow the girls as the guy got to his knees. With Anthony next to him he reached out and grabbed Anthony by the side of his shirt. Anthony's reaction was a quick, hard jab to his throat that sent the guy reeling back to the wall and then the floor while grasping his throat and gasping for air. Anthony grabbed Debbie's arm and headed down the hallway following her mother and sister.

As they neared the other end of the hallway two more guys turned the corner about fifteen feet in front of them. Everyone stopped in their tracks and started backing up. Everyone but Anthony. He reached for his gun and started to pull it out from his waist as the girls started backing into him. "Go back," yelled Debbie. After a second the four of them turned around to head back the way they came and three more guys came around the opposite corner.

Anthony and the girls stopped in their tracks and looked at the new group of guys heading their way. The three guys had automatic weapons and they began pointing them in the direction of Anthony and the girls.

Anthony looked back at the two guys that were closer to them and they were pulling out pistols. At that second Anthony got his weapon out, but he heard a familiar female voice come from the direction of the three men with automatic weapons scream "ANTONIO GET DOWN!" It was Mariana behind three of her men.

Within a second Anthony was headed to the floor along with the three girls. They hadn't been on the floor for two seconds and gun fire erupted in the hallway. Automatic fire from the right and single shots from the left. The hallway quickly filled up with shell casings and smoke. Anthony could hear the bullets fly over him and the girls as screams came from both directions of the hallway. Debbie and her mother were screaming as well, while Anthony put his hands over them and tried to keep them as close to the floor as possible.

Once the shots stopped and the last casings hit the floor Anthony looked up and to the left. The two guys with pistols were laying in a pool of blood unmoving. Anthony looked to his right and Mariana was kneeling down checking on one of her men who had been hit, he looked dead. Screams could be heard all throughout the hallway as well as shots that were still taking place out in the street. One of the other men made his way to Anthony and the girls and began helping them up. They got up and made their way back towards Mariana. She no longer had her evening gown on. She was dressed in black tight leather pants and a leather jacket with high heeled boots. Her hair was no longer free flowing. She had it tied in a very tight, but very long pony tail, the red stripe accenting her beautiful hair. In her right hand was a gold 1911 pistol. On her left hip sat another identical pistol. Even in combat she managed to look sexy and coordinated as her gold pistols matched her gold belt. "You have no idea how happy I am to see you Mariana," said Anthony.

Mariana rose up and looked at Anthony, "Are any of you hurt?"

The girls shook their heads and Anthony replied, "No. How did you get here so fast?"

"After our meeting I went to another one of my houses not too far from here." Mariana turned around quickly and when she did her long pony tail swung out like a whip. Anthony had to back up so it didn't hit him across the face. She began making her way back the way she and her men came; Anthony and the girls followed. "We don't have a lot of time, the Perez brothers must really want you bad. The street is a war zone, so we must be careful." They made their way back down the hallway to where Anthony punched the guy in the throat. Mariana got next to him, pointed her pistol at him and shot him in the head. Debbie let out a scream and her mother held her hand and quickly tried to calm her down. Mariana looked at her and then back towards Anthony. "Never leave anyone alive Antonio." Mariana turned the corner and headed down the long hallway and everyone followed. A few more of her guys appeared down the hallway and she yelled something to them in Spanish. They nodded and waited for her next command. "Where is your car Antonio?"

"It's parked right out on Parsons Boulevard."

Mariana replied, "Okay," and then said something once again in Spanish to one of her men and he then ran off. Everyone made their way to the stairwell that Mariana's men were waiting at. They held everyone in the doorway as two of her guys went into the stairwell to see if it was clear. Shots started ringing out and everyone knew it wasn't. At this point Debbie was hysterical and her mother wasn't able to calm her down. Mariana said, "You need to get a hold of yourself if you are to survive this." Anthony reached out and put an arm on her, but she just gave him a dirty look and pulled away from him.

After a minute the shots stopped and someone from the stairwell yelled, "Mariana, está claro."

Mariana opened the door and said, "Let's go." Anthony and the girls followed her and her men into the stairwell and started making their way downstairs. When they got to the bottom two more guys were dead, but they weren't Mariana's. Debbie looked like she was going to be sick. He mother held her and as they got past the bodies she tried to shield her from seeing them. They made their way towards what looked like a receiving dock for supplies where more of her men were waiting.

"You weren't kidding when you said you had an army," said Anthony.

Mariana was walking at a fast pace and a sexy stride with Anthony right next to her, and the three girls trailing behind them. Mariana smiled at Anthony as she touched his chin and said, "I'm not about to let the Perez brothers hurt my Antonio."

Anthony smiled back kind of awkwardly at her and then looked at Debbie, who gave him a burning stare at Mariana's comment. Now he began to feel uncomfortable. Mariana moved towards her men out of ear shot and started speaking in Spanish. "*Her* Antonio?" she asked, visibly annoyed, and very sarcastically.

"It's not like that. She's a flirt, but she's harmless."

"Oh really?"

Lourdes said, "Do you see her? I would be jealous." Anything to annoy her sister even more.

Anthony looked at Lourdes annoyed and asked, "Really, was that necessary?"

"How do you even know this woman?" asked Debbie, "and why is she helping you?"

Anthony swallowed hard and replied, "We do business together, and that's a really long story."

"What kind of business do you do with her?" asked Lourdes.

Anthony and Debbie both turned to Lourdes at the same time and both said, "Would you please?!"

Debbie looked back at Anthony. She was so annoyed right now and combined with being scared it was hard for her to contain herself. "You are going to have a world of explaining to do when this is all over."

Mariana made her way back to Anthony. "Antonio." Anthony moved over to her and Debbie rolled her eyes. She never heard anyone refer to Anthony by that name and it was starting to annoy her. "The Perez brothers have a dozen or so men outside engaged in a fire fight with my men, but we are starting to overtake them. You have to trust me with something."

Anthony looked at her curiously, "Go ahead."

"We will go out the exit here on 45th Avenue. A van will meet us out there. Everyone make your way towards the van. We will be under fire so get to the van as quick as possible. Once we are in the van we will go around the block to your car. We won't have time for everyone to get out of the van and into your car. You and I will jump out of the van and take your car. The girls will stay in the van and we will all meet back at my safe house in Queens."

Anthony thought about it for a minute and then looked at the girls. Debbie looked skeptical and tried to convey that she didn't like the idea but Anthony wasn't paying attention to her. He replied, "Okay."

"Wait a minute," said Debbie. "Why do you need to go with him?"

Mariana replied, "He might need cover fire and someone to shoot while he drives. Can you do that?"

"No, but why can't one of your men go with him instead of you?"

"Debbie please." Debbie gave Anthony a nasty stare.

Mariana smiled at her and replied, "If Antonio learned Spanish that would be an option, but my men don't speak English." One of Mariana's men came running to her and said something in Spanish. Mariana said, "We have to move, now!"

Anthony pulled on the girls and they all headed for a roll up door. Shots could be heard out in the streets. Mariana was right, it sounded like a war zone out there. Mariana's men began surrounding the group. There were now about eight men and they made a circle around Anthony and the girls. Mariana stood next to Anthony and the three girls stayed behind them. Mariana motioned to Anthony and he took his gun out of his waistband again. He checked to make sure a round was chambered. It was, he was ready. He noticed that fear began to settle into Debbie again, she had tears in her eyes. Brenda did as well while Lourdes was surprisingly calm. He looked back at Mariana and she smiled at him. Only she could smile at a time like this. Mariana's men all checked their weapons and they were good to go.

Mariana, addressing her men in Spanish, said loudly "Proteger la Puertorriqueña, ella es importante." Lourdes looked at Mariana in shock at what she just said, but not understanding why she said it. Mariana smiled at her. She then turned to her men at the door and yelled, "¡Abre la puerta!"

One of Mariana's men started to pull the chain that controlled the roll up door. After a second the door started rolling up and the shots that were outside started becoming louder. Several more of Mariana's men were already waiting outside. The shots sounded like they were right on top of them. Debbie held her ears from the loud blasts that were filling the street, the noise was deafening. The entire group, as if they were one, started moving out of the hospital and right into the fire fight. The men surrounding the group began laying down covering fire in all directions. Bullets were flying all over the street, coming and going in every direction. One of the men on the right side of the group took a hit and fell to the floor as they made their way quickly towards a fast approaching van. The girls were screaming and yelling as the van screeched to a halt in front of them. "Quick get in!" yelled Mariana. Everyone started jumping into the van through the cargo door that was open on the side. Bullets were pelting the van like it was a target, and in this instance it was. Mariana's men continued to lay down fire all throughout the street, taking out men from the Perez brothers at a horrifying rate. A second van screeched to a halt behind them and Mariana's remaining men started getting into that one. Once the vans were loaded they made their way down the avenue towards Parsons Boulevard. Mariana instructed the driver to stop at the corner and unload them and then head away from the fight and get the girls to safety. The van screeched to a halt at the corner and Anthony, Mariana and several of her men jumped out. After a second Mariana slid the door shut and banged on the van. The van pulled a hard right and headed away from the fight. The second van stopped behind them and the rest of her army piled out. They began firing once again at their adversaries that were lined along Parsons Boulevard.

Mariana, Anthony and a few of her men made their way towards Anthony's GNX, only to be met by fire from up the block. They all took cover behind cars in the street. Several of Mariana's men made their way past them and headed up the street spraying anything that moved. Anthony was amazed at how her soldiers risked their lives and just ran out into harm's way. Several of the Perez soldiers were taken out immediately. They were no match for Mariana's men. They were being overwhelmed. In the distance Anthony could hear sirens coming closer. "Mariana, we have to get out of here. The cops are coming." Mariana agreed, after a minute they got up and headed towards the GNX. The coast was clear, at least it seemed clear. As they got to the GNX a Perez soldier who was hiding between cars came at Anthony. He was wielding a knife and Anthony managed to grab his arm and hold off his downswing with the blade as they both locked into a grip on each other. They struggled for a moment until Anthony heard a shot ring out and the guy loosened his grip on Anthony. After a few seconds the guy slid down to his knees and then fell backwards. Standing behind the assassin on the other side of the GNX was Mariana with a smoking pistol pointed in their direction. As the guy slid down so did her arm.

"Finish him, Antonio."

Anthony composed himself from the struggle and looked up at her. He looked down to the guy, he was still alive and in a lot of pain. Anthony caught his breath and said, "Mariana, I have an idea."

"Never leave anyone alive, he must go."

Anthony replied, "I know, but he may be of use to us. I have an idea."

Mariana went quiet for a second and then reluctantly agreed. She waved to four of her men to come over and told two of them in Spanish to take the wounded guy with them. Mariana then turned to one of the others and told him to put guards near the ER for Cristina's safety, although that would be a useless move. The police would be there in a few minutes and no one was going to be near that hospital that didn't belong there. Mariana said to the last guy, "Matar a todos."

Her soldier gave her with a skeptical look and said, "Mariana, hemos genado."

Mariana walked to the car door, turned to get into the GNX and replied, "¡Hazlo! Todo el mundo!"

After a second her soldier reluctantly said, "Bien." He headed off and shortly after other men arriving from around the corner began following him.

Anthony and Mariana got into the GNX and Mariana looked around. "I like your car Antonio. It's black," Mariana paused for a second, "like my heart."

Anthony managed to chuckle and asked, "Your heart? I didn't think you had one Mariana."

Mariana laughed and replied, "I have a heart Antonio, see, it's here on my necklace." She pointed to a beautiful, but mysterious piece of jewelry that looked silver and had four points that went in four different directions. North, South, East and West. In the center was indeed a heart, and it was black. Something about the piece was disturbing. She went silent for a second and then, sounding very serious she said, "It's a soul that I do not have." After an awkward few seconds of silence Anthony started the car and went to throw it into drive and Mariana stopped him. "Wait Antonio, drive slowly up the block."

Anthony thought she was out of her mind, "Are you crazy? We need to get the fuck out of here."

Mariana smiled and pointed down the block. Anthony turned and looked. Mariana's men had what was left of the Perez brothers soldiers completely surrounded. Some of them started giving up, but her men weren't having it. Mariana's soldiers were laughing at them as they slaughtered them. They were cutting them down with bullets. They didn't have anywhere to run. At every turn there seemed to be endless supplies of bullets sent at them. Anthony watched as the Perez army that was sent to kill him was completely wiped out. "Go, Antonio, go."

Anthony pressed the gas and he made his way down the block. The street was lined with bodies all laying in blood. Mariana's men were executing the remaining Perez soldiers. They weren't even leaving any wounded. If someone was moving, a soldier would go up to them and put a bullet into their head and then move on to the next person. Anthony looked on with disbelief at what took place around him. He was almost horrified because he was the cause of this. These people's deaths were on his hands. He didn't know why he thought about it that way. They were sent there to kill him, they were getting what they deserved. After a second he snapped himself out of it. They got to the corner, turned and sped off into the night, leaving behind them two blocks full of blood, death and destruction.

Chapter 22
Sending A Message

Mike awoke to his pager going off like crazy. As he reached to shut it off for the third time it went off a fourth. He looked at it and didn't recognize the number, so he shut it off again. At the same time the house phone began ringing. He reached for the phone and answered it. "Hello," he said tiredly. After a second he woke up completely and sat straight up. It was Anthony. He listened to him intently.

"What's going on?" asked a half asleep Teresa. Mike shushed her and listened. After a minute he got up, hung up the phone and started getting dressed. "Where are you going?"

"I have to go out, Anthony is in trouble."

Teresa sat up straight and clicked on a light. "Trouble? What kind of trouble?"

Mike began looking for a different shirt. "That asshole from the barbeque, his friends went after Anthony. It's a long story."

"Oh my God, is he okay?"

"Yeah, apparently Debbie's sister is in the hospital and the Perez brother's cartel attacked the hospital while Anthony and the rest of her family were there."

"Is everyone else okay?" asked Teresa.

Mike was silent as he finished getting dressed. "I don't know Teresa. He didn't have a long time to talk." Mike made his way out of the bedroom and Teresa got up and followed him.

"Do you want me to go with you?" she yelled to him as he made his way out of the house.

"Go back to bed, I'll call you later."

Everyone had met back at Mariana's safe house in Queens. Anthony and Mariana had arrived shortly after Debbie and her family. Anthony had parked the GNX in a garage in the rear of the house and a guy was guarding the door. When Anthony and Mariana entered the house Debbie and Lourdes ran to him and hugged him tight.

"Are you okay?" asked a very visibly shaken Debbie.

"Yeah, I'm okay, are you okay?"

After a second Debbie replied, "Yes, I'm fine."

Anthony looked to Lourdes and asked her the same and she nodded yes. He looked to their mom and she was as well. Lourdes asked, "Were you followed here?"

Anthony went quiet for a minute and then replied, "No."

"How can you be sure?" asked Debbie.

Anthony replied, "Everyone's dead. No one could have followed us."

Debbie closed her eyes and gently let Anthony go. She moved to a couch and sat and started crying. Her mother came over to her and put her arm around her and tried to console her. After a second Brenda asked Anthony, "What about Cristina? We left her in a war zone."

Mariana brought a few bottles of water in from the kitchen and handed them out to her guests and replied, "She will be fine. I left several of my men in and near the ER to keep an eye on her."

"The cops started to come when we left there. I'm sure the hospital will be locked down tight," said Anthony. "Anyone attempting to go near her would be stupid at this point."

Lourdes drank some of the water that Mariana gave her. "If my sister was used as a pawn once to get Anthony out in the open what makes you think they won't use her again?"

Mariana headed up the stairs while she held Lourdes' gaze. "It will be over before they can try again."

Lourdes watched her go up the stairs and out of view. After a second she heard a door close upstairs and then asked Anthony, "Are we really safe here?"

Anthony replied, "I think so."

Lourdes sat next to her mother. Her mother reached over and held her hand with her free one. "Don't worry girls," she said, "we'll be okay here."

Debbie stared at Anthony as he sat on a chair across from her. In a low voice she said, "I don't like these people."

Anthony took a sip from his water and asked, "Why? They just saved our lives. That's more than I can say for the Italian families."

Debbie went quiet and then she heard the door open upstairs again. After a second Mariana made her way downstairs and said, "Everyone should come up to the second floor."

"Why?" asked Anthony.

"It's safer," replied Mariana. "If anyone did see us come in here and they start shooting they won't be able to hit you as easily up here."

"Oh Lord," said Debbie.

After a second everyone got up and started heading up the stairs. There were four bedrooms on the second floor. Mariana had offered up the beds for anyone who wanted to lay down. Anthony didn't want to, so the girls stayed together in one room. Anthony moved to the front room and looked out. There were two men standing at the windows with automatic weapons at the ready. The street was quiet. Anthony stood looking out the window when Mariana approached from behind and put a hand on his shoulder. He turned slightly and looked at her. "Are you okay Antonio?"

He slowly responded, "Yeah, I'm fine."

"I know what you saw tonight was something you're not used to seeing."

He looked at her fully now. "No, I have never seen anything like that except in the movies."

Mariana sat on the edge of the bed. "There will come a time when you will be involved in something that will make tonight look like a playground, and I am not referring the upcoming battle against the Perez brothers."

"Upcoming battle?"

"Yes Antonio."

Anthony shook his head and slowly paced in front of Mariana. She looked up and stared at him. "Don't you think they would get the hint after how many of their men were taken out tonight?"

"The Perez brothers don't get hints. What happened tonight will only strengthen their resolve to get their hands on you. Besides, no one from the attack has survived to carry a message back to them, other than the one you saved. I surely hope you are not planning on sending him back to the Perez brothers, are you?"

Anthony replied, "No, I have a different idea for him." He went quiet for a second and then said, "We use him to contact the Perez brothers."

Mariana asked, "Contact them for what?"

Anthony went quiet and then sat next to her. He put his head in his hands and remained quiet for a second. "As a trick."

"I don't understand."

Anthony replied, "He contacts them and lets them know they lost a lot of men, most of the assault force is dead, but they also killed me and my family in the process."

Mariana continued looking at him for a moment while she thought about his idea. "Why the trick Antonio?"

"It buys us just enough time for them to relax; they won't see or suspect our attack on them."

Mariana took a deep breath and thought about it for a minute. "Fifteen men assaulted that hospital tonight. That will put a very good dent in the Perez brother's men but we do have to finish this quickly."

"How big is their organization?" asked Anthony.

Mariana thought about it for a minute. "They have about forty five to fifty men altogether in the city. Back in the Dominican Republic I'm not sure, but we need to finish off what is here before they can request more men from DR. This could buy us the time we need. If they think they got you they won't contact DR, at least I hope they won't."

"What about DR though?"

"It will be a non-issue. If you decapitate the head, the body will die along with it. The key is the Perez brothers and the guy that put your friend in the hospital." Anthony closed his eyes and he let out a deep sigh. He got up off the bed and looked out the window. He saw a car approaching from the end of the block. Mariana's men at the window raised their weapons and pointed at the car. Mariana ordered them to lower them. "Your friend is here Antonio. Go speak to him, but don't spend a lot of time outside, it's not safe. He can't leave here now either. We can't risk it till this is over. Have him come in and stay with the girls." Anthony agreed and walked out of the room and downstairs. Mariana told her men outside via radio to allow the car to park near the house and then she made her way to the window to watch Anthony.

Mariana watched him for a few minutes and then headed towards the doorway as Lourdes came out of the other bedroom. They stared at each other for a long moment. After a second Lourdes slowly entered the bedroom. "Are you okay Lourdes?"

Lourdes slowly walked over to her and replied, "Yes." She looked out the window and watched Anthony talk to Mike. Mariana studied Lourdes for a moment and then started to play with her long hair. Lourdes looked at her out of the side of her eyes cautiously.

"You are a beautiful young girl Lourdes."

Lourdes remained quiet for a moment and felt a bit uncomfortable while Mariana was playing with her hair. After a second she managed to show an awkward smile and said, "Thank you." Lourdes stayed quiet for a minute and then asked, "Can I ask you something?" Mariana slowly shifted her gaze from Lourdes's hair to her eyes and stared at her. After a second Mariana slowly nodded her head. "Back at the hospital, when your men surrounded us before we made the run to the van, you told them to protect the Puerto Rican, she's important."

Mariana smiled while continuing to stare at Lourdes. "You understood?"

"Si," replied Lourdes.

"Yes I did say that," confirmed Mariana.

"Why did you say that?"

Mariana never took her eyes away from Lourdes'. She continued to stare into them intently. Lourdes was attached to her gaze. "I said that because you are important. Very important."

Lourdes thought about that for a minute. She wanted to break the gaze and the hold that Mariana had on her, but she couldn't. She felt like she couldn't move, as if Mariana's eyes had a hold on her eyes and they wouldn't let go. "I don't understand what you mean by important."

"You're not supposed to understand Lourdes. All I can tell you is that you are and always will be a very important person in Antonio's life. You have a destiny that you will fulfill."

"A destiny?"

Mariana replied, "Yes, a destiny." Mariana went quiet for a minute and then added, "Your destiny is a very different one than your sisters. You and your sisters will have an impact on Antonio's life like no one else ever will. You will be just as important and as powerful and as feared as Antonio."

"Feared and powerful?"

Mariana smiled at her and asked, "That intrigues you, doesn't it? Being feared and powerful."

Lourdes was silent for a second and then replied, "Yes, but I am not a person that can instill fear in others. I don't see how anyone will fear me."

"Someday you will see it Lourdes."

Lourdes thought about it for a minute and then she felt like she could finally break the gaze. When she did Mariana let her hair go and looked back out the window at Anthony quietly. "Is Anthony going to be okay? Can you help him get out of this?"

Mariana continued to watch Anthony outside the house talking with Mike. "Antonio and the rest of you will be fine." With that Mariana walked out of the room and left Lourdes to watch Anthony from the window.

Anthony and Mike made their way into the house. Mariana was standing in the living room waiting for them with her back to the door. Mike eyed her up and down while she paid no attention to him. He was in awe of her looks. Then again Mike was a dog and looked at all beautiful woman like that.

Mariana turned around and looked at Mike, "Did you enjoy your lingering gaze of my ass Michael?"

Mike snapped out of it and started turning red at her comment. Anthony held back a smile and just shook his head. Mike wondered to himself how she could possibly know he was looking at her when she had her back them. "I, I ah," he stuttered.

Mariana walked towards them and gently patted Mike on the cheek. "Let me save you some trouble Michael, you don't have a chance." She continued staring at him for a second and then said, "Antonio does, but you do not." Mariana winked at Anthony and then headed towards the basement. "You can wait upstairs with the girls Michael. Antonio, we have business downstairs."

Anthony followed Mariana into the basement. Mike shook his head in disbelief and then headed upstairs to the bedrooms.

The basement was dark, damp, and dingy and there was not a lot of light down there. Mariana's boots clanked on the wooden steps as she descended into the darkness. Anthony followed her closely behind. As they got closer he could hear the unmistakable sound of a person being beaten and tortured. When they got to the bottom of the stairs they turned towards their right and the guy from the firefight was seated in a chair with a gag over his mouth to limit his screams. His hands were tied behind his back to the chair and his legs were tied to the front legs of the chair. Two of Mariana's men were standing behind the chair, leaning on the wall, and two were in front taking turns smacking the guy around.

Anthony looked over to Mariana as she watched the beating. "He can't sound half dead when he makes the call."

Mariana looked at Anthony from the corner of her eye, "If he makes the phone call."

After a second Anthony moved towards the chair. His face was all swollen and bloody. "Do you speak English?" The guy didn't answer as he just looked up at Anthony. "We can save a lot of time and a lot of pain here if you answer what I ask you and do as I tell you. Do you speak English?" The guy smirked and looked over Anthony's shoulder towards Mariana. After a second his smirk faded away as Mariana just stared at him. Anthony glanced back towards Mariana and then swung a backhand into the guys face. The guy's head snapped backwards and to the side. After a second he leveled his head again and looked at Anthony. "Eventually I am going to find a way to make you talk to me." Mariana translated what Anthony said in Spanish in case the guy didn't speak English. He looked over to Mariana again and then back to Anthony.

Anthony moved around the chair to where Mariana's men had bandaged his wound from when she shot him. Anthony looked up at Mariana, who was watching him intently. She already knew what he was going to do next and she motioned to him. Anthony pulled back and punched the guy in the gunshot wound in his back. When he did the guy howled in pain through the gag that was over his mouth. Anthony moved over to him and applied pressure on the wound and leaned over his shoulder. The guy howled louder as

Anthony applied even more pressure. Anthony looked at him and the guy started nodding his head really fast, so he let up on the pressure. "You have something you want to say to me now?" The guy remained quiet for a second as he tried to compose himself and then he nodded his head.

Mariana instructed one of her men to remove the gag. Anthony made his way back in front of the guy. "You speak English?"

The guy took a deep breath and in a very heavy accent he replied, "Yes."

"Good, now we're getting somewhere. Do you know who I am?" The guy replied, "Yes."

"You were sent to kill me?"

"Yes."

"Antonio, we know all this already," pointed out Mariana.

The guy asked Anthony, "Why didn't you kill me?"

Anthony shifted his look from Mariana back to the guy and replied, "You're going to do something for me."

In a somewhat brazen voice the guy responded back with, "Why would I help you?"

Anthony stared back at the guy motionless and then said, "Because if not I'm going to kill you."

Anthony moved around behind the guy and looked at Mariana again. She stood motionless and continued to watch the show in front of her. The guy looked over his shoulder and said, "Either way I'm dead."

Anthony moved over to a tool bench that was set up in the corner and he looked at what was laying there. He couldn't find a pair of clippers like he used on Barry, but he did find an old rusty hand saw. He picked it up and made his way back to the guy. The guy looked at the saw and then up at Anthony. A wave of fear came across his face and he started to struggle to get loose but two of Mariana's men held him down. "Do you know what my friends call me?"

The guy stopped struggling and looked at the saw again. After a second he replied, "No."

One of Mariana's men pulled off the rope that was holding the captives left hand and held it down on the arm of the chair. The guy struggled, but the bodyguard had a firm grip on it. Anthony leaned over and grabbed the guys hand and held it out and then he put the saw on top of two of his fingers on his left hand. The guy started screaming again and one of Mariana's men put the gag back into his mouth to muffle his screams. "They call me Tony Two Fingers," said Anthony as he began sawing off two of the captive's fingers. The guy howled and screamed through the gag as blood, skin and pieces of bone filled the air. He tried to pull his arm back but between the pressure of the guy holding his arm down and Anthony holding it down from the wrist as he sawed away, he had nowhere to go.

With what seemed like an eternity Anthony finally got through the bone and the fingers fell onto the floor. Anthony bent down, picked up the severed fingers and tossed them into the lap of the bleeding man. Anthony stepped back and looked down at the guy shaking in pain.

Mariana continued to stare motionless, but now she had a slight smirk on her face. Anthony impressed her, and it took a lot to impress her. The future of fear that she saw Anthony exuding was manifesting in front of her and she liked it. After a minute of crying and screaming shock started to set in and the guys cries turned to whimpers. "Are you going to do as I ask you now?"

The guy caught his breath as the gag was once again removed. Anthony tossed a rag to one of Mariana's men and he placed it over the wounds to stem the squirting blood that was coming from the hand. He looked up at Anthony again and asked painfully, "What do you want me to do?"

Anthony replied, "You're going to call your bosses and tell them I'm dead, along with my family. You killed us in a shootout, but you lost most of your men. I had friends at the hospital with me."

The guy very nervously thought about it and said, "If I do that they will kill me. I won't have a chance, Jose and Tito will never let me live."

Anthony moved a little closer to him with the saw and said, "If you don't do this I'll start sawing something else off, and it won't be your fingers." The guy didn't fully understanding until Anthony tapped the edge of the bloody saw blade on his crotch.

The guy got scared again and started whimpering, "Oh no! No! No! No!" Anthony let the guy think about it for a minute. "If I do this for you, do you promise me you won't kill me?"

Anthony glanced over at Mariana who didn't have a happy look on her face anymore. He knew she wanted him to kill this guy, but she decided to let it play out. Anthony looked back at the guy and replied "I, will not kill you."

The guy thought about it for a minute. He didn't want to die and he didn't want to lose his dick. He was in a no win situation. If they let him go maybe he could get away from the Perez brothers, but he wasn't sure. Anything was better than being tied up here waiting for them to cut off his cock, or kill him. "Okay," he replied.

"Good," said Anthony. Mariana handed one of her men a cordless phone who then started dialing the number that the guy repeated to him. "No funny business either. You tip them off and I will cut your balls off before I kill you."

The guy never took his eyes off Anthony as the other guy held the phone up to his ear. He was still shaking with fear and pain. After a few rings someone answered on the other end of the line.

"Tito, es Raul. Esta hecho. El gringo y su familia están muertos. Perdimos muchos hombres. El tuvo ayuda alli." Anthony watched Mariana while he was talking to make sure he was saying what he needed to say. Mariana confirmed that he was. Anthony motioned to the guy holding the phone and he pulled it away and hung up.

"Good," said Anthony, "that wasn't that hard." Anthony walked towards Mariana and stood in front of her.

She locked eyes with him and he could tell she wasn't happy. "You can't let him go Antonio."

"I said 'I' wouldn't kill him." Anthony paused for a second and then handed Mariana the saw. "I didn't say anything about you or your men not killing him."

Mariana's annoyed look faded away and then she smiled at Anthony. She handed one of her men the saw and said, "Dale una corbata."

The guy looked on in disbelief and started screaming as they shoved the gag back into his mouth. He begged and pleaded but to no avail. Anthony looked hesitantly over his shoulder and then tried to look away but Mariana put her arm around him and slowly turned him around to watch the massacre that was to take place. Mariana stood close behind Anthony and leaned right up against him and placed her chin onto his shoulder and one hand onto each of his arms. She pressed tightly up against him and held him tight. "Don't be afraid Antonio."

"I'm not afraid Mariana." He could feel the heat from her body transfer to his body. Part of him was turned on by the tight grasp she had on him.

The guy with the saw moved closer to their prisoner and placed it across his throat. After a second he began to saw back and forth. Within a split second blood started squirting from his neck. The executioner continued to hack away as gurgled screams and moans came from his victim. After what felt like an eternity, the struggling, screaming and crying stopped. What didn't stop was the flow of blood, it was everywhere. After the blood the captive started to piss and shit himself. His dead body was evacuating whatever fluids were left inside him. The air smelled like piss, shit, blood and death.

The guy finally stopped sawing and what came next nearly blew Anthony's mind. The executioner reached into the slit on the guy's throat with his bare hand and felt around for a second and then pulled out his tongue. Anthony thought he was going to throw up. He didn't know how he was able to watch this. The guy laid the tongue down along his blood soaked chest. Anthony had heard of these types of executions but he couldn't believe that he just saw one. He just witnessed a 'Colombian Necktie'. When he heard people talk about it he thought they were rumors or myths, but what he just saw was no myth. He watched the guards standing around the body laughing and joking about the site in front of them.

"Are you okay Antonio?" Anthony swallowed and hardly answered her. He slowly lowered his head and then looked at Mariana out of the corner of his eye. She was still pressed up against him tightly and he didn't realize how tightly she was actually holding him. "Mi Amor, you are shivering." He was and he didn't realize that either. It made sense that he was though, after what he just saw he was lucky he didn't pass out.

"Why didn't you just shoot him, Mariana?"

"You don't send a message with a bullet Antonio." She loosened her grip on his arms a bit but still stayed pressed up against him. She was still looking at him while her chin was resting on his shoulder. She slid her face very close to his and kissed him ever so gently on the edge of his lips. "Go and get ready. We have business to finish and we have to go soon." She let him go and headed up the stairs and out of the basement. Anthony continued to stare at the body as Mariana's men filed past him and also left the basement. After a minute he followed them out as well.

Chapter 23
Into The Lion's Den

Anthony made his way slowly up to the second floor of the house. He reached the top of the stairs and turned into the dimly lit hallway and Lourdes was standing outside the bedroom door. "What are you doing out here? I thought you would be sleeping by now."

Lourdes replied, "I can't sleep with what is going on; with what went on tonight."

Anthony walked further into the hallway and stood directly in front of Lourdes. She looked deeply into his eyes. He put his arms out to her and she leaned into him and hugged him. "I know what you mean. You wouldn't believe what I've seen tonight."

Lourdes leaned into him for a second and then pulled away looking somewhat annoyed. "You reek of *her* perfume."

Anthony continued to look at her and was wondering why she was annoyed. He wondered why she put emphasis on the word her. They both looked around the hallway to make sure they were alone. Anthony spotted an empty bedroom and he guided Lourdes in there and closed the door behind them. "What's wrong with you? Why do you look annoyed?"

"If I were you I wouldn't let my sister smell that on you."

Anthony smiled at her and asked, "Are you jealous or something?"

Lourdes turned a little red from embarrassment. "No! I am telling you for your own good. You smell like a whore."

All Anthony could smell was shit and death. He took a deep breath and then sat on the edge of the bed. "She leaned on me when we were downstairs, that's all."

Lourdes moved next to Anthony and sat down. "What were you doing downstairs?"

Anthony laughed a little and then said, "That's not a conversation we are going to have right now. That falls into what we spoke about at lunch. I can't tell you everything right now."

Lourdes went quiet and looked down at the floor. "Okay, but I have to ask you something."

"What's that?"

"Are you sleeping with this woman?"

Anthony looked at Lourdes and tilted his head a bit to the side before he replied, "No, I'm not sleeping with her. There is nothing going on between us at all."

Lourdes accepted his answer, then reached over with her hand and wiped his lip and cheek of Mariana's lipstick. "This would say different Sweetheart."

Anthony looked at her hand in the dim light of the room and smiled at her. After a second she slowly smiled at him. "Trust me, that's not what it looks like. There really is nothing between us."

After another moment of silence she said, "Okay, I believe you."

Anthony sighed and laughed, "So I have to answer to Debbie and you?"

Lourdes laughed and replied sarcastically, "No, *Antonio!* I'm just looking out for you. My sister has no use for this woman as it is. She sees lipstick on your lips and you're gonna hear it." Anthony laughed at her calling him Antonio. After a second they both laughed. "I will tell you though, that woman creeps me out."

"How so?"

Lourdes thought about her experience in the front bedroom with her earlier. She had a chill go through her when she thought about it. "When you were outside talking to Mike, we were in the front bedroom and she was touching my hair, staring at me and telling me things."

Anthony thought about it and then it hit him that Mariana had done to Lourdes what she has done to him so many times in the past, she read her. "What kind of things did she tell you?"

Lourdes thought about it for a minute and Anthony could tell she was a little uncomfortable when she thought of her experience. "She told me that I am an important person to you and I will always be."

"Well, you are an important person to me, you don't need her to tell you something like that. Anyone can tell that."

Lourdes smiled at him and held his hand. "I know, and you are to me as well, but she made it seem like it was something else."

Anthony was a little confused, "I'm not sure I know what you mean."

"I don't know myself, but she also said I am going to be a powerful person and a feared person."

"She said that to you?" Anthony asked surprised.

Lourdes replied, "Yes," and asked, "Why?"

Anthony thought about that for a minute. "Lourdes, don't pay too much attention to what she says. She told me the same things. Actually she said that I am going to be in charge of the most powerful family in the world someday. How could that be possible? I can't even be made, let alone run a family. It's the same stuff I explained to you at lunch."

Lourdes looked at him, but she didn't look like he was calming her. "She told me that I wouldn't understand what she was saying but someday I will."

"I don't believe in any of that crap she claims to see."

"Anthony, I have seen these types of things before. They aren't to be taken lightly. She's a Seer, she can see things before they happen."

"You've known people that can do that?" he asked.

Lourdes was quiet for a second and then replied, "Yes, and they are usually very dangerous people. They are in contact with things that I can't explain."

"Lourdes, I don't believe in any of that stuff."

Lourdes said, "You don't have to believe any of this for it to have an effect on you. You don't have to believe in it for it to be real." Lourdes looked away and Anthony held her hand tighter. After a second she asked, "What else did she tell you?"

Anthony thought about it for a second and replied, "She told me that in the future I will make decisions that will affect thousands of people. She said she saw a city on fire, Hell on Earth, people burning because of me." Anthony went quiet for a second. "She said I will hurt and cry so much, that her heart was broken for me. She said that I would make a decision that would haunt me from that day till the day I die." Anthony went silent and Lourdes had what appeared to be a tear in her eye. "What's wrong Lourdes?"

Lourdes tried to compose herself and then replied, "I fear that she may be right about all of that."

Anthony thought about that for a minute. He was afraid that Mariana had gotten into Lourdes's head. "You don't actually believe all this do you?"

Lourdes said, "Yes, like I said, I've seen things like this before. In Puerto Rico people like that are all over the place. The Dominican Republic as well. People like that practice this art for power and money, wealth and love. Everyone has a different agenda, but I look at her and I sense evil from her. It's almost like she walks with the devil. When she walks into the room the air disappears. It gets cold and I feel death and darkness."

Anthony continued staring at her. He couldn't argue with her there. He saw horrible things in the last day and he was sure to see a lot more in the coming day, all at the hands of Mariana. He stayed quiet for a moment and then smiled at Lourdes. He tugged on her hand and they stood up. "Come on, I don't want you to think about the things that she told you anymore. I want you to go and try to get some rest. By tomorrow this whole thing will be over and everything can go back to normal."

Lourdes hesitantly nodded her head and asked, "Are you going to be okay?"

Anthony smiled at her and replied, "I'm going to be fine."

Anthony turned to walk towards the door and she pulled him towards her and hugged him tightly. Taken by surprise he hugged her back. She was squeezing him so hard he was actually having trouble breathing. He put his arms around her and held her tightly. She felt like she didn't want to let him go. He ran his hand through her long, beautiful hair and held her tightly. After a minute she pulled back and looked up at him through the darkness. "You make sure you come back to us, do you understand?"

Anthony could notice the fear and seriousness in her eyes. "I will come back to you, I promise."

After a second of staring at him Lourdes let him go. They moved to the door and went out into the hallway. Mike was just coming out of the other bedroom and he gave Anthony a curious look. At the same time Mariana was coming up the stairs. "Saying goodnight to each other?" she asked.

Lourdes ignored her and made her way into the bedroom where her sister and mother were.

Mike approached Anthony and asked, "You didn't just…"

"Really?" replied Anthony.

"He wishes," added Mariana.

Anthony looked towards Mariana and said, "You to?" Then he asked Mike, "Is Debbie up?"

"No, they're both out cold." Mike asked Mariana, "So, what's the plan?"

"You, Michael, are staying here. Guard the girls if it will make you feel better, but you're not leaving till this is over. I can't risk the safe house being exposed if you left. Not for nothing, but just because Antonio trusts you, doesn't mean that I do." Mariana handed Mike a walkie talkie and said, "You can monitor what's going on out there if you like. If you don't understand what is being said, and you won't, Antonio's girlfriend can translate for you."

Anthony looked at Mariana and said confused, "Debbie doesn't understand Spanish."

Mariana started walking down the stairs, her high heeled boots echoing through the hallway. "I was talking about Lourdes."

Anthony let out a long sigh and after a second he followed Mariana down the stairs as he shook his head to himself. Mike followed shortly. "Ant, is this such a good idea? You guys barely made it out of that hospital, and now you're going right into their territory to attack them?"

"We will be fine Michael," replied Mariana. "We have my army with us."

Mike looked at Anthony who just shrugged his shoulders. They got to the bottom of the stairs and Anthony looked out the front window of the house. There were literally dozens of men filling the street. There were also a half of dozen vans parked out there with more arriving by the second. Mike looked on in awe of the display of man power that Mariana assembled. Anthony asked, "What's the plan Mariana?"

Mariana tightened her hair into a waist length pony tail and made her way past him and out the front door. "You and me in your car, my men in the vans."

Anthony waited for more, but she didn't continue. After a minute he said, "And?"

"We go to war Antonio, we go to war." With that Mariana turned and started shouting directions to her men. They were broken into groups, each with what appeared to be a team leader. She began briefing the leaders in Spanish.

Anthony and Mike watched as the leaders got their orders and headed to their vans with their men. Anthony turned to Mike and said, "Stay here with the girls. I'll be fine. I will get in touch with you when this is done. Kiss Debbie for me."

"I will," he said, then they hugged each other tightly. They didn't say anything else, they just hugged. After a second they broke their embrace and Anthony headed down the steps. "¡Vámonos Antonio!" Mariana smiled and winked at him and said, "That means 'let's go', Mi Amor."

Anthony smiled at her and said, "Yeah I know that."

The two disappeared into the back yard as Mike watched the vans pull out and head off in different directions, onto their destinations. After a minute the GNX roared out of the back yard and shot through the alleyway like a bullet. It hit the street and made a hard right and sped off into the night to meet its destiny.

Chapter 24
Un Beso

The GNX glided swiftly through the dark night. It wasn't going to be dark much longer, dawn wasn't too far off. Anthony sat quiet as he directed the car through the tiny streets of Queens. Mariana's safe house was on one side of Queens, in Laurelton, and the Perez location was on the other side, in Corona, but they had operations all throughout the five boroughs. Mariana sat going through her arsenal of weapons, powerful calibers of hand guns and the ammo for them. She looked over at Anthony from the corner of her eye, "Are you okay Antonio?"

Anthony kept his eyes on the road and replied, "Yeah, I'm fine."

Mariana fiddled with a .45 caliber magazine as she said, "You're affected by what you saw in the basement, si?"

Anthony stayed quiet for a minute and then said, "Well, it's not every day you see someone's head nearly cut off."

Mariana smiled at him and said, "I know you weren't expecting that. In time you will learn that the life we have chosen calls for things like that."

"You could have just shot him."

Mariana laughed a little, "Why didn't you shoot him?"

"I gave him my word that I wouldn't kill him."

"And why did you do that?"

Anthony asked, "Honestly?" Marianna nodded her head. Anthony stared at her in the dimness of the car with only the lights from the dash board reflecting on her. Even in that light she looked beautiful. Her eyes sparkled and she was breath taking. "I knew you were going to kill him," he replied.

Mariana allowed a smile to come across her face. "Your word is too good Antonio. In this life that we are living there aren't many whose word are good. Especially with the Italian families. You can trust nobody."

"I can't argue with you there Mariana." Anthony went silent for a minute and then added, "But I trust you."

Mariana had a warm smile across her face. "Thank you Antonio, I trust you too. The difference is I have an advantage over you."

"What do you mean?"

"I can see things that you cannot. I already know I can trust you. You don't have that ability."

Anthony laughed and asked, "Are you trying to tell me something Mariana?"

"No, Mi Amor, I would not fuck you." She went quiet for a second and then added, "At least not in the way that you are worried about."

Anthony shifted his look to her out of the corner of his eye and couldn't help, but smile and blush a little. After a second he let out a laugh, "Behave Mariana."

Mariana went back to her weapons and laughed herself. "I know you are off limits. Not only would I have to deal with your girlfriend, but her sister as well."

"Oh stop!"

Mariana said, "Well, maybe not now, but later."

Anthony was confused, "What do you mean?"

Mariana remained quiet and continued to load a magazine. After a second she replied, "Nada Antonio, nada." She continued looking at her magazines, but got very quiet, and, almost sad. After a second Anthony looked back out the window. Mariana's radio crackled and one of her men spoke to her. She listened and then replied something back in Spanish. She put the radio back down and then looked over at Anthony. "Antonio, some things in the future are very cloudy. Usually when emotions are involved they are especially cloudy. Sometimes almost un-seeable."

Here she went again, talking to him about what she thought the future has in store for him, or her, or them. Either he was tired from being up almost twenty four hours or he was just tired of hearing it. He asked, "And?"

Mariana put down the magazine and shifted her position in the seat to face him. "I told you that there will be times in your life where you will suffer great pain and cry."

"I remember."

"These girls in your life, the three of them, they are the cause of almost all of that pain."

She had a look of sadness on her face, almost as if she was going to cry. He was no longer annoyed with her, "Are you okay?"

Mariana locked her eyes with his. A tear streamed down her face. "The one that you love the most will also make you cry the most." Another tear streamed down from her other eye.

Anthony checked the road and then looked back to her and she was still staring at him. He felt bad for her. Here was this beautiful woman telling him how he would hurt and cry and suffer in the future, and she was the one crying. Why was he beginning to buy into this? He didn't believe any of her foretelling's. At least not the way Lourdes did. "Why are you so touched Mariana? Why are you taking my pain so bad?" he asked confused.

Mariana reached over and held his free hand, not to read him but to hold him. "I cry, Antonio, because your pain is so overwhelming and so great that I feel it as well. It travels through time and feels so strong and so powerful that it's hard to bear. I can't begin to imagine what you will go through when that pain hits you. I don't know how you will get through it and survive."

Anthony's eyes started to well up from her emotion, but he held it back. He hated seeing people cry, especially girls, especially beautiful girls. More tears streamed down her face and dripped onto their hands, they felt warm. Her sadness and her emotion released heat. He never felt warm tears like that before. He pulled the car over to the corner and put it into park and looked over to her. Here was this strong, powerful, feared woman, and she was on the verge of an emotional collapse. "Mariana, what do you see that has affected you like this?"

Mariana took a deep breath in and shook her head. "That's all I can tell you Antonio. Some I can see and some I can't. What I see I can't tell you directly. I can feel it though. It's strong and it's powerful and it hurts. It hurts very much." She remained quiet as more tears came down her face. Anthony looked out the window and then back to her. He couldn't believe that he was actually starting to buy into her madness. She looked up at him through her tears and still looked beautiful, none of her make up ran. It looked as if it was permanent, or tattooed on her. Anthony reached over and cupped her face. When he did he wiped her tears away with his finger. She leaned her face into his hand and he caressed her. She had the softest and smoothest skin that he ever felt. She was also unusually warm, almost to the point of feeling like she had a fever. She shifted in her seat and when she did the magazine that she was loading slid and fell off her lap towards the floor. As it did both her and Anthony reached for it at the same time and they found themselves nearly on top of each other, faces inches apart; lips inches apart. They both stopped in their tracks and remained staring at each other. Anthony's hand still on the side of her face, holding her, caressing her. She stared deeply into his eyes, intently, and he could feel her breathe on him. Slowly she reached over closer and closed the gap between their faces and kissed him gently on his lips. Her lips were warm but they sent a chill through his body. He didn't kiss her back, at least not right away, but he didn't pull away from her either. She held the kiss for a second and then kissed him slowly again. This time he was more receptive to it and somewhat reciprocated. What was he doing? What was she doing? She had always flirted with him, but it was always just playful. After several seconds she stopped and pulled a bit back from him, but was still dangerously close. "This, Antonio, cannot happen," she whispered. "Your heart belongs to another." She paused for a moment and then added, "Your heart belongs to others."

Anthony continued staring at her. He agreed with her, but he didn't want to. He wanted to continue kissing her, but he knew that it was wrong. He wiped away the rest of her tears, but she was done crying now. He remained staring at her, as if he was in a trance. If she ever got into his head with all her readings and magic, it was nothing compared to how she was in his head now with that kiss. He slowly pulled away to a safer distance, but he was still locked into her beautiful eyes and replied, "I know." Any other person in the position he was just in wouldn't have thought twice about his girlfriend back at the safe house, but he did. He knew Mike wouldn't.

They both took deep breaths and composed themselves and sat back in their seats normally again. Mariana's radio crackled again and she listened. After a second she spoke back into it and then instructed Anthony, "Drive Antonio."

Anthony pulled out of the spot. "Are your men okay?"

"Yes, they are nearing their destinations. We must hurry. We have our own destination to reach." The car headed back towards the Corona area of Queens where the Perez brothers were held up. Mariana retrieved the fallen magazine and looked at Anthony out of the corner of her eye. He was looking back at her. She smiled and said, "Don't go falling in love now Antonio, it was just a kiss, it's not meant to be."

Anthony smiled at her and thought to himself it might be too late for that, but his reply was, "Well, don't you go falling in love either." They continued looking at each other for a minute and then both laughed.

"Are you okay?" she asked.

After a moment Anthony replied, "¡Si!"

Mariana laughed even louder and harder at his use of Spanish.

Chapter 25
The Angel Of Death

Mariana had instructed Anthony to head towards Knickerbocker Ave in Brooklyn before they made their way to Corona, Queens. The streets were still fairly empty and it was still dark out. It was true that it was darkest right before the dawn. This was not a good part of town and Anthony had the same feeling he had when he met with Mariana earlier in the night. He didn't want his car in this neighborhood.

Mariana instructed him to stop on the corner and he did. He looked down the block and noticed one of her vans slowly pulling up to a house in the middle of the block. There was another one of her vans at the other end of the block. "What are we doing here?"

Mariana continued looking down the block. "That building there is a drug den for the Perez brothers. My men are going in there to close it down." Mariana picked up the radio and said, "¡Ataque!" When she said that the side door of the van opened up and out came six of her men, weapons drawn. They immediately opened fire on the two men standing guard outside the building taking them out. Two more of Mariana's men emerged from the van with weapons aimed at the roof of the building. They began firing hitting guards on the top of the roof. When the shooting stopped all eight of them made their way into the building. Shots could be heard coming from inside the building, as well as screams. Mariana's men were conversing on the radio back and forth to each other and shots could be heard there as well. Anthony sat there watching and listening to it all, he felt nervous. Mariana picked up the radio and shouted instructions to her men in Spanish.

Anthony looked up at the building and could see flashes of light coming from the windows as the gun fire took place inside the building. Something caught his eye at the door way and he noticed two men make their way out into the street. One guy was limping and bleeding. They were not Mariana's men. They turned and started heading up the block, the opposite way of the GNX, towards Mariana's other van. Anthony pointed to them and Mariana grabbed her radio and said, "Hay dos veniendo hacia ti." After she spoke that Anthony looked down to the other van and noticed several guys jump out and began firing upon the wounded men that came out of the building, cutting them to pieces where they stood.

Mariana noticed another guy come out of the building who was also not one of hers. He started to go up the block and saw his two comrades laying on the sidewalk and decided to head the opposite way, towards Anthony and Mariana. Anthony noticed as well as Mariana, but before he could react Mariana was already out of the car. "Shit," he said as he jumped out after her.

Mariana had her weapon up and began firing as soon as her high heels touched the sidewalk. She let off three shots, all of which met their target with deadly accuracy. The fleeing drug dealer was hit and fell dead from the hail of bullets. Anthony hadn't even reached Mariana and she was already turning to head back to the GNX, her long pony tail swinging from side to side with momentum. Anthony turned and they quickly got back into the GNX.

Mariana's radio crackled again with one of her men calling out to her. She picked up the radio and said, "¿Si?"

A voice came back and said, "Siete muertos, vamos a salir."

She replied, "Bien."

Anthony noticed the shooting had stopped. Mariana said, "Let's go, two blocks over. It's finished here."

Anthony started up the GNX and pulled out of the spot. They got to the middle of the block and Mariana's men exited the building carrying two of their own that were apparently wounded. Anthony made his way around her van and headed down the block. The other van was loaded up and pulled out in front of them and made a left. Anthony got to the corner and followed the van.

Mike and Lourdes sat at a table with the radio and listened intently to what was going on. It was hard to understand, but they could hear the shots being fired as Mariana's men attacked the Perez cartel all across the city while shouting instructions to each other. Lourdes was doing her best to translate what was going on, but she was struggling. The Colombian dialect was very different from what she was used to speaking and they used words that sometimes she didn't understand. Every now and then she could hear Mariana and oddly enough she could understand her perfectly. Mike noticed how intently she was listening to the radio. "Have you heard anything about Anthony yet?"

Lourdes replied, "There is a lot going on out there and they are spread out all across the city. It sounds like multiple fights going on at the same time. Mariana is controlling it all though."

Brenda and Debbie came into the room that Mike and Lourdes were sitting in. "What's going on?" asked Debbie who was very groggy. Lourdes looked up at Debbie but didn't answer her. "Where is Anthony?"

Mike replied, "He is out with Mariana and her army, attacking the Perez brothers."

Debbie sat next to Mike and tears streamed out of her eyes. Mike put his arm around her and she laid her head on his shoulder. More shots rang out on the radio as more men yelled instructions to each other in Spanish and she jumped in her place. "I can't believe this is happening." Lourdes looked at her and she looked away with an annoyed look on her face.

Anthony's GNX turned the corner to the next street and it looked similar to the scene that played out in front of the hospital. Mariana's men had the street blocked off on both ends with their vans and there were men everywhere shooting at one another.

Anthony screeched the GNX to a halt and Mariana already had her door open. Anthony threw the car into park and they both exited it and made their way to some parked cars to take cover from the shots that were filling the street. This time Anthony finally had his weapon out and Mariana looked over to him as they kneeled down behind a car. "Are you going to use that?"

Anthony made a face and said, "I haven't needed to use it yet."

"The night is young Mi Amor," she replied smiling. She turned her attention to down the block. Shots were being traded back and forth, it looked like a bodega was the central point of the fight. Several of her men made their way to where Anthony and Mariana were holed up and she began speaking to them. Anthony watched down the block at the activity that was taking place. Mariana's men were advancing on the bodega but kept getting pushed back to their original positions unable to get any closer. They were under heavy fire coming from the bodega. Mariana glanced at Anthony and said, "This fight has to end quickly or the Perez brothers will know we are coming."

"Why can't your men get any closer to that store?" As Anthony asked that question very heavy machine gun fire could be heard filling the street. Everyone ducked behind the car and Anthony looked around the side to see three of Mariana's men get cut down from the loud, rapid fire.

"That's why Antonio. They have a heavy machine gun in that store and the building above it."

Anthony looked around again and saw an alleyway towards their right. "Look, we can get to the back of the building through there and ambush them."

Mariana looked at the alleyway, it just might work. She told several of her men to regroup and take up position where the three were just cut down and for the rest to follow her and Anthony. Several of her men made their way back up the block to be met by the same machine gun fire as the ones before them.

Anthony and Mariana made their way down the alleyway with four of her men. Two were in front of them and two took up position behind them, similar to the circle around them at the hospital, just with less people. They made their way cautiously down the dark alleyway till they got to the end of the building. One of Mariana's men peered around the side of the building, down the long alleyway towards the bodega. There appeared to be one guard standing outside the back of the store. Mariana and her men made their way down the long yard as far as they could get until the guard turned in their direction. In that instant Mariana let out a shot that hit the guy directly between the eyes. As the back of his head exploded open from the exit wound he fell to the floor gushing blood out of what remained of his head. The men behind Mariana quickly aimed their weapons towards the fire escape above the building and began unloading them toward several men, hitting all of them.

Mariana and her party made their way to the back of the bodega and the coast was clear. She instructed three of her men to make their way up the fire escape to take out the machine gun nest in the building above the bodega while she, Anthony and her remaining man were going to take out the nest inside the store. After her men started heading up the fire escape she grabbed her radio and said, "Para de dispara. Antonio y yo nos vamos a la tienda."

Lourdes's head perked up and listened intently to the radio. Debbie noticed and asked her, "What is it!?!"

Lourdes listened again and then replied, "That was Mariana. She said she and Anthony are entering a store and she told her men to stop shooting at it."

"Oh my God!" said Debbie nervously. She began to rock back and forth as she listened to the exchange on the radio as her mother and Mike both tried to calm her. Lourdes just looked away and rolled her eyes.

Mariana made her way into the store with her man in front of her and Anthony behind her. There was noise and men yelling to each other in Spanish coming from the front of the store. One of the men noticed in the front that the shooting towards the store had stopped and he became suspicious. He turned to head towards the rear of the store only to be met by a hail of bullets from Mariana's man. The rest of the men in the front of the store turned and Mariana, Anthony and her bodyguard began unloading their weapons in their direction while taking cover behind shelves of groceries. The Perez crew began returning fire, but it was too late. They were no match for what was coming their way. Brazenly Mariana walked down an aisle of the store with her two gold guns in her hands and she was unloading them at the same time cutting down Perez members like they were large targets. Mariana unloaded two full clips in a matter of seconds taking out the rest of their opposition effortlessly.

Anthony looked towards the front of the store and there were bodies lying everywhere. Mariana moved closer up the aisle as Anthony watched her pass a doorway with stairs that led to the upstairs building. She got past the door and Anthony noticed a guy running down the stairs. "MARIANA, GET DOWN!" he yelled. Without hesitation she dropped just as the guy coming down the stairs let off a shot that narrowly missed her. Anthony quickly aimed and fired several shots back at the guy, hitting him in his shoulder and chest. The guy fell back into the doorway, dropping his gun as he hit the floor. The guy slid backwards on his ass pushing himself away from the store and trying to make it back onto the stairs while clutching his chest in pain.

Mariana quickly rose and turned towards the doorway. She pressed the clip release on both of her guns and let the empty magazines fall to the floor. She reached onto her belt and pulled out two more magazines and loaded them into her guns and put one back in its holster. She walked across the store towards the fallen guy and pointed her gun at him. Before he could plead for his life she let off several shots into his face killing him instantly. She pulled her radio off her belt and instructed her men in Spanish to finish taking the building and then headed back towards Anthony who stood still watching her. On the way back she bent down and retrieved her empty magazines. Mariana reached out and touched his face when she got back in front of him. She could tell he was shaken up by shooting the guy and she tried to calm him. "Thank you Antonio, you saved my life." Anthony continued to stare at the guy laying on the stairs in a pool of blood. "You didn't kill him, I did." After a second he locked eyes with her and broke out of his trance. Her eyes captivated him and he almost instantly forgot what he had just done. "Come Mi Amor." Mariana headed out into the street with Anthony close behind her.

The street was littered with shell casings from the gun fight. Gun shots could still be heard in the building above them as several of her men made their way past them into the bodega and up the stairs to finish off the crew. "Mariana, why would there be a machine gun like that set up in the middle of a bodega?"

Mariana and Anthony made their way back down the block with two bodyguards escorting them to the GNX. Anthony pressed to keep up with Mariana's stride. All the while her high heels clacking on the pavement while she shook her tail feather. She looked like she was walking down a runway as a model, instead of being in the middle of a firefight. He didn't understand how she could walk in those heels, let alone fight in them. She glanced over her shoulder at him and replied, "Maybe they knew we were coming." They got to the GNX and she got in it giving her bodyguards more orders that they quickly went off to follow. Another guard approached her and said something in Spanish. She seemed troubled and confused as the guard walked away.

Anthony got to the driver's side and got in. "What was that about?"

Mariana gazed at him. "Some of my men in the other locations are having trouble locating their targets."

"Why do you look troubled?" Mariana went quiet for a second and then just waved his question off. He threw the car into drive and headed down the war torn block. "Where to now?"

Mariana began reloading the magazines that she picked up from the floor, "Corona Antonio."

Anthony complied and sped the car away.

"They are out of the building," said Lourdes.

"Oh thank God," said Brenda. "Where are they going now?"

Lourdes listened to the radio, but she couldn't tell. "I don't know, there is too much going on, too much chatter. Some of her men are having problems in other locations. I can't understand over some of the shooting."

"I don't understand why Anthony had to go with them," said Debbie.

"I don't know. I tried to talk him out of it," said Mike.

Debbie shook her head.

"Mariana doesn't look like someone that listens to anyone other than herself," said Lourdes. Debbie looked at her but didn't answer.

All across the city, in all the five boroughs, the same scenario was taking place all at the same time: the Perez cartel was systematically being wiped out. Wiped out in as brutal a way as possible. There was no surviving for them, they were being killed execution style. All of their locations were being hit by Mariana's kill teams and they showed no mercy. In several instances some of the top ranking members were being assassinated in their homes with their families present and their families weren't being shown mercy either.

One high ranking member of the Perez family was asleep in his bed when a kill squad busted into his house. Before he could even fully wake up his bedroom door was busted into; his wife screaming as they were both pulled into the living room at gun point. Two more men came out of the other bedrooms with the couple's two children being held at gunpoint. Even an infant was pulled out of her crib while she slept. The entire family was herded together as the mother held her children crying and begging for them to let the children go. The leader of the kill squad not paying any mind to the begging mother just motioned to his men. They all opened fire on the family as they huddled together. Four assassins fully unloaded their weapons into the family until there was no movement left. No movement from the father, the mother or the young children. The only thing moving was the blood that poured out of their dead bodies and the shell casings hitting the floor and rolling to a stop.

Making sure the family was dead, the kill squad quickly moved on to their next target to do it again.

This is what took place over and over in all the five boroughs. Brooklyn, Queens, Manhattan, Staten Island and the Bronx. No one was spared. The highest ranking members to the lowest ranking members of the Perez Cartel were identified and systematically executed. Anyone that was in the house was also executed. Men, women, children, grandchildren, parents, brothers, sisters, even grandparents; no one was spared. Age was not a factor. Anyone that got in the way like a nosy neighbor that happened to open his or her door to see what was going on got it as well. No witnesses were left, no one would be able to tell this story. This was how Mariana's cartel was taking care of this problem and there was no stopping them.

The same went on at all known drug dealing locations of the Perez brothers. Mariana's teams attacked and showed no mercy. Not even to the people that were there doing drugs. One crack den had over twenty users in it and they were all wiped out. Whoever didn't die from being shot, burned in the fire that was set after the doors had been sealed shut. Most of the locations were burned to the ground that had housed the Perez operations. Of course before the fires were set, anything of value, whether it be cash or drugs, was pulled out by the hit squads to be taken back to Mariana. It was the spoils of war, and this was war. War on an unprecedented level.

Lourdes listened intently as Mariana's men called in what was going on. She understood a lot of it, but she kept most of it to herself, playing it off that she couldn't understand the dialect or just changing what they were saying. She was hoping her face wouldn't give it away, but there was no way she was going to translate to her sister that entire families were being massacred by Mariana's army. She knew Debbie would not have put up with that. She listened and she couldn't help feel that all of this was somehow her fault. Debbie had begun to get into her head about that and she felt guilty as she heard these families being wiped out effortlessly. She tried to rationalize it in the sense that they were drug dealers and they were going to kill Anthony and the rest of her family if this had not taken place.

After viewing several more battles on the way to Corona, Anthony and Mariana had arrived at Junction Boulevard. The street was quiet and it seemed like none of the other Perez members had been able to tip off the Perez brothers as to what was going on and what was taking place across the city. More of Mariana's men had made their way to Corona and they were taking up positions on and around Junction Boulevard. There were dozens of men returning from their missions and this was hopefully the final battle. The Sun was just starting to rise. Anthony parked the GNX on the corner of Junction Boulevard and Corona Avenue. This was the very border of Corona. It was lined with shops, bodegas and after hour's bars and clubs. The Perez brothers were known to frequent a club that they controlled and Mariana's intel informed her that the brothers were in the club celebrating their apparent victory over Anthony. Little did they know they were wrong.

Anthony shut the GNX down and looked towards the club. He was tired and he had seen more death in one full day then he thought he would see in his whole life time. He yawned and Mariana turned towards him. "Tired Antonio?" Anthony nodded his head and watched her. She pulled a knife out of a sheath that was hanging off her belt and looked at it. She ran her fingers along the blade to make sure it was sharp, it was and then she put it back in its sheath. She pulled the visor down and checked herself in the mirror. She pulled out a tube of lipstick from a pouch on the other side of her belt and put it across her full lips. Anthony didn't think she needed it, but it just made her red lips even brighter. She adjusted her tight, long pony tail and ran her hand along the red stripe of hair. She then looked at Anthony out of the corner of her eye as she put her lipstick back in her pouch. "¿Qué?"

"You have enough goodies on that belt?"

Mariana smiled and closed the visor. "You should see the goodies I have when the belt comes off, Mi Amor." With that she puckered her beautiful lips and blew him a kiss. Anthony continued staring at her and then started laughing. She smiled and then got out of the car, "Let's go Antonio."

Anthony shook his head to himself and then followed her out of the car. They headed down the block towards the club. There was an alleyway a few doors down from the club where her men began assembling. She handed Anthony a full magazine for his gun and one of her men handed Anthony several more. She began talking to a few of her captains and they took their men and headed down the back alleyway to approach the club from the rear. She then conferred with her remaining men and instructed them to assault the front of the club. She motioned to her lead captain and said, "Matar a todos. Todo el mundo."

The captain replied, "Si Mariana, si." The captain instructed his men and they headed off towards the front of the club.

Another of Mariana's men came to her and spoke in a low tone. She listened intently and then spoke back to him. He ran off and Anthony approached her. "What was that about? You don't look good."

Mariana was looking at floor, thinking for a moment, and then she looked up at Anthony. "About ten of the Perez brother's soldiers are uncounted for. Their families have been found, but not the actual soldiers."

Anthony continued to stare at her. After a minute he said to her, "Maybe they are inside the club?"

"Possibly," Mariana went quiet for a minute. "Hopefully."

Anthony asked, "What about Carlos?"

Mariana asked, "What about him?"

"What if he isn't in here?"

Mariana messed with her guns and thought about it. "I have men watching his barber shop and the apartment. If he is not in here, we'll find him. It's only a matter of time."

Anthony looked back out the alleyway towards the bar. Mariana's men approached the bar and stormed their way into the club. At the same time Mariana looked down the back alleyway and the men back there were doing the same. All in all Mariana had two dozen men assaulting the club with more on their way from their previous targets. Gun shots began ringing out from all directions in the club as Mariana's men began taking out everyone that was in the inside. The people that did manage to make it out into the street were shot as they exited the club by the reserve men waiting outside. Yelling and screaming could be heard over the sounds of gun shots and breaking glass. Mariana motioned to Anthony to head into the club from the front and he started heading down the block while she made her way down the alley towards the back entrance. She unclipped her radio from her belt and warned her men, "Antonio viene al frente."

Lourdes was listening to Mariana ordering her men around when Mike asked, "What?"

"Anthony is leading Mariana's men into the front of a bar or a club while she is attacking the rear."

Debbie got up and paced back and forth nervously. "What else is going on Lourdes? They have been doing a lot of talking but you haven't been translating much." Lourdes didn't answer her. She didn't want to answer her. She knew too much of what was taking place and she wasn't going to tell her. Debbie could tell that there was more taking place then Lourdes was letting on about as well. Shots were ringing out over the radio and Debbie jumped at the sound. It was a sound she was too familiar with at this point of the night.

"Debbie, try to calm down please," begged Mike.

Debbie shook her head and continued to pace back and forth in the small room.

Anthony was at the front of the club while Mariana's men were clearing a pathway for him. The club was being cut to pieces.

Loud music could be heard on top of the screams, gunshots and broken glass as the assault continued. A guy had managed to make his way past Mariana's men and grabbed Anthony as he was coming through the doorway. What ensued was a struggle that only ended when Anthony heard two gun shots close to them. For a moment he thought that he had been shot but he didn't feel any pain. He felt the grip that the guy had on him loosen up a bit and then the guy started to slide down Anthony's body to the floor. Another shot rang out that hit the guy in the head. Blood splattered everywhere as Anthony backed up from it, but he couldn't get away from it in time and blood splashed all over him. One of Mariana's men made his way towards Anthony and pulled him into the bar.

Mariana's men were leveling the place and everyone in their way. No one was escaping. Anyone that made it to the door was just cut down as they tried to exit the bar. More vans pulled up and more men made their way into the bar. After several minutes of shooting it began to subside. Anthony met Mariana in the middle of the club and they turned their attention towards a flight of stairs that led to the upper building, similar to the bodega they assaulted earlier in the night. Mariana instructed her men to take the upstairs and some of her other men to go after the basement. Shots could be heard above and below them as the last pockets of resistance from the Perez cartel was wiped out. After a few minutes of waiting for her army to clean them out a voice could be heard on the radio telling her, "Tenemos los hermanos Perez."

Mariana smiled at Anthony. He was looking around the club for any sign of Carlos, but he couldn't find him. "Antonio, my men have the Perez brothers upstairs." Anthony smiled and made his way towards the steps. "We must hurry, the police will be here soon." Anthony went up the stairs and Mariana followed him.

Above the bar was an elaborate setup of rooms and lounges. Mariana's men had the Perez brothers secured in a room overlooking Junction Boulevard. Inside the room were kilos and kilos of cocaine stacked up so high it was hard to count. On the opposite wall there were piles of cash lying about on a table. Mariana had four of her men in the room and the Perez brothers were in the center of the room with their hands on top of their heads being tied while held at gun point.

Anthony walked into the room with Mariana right behind him. The Perez brothers looked at him and then looked over at Mariana behind him. "Hello boys," she said.

They looked nervous and surprised that Mariana was there herself. "So, you are behind this Mariana?"

Mariana moved further into the room and looked around. She surveyed the stacks of cocaine along the wall and the stacks of cash that lined the room. After a minute she turned her attention back to the Perez brothers. "Yes, it is I, Tito. You seem surprised."

"I guess you aren't dead gringo," said Jose to Anthony.

Anthony shook his head slowly while he smirked. Mariana looked at Anthony out of the corner of her eye and then she cocked her eyebrow. "You don't seem too surprised at that Jose."

Jose looked back at Mariana and had a smirk of his own on his face. "Maybe I'm not. I guess you got Raul to turn on us with that bullshit story?"

Mariana slowly walked the room and replied, "No, Raul didn't turn on you. Raul is as dead as the rest of your organization is."

The two brothers looked at each other and then back to Mariana. "What are you talking about?" asked Tito.

Mariana strolled around the room and looked out the window and then back to the two brothers. "Your organization has been completely wiped out. Every one of your dens has been torched. All of your drugs and money have been seized. All of your men and their families are dead."

Anthony gazed at her when he heard that the families were dead as well. He wasn't sure if Mariana was telling the truth or if she was lying to the two captives to fuck with their minds. It made sense to him now when she mentioned the missing men's families in the alleyway.

"You're lying Mariana," said Jose.

"Am I Jose?"

After a minute Jose struggled to get to his feet, just to be met by a blow to the head from Anthony. Jose fell back onto the floor and winced in pain. Tito went to move and Anthony struck him across the face with the butt of his gun. Mariana watched and allowed a smile to come across her face. Anthony stepped back when the two brothers stopped trying to fight back. "What the fuck Mariana? Why did you ally yourself with this gringo?" asked Jose, very much in pain.

"That's not important right now," she replied. "What I want to know is where Carlos is?"

The brothers remained quiet and then Tito replied. "I don't know what you're talking about Mariana. Who is Carlos?"

Enraged and out of patience Anthony grabbed Tito by the neck and pulled him up off the floor. Yelling he said, "Don't play fucking games with me asshole. You sent an entire hit squad after me tonight because of that asshole and his friend." Anthony got Tito to his feet and punched him in the face knocking him across the table and back to the floor. Within seconds Anthony got around the table and was pulling Tito off the floor again while laying punches into his stomach and kidneys. "Where the fuck is he?"

"Fuck you gringo," said Tito. Anthony tossed him back towards the wall with the windows and met him there quickly. He grabbed Tito by the back of the shirt and shoved his head through the glass window, shattering it with his face. When Anthony pulled him back into the room the shards of glass that were still in place ripped apart Tito's face, sending blood squirting everywhere and leaving chunks of skin on the glass. Tito screamed and howled in pain as Anthony tossed him back to the floor.

Anthony looked at Jose who was watching the beating his brother was taking. Anthony pulled his gun out of his waist band and pointed it towards Jose and starred at him. Anthony took a deep breath and continued to stare at him. "Maybe you want to talk?"

Jose stared at Mariana and Anthony. Mariana stood there with a smirk on her face, she enjoyed watching the rage pour from Anthony. She knew he wasn't far from the breaking point and then there would be no return for him. She looked out the window and saw one of her vans pull up. She grabbed her radio and said into it, "Trai los arriba."

Anthony snapped out of his rage and looked over to Mariana wondering what she was doing. She remained silent and unmoving. After a minute she said to him, "we'll try a different way Antonio." Anthony took another deep breath, calmed down and agreed to let Mariana take over.

Lourdes tapped Mike on his arm and said, "I think the fighting is over. Someone told Mariana a few minutes ago they had the Perez brothers."

"Oh thank God," said her mother. Debbie sat unmoving and looking emotionally drained.

Lourdes said, "Mariana just told someone to bring them upstairs, but I don't know who she was talking about."

Mike shrugged his shoulders. At that moment shots were heard ringing out in the street. For a minute everyone thought it was coming from the radio but when return shots were fired from the other room everyone realized it was coming from outside the house. Debbie began screaming as more shots rang out from the bedroom across the hall. Mike stood up and took his gun out and headed for the door. He turned back to Debbie and yelled, "Stay here!"

Brenda grabbed the two girls and huddled together as Mike exited the room.

Anthony remained standing where he was with his pistol aimed at the beaten Perez brothers. Noise could be heard coming from downstairs. It was the unmistakable sound of a struggle and then it made sense to Anthony. He could hear women and children crying. Mariana's men were ushering people upstairs. After a minute of her men yelling in Spanish at the people, they began entering the room at gun point. Two young women who looked to be in their early thirties, five children all under the age of ten and all boys, and one older woman somewhere in her late fifties. Mariana had rounded up the Perez brothers families.

The younger women ran to the brothers as did the children. The older woman, who was obviously their mother, stood by and watched the scene unfolding in front of her. The younger women were crying as were the kids. The wives and children huddled around their fathers hugging and kissing them. The older woman stood silent, obviously praying.

Anthony looked up at Mariana and she caught his look. He motioned his head for her to come out of the room. He walked out of the room and she followed. Her heels making their distinctive sound on the hardwood floor as she started to leave the room. She turned to one of her men and said, "Toma el dinero y el yeyo." Her captain nodded his head and she exited the room after Anthony.

They made their way to another room and Anthony turned and towards her. "I hope this is a bluff, Mariana."

Mariana gazed into Anthony's eyes. He was angry with the Perez brothers, but she could tell he was not ready to start sacrificing children. "Antonio, you should know that I don't bluff."

Anthony let out a long sigh and then asked Mariana, "You're going to kill these children?"

"Do you want to know where Carlos is?"

"Not at the expense of these kid's lives!"

Mariana softened her look and reached out and caressed Anthony's face. "Antonio, your heart is in the right place, but this is not just about Carlos anymore."

Anthony continued staring at her. "What do you mean?"

Mariana moved closer to him. "This whole thing has been about vengeance for the Perez brothers. They wanted revenge on you for what you did to their runner. Do you think these children will grow up to be normal children and just let it go for what we have done to their fathers and their organization?" Anthony looked away and after a minute he slowly shook his head to himself. After a second he looked back into her dark eyes and Mariana continued, "This same scene has played out all across the city tonight. Every captain, every soldier, every family member of the Perez organization has been eliminated." Anthony closed his eyes, he couldn't believe what had taken place. "These family members are the last ones and this will almost be over. You and your family will be safe once we learn the location of Carlos. If these children live when they get older they will come after you for revenge. There is no other way."

Anthony thought about that for a minute. He knew she was right. After a second he reluctantly agreed with her. Mariana smiled and turned around to walk out of the room. "Mariana?"

Mariana stopped in her stride and turned back to Anthony, "Si, Mi Amor?"

Anthony was locked into Mariana's dark eyes. "Don't torture those children, make it quick."

Mariana continued to stare at him and then slowly bowed her head in acknowledgment. "I am not a monster, Antonio." With that she exited the room with her signature sound as she walked away.

Anthony looked around the room and a cold chill went through his body. A wave of guilt ran through his bones and chilled his soul. He had dozens of deaths on his hands tonight. Blood that he was afraid he would never be able to cleanse himself from. Men, woman, children, it was all on him. After a minute he made his way out of the room into the hallway.

Mariana's men were taking out the dozens and dozens of kilos of cocaine and the stacks of cash and loading them into her waiting vans as they did throughout most of the night across the city. Anthony waited for the hallway to clear and he made his way back into the room with the Perez family.

Mariana circled around the Perez brothers and she kneeled before them. "Make this easy on yourselves and your families. Where is Carlos hiding?"

The defeated Perez brothers looked at one another and then Jose answered her. "Either way we're dead Mariana, us and our families. So go to Hell trying to find him."

Mike made his way to the front bedroom where two of Mariana's men were shooting out the window. "What's going on?" Neither of the two men answered him back. He inched his way towards the window and looked outside. Across the street were close to ten or more men huddled down behind cars firing on Mariana's men that were guarding the house and her men looked to be severely outnumbered. Mike looked down the block and he couldn't believe his eyes. "Oh shit!" he yelled and headed back into the other bedroom where the girls were.

Debbie asked him, "What the fuck is going on out there?"

"The Perez cartel found us and are attacking the house."

"WHAT?" yelled Debbie.

"What are we going to do?" asked Brenda nervously.

More shots rang out and now shots could be heard right in front of the house. Mariana's men were fighting back, but they were beginning to get overwhelmed. Several of the men made it back inside the house to make their last stand in there.

Mariana slowly stood up and looked towards Tito. "Do you have the same outlook Tito?"

Tito spit towards her and said, "Go fuck yourself Mariana."

Quite annoyed, Mariana reached over and picked up one of the children. The child started to cry as Mariana pulled the boy closer to her. She took her knife off her belt and put it to the young boy's throat. The child's mother tried to make her way towards her son to help him but one of Mariana's men held her back at gun point. The child shivered in her arms as she positioned the knife next to the juggler vain and then locked eyes with his father. Tears streamed down the child's face. The silence in the room was deafening.

At that moment the radio crackled and broke the silence and it startled everyone in the room. It was the voice of Lourdes, she was hysterical. "Anthony, can you hear me? Anthony are you there?!?"

Anthony turned towards Mariana and she tossed him the radio, "Lourdes? I'm here. What's the matter?"

After a second the radio crackled back, "They're attacking the safe house. Carlos is with them! He's leading them."

Anthony couldn't believe what he was hearing. He caught Mariana's gaze and she had a look of concern on her face. He never saw a look like that on her face. She released the young boy from her grasp and he ran back to his mother's arms. Shocked, she said, "The missing men!"

Tito looked up at his captors and snickered, "So now you know. We knew this gringo wasn't dead. Carlos watched what happened at the hospital and knew he got away. He followed him back to the safe house. The asshole waited too long to make his move though."

Mariana looked down at Tito and surprisingly asked, "You sacrificed your entire organization just for vengeance?"

Jose replied, "We weren't sure you were completely behind him and if you were we didn't think you would go to the extremes that you did Mariana. We expected to get hit, but not the way you struck us. Even for you, this was too far."

"We thought it would have come from the Italian families," added Tito.

Mariana looked over again at Anthony as he quickly exited the room. Mariana ran after him. "Antonio wait!"

Anthony got to the edge of the stairs and turned back to her. "There's no time Mariana."

"Take my men with you. I will reroute more men there and finish here." Anthony agreed and took off down the stairs. Mariana turned to one of her men and said, "Llevate tres hombres y vaya con él."

Mariana's man moved past her and replied, "Si Mariana," and made his way down the stairs at a fast pace to follow Anthony while calling out to several more men.

Mariana made her way back into the room and picked up another radio. She gave a dirty look over to the Perez brothers and spoke into the radio. "¡Regrese a la casa de seguridad, AHORA!"

Mariana clipped the radio to the side of her waist and surveyed the room. She looked out the window and saw Anthony exit the bar at a high rate of speed with four of her men close behind him. They made their way towards the GNX, got in and took off like a bullet down Junction Boulevard towards her safe house. Even at this distance she could hear the whine of the turbo kick into overdrive as the car rocketed by.

"He'll never get there in time Mariana, not even with that car," said Tito.

Mariana smirked at Tito and Jose. Her men had finished taking out the coke and the cash and were awaiting her final orders.

"We might have lost, but he will lose as well," added Jose.

"You don't know Antonio. Someday he will be more powerful than all of us." Mariana started to make her way out of the room. She turned to one of her remaining men and said, "Matarlos a todos, rápidamente." Her man nodded his head and she exited the room and started to head down the stairs. She got down two steps and then abruptly stopped. She could hear the women and children crying and begging for their lives. After a moment gun shots silenced the cries. Mariana noticed the older woman just standing idly by with prayer beads in her hands and her eyes closed as she slowly swayed back and forth reciting prayers quietly. Unmoved, and unnerved, Mariana continued making her way down the stairs. She heard the final gunshot and the thud of a falling body as she reached the bottom of the stairs. She grabbed her radio and tried to contact the safe house. After a minute one of her men answered and confirmed they were taking heavy fire from the remnants of the Perez cartel and suffering losses. She could hear the gun fire in the background over the radio. She thought for a minute and then said, "Recueda, proteger la puertorriqueña, ella es importante."

After a second the radio cracked back with, "Lo sé."

In the club were several more of her men beginning to exit outside. She made her way around the dead bodies that lined the club and exited out into the street. It was bright outside in the morning sun. She reached onto her belt and pulled off a pair of pitch black sunglasses, put them on and looked at one of her men. After a moment she looked back and the assassins were coming down the stairs. She motioned to a man in the doorway and said, "Quémalo." The man nodded his head as she turned with two bodyguards behind her, entered a van, and pulled away.

Seeds Of Power

Chapter 26
Race Against Time

All across the city Mariana's vans raced back towards her safe house. Many were far away, in other boroughs and would not make it back there in time. At this point Anthony was the best bet for reaching the safe house and even then he would be lucky to make it there without at least getting pulled over. Cop cars were everywhere, but they didn't seem to be paying any attention to him. They were all racing to different points across New York, undoubtedly answering calls from the chaos that Mariana and her army reeked the night before.

Anthony took a hard left and got onto an on ramp of the Long Island Expressway heading East. He was currently in Corona which was located in the Northwest area of Queens. Mariana's safe house, where Debbie and her family were, was in Laurelton. That was located in the most Southwestern area of Queens that could exist. It was on the border of Queens and Nassau counties.

Anthony hit the ramp and practically went airborne when the car reached the expressway. This would be the fastest way to reach the safe house. The streets would take too much time. He pressed further down on the gas and everyone was thrown back in their seats. He looked down at the turbo gauge on the dashboard and it was lit all the way across. When the turbo fired everyone in the car heard and felt it. Anthony gazed over to the speedometer, he was well past the one hundred mile per hour mark. Anthony weaved in and out of the small amount of traffic that was on the expressway.

The LIE was not the friendliest road to cars. It was littered with cracks and potholes and it made the ride that much more uncomfortable at this speed. Anthony was worried about flipping the car and then the girls would have no chance if Mariana's remaining men couldn't hold off Carlos and the rest of the Perez crew.

Anthony's radio made some noise and he reached over and grabbed it, it was Mariana. "Antonio where are you?"

"I'm on the LIE heading towards the Cross Island Parkway. Where are you?"

"I have a stop to make. All of my men are on the way back to the safe house. You will get there first."

Anthony replied, "Yeah, no shit!"

"Antonio, this is not something I saw. Be careful, I will be there as soon as I am done."

Anthony put the radio down and pressed the gas pedal as far as it would go. He didn't think he could squeeze much more speed from the GNX, but he was prepared to push her to the limits.

Mike made his way to the top of the stairs and looked down in the living room. There were three or four of Mariana's men positioned at the windows, but they were taking heavy fire. This attack had taken them completely off guard.

He moved away from the stairs and went back to the front windows overlooking the street. When he got in the room shots came through the window and took out the guy at the right window. Bullets filled the room and Mike hit the floor, narrowly avoiding catching one in his head.

Mike crawled over to the downed bodyguard, but he was dead. He inched his head up and peeked out the window. Carlos' group had lost several men in the fighting but they were still pinned down behind the cars across the street. Mike picked up the machine gun from the floor and started laying down fire at the men hunkered down behind cars, hitting two in the process. Mike scanned the street looking for Carlos, but he didn't see him anymore. More shots rang out downstairs and Mike returned more fire at the cars across the street. After a minute the one remaining bodyguard on the left was cut to pieces. Mike ducked and looked over at him and realized he was now dead as well. Mike dropped low as more shots were rained into the room that he was in. He knew it was now time to get out of there. He crawled to the other dead bodyguard and looked for any remaining ammo he could have but only came up with one magazine. He took it and then began crawling out of the bullet ridden bedroom and into the hallway.

Two of Mariana's men came storming up the stairs and helped Mike into the bedroom where the girls were. One guy remained outside the door while Mike and the other guy went in.

"What's going on?" asked Lourdes.

"We have to try and get out of here; Most of Mariana's men are dead. I don't think we can hold out much longer against Carlos and the Perez cartel."

Mariana's man pushed past Mike and grabbed Lourdes by the arm and pulled her up and away from the table. "HEY!" she screamed. Mike reached over to pull the guy from her and he just shoved Mike back off of him with no effort.

The guy pulled her towards the door and said, "Vamos, tienes que vivir." Lourdes stopped struggling and the guy looked at her. "¡VAMOS!," he yelled again.

Lourdes said, "Todos vamos." The guy agreed and pulled her towards the door. Lourdes motioned to her sister and said, "Come on, we're all going."

Mike opened the door and they all made their way out into the hallway. Mariana's one guy stood directly in front of Lourdes and the other stood directly behind her, forming a shield of sorts in case any bullets made their way towards her. They all made their way towards the stairs and started heading down.

Anthony glided the GNX towards the Cross Island Parkway. He exited to the right and started heading South down the parkway. At the speed he was traveling he should be by the Belt Parkway in a matter of minutes. The only problem was he picked up a cop at the parkway entrance and now he was on Anthony's tail. Even he was having trouble keeping up with Anthony and he had a powerful engine in his squad car.

The cop found a burst of speed and closed in on Anthony's car. Anthony glanced in the rearview mirror and saw the flashing red and blue lights getting closer to him, then came the loudspeaker: "PULL OVER TO THE RIGHT NOW!"

"Fuck you," was Anthony's reply. Anthony tapped the guy on his right and made a motion to take care of the situation. The guy opened the window, turned around, cocked back his AK-47 and pushed himself out the window back first and sat on the edge of the door. He brought his weapon to bear on the cop car. Before the cop could slow down and back off the guy opened fire at the windshield, spraying it with bullets. Red splattered all across the inside of what was left of the windshield. The cop car began to sway left and right and lose control. The assassin readjusted his aim and shot towards the front tires of the vehicle. Within seconds he managed to take out the passenger side tire and the car veered off into the divider and then flipped and started to barrel role down the Cross Island Parkway. The assassin pulled himself back into the vehicle as they sped along.

The living room was now being shot up much like the upstairs front room was minutes earlier. At the house, Mariana didn't have many men still left alive, but the ones that were alive were holding their own against the assault. The girls made their way to the main level of the house as the men shielded Lourdes and her family.

"Where are we going to go? It's a warzone out there!" yelled Debbie.

Mariana's men ushered them to the rear of the house and shots began coming at them from outside. So much for getting out into the yard and into Mike's car. One of Mariana's men grabbed Lourdes and pushed her towards the basement. "Come on, get downstairs!" she yelled to everyone else just as the guy who was pushing her was shot several times in his back. Debbie and her mother began screaming as Mike and the remaining bodyguard ushered them down the stairs.

Mariana's van pulled up outside of Jamaica hospital. The door slid open and she emerged with two of her men. She pulled off her belt where her guns were hanging and tossed them inside the van and instructed her men to do the same. When she was done she walked towards the entrance of the hospital with her two men directly behind her.

Anthony pulled off the Cross Island Parkway and jumped on the streets heading into Laurelton. The rest of the ride would be street driving but he was now only minutes away from the house.

The guy next to him pulled the empty magazine from his assault rifle and loaded a full one into it. He handed the empty mag to a guy in the back and he started reloading it while speaking in Spanish to his friends next to him.

Anthony made a hard right and sped down the block to make a hard left. As he did there was a guy from Carlos' crew in the middle of the street. Anthony caught him by surprise when he slammed into him sending him flying down the block. He crashed into the pavement and stopped moving.

Within seconds the two doors from the GNX were thrown open and Mariana's men as well as Anthony were piling out of the car. They couldn't get any further down the block, Carlos's men had it blocked off and were already firing at the GNX. Bullets riddled the doors and hood of the black car as Anthony and his men went for cover. Two of them took fire and fell where they were standing, leaving only Anthony and two more left.

Anthony wasn't sure how many men were left in the safe house, but from what he could see outside it was himself and the two guys left up against at least six Perez soldiers. He scanned the block for Carlos, but he didn't see him.

Lourdes and her family made their way down to the bottom of the stairs and into the basement when the smell overtook them. They headed towards the back of the room and then they saw the source of the smell. Raul was still in the chair where Mariana and Anthony left him. He had completely bled out and evacuated any bodily fluids that were left in him. The air was heavy with the smell of feces and blood.

Debbie looked at the body and she couldn't believe what she was looking at. "Oh my God!" she exclaimed. "What is that?"

Lourdes annoyingly pushed past her and said, "What the fuck does it look like? A dead body."

Debbie turned away from it, unable to look anymore and began throwing up. "Is that his tongue?" Brenda asked.

Mike came down the stairs and stopped in his tracks. He couldn't believe it either. After a second he noticed Debbie throwing up and he moved over to help her. Lourdes moved closer and looked at the body. She knew Anthony was down here earlier and he told her he wasn't going to explain what he saw. She looked around and saw two fingers laying on the floor. She stared at the fingers for a minute and then slowly backed up. She stopped moving when she bumped into her mother.

"What is it?" her mother asked quietly.

Lourdes looked at her and after a second she shook her head. She wasn't going to reveal what she just saw. Instead she pushed her mother back towards Debbie. "Help her, before they hear us down here and she gives us away."

Mariana strolled through the hospital down a long hallway and into a waiting elevator, her two bodyguards only inches away from her. They rode the elevator up towards the ICU unit on the sixth floor and exited. She scanned the signs in front of her and then made her way down another long hallway. She moved along the hallway, heels clanking with every step, as she looked at the patient names on the doors. When she found the one she was looking for she stopped in front of it. She turned towards her men and said, "Espera aquí." She entered the room as her two men remained outside.

Mariana looked at the patient laying on the bed, it was Luis. He was still unconscious, connected to all types of machines and tubes. She slowly walked over to the bed. His entire head was wrapped up in bandages from the burns that Anthony inflicted on him. He was on a respirator that was helping him to breathe. The tube ran through a hole that was cut into his neck. From the intense heat and smoke his lungs were scorched and he couldn't breathe on his own. Mariana gently ran her hand along the railing on the bed as she moved closer to Luis. "You caused all of this unnecessary death tonight and you don't even know what you did." Mariana looked around at everything that he was plugged into. IV's, monitors and the respirator.

Mariana reached out and ran her hand along the tube that was helping him breathe. She reached the center of it and squeezed it with her hand till it was completely restricted. She looked over to the respirator and it stopped moving. It stopped it's up and down motion, signaling it was no longer feeding air into Luis. Her eyes moved up from the respirator towards the vitals machine and watched as Luis' numbers started going crazy. She knew she didn't have a lot of time. Once his vitals dropped below a certain point it would trigger alarms at the nursing station and the room would be flooded with doctors. She watched his blood pressure start to drop quickly and his heart rate began to rise. She squeezed the tube tighter till it was completely crushed. She watched his vitals steadily drop and after a minute or so he began to flat line. Once she saw his heart was no longer beating she let the tube go and headed for the door quickly.

She exited the room and moved past her two bodyguards and towards the hallway. Her two bodyguards followed quickly and they headed for an elevator. She put her arm out to stop an elevator from closing and entered it. Just before the doors closed she could hear over the loudspeaker of the ICU unit 'code blue, code blue, ICU room 15, code blue.' As the elevator doors completely closed Mariana allowed a smile to come across her face.

Anthony's position was taking a pounding, as well as the GNX. He had nowhere to go and his men were running out of ammo quickly. The break he needed came from the other end of the block. One of Mariana's vans pulled up and began unloading on the Perez soldiers. Now Carlos' crew was trapped and taking fire from both sides. Anthony saw a break from being shot at and he ran across the street and headed towards the back of one of the houses' yards at the beginning of the block. He made his way along the side of the house and planned on yard hopping till he reached the safe house. It had to be safer than being out in the middle of a fire fight.

Carlos and two men stormed through the back door of the safe house. Shots flew from both directions but his men managed to take out both of Mariana's men guarding the door with only losing one of their own. As they made their way further into the kitchen shots came at them from the living room and they had to retreat back into the doorway and take cover.

Debbie had stopped throwing up and she was being held by her mother and Mike when the shots in the kitchen erupted. They were now trapped in the basement. There was a bilco door leading to the yard, but it was chained up from the outside. Mike moved to the door and tried opening it, but it would only move as far as the chain and no further. It couldn't even be shot out from inside.

"We're trapped down here," said Debbie.

By this time Lourdes had had enough. It was usually Debbie to be the one to snap, but now it was Lourdes. "Why don't you just knock it off already?"

Debbie turned to her shocked, "What?" she asked dumbfounded.

"The entire fucking night you've been like this. Stop acting like a child and try to figure a way out of here."

Their mother intervened and tried to diffuse the situation. "Now is not the time for one of your usual arguments, so both of you knock it the hell off!"

Lourdes stepped back and remained locked in a stare with her sister. Debbie had never seen her get like that before and all that was going on around them didn't seem to affect her anymore.

More shots rang out upstairs and the basement door opened up. Mike headed towards the stairs to see who it was and Carlos launched himself down the stairs in Mike's direction. The barrage completely took Mike by surprise and he started firing wildly towards the stairs. He managed to get three shots off before he ran out of bullets. Carlos crashing into him knocked the air out of him and dropped both of them to the floor.

Carlos got to his knees first and began pummeling Mike with punches to his face and body. Mike was no match for him and Mike was a tough guy, but Carlos had the complete upper hand.

Debbie moved first, she looked for something in the basement that she could use to hit Carlos with and only came up with what looked like a broom handle. She wasn't going to get far with it but she needed to give it a try. She took it and swung it down hard across Carlos' back. When it hit him it broke in half and didn't even stun him. Carlos turned his attention away from Mike and towards Debbie and swung back at her but he missed and the momentum took him off of Mike and onto his side on the floor.

Mike was completely stunned and half-conscious by now. Debbie backed up and Carlos rose to full height. He hauled his arm back and gave Debbie a backslap that threw her across the basement and into a wall and then to the floor. Stunned, her mother moved towards her to make sure she was alright.

Carlos turned around and picked Mike up from the floor. Once he had him standing Carlos slammed the side of his hand into

Mike's throat in a karate chop motion. Mike slammed into the wall behind him and lost all consciousness.

Carlos turned towards Lourdes. She shifted her gaze from Mike who was laying unmoving on the floor up to Carlos. He had a look of fire in his eyes. He shifted his gaze towards Debbie and her mother and then back towards Lourdes. He looked around the basement for his gun. After a minute he spotted it laying by the stairs. He walked slowly over towards it and picked it up. There was suddenly silence all around them. There was no more shooting coming from the street, no more yelling, no more sounds of people dying from this war. He turned his gaze back towards Lourdes and then he looked at Mike who was still unmoving. After a minute of silence he aimed the gun towards Mike's direction and pulled the trigger.

Lourdes watched in horror as she put her hands to her ears to shield herself from the sound of the impending shot, but nothing ever came. Carlos pulled the trigger again and once again there was silence. After several more tries an enraged Carlos pulled back the slide on his gun just to find he was out of bullets. Cursing he threw the gun across the basement and in a fit of rage he headed towards Lourdes's direction. Sensing she was now going to come under attack from Carlos she began backing up quickly to get away from him. She wasn't able to go very far since she was only a few steps from the left side wall of the basement. She began screaming for all she was worth.

Within seconds Carlos was on top of her position as she cowered down and tried to avoid his grasp. With his left hand he reached down and grabbed her long flowing hair and began pulling her up from her squatted position. He got her to stand fully upright and she stopped squirming and stared at him. A look of fear came across her face, a look that she never displayed before. He stepped closer to her and locked eyes with her. She nervously asked, "What are you going to do?"

Carlos looked at her for a few seconds in silence and then smirked. "I'm going to kill you Puta, you and your whole family."

Lourdes continued looking at him unmoving and then her scared look suddenly faded away. She began to look like she was actually relaxed. She let out a long breath and then allowed a smirk of her own to come across her face. "I don't think so."

Carlos' smirk faded away into a look of confusion. He continued to stare at her as he tried to process why she no longer looked scared. After a minute he asked, "And why don't you think so?"

A voice came from behind Carlos that said, "Because I'm not going to let that happen asshole."

Carlos, taken completely by surprise, turned towards his right just to be met by a crushing punch to the side of his head from Anthony.

Lourdes moved to her left to avoid Carlos crashing into the wall where she was just standing. She quickly hurried out of the way to avoid getting tangled up in the coming fight as Anthony didn't waste any time following up his punch with more. Lourdes slid further out of the way towards her mother and sister.

Carlos was completely caught by surprise by the barrage of punches that Anthony was laying into him. Anthony kept on him like white on rice, but his punches weren't having the effect that was needed to bring Carlos to the floor. Carlos began blocking the blows and now the two were entangled in each other's grasps.

This was a much different fight then the one Anthony had with Luis. For one thing Luis was drunk and Anthony was wide awake. Now Anthony was up over twenty four hours already and had been involved in more than his fair share of fighting. He was tired, he was sore and he was worn out. The only thing that was driving him at this point was pure adrenaline. He was set on fire when he came down the stairs and saw the position Carlos had Lourdes in. That was his driving force and if it killed him he was going to win this fight.

Carlos had about three inches in height on Anthony and was more than ten pounds heavier. He managed to get out of the hold that Anthony had on him and pushed Anthony back towards the other side of the basement and into the opposite wall. When he did he knocked the wind out of Anthony and then he followed up with a shot to his face that took him off of his feet. Carlos dropped down and grabbed Anthony by the throat and pulled him back up to his feet and began laying punches into his chest and stomach. Each blow made Anthony feel as if his chest was going to cave in. Anthony tried to block as many blows as he could but more managed to get through then were blocked.

Carlos pulled back and prepared to deliver a crushing blow towards Anthony. As the punch came towards him, Anthony slid to his right and Carlos' punched ended up connecting into the cement wall. Carlos howled out in pain as he pulled his obviously broken hand back into his chest to nurse the pain. The powerful blow actually managed to crack the concrete and send shards of it to the floor.

Anthony now had his moment. Quickly he reached out and grabbed Carlos' injured hand, locked onto it and twisted it back. Carlos' screams filled the basement as Anthony continued to twist the broken hand and now broken wrist much further than it was meant to go. As Anthony had the hand twisted back with his left hand and he was laying punches into Carlos with his right hand. Blow after blow Anthony was un-relentless with his attack. All his anger, all his frustration of what Carlos had done to Cristina was now coming down to this. If it was Anthony's last wish it was going to be to inflict as much damage as he could to Carlos to avenge what had happened to Cristina. "You had fun beating an innocent woman you fucking scumbag?"

All Carlos could answer was screams of pain as Anthony twisted his arm more and more. Anthony twisted it even further and Carlos dropped to his knees. Anthony was in perfect position above him and just kept raining punches to Carlos' face until blood started to flow from his mouth.

With the little bit of energy that Carlos had left he grabbed Anthony with his left hand and locked onto his side and pulled him closer to him and into a hold and the two began to struggle again. Carlos applied a bear hug to Anthony and started to squeeze the wind out of him as Anthony struggled to break the hold.

Struggling, Anthony looked over towards Lourdes and said "Lourdes, get everyone out of here, now."

Scared and not sure what to do she began to pull on her mother to get Debbie and go. Both of them helped a staggering Debbie to her feet and started to move towards the stairs. Lourdes watched Carlos and Anthony struggling with each other. "What about you?" she asked.

"Just go!" Anthony managed to get out as he struggled to breath.

Lourdes and her family headed up the stairs and out of the basement. They got into the living room and the house looked like another war zone. There were men laying all over the place, some barely moving and some obviously dead. They slowly made their way towards the front of the house and looked out into the street and then went out the front door. A van of Mariana's pulled up as the girls exited out into the street. The side door slid open and Mariana emerged from the stopping vehicle. "Where is Antonio?"

"He's in the basement fighting with Carlos," replied Lourdes.

Mariana made her way towards the girls. "Are any of you hurt?"

"No, not that bad" replied Brenda. "Debbie is just stunned more than anything."

Mariana motioned to her two bodyguards to tend to the girls and said, "Mantenerlos seguros." With her usual, sexy stride, Mariana headed towards the house.

"Mariana," called out one of her body guards.

Mariana glared over her shoulder with a look that said, 'I gave you an order, now follow it,' was all that was needed to shut the concerned bodyguard up. Mariana continued making her way into the war torn house. Several steps in and she was met by an injured Perez soldier coming down the stairs who didn't know what he got himself involved in, and now he was face to face with Mariana. He started his mistake by trying to grab her and was met by her reversing his hold. Within a second she had him in a choke hold. All it took was a few seconds more and she strangled his life out of him by crushing his windpipe with her bare hands. Once she let the body drop to the floor she continued her way towards the basement.

Anthony, still in the hold that Carlos had on him struggled to try and break it. Anthony looked over his left shoulder as he tried to pull in air and noticed a supporting beam behind him and to his left. Using his momentum and Carlos' body weight he pushed himself backwards towards the beam. As he got close enough to it he let

Carlos' weight take over and allowed himself to fall completely backwards. As he did the top of Carlos' head was driven into the beam at a high rate of speed. Once Carlos' head connected with the corner of the beam his head split open, allowing blood to gush out of the fracture, and he let Anthony go completely. From the momentum Anthony fell to the floor landing on his back, completely drained and fully out of air. From the sudden force of hitting the beam Carlos also fell backwards and as he did he smashed the back of his head on the floor.

Anthony laid there and tried to pull in air, but his right side winced in pain with each breath. He heard the familiar sound of Mariana's high heels as she descended the stairs. Looking to his right and up at her she moved over to him and bent down. "Are you okay Antonio?" Struggling to breathe he nodded his head to her. She moved her hand along his side gently feeling his ribs. "You have fractured ribs Mi Amor. Don't try to move." He tried to push himself up and pointed towards Carlos' direction but Mariana was already up and heading over there.

Mariana made her way towards Carlos, who was barely moving. He had his injured hand pulled into his chest nursing the pain while his other hand was on top of his split open head, trying to hold back the blood from flowing out of it. Mariana kneeled down next to the fallen man just to taunt him. "Antonio got the best of you I see." Carlos' eyes rolled around trying to steady his vision on Mariana, but he was unable to. She allowed a smirk to come across her face. "All of your friends are dead, including the one that started all of this." Carlos finally managed to concentrate his vision on Mariana, but he looked like he was about to slip into unconsciousness. Mariana reached out and slapped him across his face to wake him up. As he did she stood up next to his head. Anthony rolled onto his side and slowly got to his knees. Clutching his side he stopped and watched Mariana. She turned to her left and looked at Anthony. After a second of staring at Anthony she looked down to her right as Carlos laid there looking up at her stunned and dazed. She continued to stare down at him for a moment. She raised her right leg up and in an instant with powerful force she pushed her leg down and drove her spiked boot heel into Carlos' left eye. The heel penetrated the eye ball effortlessly and plunged into Carlos' brain making horrible squishing noises in the process. One loud gasp from Carlos could be heard as his body shook with a violent spasm for a minute and then his body suddenly went still. Almost immediately his body began to purge any fluids and solids that it contained. Mariana had driven her leg down so far she could almost stand on the floor while the heel was buried into Carlos' skull.

Anthony watched on and winced as Carlos caught the death blow that Mariana rained down onto him. Once again the air will filled with the smell of shit and piss, a smell that Anthony was used to by now.

After a minute of Mariana standing there, she pulled her leg up and the heel came out of Carlos' eye socket full of blood and brain matter. It didn't seem to faze her that she just killed a man with her bare hands, or in this case her feet. Nothing seemed to faze this woman at all. Nothing seemed to scare her either. Mariana strolled back over to Anthony and helped him to his feet. Anthony was finally able to get a good amount of air into his lungs but it hurt very much to breathe. Mariana helped him over to a chair and then moved over to help Mike. "Is he alive?" asked Anthony.

Mariana felt for Mike's pulse and then answered, "Yes. He's just unconscious." More vans could be heard pulling up outside. Mariana grabbed her radio and spoke into it in Spanish, instructing her men to come downstairs to help her with Anthony and Mike. A few moments went by and Mariana was able to awaken Mike while her men were coming down to assist.

Anthony got to his feet once again and went to his hurt friend. "You okay Bro?"

A dazed Mike nodded his head but was barely able to speak from the blow that Carlos gave him to the throat. Mike looked over to the body and then back to Anthony. "You did that?" he asked in a sore raspy voice.

Mariana started to make her way up the stairs and replied, "No Michael, I did. Come along we must go." Mariana's bodyguards helped the two wounded friends make their way out of the basement.

Mariana's men went through the house looking for any Perez soldiers that were still alive. Every now and then a shot could be heard coming from either inside the house or outside and that indicated that another one was found alive and executed. Any of her men that were alive were helped up and headed out of the house. All but one that is.

Three of her men were heading in Mariana's direction. Two of them were holding up a wounded man. She stepped in front of them and they stopped. She looked at the wounded man and he looked up at her. She had a dark look on her face. In an instant her expression changed to a look of anger. She looked in Mike's direction and said, "Michael, wait outside with the girls." Mike nodded at Anthony and then made his way out of the house.

Mariana stepped closer to the wounded man and he had a look of fear come across his face. "¿Tu tinias que proteger la puertorriqueña?"

The two men holding up the injured man let him go and stepped to the side. He looked at them and then looked back at Mariana, he began trembling. Mariana continued staring at him intently. After a second he slowly and cautiously replied, "Si, Mariana." Between the pain that the guy was in and the fear that had come over him he could barely speak and he could hardly stand. He shook uncontrollably with fear. He locked eyes with Mariana and she stared at him patiently. Behind her dark beautiful eyes he could tell a fire raged.

After a second Mariana spoke again, "Fallaste."

Tears streamed down the wounded man's face. Anthony couldn't tell if it was from what Mariana was saying to him or if it was from his wounds. After a second Mariana took a step back from him, reached onto her belt and pulled out her knife. In a split second she slashed the guy's throat. Anthony stepped back and watched in horror as the guy clutched his gushing throat. Blood spewed out of his neck, like a faucet had been turned on at a sink. Mariana's men stood unmoved. After a second or so the guy dropped to the floor and began gurgling on his blood. He withered around for a minute and then he finally stopped. Mariana looked down at him and then put her bloody knife back into the sheath on her belt.

Mariana picked her gaze up from the fallen man and motioned to her other two men. "Incendie la casa."

Both men said at the same time, "Si Mariana," and went to obey their orders.

Mariana did an about face and headed out of the house and Anthony followed. "What just happened there Mariana? He was your own man."

"He failed to protect Lourdes." Mariana moved over to one of her men as Anthony stayed behind and watched her.

After a minute he moved away from the house towards Debbie and her family. Debbie broke free from her mother and ran to him in tears. He put out his hands to her, not so much to hold her, but to prepare for the pain of her crashing into his fractured ribs. "Easy Sweetheart, easy."

"Are you okay?" she asked concerned.

Anthony gently hugged her and replied, "Yeah, I'm fine. Just a few fractured ribs, that's all." He held her for a second and then pulled slowly away from her and looked at her bruised and swollen face. "Are you okay?"

Debbie had tears streaming down her face. It hurt to cry, Carlos had hit her hard. She now knew partially what Cristina had been through and she understood why Anthony was so angry. She could see that Anthony was angry and she didn't want to enflame the situation anymore then it was. "Yeah, I'm fine." She went quite for a second and then asked him, "Where is Carlos?" Anthony gave her a look as if to say, 'Don't ask.' She stared at him for a second and then asked, "Did you…?"

Anthony responded, "No. Mariana did." Debbie closed her eyes and gently placed her head on his chest. He looked up at Lourdes who was staring at them. "Are you okay?" he asked.

Lourdes nodded her head and smiled at him, he smiled back. Mariana made her way towards them and said, "I hate to break this party up but we have to get out of here. My men are burning down the house and the police will be here soon."

Anthony said to Debbie, "Go with your family to the GNX. I'll be right there. Mike, you head out too."

Debbie, her mother and sister headed over to the shot up Grand National, Mike headed towards his Cutlass. Anthony asked, "Mariana, where are you going?"

"To one of my other safe houses. I will be in touch with you shortly. You and your family will be safe now."

Anthony replied, "I know." He went silent for a second. "Thank you."

Mariana smiled at him and touched the side of his face gently like she did so many times throughout the last day and night. "Go home and rest Mi Amor, I will talk to you soon."

Anthony smiled and made his way to the GNX. Mariana looked at her shot up safe house. Smoke could be seen coming out of the windows and flames started crackling. She looked around the street. Her men had cleaned up the street of any bodies and placed them in the house that was now quickly going up in flames. Mariana moved to her van and her two trusty bodyguards took up their usual place behind her. She one last look at the house. Explosions could now be heard going off inside the house as the other vans started pulling out and away from the inferno. Mariana got inside the van and her two men followed and closed the door. After a second the van pulled away as the GNX sped past her heading in the opposite direction with the Cutlass close behind. As Mariana's van got to the corner it stopped next to Carlos' blue Corvette. The driver rolled the van window down and tossed a flaming cocktail bomb into the driver's side window of the car and then sped off as the Corvette burst into flames. Mariana watched in the rear view mirror as the house let out one final explosion and was consumed into a total fireball. One of many fires that she was responsible for setting across the city in the past day.

Chapter 27
News Flash

As much as Anthony tried to rest he couldn't. It had been two days since the attack on Mariana's safe house and all he could do was go over it in his mind. He kept replaying everything that happened from Flushing hospital to the burning of Mariana's house. He had gotten very little sleep over the last two days and he wasn't sure how much longer he could go without a full night's sleep.

He slowly sat up in bed and winced in pain as he righted himself. Brenda had patched him up again, but she warned him that his ribs would take several weeks to fully heal. He looked around the dark bedroom for a minute and then slowly stood up and headed out into the hallway. He paused for a second and listened to Debbie downstairs watching TV. She had gone back to being quiet again after the war. She hadn't fought with him, but he could tell that she was really affected by what went on. She had issues with his friendship with Lourdes, issues with his job, issues with Mariana, issues all the way around.

He made his way slowly and painfully down the stairs and into the living room. Like he thought, Debbie was on the couch watching TV, the news to be exact. The news was flooded with information regarding the war between the two cartels.

Without shifting her eyes from the TV to Anthony she asked, "Do you want something to eat?"

Anthony stood quietly in the living room looking at her for a minute before he replied, "No." Slowly he made his way to the couch and carefully lowered himself into the seat next to her. "Watching the news?"

"Yep," she replied.

After letting out a long, deep, painful breath Anthony turned to Debbie who never looked back, she just stared at the TV set. "Why?" he asked.

After a moment of silence she replied coldly, "I have to find out from somewhere what happened."

Anthony closed his eyes and took in another deep breath. "Debbie, I really don't want to fight with you."

"I don't want to fight with you either."

Anthony turned back to the TV set as she raised the volume when the news came back on. On the screen were pictures of burning apartment buildings, factories and houses all across the city. After a minute of the images a news reporter was shown with a burnt out house behind him while he spoke into the camera. 'This story has played out so many times over the past three days all across the five boroughs of New York City. Apartment building after apartment building, house after house. Nothing has been left untouched. Bodegas, factories, businesses, even hospitals. You name it and it has been attacked in some sort of way. The body count as it stands now is one hundred and sixty four dead and that is sure to go up. What appears to be all the signs of an underground war between drug cartels, also appears to be completely one-sided. Almost all the bodies that have been identified seem to belong to a known drug cartel run by the Perez brothers, based out of the Dominican Republic.'

Pictures of the fallen brothers were flashed on the screen.

'We say one sided because none of the other bodies have been identified belonging to any other cartel or crime family. About sixty of the victims actually belonged to the cartel the rest of the people have been identified as family members of the victims.'

Anthony sat uncomfortably in the seat as Debbie ventured a glance out of the corner of her eye at him. "Family members huh?"

"Deb, I didn't go around killing people. It's not what you think."

Debbie turned her gaze back at the news broadcast. "You don't even want to know what I think."

'We have been told by some of the responding police and EMS units that some victims of this massacre are infants, only a few months old and seniors in their seventies and eighties as well. What investigators are trying to determine now is who is responsible for this. There have been no witnesses to come forward regarding any of the shootings or the fires across New York City and police have come up completely empty in their search for an opposing force. Some are speculating it was a rival cartel and the motive was a bad drug deal. Never before has an underground war been fought that caused so much bloodshed in a two day span. Investigators are certain of one thing though. The police are sure the body count is going to continue to rise and some fear this is only the beginning.'

Anthony struggled to stand up as Debbie turned off the TV. Slowly he made his way into the kitchen to get something to drink. After a minute Debbie followed him into the kitchen. After an awkward moment of silence she asked him, "Why won't you talk to me about this whole thing?"

Anthony moved to a chair and slowly lowered himself into it. He motioned for her to come and sit next to him and she did. "Deb, it's not that I don't want to talk to you about this."

"Then what is it?"

"This wasn't easy for me to see or to be a part of." Anthony paused for a second and then exhaled. "This wasn't easy for me to do."

Debbie let out a sigh of her own. "I know that none of this could have been easy." She reached over and took a sip of his drink.

Anthony reached out and touched her hand. "I didn't go out and kill people Debbie.

A tear streamed down from Debbie's right eye. "The news said infants were murdered."

Anthony shrugged away at the news. "Don't believe half of what they are reporting Debbie."

"They wouldn't make up the deaths of children Anthony."

Anthony took a sip of his drink and then poured another. "Deb, I am not going to deny that terrible things were done. I didn't witness infants being killed, and you can bet that if that was going to take place in front of me I would have put a stop to it."

Debbie remained quiet for a minute. "This woman that is your friend, she is responsible for all this?" Anthony remained motionless for a minute and then he slowly nodded his head. Debbie closed her eyes as if she didn't want to really know the answer to that question. "How do you know this woman again?"

"I told you, she's part of a Colombian cartel and is in charge of their operation in the Northeast. I've been on a few deals with her and her organization."

"A few deals and she declared war for you like this?" Before Anthony could answer her she said, "I'm sorry, but I don't buy that. There is more there between you two for her to do this."

"It's really not like that Debbie."

"Explain it to me then," she shot back.

Anthony thought to himself how he could possibly explain to her what Mariana's motives were and why she did what she did. There was no way she would believe him about Mariana when he himself didn't believe her. "Well, this woman claims she can see things."

Debbie looked at him with the look that he knew she was going to give him. "See things?"

"Believe me Debbie, I am right there with you when it comes to her abilities that she claims to have."

Debbie smirked and laughed out loud. "What does she say she sees?"

Anthony allowed a smirk to come across his face before he continued. "She claims that somewhere in the future she sees me as a very powerful person in my line of work."

"A powerful person?" she asked.

"According to her, yes."

"And according to you, you can't even be made so how is it possible that you are going to be this powerful person?"

Anthony put a frown on, "I don't know, but that is what she said she saw. I don't believe it myself, but after the conversation I had with my associates and their lack of interest in my situation, I had no choice but to align myself with her. She offered to help me with the Perez brothers because of this vision she claimed she had. She said she sees the two of us running things down the road and she would need to intervene if I were to survive." Debbie shook her head again in disbelief. "Debbie I know how it sounds, but what else could I do? What else could we do? This guy put your sister in the hospital just to get to me. You saw how they attacked the hospital. Do you think after that mess they were just going to go home and forget about it?" Debbie thought about it for a minute and then conceded the point. "There was no way Carlos or the Perez brothers were going to let me, your sister or anyone else in your family live after what took place at the hospital, including you." Debbie looked him in the eyes. "There was nothing else that could be done. The people I work for weren't going to get involved; not the way I needed them to."

Debbie thought about that for a minute and then asked him, "How did you want them to deal with it?"

That was a question he didn't want to answer, but he knew he needed to so she could understand why Mariana intervened. "I asked them to take out the Perez brothers, Carlos and Luis, but they refused. They told me that I'm not made and what I was asking for wasn't about business. They didn't want to get involved."

"I told you about this job. You have done so many things for them, and God knows what else I don't know about, and this is how they repay you."

"They told me to handle it myself." Anthony paused. "It was obvious that I wouldn't be able to handle something like this alone so that's when Mariana got involved."

Debbie shuddered at the mention of Mariana's name again. "I can't stand that woman!"

Anthony remained quiet for a minute. He squeezed her hand, "Deb, listen to me. I know this entire thing with her sounds crazy, but what I am telling you is exactly how it went down." Anthony went quiet for a second and then continued, "No matter how you look at it, no matter how you feel about her, one thing is certain."

"What's that?" she asked.

"If it wasn't for her, all of us would probably be dead right now. I can't count the times she saved my life. Believe me, I don't buy any of her stories, but I can't deny that if it wasn't for her I wouldn't be here right now having this conversation."

Debbie sat there and let that sink in for a minute. She knew Anthony was right, he was always right. When Carlos hit her that was only a small fraction of what he inflicted on her sister. She now understood why Anthony felt like he did towards Carlos. Overall it was a series of unfortunate events that led to what took place. She dreaded the night at the club when she introduced Anthony to her two sisters. If it wasn't for that night, all of this would have never taken place. She couldn't dwell on that now, she had to put that thought out of her head. She wasn't happy with what took place over the past few days, but she needed to try and move on. She said to him, "Well, there has been one good piece of news over the last day."

"What's that?" asked Anthony.

"Cristina is breathing on her own again."

Anthony's eyes lit up, "That's great!"

Debbie replied, "Yeah, it is. They took her off the respirator last night and she has been breathing on her own since. They don't think they will have to put her back on it."

Anthony closed his eyes and said, "Thank God. I'm glad to hear that."

Debbie squeezed Anthony's hand and he squeezed it back. After a minute she got up from her chair and moved over to his and sat gently on his lap. She put her arms around him and laid her head on top of his. He put his arms around her and held her as tight as he could without hurting his fractured ribs. "I love you Anthony."

"I love you to Debbie, more than you can imagine."

Debbie knew he loved her. He had to if he did what he did over the past several days. She didn't doubt his love for her. She knew he loved her sisters too. She thought about that for a moment. It was that loved that frightened her more than anything else though.

Chapter 28
Setting The Peace

Activity at the social club was busy today. There were legions of made guys, capos, associates and wise guys alike up and down the street. A boss was on his way to the club today to discuss the war between Mariana and the Perez brothers. This was known as showing the flag. Almost the entire organization was out in full force, in full dress, to show their allegiance to their leader. It was a sign of respect. It was a sign of fear.

As Anthony had predicted, the elimination of the Perez brother's organization had created a power vacuum. Now, anyone could step in and try to replace them. Chinese, Russian, Jamaican; the list was un-ending. Mariana was not about to let that that happen. She had her foot in the door with her cartel and knowing her she wasn't going to let another organization step in where she was poised to be.

Anthony received the call the night before. He needed to be at the club, well dressed. Not only to show the flag, but to be part of a sit down regarding the Perez brothers. He was nervous about it. When he heard the club was showing the flag he knew a boss was going to be there. He wasn't sure where this was going to lead. He knew the family wasn't providing back up with his problem, but he also knew Mariana might have gone overboard with her response to the situation. She was also slated to be part of the sit down. As he thought more and more about it he knew it was going to be an interesting day to say the least.

Mike and Anthony arrived at the club together. Enzo was seated outside talking to a few of the other guys. They made their way through the crowd as they said their hellos to some of the other guys. Enzo stood up when Anthony approached and offered out a hug to him. They greeted with a kiss cheek to cheek after the hug. Enzo then locked eyes with Mike and nodded at him. "How are you feeling Ant?"

"I'm okay Enzo, you?"

Enzo replied, "I'm fine," and eyed Anthony up and down. "You look like you had quite the ride the other night."

Anthony smiled and tried not to make too much of what Enzo was saying. "Not really."

Enzo patted him on the back as the crowd of people began to turn their attention towards the street. A black, stretch, Cadi limo pulled up and everyone began quieting down. Anthony looked through the crowd and watched as the driver got out and made his way towards the back door and opened it. An older man, dressed in a very expensive suit and fedora hat, emerged from the back of the car. The driver placed an over coat on his shoulders and guided him onto the curb.

The Old Man, as he was referred to, looked around at the gazing crowd of men while he smoked his cigar. No one dared say anything to him as he stood looking at his organization. He was in charge of this family. As he stood there, taking in the site before him, he exuded pure power. Not quite the same power that Mariana portrayed. It was similar, but different at the same time.

After a minute another older gentleman got out of the limo and walked up behind him. He too was dressed in an expensive tailored suit and wore a fedora hat. They conversed for a minute and then made their way through the crowd and into the social club.

Once they were fully inside and out of sight, conversation resumed amongst the organization, but at a lower tone. Anthony and Mike had walked slightly away from the club, but still in sight of everyone. Mike looked at Anthony who held his gaze. "How do you think this is going to go?"

Anthony thought about it for a minute. "Honestly, I don't know. I will make sure you're not part of it though."

Mike waved Anthony off and said, "Listen, we're in this together. You would have had my back the same way I had yours. I'm just sorry I couldn't do more against that asshole when he charged me."

"Mike, you got nothing to apologize to me for. The way you described it there was nothing you could have done. The only reason I got the drop on him was because he was preoccupied with Lourdes."

Mike thought about it for a minute and then agreed. Mickey made his way through the crowd towards Anthony and Mike. "Hey guys," he said. Mike and Anthony turned towards their friend. "How are the two of you doing?"

Anthony reached towards his ribs and replied, "A little sore."

Mickey smiled and said, "I could only imagine." He looked around for a minute and then tilted his head towards the club. "Come on, they are ready to talk to you."

Nervously Anthony looked at Mike, who returned the look back. Mike slapped Anthony on the back and they made their way into the club. The club itself was packed with guys, all talking business. It was lined wall to wall with people; Anthony had never seen it so crowded. It looked like the entire family was here. There had to be over two hundred people located inside and out.

Mickey guided them towards a small room in the back and opened the door. Already seated was Frankie the Hand and seated next to him was the second guy to come out of the limo right behind The Old Man. Anthony and Mike entered the room and Mickey closed the door behind them.

Frankie stood up and motioned for the boys to come in. They entered the room further and the other guy stood up from his seat. Frankie said, "Leo, this is Anthony and Mike. Guys, this is Leo, the Underboss to The Old Man."

Anthony and Mike both made their way towards Leo and when he extended his hand they both shook it. "It's nice to meet you Leo," said Anthony.

Leo nodded to both of them and then motioned at the chairs in front of them. "Take a seat boys." He talked in a raspy voice with a bit of broken English. "Do you two want something to drink?"

At the same time both Mike and Anthony replied, "No, thank you."

Leo motioned and everyone took a seat. He took a long drag from his cigar and looked at the two of them. After a tense minute of long silence he pointed at Frankie and said, "Frankie here tells me good things about the two of you." Anthony and Mike both looked over at Frankie, who gently nodded his head towards them. "He tells me that the two of you are good earners."

Feeling he should say something Anthony replied, "We try our best."

Leo locked eyes with Anthony as he took a long drag from his cigar. After a few seconds it felt like a staring contest. Anthony was unwilling to break the contact, no matter how uncomfortable he began to feel. After a moment it was Leo that broke it. "Frankie tells me you two have done good work with the business that we have given to you, so I was surprised to hear all over the news this unfortunate incident that occurred with some of our friends. Frankie told me of the issues you had with the Perez brothers."

Anthony looked at both Frankie and Leo, "There were some things that couldn't be avoided."

Leo pulled another long drag from his cigar and stared at Anthony again. "Really now?"

Before Anthony could answer there was a knock on the door. Frankie motioned for Mike to answer it and he got up and did. Mickey walked into the room and said to Frankie, "Mariana is here."

Leo replied, "Send her in, we're just getting started."

Mickey backed out of the doorway and after a second Mariana walked into the room with two of her trusty bodyguards behind her. This time they didn't have AK-47's in their hands but you can bet they had some kind of firepower on them. Leo looked up at them and said, "Tell your guys to wait outside. This is a meeting, not a fucking shakedown."

Mariana brazenly locked eyes with Leo and gave him a look that could melt ice. Anthony had never seen anyone talk to her like that, but then again Leo didn't work for her and she didn't work for Leo. Like he thought before, this was going to be interesting. Mariana slowly guided her eyes towards Anthony and he slowly motioned to her that it would be okay. She looked at her bodyguards and motioned for them to leave the room. Mariana then made her way around the table and sat next to Anthony.

Frankie said to Mariana, "We were just getting started. Mariana, this is Leo, the Underboss of our family. Leo, this is Mariana. She is in charge of her organizations interests here in the Northeast."

Leo locked in Mariana's icy look and acknowledged her. After a second she did the same. Leo then turned his attention back at Anthony. "I want to know what the hell went on in this city with the Perez brothers. I heard what Frankie told me, but I want to know how an entire cartel, along with their families, were completely wiped out."

Mariana looked at Leo before Anthony could answer. "My organization had some internal problems with the Perez brothers." Leo shifted his look from Anthony to Mariana to Mike and then back to Mariana.

"Internal problems huh?" asked Leo.

Mariana smirked. "It's between the Spanish organizations. This had nothing to do with your manpower or family."

Leo took a drag from his cigar. "I'm having problems buying that load of shit Mariana."

Very nonchalantly Mariana replied, "I really don't care what you buy or not." Anthony and Mike were completely taken back by Mariana's response to Leo. They both caught each other's gaze out of the corners of their eyes. "Your men might have had an issue with the Perez brothers, but the conflict that arose between my organization and theirs had nothing to do with it."

Leo let out a puff of smoke and stared at Frankie, who remained quiet. After a second he gazed back at Mariana again. "What kind of an issue did you have with them Mariana."

"That's my concern Leo. When your family has an issue with one of the other four families we don't get involved, so I would appreciate it if you stay out of my issues. What went on was between them and I, and I settled it."

Leo let out a long and annoyed sigh. Then he asked Anthony, "Is that your story too?"

Anthony looked at Frankie who remained motionless. Frankie knew the truth, but he wasn't guiding Anthony in either direction. After a minute he agreed. He wasn't going to admit to the Underboss of the family that he did most of his work for, that he was part of a massacre over his girlfriend's sister at a barbeque. He figured let Mariana take the lead on it. She seemed to be holding her own against Leo as it was and he was impressed.

Leo shifted his gaze towards Mike, who after a second also agreed. It was evident that Leo was frustrated with the situation and quiet had set into the room as everyone tried to figure out where to go next. Mike tried to break the ice. "Listen, whatever happened here happened and it's over. The idea now is to move on and figure out the best way to do that."

Leo said, "You think it's that easy?"

Anthony thought about it for a second and then responded, "Yeah, it actually is."

Leo sat back in his seat, surprised by Anthony's answer. Frankie cocked an eyebrow towards Mike who now just remained quiet. "We had a long standing relationship with the Perez brothers. We made a lot of money with them and we always worked peacefully with them. This massacre isn't going to go away that easy. There are issues within the Dominican Republic now and they're going to want answers."

"The issue here is what happens in New York, not DR" said Mariana.

"And we're supposed to just ignore DR?" asked Leo.

Mariana thought about it for a minute. "I will deal with any fallout from DR."

Leo ventured a look over to Frankie. After a second Frankie asked, "Why do I get the impression that DR has already been dealt with?"

Mariana allowed a rare smile to come across her face, but it was more of a smirk. After a second she nodded her head without verbally committing that she had already dealt with DR. This admission appeared to shake up Leo and Frankie. Mariana could tell that they were now nervous. "Gentlemen, the issue here at hand is what happens to the void that the Perez brothers have left."

Leo said, "Why do I think you already have a solution to that problem?"

Mariana smirked again and replied, "I am able, and willing, to step into that void. My organization is prepared to fill in any distribution losses caused by the Perez brothers."

Leo sat up straight and glared at her across the table. "You think you can really fill that void?"

"Completely."

"That's a tall order Mariana. The reason why we deal with multiple cartels is because no single one can fulfill the high demand that we have. What makes you think you can fill that order now?"

Mariana thought about the question for a while. "When you began dealing with my organization we were small. In the time that has passed we have since grown and have tripled our production of your product."

Frankie looked at Anthony and Mariana. He now lit up a cigar and blew the smoke across the table. "With this increase of supply what is it going to cost us?"

Mariana thought about it for a second. "I'm not looking to be greedy. I will continue selling to your family at the current rate that we have now."

Leo sat back in his chair to think about it. Frankie leaned over and whispered something in his ear and they began quietly talking to each other in Italian. Feeling there was an opportunity to put this to bed Anthony cleared his throat. Leo and Frankie halted their private conversation and looked at him. "You have something you want to add Anthony?" asked Frankie.

"Possibly." Feeling more relaxed now Anthony stood up and made his way to the bar and poured himself a glass of wine. Mike gazed at him across the room, marveling at how Anthony began to carry himself. Anthony composed his thoughts as he made his way back to his seat with his glass of wine, everyone in the room hanging on his coming words. "Well, I am thinking, in the spirit of peace and putting this whole thing behind us," Anthony turned his attention towards Mariana and continued, "with the increased supply of your product, your cartel is going to be looking at more than double the profits."

Mariana asked, "What are you thinking Antonio?"

"Since our family will be pulling in more of your product, and there is no real competition for you anymore, why don't you keep selling your original amount of kilos at the original price and anything over that amount that you have to cover from the Perez brothers you do at a discounted rate."

Mariana locked eyes with Anthony and thought about his proposal. She slowly looked at Leo and Frankie and then back at Anthony. After a minute she sat forward and looked again at Leo. "How much of a discount are you looking for?"

Leo and Frankie gazed at one another, but neither had an answer. They were just about to agree to pay everything at the set amount before Anthony jumped in with his idea, now they were at a loss for words by being caught off guard. Leo motioned towards Anthony and decided to shift the burden to him. "This was your idea, *Antonio*, you come up with the number."

All eyes in the room shifted back towards Anthony's direction. Anthony allowed a slight smirk to come across his face at the way Leo pronounced Anthony's name. He thought about it for a long minute before he asked Mariana, "One thousand a key less?"

Frankie gave Leo a look that said she would never go for it. There was silence in the room, you could hear a pin drop while Mariana mulled Anthony's proposal. After a long second she countered with, "Five hundred."

Before Leo or Frankie could answer Anthony came back with, "Let's split the difference, seven fifty."

Mariana thought about it again for a long minute and then agreed, "Seven fifty it is." She slowly smiled at Anthony who returned her smile. After a second he looked over to Leo and Frankie for their approval.

Leo and Frankie looked at each other and then nodded in agreement. Leo sat forward again and said, "Deal."

Mariana stood up and said, "Very good."

Leo and Frankie stood up and then Mike and Anthony rose. Frankie gave out glasses of wine to everyone who didn't have them and Leo offered up a toast: "To our business."

Everyone in the room raised their glasses and everyone toasted, "To our business," and drank their wine.

Mariana put down her glass. "Remember gentlemen, this was your man that brokered this deal," Mariana said as she pointed towards Anthony. "I am glad we could come to an agreement here today."

Frankie replied, "I am glad as well Mariana."

Mariana bowed her head slightly and headed towards the door. Anthony looked towards Frankie and Leo and Frankie said, "We're done guys."

Mariana opened the door and she, Mike and Anthony headed out of the room. Leo motioned to Frankie, who moved towards a window on the far end of the room that looked into the club. He pulled the curtain back and watched Mariana and Anthony head towards the exit of the club talking amongst themselves. "What do you think Leo?"

Leo was quiet as he moved towards the window next to Frankie. "I don't fucking like her. You're not going to tell me it was a coincidence that her cartel had an issue with the Perez brothers at the same time your guy had an issue with them." Frankie shrugged his shoulders towards Leo. "You made it clear to him we weren't sanctioning anything against the Perez brothers?"

"Yeah, of course I did. I told him to protect himself. I didn't think he would do what was done."

Leo stared at Anthony and Mariana in the distance talking to each other. "He's close to her."

"He would have to be if she did that for him." Frankie thought about it some more. "Who knows, maybe they had their own issues with the Perez brothers and it's all a coincidence."

Leo took a long drag from his cigar. "I didn't get as far as I have in this thing of ours taking stupid chances or believing in coincidences like that. Maybe he's fucking her." Leo thought about it some more. "He's dangerous."

"Anthony?" asked Frankie.

Leo replied, "Yeah, if he did get her to do that to the Perez brothers, what else can he get her to do?"

Frankie thought about it for a minute. "Leo, that's the Colombians. They go to the extreme when they do something. You remember that thing on Valentine's Day about ten years ago over in City Line. They whacked an entire family in an apartment, something like eleven people got clipped. The guy they really wanted, they left him alive so he would suffer from the loss of his family."

Leo looked at Frankie out of the corner of his eye while he puffed his cigar. After a second he shook his head, he picked his hat up from the table. "I don't like her, I don't like dealing with women and I don't like dealing with Colombians. You can't trust them." Leo thought about it some more and then repeated again. "He's dangerous, that's all I'm going to say." Leo headed towards the door and reached to open it. He gazed back at Frankie. "He's dangerous, him and his boy." With that Leo opened the door and walked out of the room slamming the door behind him. Frankie shook his head and looked back out the window.

Anthony and Mariana exited the club, the street had started to thin out a bit. Mike remained inside the club, talking to a few guys while Anthony and Mariana walked slowly down the block, her two bodyguards in tow about twenty feet behind them. "I guess that went well," Anthony said.

Mariana replied, "It did. They didn't even suspect we planned that negotiation."

Anthony smirked, "Do you think they really bought that the Perez brothers being wiped out had nothing to do with me?"

It didn't take long for Mariana to reply, "No, not at all." Anthony thought the same. "That's why I agreed to a reduced price for you. I am not sure how much good it did though."

"Why do you say that?"

Mariana looked around the street. The Sun shone on her jet black hair and highlighted her red stripe. She looked as beautiful as always. "They are afraid of you."

Anthony laughed a little, "I doubt they're afraid of me."

"They are Antonio, and it's not a good fear."

Anthony stopped laughing when he realized Mariana was not laughing or smirking. "What do you mean?"

Mariana took a deep breath. "They are worried about you. They don't know where you stand, especially since they weren't the ones to help you and I was." Anthony moved over towards Mike's car and leaned on it, Mariana followed. "You make them nervous because they don't know what you are capable of at this point. You or I."

Anthony thought about that for a minute. "Are you worried about them?"

Mariana now smirked, "I am not afraid of them, but you should be." Anthony locked eyes with her and she reached out and touched his hand. "You have to be careful Mi Amor. In the families you are associated with, it's your friends that come to take care of you, and not in a good way."

Anthony continued staring at her and then replied, "I know."

"Remember what I told you. You can be in power only once these families are gone. You will be a powerful person. The seeds of power have been planted, but they will need time to grow."

Anthony thought about that and looked down the block. Enzo was outside talking to a few guys when Frankie came out and took him inside. Anthony turned his attention back towards Mariana. "Are you going to be okay with everything that went on?"

Mariana smiled at him. Anthony was the only person that could make her smile like that. Anthony was the only person that she ever showed soft emotion to. She replied, "Yes Mi Amor, I will be fine. Don't worry about me."

"How many people did you end up losing in this whole thing?"

Mariana thought about it for a minute and replied, "Seventeen."

Anthony closed his eyes at the number. "All over a drunk asshole at a barbeque." Mariana stared at him with her dark eyes. "Maybe Debbie was right, maybe I overreacted."

Before Anthony could finish she put her finger over his lips to stop him. "It's done. You did what you had to do for someone that you love and there is no changing history. Move on from here."

Anthony smiled at her and said, "Thank you again for everything Mariana. I don't know what I would have done without you and your help."

Mariana smiled warmly at him. She reached over and gently kissed him on the side of his lips. "You're welcome Antonio." Anthony smiled back at her. "I have to go. Remember what I told you, be careful. Trust no one in your organization." Mariana looked down the block at the assembled organization and then back to Anthony. "Your first great pain is nearly upon you. No matter how much this pain hurts you, remember something. This is the least of the three pains that you will go through. They only get worse." Anthony still didn't buy her fortune telling stories, but he decided to listen to her. "This pain that I am talking about is not a physical pain either. It's emotional pain, but it gets so bad that it will feel like physical pain." Anthony reluctantly let that sink in to his mind. "Remember, three women, three pains." Anthony thought about that for a minute longer. Mariana let go of his hand and looked at one of her body guards and motioned for him to get the car ready.

Anthony continued to stare at her as she slowly backed away from him. "Be careful Mariana."

Mariana smiled at him and said, "You to Mi Amor, you to." With that she walked away towards her car, got in and pulled away.

Anthony stayed leaning against the car and lit up a cigar. After a minute Mike came walking over to him and asked, "You okay Bro?"

In deep thought Anthony turned to his friend and said, "Yeah Bro, I'm fine. You?"

Mike replied, "Yeah. Intense meeting huh?"

Anthony continued watching Mariana's car as it drove away. "Yeah."

Mike noticed his friend really wasn't there and tried to snap him out of it. "You sure you're okay?"

"Yeah," replied Anthony.

"Please tell me this girl is not in your head now too."

Anthony laughed at Mikes comment and said, "No, she's not in my head. Come on, let's go get something to eat and then head home."

With that the two friends got in the car and headed away from the club.

Chapter 29
Welcome Home

About a month went by and business was back to normal and the news had died down about the Perez brothers. It was no longer being talked about on the radio or in the newspapers. Mariana's production had ramped up and she was now filling the void that the Perez brothers had left behind in their deaths.

Things between Anthony and Debbie had been on slippery ground since the attack at the hospital. They hadn't spoken about it much, but Anthony could tell she was still bothered by it and still greatly bothered by his work. At some level though Anthony was bothered by his work as well. Something that Mariana had said had gotten into his head and now he was looking over his shoulder at every pass. Maybe she was just being paranoid and she set him off on a paranoid path, but he felt like the hammer was going to drop and something was going to happen to him.

He was trying to put that thought out of his head as today was supposed to be a happy day, Cristina was coming home from the hospital. Anthony was driving over to the hospital to pick her up while Debbie, Lourdes and their mom headed over to Cristina's apartment to clean it up from the mess that was created when Carlos beat her. The girls didn't want Anthony to see the place like that for fear of invoking thoughts of what Cristina went through that night.

Anthony pulled up at the entrance of the hospital and parked the GNX. He had gotten it back only two days before from the body shop. It was badly in need of repair after the war. He had his baby back, now he was getting his friend back. He stopped and looked around the street and flashbacks shot through his mind of the night the Perez brothers assaulted the hospital. He looked down the block towards the loading dock that their group emerged from under heavy fire. He could still hear the bullets flying past him and the smoke of gun powder and death in the air.

He purged the thoughts that were going through his mind and moved up the steps and into the hospital. He looked around and noticed a heavy security presence in the hospital and he was sure it was due to the war. He turned to his left and made his way towards the information desk, when something to his right caught his attention. He turned to look and it was Cristina in a wheelchair being wheeled down the hallway towards him. When they locked eyes Cristina lit up like a Christmas tree. Anthony quickly made his way towards his friend. Cristina attempted to get out of the chair, but the orderly wheeling her out gently held her down saying, "I'm sorry, but you can't leave the chair until you're outside."

Anthony quickly came to her side, knelt down and grabbed hold of her and hugged her tightly as she did the same. At that moment all the emotion from the past month poured out of both of them as they hugged and cried in each other's arms. "I'm so happy to see you Cristina," said Anthony in a very emotional state.

Cristina hugged him tightly and cried at the site of her friend, feeling like she didn't want to let him go. "I'm so happy to see you too!"

Anthony pulled back a bit and gazed into her soft, pretty eyes. Most of the bruising was gone from the assault she had suffered over a month ago. Doctors had managed to set her nose back. You could tell it was broken, but they were sure she would heal and go back to looking completely normal, as if it was never broken. Her arm was still bandaged from the burn. She would have a scar there for the rest of her life, but for the most part she would heal. Her ribs were still sore and that would take time to heal completely. Anthony reached over and gently wiped the tears from her face. When he did she smiled and held his hand close to her face. "I'm sorry, does that hurt to touch?"

Cristina smiled and replied, "No Anthony. On the contrary, it feels so good!" Through all of her hurt, through all of her pain and suffering, she managed to have the warmest smile and the brightest eyes. For the first time since Anthony met her she looked completely at peace and comfort.

Anthony smiled back at her and kissed her softly on her cheek. The orderly touched Anthony on the arm and said, "She has to sign some papers at the desk and then you guys can be on your way." Anthony smiled and stood up as the orderly turned the chair and headed towards the desk.

Anthony watched her at the desk as he wiped his own tears that came with the emotional meeting. He hadn't seen her since the night of the attack and she was hardly conscious then. He couldn't bring himself to look at her after that night. All the rush of the hurt came back to him when he thought about it. She looked broken and he didn't want to see her like that. Debbie had explained it to her and she was more than understanding. He also needed to avoid the hospital in case the police wanted to talk to him about the attack. By now it had died down enough where he felt he could go back there. While in his thoughts he heard his name called from behind, "Antonio."

Anthony turned around and saw Mariana's two main body guards coming towards him. The younger one stopped as the older one, known as Roberto, approached him. "Hola Antonio, how are you?"

Caught by surprise that they were there and that one was actually speaking English to him, smiling, he said, "I'm okay. What are you two doing here?" Nervously he looked around but he didn't see Mariana.

Laughing, the bodyguard replied, "It is okay Antonio, don't be nervous. Mariana is not here and we are not here to hurt you. We have had a guard or two here since the night of the attack and Mariana wanted to make sure your friend was safe, even after the war."

Anthony calmed down a bit and smiled. "Thank you for all you and your organization have done."

Roberto put his arm on Anthony's shoulder and then gently slapped him on his back. "Mariana sends her regards."

"How is she? I haven't seen her in a few weeks."

Smiling, Roberto said, "She is doing well. She worries about you though. She doesn't trust your friends."

Anthony laughed out loud, "Tell her I am doing okay." Roberto smiled and looked over towards Cristina checking out. "I didn't know you spoke English Roberto."

Roberto replied, "Not many in our organization do. I have been guarding Mariana for such a long time I figured when we were sent to America I better learn."

Anthony laughed and asked, "How long have you been guarding her?"

Roberto thought about it for a minute and said, "Since she was a very little girl."

Anthony laughed, "I can't imagine Mariana as a little girl."

Roberto now laughed out loud and said, "Even then she was a handful."

"I bet."

After a second they both began laughing again. "I just wanted to say hello Antonio. I am glad your friend is better and leaving this place. Our job is done here, she is your responsibility now. Take care of her and yourself Antonio."

They strolled towards the entrance of the hospital as the orderly began wheeling Cristina towards them. Anthony turned towards Roberto. "I will Roberto, thank you again for everything. Give Mariana my love."

Anthony shook Roberto's hand and Roberto slapped him on the back again and said, "I will." Roberto smiled at Cristina, then motioned to his companion to follow and left the hospital.

"Who was that Anthony?" asked Cristina.

Anthony watched Roberto and his friend leave and then replied, "Just a friend. Come on, are you ready to go home?"

"Yes!" she excitedly replied.

Anthony laughed and they went outside. Once through the sliding door of the entrance the orderly said, "Okay, now you can get out of the chair." Anthony reached down and took Cristina by the hand and slowly helped her out of the chair. She smiled at the orderly, who smiled back at her. After a second the orderly pulled the chair back and headed back into the hospital.

"Are you okay?"

"Yes," replied Cristina.

"Good, let's take you home." Cristina smiled and they made their way to the GNX. Anthony helped her get in and then they headed out of there towards home. She only lived a few minutes away, so it would be a short ride. Anthony said, "There are a few things we should talk about."

Cristina replied, "Okay."

Anthony trained his eyes back on the road. "Your sisters and your mom cleaned up the house so you don't have to worry about any of that. Have your sisters or anyone told you about anything that happened from the night that you were attacked?"

"No, I have seen some of the news though about the attack on the hospital and the fighting that took place afterwards throughout the city. Was that all related to me?"

Hesitantly, Anthony replied, "Kind of, but it's a little more complicated than that."

"What do you mean?"

Anthony tried to figure out how to word what he wanted to say, but there was no easy way to say it. "This whole thing was sparked from the barbeque and the guy I burned on the grill. When Carlos beat you that night and put you in the hospital, he did that as a trap to get me."

Confused, Cristina was not understanding what he was saying. "I don't think so Anthony. The last thing I remember was talking on the phone to Lourdes about the barbeque. I said something like 'fuck Luis' and Carlos was standing behind me. I didn't know he was there. When he heard that he went into a rage. He beat me for what I said."

Anthony hated hearing that. "Sweetheart, listen to me. One of the first things you have to try and do is stop taking blame for him hitting you. You didn't do anything wrong or say anything wrong to warrant him hitting you and doing the things to you that he did."

Cristina thought about that for a minute and then said, "I know, you're right."

"Did you have any idea that Carlos was tied to a drug cartel run by the Perez brothers?"

Cristina thought about it for a minute and then replied, "No, he never mentioned anything like that. I know his friend that you put in the hospital had ties to them and he hung around Carlos' shop all the time. They were close friends."

Anthony thought about it and tried to put the pieces of the puzzle together in his mind. After a minute he said to her, "I think Carlos let his friend and that cartel run things through his shop. Carlos contacted the Perez brothers shortly after the barbeque about what happened to Luis. In turn the Perez brothers went to the Italian families that I work for and made a beef; they wanted me. The families wouldn't turn me over to them, but they wouldn't help me against them either." Cristina shook her head in disbelief. "They put a price on my head and when Carlos beat you he was using you as bait to draw me out in the open. He thought that I would have come to the house that night to help you, and I would have, but I left to go to work and I didn't have my pager on me when Lourdes was trying to get in touch with me. I forgot it at home. Your family came to the house and took you to the hospital and his trap didn't work."

"I don't remember any of that, I barely remember being at the hospital that night."

Anthony continued, "You were pretty out of it. Carlos had a hit squad outside the house waiting for me to come. When I didn't and your family took you to the hospital they moved the hit squad to the hospital. I got here minutes before they did. Five minutes later and they would have got me coming up the steps of the hospital."

Cristina closed her eyes and tried her best to hold back the tears. Anthony reached over and held her hand as she squeezed his tightly back. "Oh my God, is that when the shootout took place that everyone in the hospital was talking about?"

Anthony replied, "Yeah, I noticed some weird looking people outside the hospital near my car and then I started noticing more people up and down the street."

"What did you do?"

"I called someone that I knew was going to help me and she came with some people." Anthony thought about it for a second and then said, "People is an understatement, she came with an army, the shootout then took place, inside the hospital and outside." Cristina listened intently. "She got me and your family out of the hospital and to what we thought was a safe place."

Cristina asked, "What do you mean what you thought was a safe place?"

"Carlos was parked someplace outside the hospital watching the firefight. My friend's army completely overwhelmed and eliminated the hit squad that was sent for me. We all went back to her safe house and she gathered a bigger army for a counter attack on the Perez brothers."

"That was the gang fighting that took place across the city that I've been seeing on TV?"

Anthony replied, "Yes, what we didn't know was while we were out attacking the Perez brothers throughout the night, Carlos had followed us back from the hospital to the safe house."

"Oh no! What did he do?"

Anthony thought about it for a minute. "When we were out fighting he was gathering another army, about ten or so men, and he attacked the safe house while we were finishing up our fighting with the Perez brothers. We found out about it from Lourdes as he was attacking and I headed back to the safe house." Anthony went silent while he replayed it in his mind.

Cristina could tell that he was reliving it and she squeezed his hand. After a moment she asked, "Are you okay?"

After a second he replied, "Yeah."

"What happened then?"

"I got to the house just in the nick of time. He had your family trapped in the basement and had knocked out my friend Mike. He pretty much knocked out Debbie and he had Lourdes pinned against the wall. I came in quietly and snuck up behind him. Before he could do anything to your sister I stopped him and we fought."

Cristina closed her eyes and shook her head slowly. Anthony turned the GNX on the corner of her block and she looked out the window. "What happened then?"

Anthony pulled the GNX into a spot across the street from her house and shut the car off. After a moment she shifted her look from out the window into Anthony's eyes. Anthony stared into her beautiful eyes for a moment and noticed them start to well up with tears. He let go of her hand and cupped her face and wiped her tears as they slowly streamed down her pretty face. She gently rested her face into his hand and stared at him intently. "We fought, furiously, back and forth until I got the better of him, but in the process of it I was hurt myself. He got me in a bear hug and squeezed until he fractured several of my ribs."

Cristina cried harder now at the pain that Anthony went through. Anthony reached with his other hand and wiped the tears coming out of the opposite eye. "Go on," she said, her voice cracking with emotion.

"We were both down, him worse than me. At that time my friend Mariana arrived and she checked on me, then went over to him. He was pretty out of it, bleeding from his face and the top of his head. He had a shattered hand and wrist, his head was fractured as well." Anthony went silent and looked outside. After a minute he said, "The rest is history, you don't need to know the details."

Anthony tried to let her go, but she put pressure on his hand not wanting to move her face away from it. "No!" Cristina went into silence for a minute. "I want to know what happened, please."

Anthony took a deep breath. "Mariana stood up and looked over at me as I was trying to get to my knees. Then she looked down at him, lifted up her leg and drove down her high heel through his eye and into his brain. She killed him almost instantly."

Cristina closed her eyes for a minute and then let his hand go. Anthony reached over and stroked her long hair away from her face. "Are you okay Sweetheart?"

After a second she opened her eyes. After another minute she smiled at him and replied, "Yeah, I'm fine."

Anthony shifted himself in the seat and took her hands. "Listen to me, okay? This is important." Cristina hung on his every word. "If anyone comes to you like police, law enforcement or anyone at all looking for him, the last time you saw him was when he beat you up. They took you to the hospital and you never saw him again. You have no idea where he went or where he could be. Do you understand?"

Cristina looked at him intently, wiped the remaining tears from her face and then responded, "I understand."

"Good." Anthony tried to get out of the car and she grabbed his arms and reached out and hugged him.

"Anthony, I am so sorry you had to go through all of that over him and us."

Anthony hugged her for a minute and then pulled away. "You have nothing at all to be sorry for. Do you understand me?" Cristina agreed with him. "You, Lourdes, NO ONE! You don't ever have to apologize to me. You never did anything wrong and you have nothing to be sorry for." Cristina thought about it and looked at him intently. "Listen, for what it's worth he died quickly. If anyth…"

"Anthony," Cristina cut him off, "I don't care if he felt pain or not. He doesn't mean anything to me and as far as I'm concerned, any pain that he did feel wasn't enough."

Anthony let that sink in for a minute. After a second he smiled at her and said, "Come on, let's go inside."

Cristina smiled at him and said, "Okay."

They both exited the car and headed across the street towards her apartment. Cristina opened the front door to the building and they headed down the long hallway to her apartment door. Before she could reach for the knob the door opened and standing inside were her two sisters and her mother. Cristina was met by the three of them yelling "WELCOME HOME!"

Overcome with emotion, Cristina's family pulled her into the apartment and began hugging her and crying. Anthony stepped back into the hallway and watched the reunion between the four women with tears in his own eyes. After a minute or so everyone made their way into the apartment and closed the door behind them.

Everyone moved in from the hallway into the living room as Cristina looked around. Clearly thoughts were going through her mind as she relived the night that Carlos beat her. She surveyed the apartment and fought back the emotion that was welling up inside of her. Her mother moved her deeper into the living room and brought her to the couch to sit. "Are you okay Sweetheart?"

Cristina smiled at her mother and replied, "Yes Mama, I'm fine."

Debbie sat next to her and held her hand. "Listen Cristina, if you don't want to stay here, Mama said you can go back to her house or if you want you can come and stay with Anthony and I, whatever you want to do, it's up to you."

Debbie looked over to Anthony who shed a slight smile on his face at her offer. Cristina looked around at her apartment again and then to her sister Lourdes who had a smile on her face. After a second Lourdes said, "There is another option to."

Cristina continued to look at her and asked, "What's that?"

Lourdes moved over to the other side of her sister and said, "Well I talked to Mama and she said that if it was okay with you then it would be okay with her and I could come and stay here with you."

Cristina looked up at her mom and then at her sisters. With tears in her eyes she said to everyone, "You are all so sweet, thank you for everything." Cristina said to Lourdes, "Sure, I would love for you to come and live here with me."

All excited Lourdes reached over and hugged her sister. "COOL!" she said as everyone in the room laughed out loud.

Anthony smiled and made his way into the kitchen, stopped in the doorway and looked over at the stove. All he could picture in his mind was Cristina being dragged by Carlos to the stove and being forced onto the hot burner. He could imagine her screams of pain and terror as he tortured her that night and he felt himself get red with anger. After a second he felt Debbie behind him as she rubbed his back and brought him back to reality. "Are you okay Babe?"

Anthony looked over his shoulder and replied, "Yeah, I'm just thinking about what that poor girl went through in here that night." Anthony moved further into the kitchen and grabbed a can of soda, opened it up and took a sip of it.

Debbie moved further into the kitchen. "Don't let your mind take you on a wild ride, all of that stuff is over."

Anthony said, "Thanks for offering our place to your sister."

Debbie smiled and looked back into the living room at her sisters and mom talking. Her younger sister was clearly excited about moving in with her older one. "You see how I am the outcast, right?"

Taking another sip from his soda he said to Debbie, "I don't understand what you mean Sweetheart."

Debbie thought about it for a minute. "Well you see my mom offered her place and we offered ours and she chose for Lourdes to come and live here."

Anthony shrugged his shoulders and said, "Don't make something where there is nothing. You said yourself a while ago, she's too old to go back and live with your mom again and she probably wouldn't have felt comfortable staying by our house. You know, like maybe she would feel like she was intruding."

Debbie thought about it for a minute and then replied, "Maybe you're right."

"This was a good move. Lourdes is getting to a point that she could use her own place so this will work out well for both of them."

Debbie smiled at him. He leaned down and kissed her as she leaned into him and they watched her family laughing and joking with each other.

Chapter 30
One Last Deal

Debbie was in an especially annoyed mood, even for her. Anthony and Debbie both finished eating lunch and were in the living room watching TV. For some odd reason a news report had been broadcast about the war between Mariana and the Perez brothers. No real new information had come forward, but a final body count had been tallied and it now stood at one hundred and eighty six dead. Many of that number included children. What that number didn't include was the seventeen people that Mariana lost. They weren't included because Mariana had made sure to collect all her dead so nothing could be tied back to her cartel. It was smart, and that's how she managed to keep the authorities in the dark of her involvement. With the combined numbers there were over two hundred dead from this conflict.

Anthony switched off the television when he noticed that Debbie was annoyed. His pager started going off, it was Enzo. He let out a long sigh and headed for the phone. He called him and Enzo answered on the second ring. "What's up En?" Anthony listened to his friend on the other end of the phone complain that he was looking for his stuff and he couldn't locate Mike. Anthony locked eyes with Debbie as she brushed past him to take the dishes to the kitchen. "En, I have no idea where he is. I haven't spoken to him today." Anthony listened to him drone on more and more. "En, you two have gotten along a little better. Do you really need me to get involved with this shit?" Debbie brushed past him again, this time grabbing the cups and taking them back into the kitchen, still visibly annoyed. Anthony looked over to the clock hanging on the wall and then said, "Okay, I will find him and have him there." Before he could hang up Enzo went on another tirade and Anthony had to pull the phone from his ear from the volume of Enzo's voice. "What the fuck do you need me there for?" Anthony listened to him some more, let out a long exhausted sigh and said, "FINE, I'll see you there," and he hung up the phone.

Anthony closed his eyes and let out another long annoyed sigh. "What was that all about?" asked Debbie as she walked past Anthony and made her way back to the couch.

Anthony remained quiet as he made his way into the living room behind her and sat back down on the couch next to her. "That was Enzo."

"What did he want?"

"He is all up in arms because he can't find Mike and he is looking for his stuff."

Debbie rolled her eyes and thumbed through a magazine that she clearly wasn't interested in reading. "I guess you have to bring him his stuff?"

Anthony shook his head in disgust as he grabbed the cordless phone and called Teresa's house. "Not exactly. Enzo wants me to meet both of them. Why? I can't tell you."

"What?"

Anthony hushed Debbie up as Teresa picked up the phone. "Hey Sis, is your boyfriend there? Can I talk to him?"

"Why do you have to go?"

Anthony glanced over at Debbie while he waited for Mike to get on the phone. "I have no idea but Enzo sounded weird, really strung out."

"I don't believe this."

"Hey Mike, its Anthony. You know Enzo has been trying to reach you?" Anthony listened to Mike on the other end of the line. "Well why didn't you return any of his calls? Do you have his stuff? He's calling me and now he wants me to meet you guys." Anthony listened to Mike. "I have no idea why he wants me there. Meet up at the park at two o'clock." Anthony listened some more. "Okay, bye."

Anthony hung the phone up and noticed Debbie was fuming. After a second he asked her in a somewhat annoyed tone, "What?"

"Why do you have to go?"

Anthony thought about it for a minute. "I don't know. I'm in no mood to go either, but I have to. These two sound like they are going to explode on each other."

"And you have to go there to stop it?"

"Debbie please, I'm not in the mood to argue with you."

"I thought you were done street dealing? Now you're back to playing middle man between these two guys?"

Anthony sat there looking off into space thinking about the whole situation. Besides that he now had his girlfriend on a tirade about him having to go to a street deal; something he hasn't had to do in a while. "I am not getting back into street dealing. It's not like I am going to meet a couple of strangers Deb."

"That doesn't matter. When are you going to give all this shit up?"

Anthony got up and started to head upstairs and Debbie followed him. "Give what shit up? This is my job. We spoke about this."

"I thought your days of being a street dealer were over?"

Anthony grabbed his 1911 out of the closet safe and slipped it in his waistband. "They are, I'm only going on this one deal."

They walked out of the bedroom and headed back downstairs. Anthony grabbed his pager off the table and clipped it onto his belt. Debbie moved and sat back down on the couch trying to hold back tears. Anthony moved next to her on the couch. "Why are you crying? Why are you so upset about this?"

Debbie tried to calm herself down. "I don't know how much more of this I can take."

"What do you mean?"

"You leave at all hours of the night, you do things that I can't even bring myself to think about. I lay in bed at night wondering if you're okay, if you're alright. I don't know half the time if you are living or dead. When you walk out the door I don't know if I am ever going to see you again." Debbie began crying harder and Anthony reached out and held her hand.

"Debbie this is my job. I have been doing this stuff since you met me. This is how I pay the bills. This is how I give you things."

Debbie wiped her tears. Raising her voice she said, "I DON'T WANT THINGS! I want a normal relationship. I want a normal boyfriend."

Anthony placed his hands over his face trying to contain his annoyance. He reached behind his neck and undid his chain and held it in his hands. After a second Debbie reached over and took the chain from him and started playing with it. "Debbie listen to me, I am not going back to street dealing. I just have to go to this one deal that's all."

Debbie, concentrating on the chain, replied, "I've heard that before. Months ago you said you didn't plan on doing this your entire life. It seems to me that you have gotten deeper and deeper in this lifestyle and I don't see a way out for you. Nine out of ten times this lifestyle either leads to jail or to a funeral. I can't live like that."

Anthony couldn't argue with that. She was right, but the last thing he could do was actually admit to that. "Listen, why don't we plan on going away for a little while together? You have some vacation time, maybe we can get away."

Debbie laughed a little, but she wasn't amused. "Do you think that is going to make everything better? Do you think that is going to make me forget what you do for a living? Do you think that is going to make me forget about this street war that you were a part of? Almost two hundred people died, all because of my sister!"

Anthony was tired of hearing that. "We are not going to have this conversation again."

"Why can't you just get a normal job? Why can't you just find normal work and be a normal person?"

"Cause I can't."

"Why? You went to high school. You have an education."

"Because I can't!"

Yelling, Debbie asked, "WHY?"

Standing up and yelling back Anthony said, "BECAUSE I'M A LOSER!"

Shocked, Debbie yelled "WHAT? You're not a loser! You have a brain. I don't understand why you can just get a regular job."

Anthony paced back and forth for a second and then sat back down next to her. "Debbie, I make more in one day doing this than I can make in a year on a regular job."

Debbie let out a sigh. "That's all good until you get caught!"

"I'm not going to get caught."

They both went quiet for a minute and Debbie reached over to hand Anthony back his chain. He looked down at it in her hand and then pushed it back towards her. "You wear it."

Debbie, somewhat shocked, continued to look at the chain in her hand. "You never take this chain off. You didn't take it off the night of the hospital attack. Why would you take it off now?"

"I don't want to lose it and it's hurting my neck," he lied.

Debbie looked hurt and held the chain tighter in her hands. "I don't know how you can look at me and lie like that."

Annoyed, Anthony stood up and turned away from her. "Oh stop, now I'm lying about a chain?"

"You're afraid you're not going to come back from this deal, aren't you?"

Anthony needed to keep her out of his head. "No, I just told you, it's annoying my neck."

"Where is this deal?" Before he could answer she followed up with, "Can I come with you?"

Anthony gave her a puzzled look. "What? You're not coming with me on a drug deal Debbie."

"Why? I came with you when you delivered the drugs to Enzo at the garage. What's different about this one?"

He didn't have an answer for her question. Something indeed did feel different about this deal. There was no way he was letting her come with him though. "You're not going to come on a drug deal. I am not going to sit here and debate this with you."

Debbie began to cry again. With tears streaming down her face she said, "I can't do this anymore. I can't live like this anymore and I can't see you anymore. I am losing my sanity and you are losing your soul."

"So what are you saying?"

Debbie, crying harder now, said, "Leave, leave and get out of my house."

Taken aback, Anthony slowly stood up and stared at her crying, now uncontrollably. He reached down to her and said, "Deb."

Yelling on the top of her lungs she said, "GET OUT!"

Anthony fully stood up and looked at her motionless. After a minute he walked through the dining room, punched the table and stormed out of the house.

Anthony pulled up outside the park and found Enzo standing near a bench waiting for him. Anthony turned off the car and exited it. The park was pretty empty. It was starting to get cold now as fall was almost near. There were only a few people in the park, some children playing on the far side of it, every now and then a jogger would run by. Enzo was pacing back and forth, clearly in need of a hit.

Anthony made his way over to Enzo. Enzo gazed at him and then finally extended his hand. Anthony shook it and then reached in for their usual check to check kiss but Enzo seemed to shy away. Anthony backed away and let his hand go. "How are you doing Enzo?"

Enzo paced back and forth, "I'm fine."

"You don't look so good."

Enzo replied, "I'm fine, I would be better if I had my shit."

Anthony stood motionless. Enzo was in need of a hit for sure. He must have run out and now he was starting to show early signs of withdrawal. "En, maybe it's time we had a difficult conversation."

"What kind of a conversation?"

Anthony swallowed hard. "About your drug use. I think you are going a little overboard with it."

Enzo glared at Anthony with a look that could kill. He never saw his friend look at him like that. He tried to take it that it was due to the withdrawal symptoms. "Maybe you should keep your opinion to yourself, how's that?" Annoyed, Anthony let it go. He turned around, visibly annoyed and scanned the rest of the park looking for Mike, but he wasn't around yet. "Where is this fucking asshole? Did you talk to him?"

"Yeah, right after I spoke to you."

"AND?" asked Enzo loudly.

By this point Anthony pretty much had enough of Enzo's attitude. "HEY," he shot back, "I don't know who the fuck you think you're talking to, but you need to calm the fuck down!"

Taken back by Anthony's retaliation Enzo started pacing back and forth again. It wasn't enough what Anthony just went through with his apparent break up with Debbie, but now he had his friend giving him an attitude. He was in no mood for this shit. He looked across the park again and now he saw Mike making his way towards them. Relieved that this was almost over, Mike approached them and extended his hand towards Anthony. They kissed their usual cheek to cheek greeting and then Mike said, "What's up En?"

Enzo turned his gaze towards Mike and replied, "I'm standing here waiting for you, that's what's up!"

The two faced off and looked at each other with Anthony stuck in the middle. Anthony gazed between both of them and said, "Really guys? Let's just give each other what we all came here for and be on our way."

Enzo backed up a little and looked around the park. Anthony and Mike did the same, just to make sure there were no cops. Why Enzo picked a park to meet at was beyond comprehension, but when someone is high twenty three hours a day there is no rational thinking taking place.

Mike reached into his duffle bag and handed Enzo a brick of weed. In turn Enzo handed Mike a stack of money, all of which looked like hundred dollar bills. At that point Anthony's pager started going off. He reached down and struggled to get it off of his belt clip. He pulled harder and it finally came off. Before he ventured to look to see who was paging him he looked up and Mike was now handing Enzo a kilo of cocaine while Enzo was handing over two more stacks of cash to Mike. Confident that this deal was almost over he looked at the pager, in anticipation, in the hope of it being Debbie. It wasn't, it was Cristina.

Enzo tested the cocaine and suddenly dropped the kilo on the floor. Anthony's eyes darted from the pager to the dropped kilo. Anthony looked over towards Mike who was concentrating on counting the money. "This isn't real."

Never taking his eyes off the money Mike replied, "What?"

Anthony looked back down at the pager as it started to go off again as he was clipping it back to his belt. He shut off the alert and by the time he had his eyes picked back up to what was going on in front of him Enzo had his pistol pulled out and pointed at Mike. Anthony's eyes opened wide at the site before his eyes. It didn't register to him what was going on. It took all of his energy for him to get the words out of his mouth, "ENZO, what are you doing?"

The look on Enzo's face was something that Anthony had never seen before. He looked completely crazed. "This isn't real!" Enzo repeated, this time followed by a gun shot that sent a bullet racing into Mike's stomach. Mike never knew what hit him. His eyes never came up from looking at the money. The shot sent Mike reeling backwards, the stacks of money into the air. Mike hit the floor on his back as all the money rained down around and on him.

"Enzo, what the fuck are you doing?" yelled Anthony.

Enzo wasn't listening, he continued to stare at Mike with an evil look. Enzo took a step closer to Mike and raised his gun. Anthony started to reach into his waist band and grasped his 1911, he didn't know what to do. Before he could pull it out Enzo fired another point blank shot, this time hitting Mike square in the chest.

Anthony got his gun out of his pants, but before he could raise it and train it on Enzo there was a screeching noise coming from the street behind him. Anthony looked over his right shoulder to see a flashing red light on top of what appeared to be an undercover cop car coming to a hard stop. Enzo quickly took off and started running up the street and away from the scene. Anthony turned fully to his right as a guy was jumping out of the car with a gun trained in his direction yelling, "FREEZE!" Anthony started turning back to his left with his pistol drawn is his right hand and then it came. The cop let off a shot that struck Anthony on the right side of his head. All Anthony felt and saw at that point was blackness. He fell towards his left side and hit the floor unmoving.

The cop looked at the two bodies lying on the sidewalk and then looked to his left up the block. Enzo was running down the block and coming close to the corner at the end of the park. He jumped back into his car, threw it into reverse and screeched out down the block in pursuit of Enzo.

Enzo turned the corner at the right side of the park and took off at a rapid pace up the block. The cop reached the corner and made a hard right and sped up the block after him.

Debbie had followed Anthony to the deal, parked a block away, and watched the deal unfold and fall apart. Once the cop pulled away Debbie threw her car into drive and came out from the block where she watched everything from. She made a hard left and pulled up to where Anthony and Mike were laying, but when she arrived at the scene it was more then she could handle. Debbie saw Anthony and Mike laying in the street and she went into hysterics.

She jumped out and ran to them, both of them were lying in pools of blood. Mike's chest and stomach were pouring blood out at an unbelievable rate. Mike was unmoving and his eyes were open. Debbie gasped for air at the site that was in front of her. She put her hands over her mouth and started to scream. She didn't know what to do. She quickly moved towards Anthony and kneeled down to him. Blood was coming from the right side of his head and he was unconscious. "ANTHONY," she yelled. "Anthony, answer me," she said while hysterically crying.

At this point people started to gather around her while she was trying to get Anthony to respond to her. She looked towards Mike and then back to Anthony. She looked up at a guy that came running towards them. "Please, somebody help me!"

The guy came to her and asked, "What happened?"

Hysterically she looked around and then lied as she said, "I don't know, but please help me!"

"What do you want to do?"

"Please help me get him into my car, I need to get him to a hospital."

The guy nodded as Debbie got up and ran to the passenger side of her car and opened the door and then ran back to Anthony. The guy was already picking Anthony up when Debbie got back there to assist him. They each put an arm of Anthony's around their shoulders and lifted him off of the ground. After a second of steadying him they moved him over to the car and sat him down on the passenger side of the car. Debbie closed the door and made her way back over to Mike.

The guy that helped her get Anthony in the car came over next to her and looked down at Mike, but it was apparent that he was gone. Debbie began crying again as she also came to the realization that Mike was dead. He was pale white and no longer breathing. His eyes were wide open, staring at the sky. Debbie reached out and touched his hand. She glanced up at the guy and he slowly backed away. "You better hurry if the other one is going to survive."

Debbie agreed and then looked at Mike one last time before she got up and ran to her car. She got in, backed up and headed out and away from the park and towards the hospital just as other cops and ambulances started heading towards the park from the opposite direction.

Chapter 31
Waiting Patiently

Debbie paced nervously back and forth in the emergency waiting room at Saint John's Medical Center. There was nothing else she could do except pace and wait and cry. She was beside herself. She looked through a window that overlooked the emergency room, but she could no longer see Anthony. When she arrived at the hospital she ran into the emergency room hysterically crying and hospital staff ran to help her. They immediately pulled Anthony from the car and into the emergency room and that was the last that she saw of him. Now all she could do was wait. She sat and tried to relax, but all she did was cry. She put her head into her hands and held it tightly as she sobbed. She was jarred out of her thoughts by a hand on her shoulder. She looked up and it was Cristina's, Lourdes was standing next to her.

"Oh my God Debbie! What happened?" asked Cristina. All Debbie could do was shake her head while she cried. Her sister sat next to her and wrapped her in a tight hug while Lourdes stood over them with tears in her own eyes. "It's okay Sweetheart," said Cristina, now with tears in her eyes as well.

Lourdes moved to the other side of Debbie and sat next to her. After a second she put her hand on her sister's shoulder and rubbed her gently. Debbie looked over her shoulder and then touched her hand. After a moment the three sisters hugged and cried together. They stayed motionless for a minute and just held one another as they all cried in one another's arms. After a long minute Lourdes said, "Debbie, what happened?"

Debbie began composing herself and then sat back and said to her two sisters, "Anthony went on a drug deal and he was shot." Lourdes closed her eyes and shook her head slowly. "He was shot in the head." She started to cry again as Cristina tried to console her.

"Sweetheart, how was he when they brought him in here?"

Debbie thought about it for a second. "I brought him in here."

"You brought him in?" asked Lourdes.

"Yes," replied Debbie.

"Were you with him at the deal?"

"No, not at all!" Frustrated with all that took place Debbie sat up and started to get up but Cristina gently held her down. She looked at her sister and started to relax. After a minute she looked back at Lourdes and softened her look. Lourdes reached over and held her hand and after a minute she continued. "Anthony and I were home, we had just finished lunch and watching TV when his pager started going off. It was his friend Enzo, who Anthony has been getting drugs for from Mike."

"I thought Anthony wasn't street dealing anymore?" asked Lourdes.

Debbie tried to push the annoyance that she had out of her as she realized the extent that her sister knew of Anthony's work. "He hasn't been street dealing in a while. He's been playing middleman between Enzo and Mike for a while because they really can't stand each other. I thought he was done with that since they have been dealing with each other for the last few months now, but Enzo called him all agitated and insisted that he come. Anthony tracked Mike down and set everything up." Debbie went quiet as she stared at the floor with tears in her eyes.

"What else happened Sweetheart?" asked Cristina.

Debbie looked up from the floor and continued, "We had a very bad argument regarding the deal, regarding his work and his life in general." Debbie went silent for a minute as she replayed the argument over in her mind. "We've had arguments before about this stuff, but this argument was different."

"What do you mean?" asked Lourdes.

Trying to control the emotion in her voice she said, "We broke up."

Shocked, Cristina asked her, "You what?"

Turning her tear filled eyes to her other sister she repeated, "We broke up!" She tried to contain herself but she couldn't any longer. She stared at her sister and repeated again, "We broke up. I told him to leave and get out of the house, and that I didn't want to see him anymore."

"Sweetheart, why did you do that? What made you break up with him?"

"Cristina, I couldn't take it anymore! Like I told him, I lay in bed at night not knowing what he is doing, who he is with and if he is okay or if he is going to ever come home." Debbie went silent for a second and then added, "I just can't do it anymore. Not after what took place when you ended up in the hospital."

Cristina sat back and caught the look that Lourdes was giving her while Debbie cried in between the two of them. The look spoke volumes to her and she felt there was an argument once again brewing between her two sisters, and that was the last thing that needed to take place at that moment. Cristina gently shook her head as if to convey to Lourdes, 'Not now.' Cristina reached out and stroked Debbie's hair. "What else happened?"

"He left the house pretty angry. I wasn't sure if he was going to come back. I wasn't sure of anything at that point but something was weird about him."

"What do you mean?" asked Lourdes.

Without looking over to her sister she responded, "He took his chain off, this chain." Debbie pulled the chain out from under her shirt that she was now wearing and showed it to her sisters. "He never takes this chain off, but he did and he told me to wear it. He said it was bothering his neck." Debbie thought about it deeper. "It was like he knew something was going to go wrong and he didn't want to lose it or something, so he gave it to me to wear. After that the argument got worse and he left."

"How did you end up at the deal?" asked Cristina.

"I didn't want things to end between us the way they did, and by that point I was starting to think something bad was going to happen. It's like I had a premonition or something. I waited till he pulled out and then I jumped in my car and followed him. The deal was at a park close to the house. I parked about a block away, on a corner, and I watched them. Enzo looked weird, walking back and forth. After a few minutes Mike showed up and they started to deal. From what I saw Enzo pulled out a gun and shot Mike at point blank range in the stomach."

Lourdes said, "Oh my God!"

Debbie said, "I know, imagine seeing it firsthand." Debbie paused for a second and then said, "It happened so fast. Anthony looked like he was caught off guard by what took place. Then I saw

Enzo step forward and shot Mike again, this time in the chest. I was frozen in place, I didn't know what to do."

"Did Enzo shoot Anthony?" asked Lourdes.

Debbie replied, "No. When the second shot came Anthony pulled out his pistol and at the same time an undercover cop pulled up. Anthony turned around and the cop shot him."

"Just like that?" asked Cristina, stunned and confused.

"Yeah, that doesn't make any sense," added Lourdes. "If Enzo was the one doing the shooting, why did the cop shoot at Anthony?"

Debbie replied, "I don't know. I saw Enzo take off running at the same time the cop showed up. Maybe since Anthony had his gun out and he turned toward the cop, maybe he thought Anthony was going to shoot at him, I don't know. After he shot Anthony he got back in his car and took off after Enzo. That's when I drove over there. I started screaming and people started coming over. Some guy helped me pick Anthony up and put him in my car."

Everyone went silent for a second and then Lourdes asked, "What happened to Mike?"

Debbie swallowed hard. Before she could reply everyone knew the answer. "I went back to get him, but it was too late; he was dead."

"Oh Debbie, I'm so sorry," said Cristina. "I don't know what to say."

Debbie sat motionless thinking about it. "You have no idea what Mike's face looked like. He was just staring off into nowhere. I've never seen anything like that. Not even with what we went through after the barbeque." Debbie went quiet for another minute. "I knew at that point there was nothing that I could do for Mike, so I got in the car and raced over here. I wasn't even sure if Anthony was going to make it on the way here. Doctors, nurses, people came running out and pulled him out of the car and right into the ER. He was still breathing when they took him in."

"Has anyone been out here to talk to you since you brought him in?" asked Lourdes.

Debbie responded, "No, about twenty minutes after I brought him in they ran through here with Mike though." Everyone was silent. "I know it was useless though. He was gone in the park."

Cristina put her arm around her sister again. "I know how close you were with Mike."

Debbie thought about that and Lourdes asked, "Does Teresa know yet?"

Debbie said, "I couldn't bring myself to call her. They're probably going to call his mother, if they haven't already. I'm sure she will tell her."

"Sweetheart," started Cristina, "look at me." Debbie turned her gaze from Lourdes to Cristina. Cristina looked around and lowered her voice a little. "Have any cops been around to talk to you?"

Debbie replied, "No, why?"

Cristina looked around again and replied, "It's inevitable. Since a shooting is involved they are going to have questions, especially since it was a cop that shot him. Don't talk to anyone until you have a lawyer with you. Don't give them any information, and under no circumstances tell them what you saw take place at that park."

"Cristina is right, whatever you say can get Anthony in a world of trouble, even more than what he can be in right now. I wouldn't say a word to anyone until you talk to a lawyer."

Debbie agreed and said, "Okay, I'll have to get in contact with Mickey. Anthony told me to only deal with him if he ever got in trouble and needed a lawyer."

Cristina looked to her left and saw Teresa coming into the hospital. Cristina pointed her out to Debbie. "Deb, you're going to have to talk to her."

Debbie sadly said, "I know."

"Do you have Mickey's number on you?" asked Lourdes. "We'll call him while you talk to Teresa."

"Yeah, it's in my phone book." Debbie reached into her purse and took out a small address book and gave it to her sister and then stood up. Cristina let her hand go and watched her as she walked off to console her friend. Once Debbie got to Teresa they both grabbed each other in a tight hug and began crying.

Cristina and Lourdes watched from across the waiting room for a moment and then headed towards the payphones. Half way to the payphones the two sisters heard a loud, chilling scream come from Teresa. As they turned around to look, Debbie was holding her friend up while Teresa looked like she was about to collapse to the floor. She was in complete hysterics. Lourdes and Cristina, both with tears in their eyes, turned around to continue on to the payphones. Cristina said, "You call Mickey, I'll call Mama. If this doesn't go well we're not going to be able to contain Debbie by ourselves."

Lourdes thought about that for a minute and agreed. After a minute of thinking she said, "I hate to say this but I think Mama will have a harder time containing us then Debbie."

Cristina looked at her sister and contemplated what she just said.

Several hours had passed and the hospital waiting room was crowded now. More people had arrived. A few of the guys that Anthony worked with from the club had shown up to see if any one needed anything. Some had come and some had gone. It was like a revolving door for them. Mickey was there now and he was stapled to Debbie's side. They had gone off to a quiet corner for a while so Debbie could tell him what happened. He agreed with Lourdes and Cristina in the sense of not telling the cops what she saw, at least for now. Luckily no cops had yet come to talk to her, which was odd, but everyone was sure they would eventually come.

Debbie's mom had come as soon as she got off from work and she did her best to comfort her three daughters. They were all close with Anthony and she hated to see them so upset. They had just gotten past a traumatizing experience with Carlos and the war, now they felt like a new one was about to start. She had her hands full with her three daughters.

Teresa had left, there was nothing that she could do and she was a hysterical mess. The doctors had come out and confirmed to her that Mike was indeed deceased. They tried to revive him, but he was dead on arrival. Debbie didn't need a doctor to confirm that though, she witnessed it first-hand. It was not something she ever wanted to see again. Teresa wanted to stay for Anthony, but Debbie insisted that she go and be with Mike's family.

Lourdes and Cristina had filled their mom in on everything that had happened. Brenda tried her best to be there for her three girls. All she could do at this point was to offer support and comfort.

She could also do her best to try and avoid any flare ups between Debbie and Lourdes. Even in this hard time the two of them managed to get under each other's skin. Lourdes was usually the graceful one and tried the best to avoid the confrontation, but sometimes, most of the time, Debbie was impossible.

It was actually quiet at this point in the emergency room. Everyone was seated, some had their eyes closed, either resting, praying or just trying to get rid of the images of the day's events. A doctor had emerged from the emergency room area and started heading towards Debbie and her family. Brenda noticed this and tapped Debbie on her shoulder to take notice. When Debbie opened her eyes and saw the doctor walking over, her eyes immediately filled up expecting to hear the worst. Her mother stood up and helped her daughter stand and then put her arms on her shoulders as the doctor approached. The doctor came over as a crowd of people started coming around to hear what he had to say. He introduced himself to everyone and then motioned for Debbie to sit and he sat across from her. "We rushed Anthony into emergency surgery after we assessed the situation. He was shot in the right side of his head, but it was at an angle that didn't allow the bullet to penetrate very far into the skull. The bullet did fracture his skull but never made it past the skull into the brain."

Everyone let out a sigh of relief once they heard the news. "Is he okay?" asked Debbie.

"He is okay. He is alive, but he did lose a lot of blood. We have his condition listed as critical but stable. We do expect him to make a full recovery, but it's going to take time. A lot of time and a lot of patience."

Brenda asked, "Is he going to have any disfigurement?"

The doctor replied, "Well, temporarily we had to shave one side of his head so we could get in there to work. The bullet was lodged pretty well and we had to cut into his skull a bit to get it out. There will be some scarring, but when his hair grows back it will cover most of it. Some scarring will protrude past the hairline, but it should be minimal. As far as misshaping of his head or skull, I don't foresee anything like that."

"Thank God," said Brenda. Everyone nodded their heads in agreement.

The doctor looked around again at everyone and then said, "As far as the bullet, we pulled it and I examined it quickly and compared it to his friend that was also brought in shortly afterwards." Debbie and Mickey looked at each other without moving. "I'm not a forensic expert, but they are two totally different calibers, which means they came from different guns. As you know since this involves a shooting, multiple shootings, the authorities are going to have to be notified and they are probably going to have questions for you since you brought him in." Debbie stared at the doctor. "Were you there with him?" he asked.

After a minute she replied, "No. When I got there he and Mike were already shot." It wasn't a complete lie.

The doctor thought about it for a second and then asked, "Do you have any other questions?"

Cristina asked, "What is his recovery time going to be like?"

The doctor took in a long breath and then let it out. He replied, "Well, that is hard to predict. He is going to be in a large amount of pain. A wound like this and the following efforts to remove the bullet is a very traumatizing event. We have to worry about infection for one thing. Something else will be his mental state of mind when he wakes up from this whole thing. An injury such as this one can alter your mental state, usually towards depression." The doctor asked Debbie, "The other guy that came in after him that passed, were they close?"

Debbie replied, "Yes, very close."

The doctor made a weird face, almost uncomfortable, and said, "I would think he has a pretty long road ahead of him." The doctor paused for a moment and added, "Listen, I don't know all the circumstances here, and I really don't want to venture a guess or to pry, but guns were involved and one person is dead. I am sure that when he comes out of here there are going to be tough times ahead regarding legal ramifications and a lot of questions that need to be answered. Depending on his role in the whole thing, that is something else that can play with his mental state during recovery."

Debbie asked, "Is it possible to see him?"

The doctor replied, "Not at this time. He is in recovery and we have him heavily sedated, mostly because of the pain. It will be a long while before we will even start to think about waking him up.

My suggestion is for you to go home, get some rest and we will call you when he is alert enough for visitors."

Brenda agreed and said, "He's right girls. Let him rest and as soon as we can see him we will come back."

The doctor smiled at Debbie and stood up. He started to walk away and then said to Debbie. "You know, he is very lucky. A gun shot like that, in that location of his body, things could have been very different. An inch over and he could be dead. If it wasn't for you bringing him in when you did, even with the wound that it was, he would have bled out in that street and died."

Debbie smiled at the doctor. "Thank you doctor." He smiled and walked away as Debbie sat back down and looked at her family.

Mickey rubbed Debbie on her shoulder and said, "I am going to go and make a few calls. I want to see what I can find out about Enzo and this whole situation. I'll be in contact with you shortly. If something comes up don't hesitate to call me."

Debbie squeezed Mickey's hand and smiled at him. "Thanks Mickey, I will." Mickey smiled and walked away.

All that was left was Debbie and her family now. Everyone sat back in their chairs, all looking exhausted. Debbie let out a long, tired sigh. Lourdes said, "This is really good news Debbie, he's going to be okay."

Debbie allowed a slight smile to come across her face. Cristina asked, "What's wrong Debbie? I thought you would be happy with this news."

Debbie shifted her look from one sister to another and replied, "Of course I'm happy, but after the argument I don't know how he is going to wake up. I don't know what to expect out of him, or myself."

"Well," started Brenda, "you guys have a few things to work out, but right now I wouldn't think about that."

Debbie said, "The thought of him recovering, who knows what he is going to go through. You heard the doctor, he has a long road ahead of him. Who knows what kind of legal issues he is going to have as well."

Cristina replied, "Debbie, you are not alone in this. I am here to help you. I will be more than glad to help while Anthony is recovering."

Debbie smiled at her sister. Lourdes added, "You can count on me as well. Anthony is like a brother to us and I will do anything to help him get back on his feet. I'm planning on staying local for a while, so I will be here as well for anything you two need."

Debbie shifted her look towards her other sister. She smiled at her, but even she knew it wasn't a genuine smile; not like the one that Cristina received just moments ago. "I know how much Anthony means to you," Debbie shifted her look from Lourdes towards Cristina, "to both of you. I understand how much you both mean to him as well. He loves the two of you; you're like sisters to him. Thank you, both of you."

Brenda looked on and smiled at her three daughters. "Anything you or Anthony need Debbie, we're all here for you."

Debbie smiled and put her head down. Tears welled up in her eyes again as her sisters and mother came over to her and hugged her tight.

Chapter 32
Goodbye Friend

Dressed in black from head to toe, Debbie made her way slowly down the stairs at home. She was tired and felt beaten up. She had been at the hospital every day and night for the last five days. Tonight was the one night that she was taking off from doing it. She would gladly go if it would change where she had to go tonight, but she knew that was impossible. Tonight was Mike's funeral.

She stopped at the bottom of the stairs, lowered herself down and sat on the last step. She placed her head in her hands and began to cry softly. It still didn't register to her that Mike was gone. She knew it wasn't a dream, but she just couldn't bring herself to believe it. She replayed the scene at the park over and over in her mind. She could hear the shots ring out in her head.

She sat for a long minute and just cried. She heard her front door opening and looked up. Brenda, also dressed in full black, was coming into the house. When she saw her mother she completely broke apart. "Oh Sweetheart! Are you okay?" she asked as she ran to her daughter and wrapped her arms around her in a loving hug. Debbie held her mother tightly and let all her emotion pour out of her. "Did something happen? Is Anthony okay?"

After a minute of crying she pulled back from her mother and replied, "Anthony's fine, there hasn't been any change."

Brenda sat next to her and said, "Does it have to do with going to your friend's funeral?"

Debbie wiped her tears away and replied, "I don't know if I can do this; I'm not ready to say goodbye to him."

Brenda wiped her daughter's tears away and replied, "Sweetheart, we are never really ready to say goodbye to someone, especially under these circumstances." Debbie listened to her mother, after a minute she added, "Maybe you shouldn't go there if you can't bear to see him. I'm sure Teresa and his family will understand with all that you are going through right now."

Debbie replied, "No Mama, I have to go. I could never forgive myself if I don't go and say goodbye to him."

Her mother watched her daughter looking at the floor and asked, "What are you thinking about Sweetheart?"

Debbie replied, "I was just thinking that Anthony is not going to have that chance to say goodbye to his friend. That's going to destroy him when he wakes up."

Brenda thought about that and slowly stood up, helping her daughter get up at the same time. Debbie hugged her again and then suddenly let her go. "What's wrong?" she asked as her daughter pulled away from her abruptly. Debbie put her hand over her mouth and held her stomach as she pushed past her mother and ran towards the bathroom quickly. "What's the matter?" she asked nervously. Debbie ran into the bathroom and shut the door and began throwing up. Brenda stopped at the door when she heard her, realizing why she ran from her so quickly.

After a minute she moved to the kitchen and poured a glass of water and waited for her daughter to come back out of the bathroom. As she waited her two other daughters entered the house and walked back into the kitchen, both of them dressed in black as well. "Where is Debbie?" asked Cristina.

"She is in the bathroom, throwing up."

"Throwing up?" asked Lourdes. "Is she sick?"

Their mom sat at the table, let out a long sigh and shrugged her shoulders. "I don't know Lourdes, I think it's her nerves. Between the war, the shooting and now this funeral, I think she is at her breaking point."

Debbie emerged from the bathroom and went into the kitchen. She barely said hello to her sisters. She sat down next to her mother and took the glass of water from her. "Are you okay?" asked Lourdes.

"Yes," she replied.

"Are you sure you want to go and do this Debbie?" asked Brenda again.

Debbie took a sip of the water and replied, "Yeah, I have to."

Cristina walked over to Debbie and rubbed her shoulders. "Well, we are all going with you."

Debbie smiled at her sister, "Thank you." Debbie looked over at the clock and then slowly stood up. "Come on, we better get going."

Brenda stood up and said, "Okay, let's get going." They all got their coats and headed out of the house.

Arriving at the funeral home Brenda walked up next to Debbie and slipped her arm into her daughters arm. She knew this was going to be hard for her. She knew her daughter was in for a world of hurt when she entered the funeral home to say goodbye to Mike. That's why she was there, that's why her other daughters were there; to help her through what could be one of the hardest times of her life.

Sensing that this was going to be a difficult time, Cristina moved in on the other side of her sister and slipped her arm in Debbie's as well. Lourdes took up behind the three of them and they made their way up the steps towards the door.

Outside the funeral home were dozens and dozens of people. Debbie looked around and then it clicked in to her, these people were all here for Mike. They were soldiers, capos and associates from the various New York families. They were wise guys, and they all looked like wise guys. All of them in expensive suits and fancy dress shoes. Some people she recognized from the barbeque for Anthony's birthday. Some she had never seen before, but she could tell they were from the clubs.

Once inside the funeral parlor there was no shortage of people. It was packed to capacity with more wise guys. Leaning towards her daughter's ear, Brenda asked the obvious question, "All these people are here for Mike?" Debbie answered her with just a look. "Friends?" she asked.

"Kind of," replied Debbie.

"Are these the same people where Anthony got all the get well soon flowers from?" Debbie looked at her and agreed, not wanting to say out loud they were wise guys.

They made their way closer to the room that Mike was laid out in and the crowd got thicker. Debbie and her mother made their way slowly through the crowd and was met by a tearful Teresa at the entrance of the room. Teresa immediately reached out and embraced

Debbie with a tight hug and the two girls cried hard in each other's arms. Cristina and her mom both let Debbie go and stepped back for a minute. Debbie and Teresa stayed in a tight embrace for a long minute before letting each other go. "How are you doing?" asked Debbie.

After composing herself Teresa replied, "About as good as I could be doing right now."

"I know, that was a stupid question."

"No, not at all Debbie." Teresa went quiet for a minute and then said, "Thank you for coming." Teresa looked at Debbie's family and added, "All of you, thank you." Everyone smiled back at Teresa. Teresa asked Debbie, "Do you want me to go up with you?"

Debbie nervously looked around at the packed room. She couldn't see the front of the room through the sea of people. After a second she said to Teresa, "Yes." She looked towards her mom and sisters and said, "We'll all go up together?"

Cristina looked at her with her usual soft look and said, "Oh course Sweetheart."

Slowly the five girls made their way through the crowd and headed towards the front of the room. After a minute of getting past everyone they got towards the front row. Instead of looking towards the casket Debbie turned her head towards Mike's family, sitting and weeping at the site of him lying in a casket. Teresa noticed and didn't force her towards Mike, but guided her towards his family. Debbie made her way towards them with her mother and sisters behind. One by one they paid their respects to Mike's family.

Once they were done Debbie took a deep breath and then slowly turned around to look at Mike. As she turned she kept her eyes closed until she was fully facing him. Her mom moved closer behind her and put her arms on her shoulders as Cristina moved next to her and held her hand. Debbie grabbed back and squeezed tightly. After a second Debbie slowly opened her eyes and allowed herself to see her friend. The site hit her like a ton of bricks as all her emotion came out again. She cried hard as her sister and her mother held her tightly. She thought she was going to pass out when she caught the sight of Mike lying in front of her. Steadying her, Brenda whispered in her ear, "It's okay Sweetheart."

Slowly Debbie looked around the room and moved closer to the casket with Teresa on one side of her and Cristina on another. Lourdes took place next to her mother as Debbie inched her way towards the casket. Slowly the five girls made their way up to Mike to pay their respects. The only thing that was close in number to the people that were in the room was the amount of flowers. The casket was surrounded by dozens of arrangements of beautiful flowers. Baskets, crosses, hearts, bleeding hearts and rosaries.

Still very emotional Debbie and Teresa broke away a bit from Debbie's family and kneeled before the casket. Holding each other and crying they looked at Mike, unable to contain their emotion. Debbie slowly reached out and touched Mike's hand. She cried harder as she did and Teresa did the same.

Debbie slowly looked up the casket into Mike's face. He looked very peaceful, like he was sleeping. He was dressed in a light gray suit and his face looked very natural. He looked very different from when Debbie saw him lying in the park. She wished she could get that memory out of her head, but she feared it was forever burnt into her memory. After a minute she looked at Teresa who was looking back at her. "I can't believe this Teresa."

After a second Teresa replied, "I know, I can't believe it either Debbie. I can't believe it, I don't know how this happened."

Debbie remained quiet, after a minute she said, "I don't know."

After a long minute of paying their respects they got up and made their way towards a few empty chairs and sat. More and more people streamed in, paid their respects and moved on. Teresa asked, "Anything new with Anthony?"

Debbie replied, "No, he is still unconscious." Teresa shook her head and went quiet again. After a minute of silence Debbie said to her, "Teresa it must be hard staying home all alone. You know if you want you can come and stay by me."

Teresa smiled at her friend and replied, "I know, thank you. My mom has been staying with me, but I don't think I can continue living there. Everywhere I look I see Mike."

"I can imagine."

All throughout the room you could smell cigar smoke. Almost all the men in the room lit up cigars, in honor of Mike.

Debbie looked around and allowed a smile to come across her face through her tears as she realized what they were doing. Teresa had the same smile. Debbie said to her, "I can almost see Mike and Anthony now, sitting at Ascension, kicking back with cigars in their mouths."

Laughing and crying, Teresa said, "Yep, I can see that too." Teresa went silent for a minute and said, "Debbie, he's going to be okay." Debbie had tears in her eyes. "He's strong, he's going to come home. We're not going to lose both of them, we can't."

Softly, Debbie replied, "I know, I know."

After what felt like an eternity of silence and watching people stream through the room and past the casket to pay their respects, the rest of the service went on. Most of the wise guys had gone and mostly family and friends that weren't associated with the social clubs were left. A young priest had come to close out the service and give the final blessing. It was still very emotional for all that remained. Mike was young, too young to die the way he did, to die period.

Debbie had decided to leave the room after the blessing and get some air in the lobby. She left her family sitting with Teresa and Mike's family. She slowly walked through the funeral home and found an empty room that wasn't being used. She entered the room and sat quietly crying and praying. Praying for Mike's soul to find rest, for Teresa to find peace, for Anthony to get better, and for herself to find clarity.

As she sat weeping the young priest walked into the room and gently placed his hand on her shoulder. Slowly she looked up at him. "Are you okay?" he asked. Slowly she wiped her tears away and said, "Yes, I'm okay.

"You were close with Michael?"

"Yes, he was one of my best friends. Mine and my boyfriends."

The priest gestured at the seat next to Debbie. "May I sit with you?"

Debbie smiled and replied, "Sure."

The priest moved around the chair and sat next to her. "My name is John."

"I'm Debbie, Father."

"It's nice to meet you Debbie. I can see that you are very, very troubled by the loss of your friend."

Debbie began to cry again and the priest reached out and held her hand. "I am Father."

"Rest assured that Michael is resting now with our Father. He is in paradise today." Debbie thought about that for a minute. She really didn't know what to think. She knew the lives that Mike and Anthony lived. They were pretty far from what God had intended them to live in and she wasn't sure if Mike was in paradise. Noticing the look on her face Father John said to her, "You don't look like you take comfort in that."

Debbie looked around the room and then said, "I don't Father."

"Why is that? Do you not believe in God?"

Debbie thought about that for a minute. "I do believe in God."

"So what is troubling you then?"

Debbie let out a long breath and replied, "Father, Mike and my boyfriend were into some pretty shady things."

Father John thought about that for a second and then asked, "Is your boyfriend the other young man that was shot when Michael was shot?"

Debbie replied, "Yes," and asked, "You've heard?"

Father John replied, "Yes, it's been all over the news and in the newspapers. Something about a drug deal gone wrong."

Debbie replied, "Yes, so you see why I have trouble wondering if Mike is in paradise right now."

The priest awkwardly smiled and then said, "You must have faith in God. It is not our place to judge or to decide if Michael is in paradise. All that we can do is pray. Pray for his soul and pray that God has mercy on his soul to allow him to come into paradise." Debbie thought about that. "Tell me about your boyfriend."

Debbie looked around the room again. "I fear that my boyfriend has done bad things. He hangs around with bad people. I have managed to work past it for a while, but lately things have gotten worse and I am afraid he has done unspeakable things to people. Unspeakable things to innocent people, even to innocent children."

The priest thought about it for a minute and asked, "Are you referring to the news stories about a month ago regarding the gang fighting in the city?"

Debbie looked at Father John nervously and said, "I'm sorry, I can't talk to you about this."

Starting to get up, Father John put his hand on Debbie's shoulder and she sat back down. "It's okay Debbie, you don't need to talk about something that you don't want to talk about."

Debbie sat motionless for a moment, thinking about what she wanted to say. "My boyfriend has changed. He's different from the person that I met, from the person that I fell in love with and moved in with."

"You live with him and you are not married?"

Embarrassed, Debbie put her head down. "I know that is wrong." The priest smiled in agreement with her statement. "I know the things that he gives me is wrong. The money, the jewelry, the car, it all comes from blood money. I can't take it anymore and I feel like I am losing my soul in the process and I don't know what to do. I can't breathe anymore."

"It's not too late for you Debbie. You must do what your heart tells you to do. You must listen to God talking to you."

"What about Anthony?"

Father John thought about her question for a minute. "Do you feel that you can save him?"

Debbie thought about that for a very long minute and then said, "I don't know, I don't think so."

"You can only try, only he can want to save himself. In the end you can only try, he must follow his own path and you must follow yours." Debbie thought about that for a minute. The bells in the funeral parlor began chiming, signaling that it was time for everyone to go. "Come by the church when you have some time. We can talk about it in more detail if you like."

Debbie smiled at him, for once she felt better. She felt like she had someone that would listen to her. Maybe this priest could show her how to bring Anthony out of the darkness that he was living in. If not, maybe he could help her come out of the darkness. "I will Father, I will. Thank you."

Father John stood up and rubbed Debbie's hand. "Good, you're welcome. I look forward to it. Until then, keep praying." Father John walked out of the room, leaving Debbie alone to her thoughts.

Chapter 33
It's Time To Wake Up

One week had passed since Mike was buried. Enzo was now formally under arrest for shooting Mike. He was being held on Riker's Island with no bail. The authorities had talked to Debbie, just as Mickey predicted. She gave her statement, with Mickey by her side and they went on their way.

Cristina had gone back to work; her mother did as well. Debbie still wasn't ready to go back and Lourdes was putting off photo shoots. The two sisters both spent a lot of time at the hospital, but they weren't getting any closer to each other. If anything, they were growing further apart. Debbie felt resentment towards her younger sister and it was almost impossible to hide it. It had always been like that, but lately it was worse and Lourdes felt it. Not to make a hard time worse, Lourdes tried to ignore it, it didn't always work.

It had been nearly two weeks and Debbie had gotten the call that they were beginning to bring Anthony back to consciousness. They waited longer since an infection started to set in, so they wanted to keep him sedated while they fought off the infection.

Today was the day that Anthony would be fully awake. No one knew what Anthony would remember about the park, so someone had to break the news to him that his best friend was dead and his other best friend was responsible for it and now sitting in a jail cell.

Debbie didn't know what to think, she didn't know where today would lead her. The last thing she said to Anthony was to get out of her life. She didn't know how he was going to wake up and react to her. She herself didn't know how she wanted to react. She didn't know where her life was going to take her and she wasn't sure if her life still included Anthony. She wasn't sure of anything.

Debbie was now arriving at the hospital. Her family was going to come later. She knew that she needed to see Anthony alone at first. She made her way through the hospital toward the ICU area. There she was met by the same doctor that attended to Anthony when she brought him in. She spoke to the doctor briefly about his condition and then the doctor led her to where Anthony was.

Debbie stood in the doorway and stared at him for a long minute. He had his head turned to the left and seemed to be looking out the window. He had a lot of machines hooked up to him: monitors, IV and endless wires and probes. His head was wrapped tightly from the gunshot wound, he almost looked like a mummy. Debbie slowly made her way into the room and Anthony gently turned his head towards the right to look at her. She made her way over to him and began to cry. He slowly lifted up his right arm and she reached out and touched his hand gently. "Hi," was all that she could say.

In a raspy, tired voice he replied, "Hi."

Debbie reached over the bed and kissed Anthony gently. She thought she wouldn't ever see him alive again. All her emotion welled up. "How do you feel?"

"I'm in a lot of pain."

Debbie fought to hold back more tears. "I know, the doctor said that you're going to be in pain for quite a while." Anthony reached down and grabbed a morphine drip activator and pressed it several times. "Go easy with that." Anthony pressed it a few more times and relaxed a bit as the morphine kicked in. "Do you remember anything that happened?"

Anthony thought about it for a second and then said, "I remember the park."

"Do you remember what happened at the park?"

Groggy, Anthony responded, "Cristina paged me."

"My sister paged you at the park?" Anthony slowly nodded his head. "What else do you remember?"

Anthony thought about it again and then replied, "A gun shot, I looked up and Mike was on the floor." Debbie closed her eyes as she remembered the look on Mike's face. "Then everything went black, I don't remember anything else." Debbie moved closer to the bed and held his hand again. "Where's Mike?"

Debbie swallowed hard while she searched for the words to tell him. She wasn't even sure if she should tell him at this point, but if she hid it from him he would be furious. She stroked his hand with her free one while holding it with her other one. "Anthony, Mike was shot twice." Anthony looked up at her and at that point it became apparent that he knew what she was going to say next. "Anthony, Mike passed away at the park, he didn't make it." Anthony turned his head back towards his left and stared out the window, burying the emotion that came with Debbie's revelation. Debbie squeezed his hand gently, but he didn't respond. "Anthony, do you want to talk about it?"

After a long minute of silence he asked, "Enzo shot Mike?"

"Yes," she replied.

Anthony looked back towards his right, at her. "Enzo shot me too?" he asked.

"No, Enzo didn't shoot you. A cop arrived just as Mike was shot. The cop shot you."

Anthony was quiet for a long minute and then asked, "Why didn't I die?"

Shocked at his question Debbie replied, "I followed you to the park. When you were shot Enzo ran away and the cop went after him. I came over and picked you up and drove you here."

Anthony stared at her for a long moment and then said, "You didn't want me in your life anymore. Why did you follow me to the deal?"

Debbie began to cry again and gently leaned into him. She squeezed his hand again and said, "Let's not talk about that now, that's not important."

Anthony looked back out the window. With Debbie leaning on him crying he asked, "Why did Enzo do that?"

Debbie thought about it for a minute. "I don't know."

Anthony thought about it some more, he was tired and in a lot of pain, but things started coming back to him. "I remember Enzo yelling something about the stuff that Mike gave him."

"What do you mean?"

"He said the drugs weren't real."

Debbie took a deep breath and asked, "Is it possible Mike gave Enzo fake drugs?"

Anthony gave Debbie a look that she hadn't seen before. "NO!"

"Okay, calm down, don't get yourself excited."

Anthony began to relax and then looked towards the window again. A nurse came in and began looking at one of the machines that Anthony was connected to. Debbie let his hand go and she moved towards the window and began to look out. She looked out at the city and thought to herself, about what had happened ever since the barbeque. The fight with Luis, the night of the massacre at the hospital and all that followed. She turned around quick and felt nauseous. She held her stomach and then ran into the bathroom. She barely made it in there when she began throwing up yet again. The nurse noticed how Debbie ran off and she followed her. "Miss, are you okay?" she asked.

Not answering right away Debbie continued to throw up. She was mentally drained and now it was taking a toll on her physically. Once she could stop throwing up long enough to answer she replied, "Yes, I'm fine."

After another minute of sickness she emerged from the bathroom. The nurse made sure she was okay and then left the room. Slowly, she made her way back towards the bed. Anthony asked, "What's wrong with you?"

Debbie put her head down and said, "I'm just not feeling well. I haven't slept in weeks, I haven't eaten, and everything is catching up to me."

"You need to take care of yourself."

Debbie rolled her eyes. She didn't want to fight with Anthony, but she was on edge. "Yeah, you tell me that and look how you take care of yourself." Anthony looked away. Feeling a fight coming on she decided to excuse herself. "I'm going outside for a minute." She reached over and kissed him on his cheek and then abruptly walked out of the room.

Once outside she exhaled and began to cry again. She didn't know what else to do anymore. She was lost and didn't feel well. She leaned up against the wall and let out another long, deep sigh. She closed her eyes and remained like that for a minute until a hand on her shoulder jarred her back to reality. She opened her eyes to find Mariana standing next to her; two of her bodyguards standing behind her. "Hello Debbie."

Startled and unable to hide it, she replied back with a very cold, "Hello Mariana."

"Are you okay?" Debbie remained silent for a moment until she forced a smile onto her face. "Is Antonio okay?"

Debbie hated when she heard Anthony referred to as Antonio, it made her skin crawl. She disliked Mariana very much, she was beautiful and she knew Anthony found her attractive. She wasn't sure of Anthony's link to her and she wasn't entirely sold on his version of how he knew her, so she let her mind run away with it. After a minute she replied, "*Anthony*, is fine," placing a large emphasis on Anthony, not Antonio.

Mariana caught Debbie's sarcasm and allowed a smirk to come across her face. She motioned for her bodyguards to give them some space. They retreated about twenty feet away down the hall. She turned back to Debbie and motioned for them to sit on some seats in the hallway. Reluctantly Debbie moved to the chairs and took a seat. "If he is okay, what is troubling you Debbie?"

Debbie let out another of her long exhausted sighs and then replied, "Do you really need to ask me something like that? Look at everything that we have been through in the last several weeks. I don't know how much more of this I can take or how much more Anthony can take."

Mariana looked towards Anthony's room and then back towards Debbie. "Antonio is a very strong person. He will get through this and he will come out stronger than you can imagine."

Debbie remembered the conversation she had with Anthony right after the war. She also had several conversations with Lourdes regarding Mariana. Lourdes was always very careful about what she told her regarding the conversations but Debbie knew there was more then what Lourdes had led on about, especially during the night of the assault on the Perez brothers. "How do you know so much about Anthony and his future?"

Mariana smiled and stared into Debbie's eyes. "It's something that I can do."

Debbie rolled her eyes. She, like Anthony, didn't believe any of that stuff. She thought about it for a minute and said, "Anthony mentioned to me you told him he would be a powerful person." Mariana smiled at her. "What did you mean by that?"

Mariana looked down the hallway at her two men, they were staring at her intently. She looked down the opposite way to make sure there weren't a lot of people around them and then spoke in a hushed tone. "I see Anthony in charge of a very powerful organization. The Italians refer to these organizations as families." Debbie agreed with her. "In my opinion they are nothing like a family." Mariana paused for a moment. "Maybe when it's Antonio's turn it will be though."

Debbie looked around the hallway now. "What I don't understand is Anthony is not fully Italian, he can't be made. How do you see him in control of a family?"

Mariana stared at her intently, reached over and took Debbie's hand and held it tightly. "Antonio will change all the rules. Nothing that you know now will apply. Look into my eyes."

Trying to burn images into Debbie's mind, Mariana concentrated on something in the future while holding Debbie's gaze. This was something very different then she usually did. When she gazed intently into someone's eyes she was usually reading them, reading their future, their soul. This time Mariana reversed it and allowed a window to be opened into what she saw. After a second Debbie tried to resist it. Mariana quickly reached out and held Debbie by the face and wouldn't let her break the stare. Debbie was helpless and she couldn't move. Debbie saw things, things she couldn't understand, didn't want to believe. She shook with a chill and fear. After a minute Mariana broke the look and sat back, visibly tired and drained. Debbie, now out of breath herself looked away and tried to compose herself. "How...how did you do that?"

Mariana, looking at the floor tried to regain her composure and shook her head. "That is not important. What is important is that you saw. You see, I tell the truth."

Debbie looked around the hospital. Still not sure of what she believed at that point she said, "I don't know what I just saw."

Mariana replied, "You saw the future."

Breathing heavy, Debbie replied, "He told me he was going to give all this up someday."

After a moment of long silence Mariana began to stand up. She looked down at Debbie and said, "You already have your mind made up Debbie."

Debbie asked, "He will be in charge of a family someday?"

Mariana continued, "Like I said, when his time comes, family will mean something." Debbie swallowed hard and looked nervous. She wanted to scream, she wanted to cry. She felt like she was going to explode. She once again felt like she was going to be sick. Mariana's two men approached. "I can't stay, I must go. Give Antonio my regards." Debbie, remaining silent, just looked at Mariana as she walked away with her two bodyguards in tow. Debbie watched her walk down the long hallway with tears in her eyes. After a moment she got up and ran to a bathroom in the hallway, only to be sick once again.

Mariana made her way slowly up the stairs into one of her safe houses. She too felt like she was going to be sick. One of her bodyguards went to park the car as Roberto made his way up the stairs behind her. She looked around in the dimly lit hallway. Another bodyguard was standing outside the entrance to the apartment. He looked scared and pale. He wouldn't look at Mariana. He would only stare at the floor. Mariana said to Roberto, "Something is wrong."

Now beginning to become alarmed Roberto looked around the hallway and made his way past Mariana. He headed towards the door and motioned for Mariana to stay back. Taking out his pistol he opened the door and looked into the apartment. Standing before him was a dark figure at the opposite end of the hallway. Before Roberto could raise his weapon the pistol began to heat up. He tried to hold onto it as long as he could, but the black gun began to glow red and orange from the immense heat that was radiating from it. Immediately, he howled out in pain, dropped it and pulled his burned hand into his chest; the skin on his palm quickly blistered from the burn. The pistol hit the floor with smoke coming off of it. Roberto backed up into the wall behind him as Mariana walked towards his side. She looked into the apartment and the dark cloaked figure began moving down the hallway towards her. "¡Mariana, es Ana Maria!" said Roberto.

Looking back at Roberto she replied, "Si."

The figure emerged from the dark apartment into the hallway and Mariana gazed at her. She was dressed in a long, hooded, black silk cloak. The inside of the cloak had a stunning purple lining as if it was a royal robe fit for a king or a queen. She wore a very short, tight, black dress under the robe, revealing perfect legs that didn't seem to want to end. She stood about five feet seven inches tall, but the heels she had on sent her near the six foot tall range. After a second the figure pulled back the hood to reveal a stunningly beautiful girl with dark black hair, very similar to Mariana's hair color, but not quite as long. She had two purple stripes of color in her hair, one flowing down on each side of her head. The purple color matched the inside of her robe almost perfectly. She had on a silver necklace; not as large as Mariana's but somewhat similar. It appeared to have a dark colored stone in the center and was surrounded by thorns. "Hola, Mariana," she said.

After a second of silence Mariana replied "Hola, Ana Maria."

Ana Maria looked over at Roberto clutching his burned hand. She reached out to touch him and he pulled away from her in fear. She stopped for a second and then reached again and touched his hand gently. "Lo siento." Roberto shook for a second and then looked up at Ana Maria. After a few seconds of her touching his hand he was no longer in pain. He looked down and his hand no longer had a burn mark on it. The blister was gone. "I couldn't risk you shooting me by mistake." Roberto looked back up at her and shuddered with fear.

"What are you doing here Ana Maria?" asked Mariana, clearly annoyed by her presence.

Ana Maria broke her gaze from Roberto and looked at Mariana. "La Reina sent me."

Roberto looked nervous when he heard the name. Mariana looked at him for a second and then back to Ana Maria. "¿La Reina, para qué?"

Ana Maria replied, "She wants you to come back to Colombia, immediately."

Mariana now began to look nervous, her eyes danced between Roberto's and Ana Maria's. "I cannot come back right now Ana Maria. I have business to attend to here."

Ana Maria made her way back into the apartment. After a second Mariana followed her. Roberto reached down and picked up his pistol and quickly holstered it. He entered the apartment and shut the door.

Once inside the apartment Ana Maria said to Mariana, "There is a jet waiting for us; La Reina wants you back in Colombia tonight." Ana Maria tilted her head to the side and asked, "Do you really want to keep her waiting?"

Mariana thought about it for a minute. A look of fear came across her face at the thought of having to go back to Colombia. "No." Fear was a rare emotion that Mariana felt, let alone expressed.

"Good, I will wait for you outside." Ana Maria made her way past Roberto, her long cloak sweeping past him as she made her way out of the apartment.

Mariana stood still. She said to Roberto, "Give me four of your men."

"Mariana! I am going back with you."

Mariana moved towards a bedroom. She went into the room and then behind a divider in the room and began changing her clothes. Roberto waited in the doorway. "No you're not Roberto, I need you to stay here."

"Mariana, you can't face La Reina alone. Let me come with you."

"You will be of no help to me there. You saw what Ana Maria just did to you, imagine La Reina!"

"Mariana, if that is the case then four of my men will be of no help either."

After a minute Mariana emerged from behind the divider. She now had on a short black dress similar to the one Ana Maria was wearing and a pair of high heels. "I don't expect your men to be of any help to me there, but I am not bringing you back there." Mariana stopped and looked at Roberto. "I need you to stay here, for your own good Roberto. If you come back with me you will be no good to me dead."

After a few seconds of thinking about it he replied, "Bien."

"Good," replied Mariana. She moved towards a closet, opened it and looked inside. She gazed towards Roberto before closing her eyes for a long minute. "I could be gone for a while. Keep an eye on Antonio for me, from a distance."

"Si, Mariana."

"Get the men ready and make sure they are men you won't miss."

Reluctantly, he agreed. Roberto took a radio off his hip and spoke into it ordering four men to meet Mariana outside and to go with her.

Mariana reached into the closet and pulled out a black silk robe just like Ana Maria's. The only difference was hers had a deep red lining in it, similar to the red stripe in her hair. She wrapped the cloak around her shoulders and pulled the hood over her head. After a second Roberto lowered his head and bowed to her. She turned and walked out of the room at a fast pace.

Chapter 34
Meeting Of The Coven

Mariana's jet touched down in Colombia in the very early hours of the morning. The black sky only yielded light from the moon and stars. The dawn light was far off. Landing at José María Córdova International Airport, cars were waiting for Mariana, Ana Maria and their respective bodyguards.

The small motorcade made their way through the city of Rionegro, a town located in the sub-region of Eastern Antioquia. It was officially called Ciudad Santiago de Arma de Rionegro, but more commonly called just Rionegro. The city was located East of Medellin and West of Marinilla, closer to the latter. It was a rich city due to its location and many industries of trade.

Just on the outskirts of the city a large house arose into view. Mariana looked at it and swallowed hard. She began to get nervous and it took a lot to get Mariana nervous. She hadn't been back to Colombia in a long time and she had a bad feeling about going to meet with La Reina. She looked over to Ana Maria who just gazed at her. They hadn't spoken a word on the flight from New York to Colombia.

The motorcade turned off the main road onto a dirt road that led to the sprawling estate. After several minutes of riding on the dirt road, they pulled into a huge courtyard in front of the house. The cars came to a stop and several men approached them and began to open the doors. Everyone emerged from their cars and began heading towards the estate. Mariana had two bodyguards in front of her and two more behind her. Ana Maria followed Mariana's group with two of her own bodyguards behind her.

Everyone walked at a brisk pace through a beautiful, long garden. Mariana pulled her hood over her head and Ana Maria did the same. They came to a high gate that began opening as soon as they approached it. Mariana stopped and looked down the long flight of stairs that were ahead of her. They appeared to lead under the estate. "You won't need your bodyguards any further Mariana."

Mariana smirked at Ana Maria, "My bodyguards will accompany me."

Ana Maria reached out and touched Mariana's arm and said, "Leave your bodyguards here, for their own sake Mariana."

Mariana stared at Ana Maria's hand for a long minute until she removed it. "You have no charge over me, Ana Maria."

Ana Maria gazed back at her and replied, "Very well." Mariana then proceeded through the gate with her bodyguards. Ana Maria motioned for hers to remain behind and then she followed Mariana down the dark steps.

Nothing else was spoken along the trip down the dark, dingy corridor. The only light along the path was provided every twenty feet or so from torches that lined both sides of the stone walls. Water could be heard rushing along the Negro River in the distance. Mariana and Ana Maria's high heels echoed along the stone pathway as they made their way towards a dark door. In front of the door were two guards standing duty. They became alert as Mariana's bodyguards got closer but then relaxed when they saw the two hooded women accompanying them.

Ana Maria motioned to one of the guards and he reached over and started opening the large wooden door. Mariana watched nervously as the door came open. Once fully opened she motioned for two of her men to enter and then she followed slowly behind them. Following her were her other two bodyguards and behind them was Ana Maria. Once everyone completely passed through the doorway the door was shut. When the door banged closed Mariana jumped slightly from the noise.

They were now in a long, wide cavernous room that was situated deep under the estate above them. The walls were made of the same stone that comprised the long pathway that led them here. All along the walls were torches that lit the entire room. From floor to ceiling were large stone columns. These beams were part of the foundation of the estate above them. There were a dozen of them in the room and each one was several feet in diameter.

Ana Maria stepped forward first and Mariana followed. She instructed her bodyguards to stay close behind her. As they made their way further into the room an altar at the front could be seen. There were many religious statues lining the room, much like

Mariana's safe house. All had candles in front of them with the same ritualistic offerings. The bodyguards looked at their surroundings and then at each other, all with the same look, wondering what they got themselves into by accompanying Mariana here; as if they had a choice.

Above the altar was a huge pentagram, each point of it was highlighted with a red stone. The altar was made of stone and it looked like it was stained with blood that had dripped from the top of it and that poured over the sides.

Another hooded, cloaked figure emerged from behind the altar. When the figure came into view Mariana and her bodyguards stopped in their tracks. Ana Maria looked over her shoulder at Mariana. Mariana caught her gaze and then slowly began walking again towards the altar. The two girls made their way about fifteen feet towards the other cloaked figure before they stopped.

The cloaked figure remained with their back towards the girls, facing the altar. The figure lit several large candles on the altar and then turned to face Mariana and Ana Maria. The figure was wearing an identical black silk robe, but this one had a bright silver lining inside. "So I finally have in front of me the Star of the Sea and Bitter Grace at the same time."

At the same time both Mariana and Ana Maria said, "Yes, Mi Reina."

"It has been a while." La Reina made her way slowly down the steps in front of the altar. She reached the bottom and walked over to Mariana and Ana Maria. She stopped in front of them and then lowered her hood, revealing a very pretty woman in her early forties. She had straight black hair with a silver stripe flowing down the right side of her head. The silver stripe matched the silver in her robe, the same as Mariana's and Ana Maria's matched their robes. She wore a silver pentagram necklace that matched the huge one on the wall behind her. She had a long black dress on under her robe and black high heeled boots. She stood much shorter than the two younger girls in front of her. Only about five foot one inch tall. Even with the three inch addition that the boots offered her she was still shorter than Mariana and was dwarfed by Ana Maria.

Ana Maria and Mariana immediately lowered their hoods when La Reina brought hers down. After a second of silence both girls lowered their heads in a bow to the older woman. La Reina stood motionless and stared at her two subjects in front of her as a queen would. She gazed over the girls shoulders and looked at the four bodyguards. "Who, brought bodyguards in here?"

Mariana remained in her bow but brought her eyes up to look at La Reina. She was clearly scared as she did. As she attempted to answer, La Reina turned her gaze from the bodyguards towards Mariana, already knowing the answer. Mariana quickly looked back towards the floor and replied "I.., I did."

La Reina glared at Mariana for a long moment. Unwilling to look up at her, Marina felt a cold chill run through her body. She tried to control her breathing, but it wasn't working. She closed her eyes and tried to concentrate on her breathing until she finally started to get it under control. The control didn't come until La Reina took her cold stare away from her. Once that occurred she felt like she could breathe normal, again. "I am very disappointed in you Mariana."

Trying to get the courage up to speak Mariana took another deep breath and asked nervously, "Why, Mi Reina?"

La Reina gazed at the bodyguards again and then back to Mariana. "You have created a bloodbath in New York."

Still with her head lowered in a bow Mariana continued, "It was unavoidable Mi Reina." Mariana swallowed hard awaiting La Reina's response.

"It was avoidable Mariana. Antonio could have handled the situation on his own. Your response was too extreme."

"I felt extreme was needed in this instance. The Perez brothers were not backing down after the attack on the hospital."

La Reina's eyes opened wide in response to Mariana's and she didn't seem pleased. "You eliminated the entire cartel, as well as family members that included children and infants." Mariana remained quiet. "It is actions like that which give organizations like ours a bad reputation. The Italian families look down on us because of it." Mariana continued to remain quiet for a long minute. La Reina looked toward Ana Maria who never looked up at her, but remained with her head in a bow as well.

After a moment Mariana broke the silence, "Mi Reina, we have secured a stronger partnership with the largest of the Italian families. In turn we will be the major supplier into New York for a long time to come."

La Reina thought about it for a minute. She made her way back up the steps towards the altar. After a second both Mariana and Ana Maria brought their heads up and looked at La Reina. "Do not trust your partnership with the Italian families Mariana. They are not to be trusted."

Mariana replied, "I don't trust them Mi Reina."

La Reina held her gaze and replied, "Good." She moved to light more candles along the steps and then she looked over her shoulder at Mariana. "What is it that you see in Antonio?"

After a moment of silence Mariana said, "He will be powerful Mi Reina."

La Reina continued lighting candles and then closed her eyes. She sprinkled some powder into the air in front of her and blew gently until the powder hit the flame of the candles. It made a small popping sound and filled the room with a pleasant odor. "I know he will be powerful. You have a different vision for him than I do though, don't you?"

Mariana began to get nervous again as La Reina walked back down the stairs. Mariana went to bow her head and La Reina waved her hand. Immediately Mariana could no longer lower her head any further than she did. She tried, but she was locked into the position that she was in. Slowly, La Reina moved her right hand up in mid-air, as she did Mariana's head rose as well until she was looking directly at her. A look of fear came across Mariana's face and she couldn't contain herself. She began to shiver with fear and she made a squealing noise, showing that she was uncomfortable. One of her bodyguards stepped forward but La Reina's gaze caught the bodyguard's eye as she waved her left hand. When she did this he was spun to his right and taken completely off his feet. The three other bodyguards tried to spring into action but La Reina was too quick for them. With a turn of her head toward her right the three bodyguards were all forced backwards, each into a column. Crashing back first into the stone pillars, they all dropped their primary weapons and fell forward onto their faces.

Ana Maria turned around and looked at the four bodyguards thrown throughout the room writhing in pain and astonishment. She turned towards Mariana and said, "I told you to leave them outside."

La Reina shifted her gaze from the four men towards Ana Maria and then she released her hold on Mariana. She glanced back at Mariana and said, "You should have listened to your sister."

Shaking with fear, Mariana backed away from La Reina a little bit. Wind could be felt traveling throughout the room as Mariana looked around nervously, trying to find the source of it. Ana Maria moved away from Mariana and began walking up the steps and took place behind La Reina on her right side. "Please, Mother, what are you going to do to me?" asked Mariana, while shaking.

"My daughter, you need to be disciplined." La Reina pulled her right hand back and then pushed it forward. When she did a burst of unseen energy hit Mariana like a brick wall.

"NO!" screamed Mariana as she held her hands up trying to block the blast of energy. For a brief second she could contain it, but then it overwhelmed her and threw her backwards into one of the columns five feet behind her as it did her bodyguards; this blast being much stronger.

The first bodyguard got to his feet and began pulling his pistol from his holster. La Reina looked at him and motioned with her left hand again. When she did the pistol left the man's hand and flew towards the left side of the room. Stunned by what just took place he stood in complete shock. He glanced at Ana Maria who just shook her head gently from side to side. He tried to move away but now he couldn't. La Reina threw more powder in the air towards the candle in front of her. This time she blew a harder breath towards the flame and like a flame thrower, fire spat out towards the frozen bodyguard. Within seconds the flame engulfed him and all he could do was scream as the fire intensified. Everyone in the room watched on as the bodyguard hit the floor, unmoving and on fire.

La Reina made her way back down the stairs towards her daughter. "We have very different views on the destiny of your friend Antonio."

With tears in her eyes Mariana looked up at her mother, "Please Mi Reina, I beg of you!"

"Antonio has one purpose: to rise against the five families. When they fall he will fall!"

"NO!" yelled Mariana.

Annoyed by the lack of respect that Mariana just showed her La Reina gestured once again with her hand. Another burst of energy caught Mariana and it sent her rolling in a tumble roll across the floor. Mariana rolled fifteen feet across the gigantic room, screaming and begging for her punishment to stop.

La Reina continued walking towards her when the three remaining bodyguards got to their feet and tried to aid Mariana. Stopping the pursuit of her daughter she shifted her attention towards the bodyguards. Foolishly, two of them continued on towards her while one went towards Mariana. La Reina gave them an evil glare as they un-holstered their remaining pistols. As they started to train their weapons on her she reached out with both of her hands and made a motion of drawing them together, almost as if she was going to clap her hands. As she did this the two bodyguards slowly turned towards each other. Unwillingly aiming their weapons at one another La Reina then made an outward motion with her hands causing the two bodyguards to fire on one another at point blank range. La Reina stepped back and watch the two bodyguards cut themselves to pieces in a hail of bullets; both dropping to the floor dead.

La Reina glanced over her left shoulder and watched the one remaining bodyguard helping Mariana towards the door. She shook her head in disgust as she made her way towards her escaping daughter. The bodyguard reached out and opened the door only to have the handle fly back out of his hand and have the door slam shut in his face. Mariana saw her mother approaching them in a steady pace, Ana Maria trailing closely behind. "You should know Mariana that there is no place to go."

Dropping to her knees as if to beg for forgiveness tears once again began to stream down Mariana's face. "Please Mi Reina, no more!"

Before the bodyguard could turn around La Reina opened her mouth and a shrieking, blood curdling noise emerged from it. It was such a high octave that the bodyguard tried covering his ears as he shook with pain. Mariana too covered her ears in the vain attempt to hide from the noise, but she was unsuccessful. After what seemed like an eternity of pain and suffering, the last bodyguard dropped to his knees. He seemed to be taking the brunt of the force from the yell, but Mariana was still suffering as well. Already on the floor holding her ears from the piercing pain she rolled herself into a fetal position to try and absorb the horrific sound. Ana Maria stood idly by behind her mother, watching the scene unfold in front of her, unaffected by the punishment her mother was dishing out to her sister and protector.

The bodyguard let his hands drop to his sides, completely out of energy from the noise that was assaulting his senses. He looked up at La Reina as blood started dripping from his ears. He began to shake violently and then blood began to pour from his eyes and nose. After several long seconds of bleeding and twitching he collapsed over to his side and stopped moving, blood now rapidly pouring from every orifice in his head. La Reina closed her mouth, causing the sound to stop.

Mariana, who was curled up in a ball and crying, finally removed her hands from her ears. Bringing herself to speak she tearfully said, "What is it that you want from me Mother?"

La Reina glared down at her beaten daughter. "You have shown too much to your friend. You have planted the seeds of power in him."

Confused, Mariana asked, "Isn't that what you wanted?"

La Reina kneeled down next to her daughter. As she did Mariana slid slowly and fearfully away from her. "You and I have a very different vision for him. I know the vision you have presented to him. You revealed three pains to him and you revealed the city of fire."

"I.., I was trying to get him to believe me. He doubts what I tell him when it comes to the future."

"The future you speak of, I know that you see yourself in charge with him. That will not come to pass." La Reina stood up and walked back towards Ana Maria. She turned back towards Mariana and hit her with another invisible burst of energy. This one was different as it didn't send her across the room or into a wall. It hit her internally, causing her to feel pressure and pain inside her body. Wind began whipping through the room once again as La Reina rained down judgment on Mariana. Laying on the floor in great pain,

Mariana begged her mother once again to stop the onslaught of torture that she was putting her through. Heat ravaged the inside of her body and she felt as if she would burst into flames any second. "You think you can replace me as the head of this organization, but I won't let you do to me the same that happened to your father." After another long minute of the punishment, La Reina ceased her attack on Mariana and allowed her to gain her composure.

Mariana said fearfully, and in pain, "I will bring your vision to pass."

La Reina now had a smirk across her face. "Antonio must not be allowed to endure his second pain. Once he makes his moves on the other families then you will make your move on him. Do you understand me?"

Mariana caught her breath and then hesitantly replied, "Yes Mi Reina."

La Reina smiled and said, "Muy bien." She stepped over her daughter and opened the door and instructed the two guards standing outside to come in.

The two guards entered the room and looked around at the sight before them. Knowing better than to ask questions of what happened in the room they bowed their heads to La Reina and asked, "¿Si, Mi Reina?"

"Llevala a un cuarto."

Stunned, Mariana looked to her mother as the two bodyguards helped her up. "What? Why must I stay here?"

La Reina smiled at her daughter and replied, "For what you have caused in New York, and for your disobedience with Antonio, you will remain here until you learn your rightful place amongst us."

Defiantly, Mariana protested, "I have an operation in New York to oversee."

"Ana Maria can see to your operation while you sit here and think about your actions. It will be a few years before Antonio is back in play. That will be enough time for you to embrace our true cause." La Reina motioned to her two guards and they reached over and began pulling Mariana out of the room while she continued to resist them. Weakened by the assault her mother gave her she couldn't resist much. No longer paying any attention to her daughters whining, La Reina headed back towards the altar with Ana Maria by her side. The door to the room closed as the guards led Mariana away.

"Do you really think she will see your vision through Mi Reina?"

La Reina glanced at her daughter as they slowly walked deeper into the room. "She will have to. She has Antonio's trust. When it comes time for him he will only rely on her."

"She has bonded with him."

Turning her head quickly to look at Ana Maria she asked, sounding shocked, "How do you know this?"

Glancing back at her mother she replied, "I have felt it. She kissed him. They are intertwined now."

Looking away La Reina thought about it for a minute. "He has great love for these sisters, Mariana will not be able to break that bond."

"If he reaches his third pain she will."

La Reina thought about that comment. "If he reaches his third pain then we would have failed anyway." La Reina walked up the steps towards the altar.

"What do you want of me Mother?"

La Reina looked at her daughter. "Go to New York and take control of Mariana's forces. Beware, they are loyal to her, and you will meet resistance."

Ana Maria asked, "What of the deal she made with the Italian families?"

"Honor it. In the end it was a good move."

Ana Maria agreed and then asked, "What about Ecuador?"

La Reina thought about her question. "Ecuador is on the rise. They will be the key to Antonio coming back into the life. It is something that must be allowed, for now."

"He will not deal with me."

"When the time is right I will send Mariana back to New York to help Antonio with his struggle. When that comes to pass she will eliminate him. You will be there to make sure she does."

"What if she doesn't eliminate him?"

Without hesitation La Reina replied, "You will eliminate him and then you will eliminate her."

Ana Maria bowed her head and then started heading down the stairs. Halfway down she turned back around and caught her mother's gaze. "What if she does eliminate him as planned?"

La Reina gave Ana Maria a piercing gaze and replied, "Eliminate her anyway. I will not end up like your father."

Ana Maria smiled at her mother, bowed her head again, and headed down the stairs and out of the room raising her hood as she departed.

Chapter 35
Done

One week had passed since Anthony woke up and he was recuperating much faster than anyone had anticipated. The hospital was even talking about releasing him over the next few days.

Anthony sat up in his hospital bed as Mickey went over what he knew about the case. Enzo was under arrest for the murder of Mike. The authorities were planning on bringing charges against Anthony for drug trafficking and weapons possession. They were still considering an attempted murder charge since Anthony had his weapon pulled and turned towards the cop. Anthony sat and listened intently as Mickey laid everything out for him as Debbie sat by his side. "What is your opinion Mickey?" asked Anthony.

"Well," he replied as he thought about it, "I think this case can be won, but it's not going to be easy." Anthony listened intently to his friend. "The weapons charge will be hard to beat. You had the gun in your hand and you did turn towards the responding officer. If they do file attempted murder charges that is going to be tricky." Debbie sat quietly and listened closely.

"I turned when he yelled freeze, I didn't have it in my hand to shoot at him. I pulled it out in case Enzo was going to turn his on me."

"I believe you, it's a matter of getting twelve jurors to believe you. With this whole situation, that's going to be tough."

"Why is it going to be so tough?" asked Debbie.

Mickey shifted his look from Anthony to Debbie. "Well, it was a drug deal taking place in the middle of a park. Three guys there with guns and drugs; children playing in the distance. Considering what just went on with the Perez brothers and that whole war in the streets thing, they are taking this seriously and cracking down on things like this." Debbie had to agree with him.

Anthony let out a frustrated sigh, "That fucking cop jumped the gun. I wasn't even facing him when he let that shot off." Mickey continued staring at him and Anthony thought about it for a minute. "This whole thing just doesn't feel right."

Annoyed Debbie got up from her seat by the bed and asked Anthony, "This doesn't feel right?" Why would this feel right?" Before Anthony could answer her she said, "I told you not to go to that fucking deal, but you didn't listen to me. Now look at the world of shit you have yourself in." Debbie moved around the bed and looked out the window.

Mickey, watching her for a second, shifted his gaze from her to Anthony. "There is always the other option that we spoke about."

Anthony caught Mickey's gaze and then agreed with him. Debbie turned away from the window and asked, "What other option?"

Anthony continued staring at Mickey. After a second he looked back at Debbie. "It's a backup plan."

Mickey added, "Something to ensure Anthony won't go to prison."

Anthony asked Mickey, "Can it be done?"

Debbie asked, "What kind of backup plan?"

Mickey replied, "This is something we always planned for, so yeah I think so."

"What are the two of you talking about?" asked Debbie.

"Get it rolling, I don't want to take any chances with this." Anthony thought for a minute as Mickey stood up and headed for the door. "Take care of both issues Mickey."

Mickey replied, "You got it." He walked out of the room as Debbie made her way back towards the bed.

"What the hell are the two of you planning?"

Anthony replied, "We just told you, it's a backup plan to ensure that I won't see jail time."

"What are you looking to do, eliminate people so you don't have to go to jail?"

Annoyed, Anthony asked, "What the hell are you talking about? Who would I eliminate?"

"I don't know, the cop maybe?"

Anthony took a deep breath, "I am not eliminating anybody. Calm down, who do you think I am? Mickey has connections in the courts. He might be able to get a judge on this case that can affect the outcome of the verdict, even get the charges reduced or dropped, that's all."

Debbie shook her head again and moved back to the window. "You'll have to excuse me if that is the first thing I jumped to thinking," she said sarcastically. "I see how you handled the Perez issue."

"Here we go again," said Anthony.

Debbie said, "No, we're not!" With that she stormed out of the hospital room.

"Deb, where are you going?"

Debbie left the hospital, made her way home and sat in the driveway for a few minutes and just cried. She didn't believe Anthony, she felt he was doing something other than swaying the outcome of the trial the way he said he was going to. She felt he was up to something more devious.

After a few minutes of crying she got out of her car and made her way into her house. As she opened the door she could smell food cooking and hear music playing in the house. She listened for a minute and heard Spanish music playing and she knew then her sisters were there. She closed her eyes and rested her head on the door. She was not in the mood for them right now. Even Cristina had begun to get under her skin more than usual. She listened some more and once she heard her mother she then made her way into the house.

"Hi Sweetheart!" said her mother. "How are you doing?"

In what was becoming a normal tone for her, she replied, "I'm tired Mother. Very tired."

Feeling the annoyance of her daughter she went about her cooking while catching Cristina's look. She motioned towards Lourdes to shut off the radio and she did. After a few minutes of silence Cristina asked, "Are you okay Debbie?"

Debbie moved towards the refrigerator and took out a can of soda and opened it. Not really in a rush to answer her sister she simply nodded her head. After a minute she finally said, somewhat sarcastically, "Just wonderful." With that she moved into the dining room and began looking at the mail.

Cristina went back to cooking while Lourdes stood quietly and rolled her eyes. "Sometimes I don't understand her."

Charging back into the kitchen from the dining room Debbie asked, "What's for you to understand Lourdes?"

Slamming down a pot on the stove Lourdes turned towards her sister with a nasty reply of her own, "You Debbie! What the fuck is your problem?"

Stepping in between the two sisters, trying to diffuse the situation, was their mother. "Come on girls, we're not going to do this tonight."

"My fucking problem is you Lourdes, it's always been you!"

"DEBBIE!" yelled Brenda. "That's completely uncalled for. Your sister, both of your sisters, are here to help you."

Looking back at her mother with a glaring stare she replied. "The only reason she is here is for Anthony, not me!"

"What is that supposed to mean?" asked Lourdes.

Turning to look at Cristina, Debbie then said, "Both of them."

Stunned, Cristina asked, "What are you talking about Debbie? Where is this coming from?"

Turning away frustrated Debbie made her way into the dining room and then the living room. Brenda said to Cristina and Lourdes, "Let her go and calm down."

Pushing past her mother Lourdes said, "Fuck that."

Cristina reached out to stop her sister from pursuing Debbie but was unsuccessful. "Lourdes, let it go."

Not listening to her mother or her sister she followed Debbie into the living room only to be met with a nasty stare. "Lourdes, leave me the hell alone."

"Leave you alone? You came in the house with this shit mood yelling and screaming at us."

"Yeah I did. I came in MY house. My house to loud Spanish music and you all up my ass."

"Oh, I'm sorry the SPANISH music ruined your day."

Walking away Debbie said, "Fuck off Lourdes."

At the end of her rope with her sister, Lourdes reached out and grabbed Debbie by the shoulder spinning her around. Before it could escalate any further Brenda jumped between the two of them and pulled them apart while Cristina pulled Lourdes away from Debbie.

In a bit of shock by being grabbed by her sister, Debbie backed off a little and then began crying.

"What the hell is wrong with the two of you?" asked Brenda.

Debbie made her way to the couch and sat as her mother followed her. Crying she leaned into her mother. "Yeah, coddle her," said Lourdes.

Fed up, Brenda replied, "That's enough Lourdes!" Looking down at her daughter she asked, "Sweetheart, what is going on with you?"

After a minute of composing herself she replied, "I have had it with everything. I have had it with this lifestyle of Anthony's. I've had it with this whole situation."

Lourdes rolled her eyes again and moved to sit in a chair across the room. Once Cristina was sure Lourdes wasn't going to charge at her sister she went and sat on the other side of Debbie. "Sweetheart, I know you have been through a lot up until now, but things are going to get better."

Debbie gave Cristina a look. "You have no idea what it is to live like this."

"Live like what?" asked Lourdes. "You have a boyfriend that loves you and would do anything for you."

Debbie gazed at her sister across the room. "You think so? He would do anything for the two of you, not me. Look at what he did all across the city for the two of you. I asked him not to go to a drug deal, did he listen and do that for me?"

Cristina asked, "So that's what this is about Debbie? You're going to blame everything on your sister and me?"

Shocked Debbie turned back to Cristina. "You have got to be kidding me. We were fine until I introduced him to the two of you. He had to get involved in your issues with Carlos." Turning to look at Lourdes she said, "He had to be your fucking knight in shining armor at the barbeque."

Responding back to her sister, Lourdes said, "Neither one of us asked him for help in either of our situations."

Shaking her head Debbie said, "No, of course not."

Cristina said, "I am really surprised at you Debbie."

Debbie got up and walked away from Cristina. Halfway across the room she turned around and said, "What are you so surprised about?" Before Cristina could answer her she said, "Surprised that I feel the same way towards you that I do towards Lourdes?"

Brenda got up from the couch and made her way towards her daughter. "Sweetheart, once Anthony comes home things will be better, you'll see. He said he's going to get out of this lifestyle."

After a minute of silence Debbie said, "It's never going to get better Mama. He was sitting in the hospital room with his lawyer today talking about how to fix his trial. For all I know he could be planning to kill the cop, the prosecutor and God knows who else."

Stunned by what she just heard, Brenda backed up and questioned, "Does he have the ability to do that?"

Shrugging her shoulders Debbie replied, "Probably, who knows what he is capable of! Look at what he and Mariana did to the Perez brothers and their organization."

"Debbie," started Cristina, "why don't you give him a chance? Like Mama said, he told you he isn't going to stay in this lifestyle."

Staring at the floor and thinking about what Mariana made her see she looked up and said, "I can't do this anymore. I don't want to do this anymore. I won't do this anymore."

Standing up Lourdes asked, "What are you going to do?"

Taking a deep breath and calmly looking at her sister Debbie replied, "I'm getting out of here."

Walking towards Cristina, Lourdes asked, "What do you mean Debbie?"

Looking over at her sisters with tears in her eyes she replied, "I am doing something I should have done a long time ago; I'm leaving him." Stunned by her revelation Cristina, Lourdes and their mother all looked at each other not knowing what to say. After a moment of silence Debbie continued, "I can't live like this anymore. I don't know what he is capable of anymore. After this shit with Carlos and with what Mariana showed me I know he is never going to leave this life."

"What are you talking about with Mariana?" asked Lourdes.

Debbie replied, "Mariana told me how Anthony is going to be in charge of a family someday."

"In charge of a family?" asked Brenda.

Debbie replied, "Yes, in charge of a family. Running things like a family, with his family."

"You can't listen to that woman," said Lourdes lying. She knew what Mariana spoke of and she believed her as well. She couldn't let her sister know that she knew and believed her, but she needed to try and stop this situation before Debbie did something that would hurt Anthony. "She has these fantasies. You know yourself Anthony can't even be made, how is he going to run a family?"

Covering her eyes and shaking her head she yelled, "I DON'T KNOW!" After a minute of composing herself she continued, "I saw things."

"What kinds of things Debbie?" asked her mother as she approached her daughter again.

"She held my hand and did something to me and made me see these visions. Visions of him killing people, ordering people to be killed. I saw him rich, powerful and ruthless. I never believed any of that fortune telling shit, but I know what I saw."

"Debbie," said Cristina, "that's not Anthony."

Debbie let out a long breath and said, "You don't know him. What I saw is not the Anthony that any of us know, but believe me he is capable of it. I can see it."

"What are you going to do Sweetheart? What do you want to do?" asked Brenda.

"I know that I'm going to leave here."

"Where are you going to go?" asked Lourdes.

Shaking her head she said, "I don't know, but I can't be with him anymore. I can't be here anymore."

Walking over closer to her sister Cristina asked, "Debbie, are you sure you want to do this? He is going to be coming home from the hospital soon. He is going to need someone to take care of him. Why don't you give it some time?"

"I'm leaving here before he comes home."

"What?" asked Lourdes shocked and surprised.

Cristina and Lourdes stared at each other for a minute. "Debbie, he is going to need help."

Debbie replied, "I can't give him that help. For me it's over. I'm done here and I'm done with him."

Cristina caught her mother's attention and gave her a look to try and intervene and change Debbie's mind, but the look on her face spoke something different. "You have to do what makes you happy Debbie. You can come and stay with me if you want."

Cristina continued staring at her mother in total shock. "You agree with her line of thinking Mama?"

"This is your sisters decision Cristina, we can't get involved with it. The same way we couldn't get involved with you and Carlos."

"I don't believe what I am hearing," added Lourdes. "This is nothing like her and Carlos. Anthony doesn't abuse her."

Debbie sat back down on the couch crying once again. "I need to get out of New York. I need to get as far away from here as possible."

Brenda looked at her curiously, "Why?"

Debbie replied, "I just need to. I don't know what he is going to do when he comes home and sees that I'm gone. He'll go looking for me at your house first."

"Hello!" said Lourdes. "You are talking about him like he's Carlos. That's not Anthony. He is not going to do that, but you have to at least tell him things are over. You can't just get up and leave."

Debbie stood up and said, "No. He will never let me go or he will try to talk me out of it and I can't do that. I need to leave and I need to leave now." Debbie started to head upstairs. As she got to the base of the stairs she looked back at her family. "We all need to go." Staying in silence everyone just stared at her. Realizing her sisters weren't going anywhere she said to them, "You're my family, you have to go as well."

Lourdes was the first to break the silence, "Now you want to call us a family?"

"Lourdes!" said her mother.

Shaking her head she took a step towards Debbie. "All these years you never thought of me as a sister. Your hatred towards me has been evident for as long as I can remember. Now you want to hurt the guy that loves you and you want us to play a part in that?"

"I don't want you to play a part in it. You are my sisters, you should stay by my side in this."

Cristina moved next to Lourdes and said, "Debbie, Lourdes is right. She has caught the brunt of your hatred throughout the years a lot more than I have, but I don't agree with what you're doing."

Debbie looked at Cristina with disbelief in her eyes. If anything she would have thought that Cristina would have stuck with her. She knew Lourdes would have been a stretch, but not Cristina. "I don't believe this."

"After everything Anthony did for me. After everything he did for all of us to keep us safe, I can't turn my back on him," said Cristina.

Debbie shifted her eyes from Cristina to Lourdes. She knew it was a useless point, if Cristina didn't come with her, Lourdes wouldn't either. Without any words spoken Lourdes moved next to Cristina and held her hand. Debbie turned her look towards her mother and asked, "You?"

Brenda walked over to her, "You're my daughter. Are you sure this is what you want to do?"

Without hesitation Debbie replied, "Yes, I'm sure."

"Okay, go and pack your things." Debbie looked at her two sisters once again. As her eyes met theirs they both looked away from her. After a second she headed up the stairs crying. Once she was out of the room Brenda walked over to them. "You two need to think about this harder."

"We need to think about this?" asked Lourdes.

"Yes, that's your sister. If she is right about one thing it's that family sticks together."

Cristina interrupted and said, "Lourdes is right. She never thought of us as sisters. Now that it's to her advantage she wants to call us that?"

Lourdes quickly agreed with Cristina. "I won't be a part of hurting Anthony like that. He needs help, he needs us."

Stunned, Brenda turned to head up the stairs after Debbie. "This is your final answer?"

Cristina and Lourdes looked at each other for a second, both with tears in their eyes now. After a second they looked back at their mother and both replied, "Yes."

"Okay, then I have to turn my back on the two of you." With that Brenda made her way up the stairs.

The Sixth Family

Cristina hesitantly moved a few inches towards the stairs and then stopped, looked at Lourdes and threw her arms around her and hugged her tight. Both stayed quiet, crying in each others arms for a minute before Cristina pulled on her sister and said, "Come on Lourdes, let's get out of here." Agreeing with Cristina, the two sisters left the house, arm in arm with each other.

Chapter 36
Pain

Three days had passed since Debbie left her house with her mother and now Anthony was looking at coming home. He stood in front of the window looking out across the city in deep thought. He hadn't seen Debbie since she stormed out of the hospital room. Lately it wasn't unusual for them to go several days without talking. Debbie had been in a very set off mood and Anthony was not looking to get into it with her. He didn't know that she left though, Cristina and Lourdes hadn't told him; they wanted to wait until he came home.

As he looked out his window an orderly came into the room with a wheelchair and began bitching to him that he wasn't supposed to be out of bed and on his feet. Much like when Cristina came out of the hospital, he wasn't supposed to be walking until he left. Reluctantly, he made his way to the wheelchair and sat. His head was bandaged on his right side tightly. He needed to clean the wound three times a day to prevent the infection from coming back and he needed to come back for follow up visits twice a week to monitor his condition.

Mickey had managed to get the authorities to back off some since he had a complicated medical condition, but it was only an amount of time before the authorities would press on with their case against him.

Sitting in the chair gave him time to think. He thought of the loss of his best friend. Mike was gone and Anthony wasn't conscious to go to his funeral. He was strong when people were around, but when he was alone he allowed himself to cry at the loss of his friend. They were like brothers and Anthony felt the emptiness now. Even with all his impending legal troubles on his mind, he still thought of Mike.

Teresa had come to see him and that made it harder to think about his friend. Teresa was thinking about going down to Florida with some of her family. She could no longer stay up here and stay in the house. Now Anthony was looking at losing another friend as well.

Everywhere Anthony looked there was loss, Mike was gone, Teresa was leaving and to him Enzo was now gone as well. Even if he wasn't in jail he could never bring himself to look at Enzo again. Enzo took his friend away, for that Anthony couldn't have him in his life at all. He had other plans for Enzo now.

There was more loss that he was going to have to face, still not knowing about Debbie, he knew nothing about Mariana. He didn't think it was odd that Mariana hadn't been around to see him, he just thought she was busy. He didn't know she did in fact come to see him and he didn't know what she revealed to Debbie. He also didn't know Mariana unwittingly helped seal Debbie's mind on what she needed to do. It was right after that encounter that Mariana was summoned back to Colombia to face her mother. Anthony had no idea what kind of trouble Mariana was actually in. For all intents and purpose she was among the missing now as well.

He sat quiet and looked around the room at all the flowers that were sent to him, wishing him to get well. The room was packed and looked more like a florist then a hospital room. Dozens and dozens of arrangements from all the wise guys from all the different clubs that he worked out of.

Even that was gone to him now as well. He was done with the clubs, done with the families, done with the work. He sent Mickey back to the families to tell them he was finished. Mickey confirmed they would let him out of his commitments. He wasn't made, so it was a little easier for him to walk away from this life than most people. Still he knew a lot about the businesses that went on in the clubs and he was worried that they would take action against him, worried that he might flip to save his skin regarding the drug charges. Anyone that really knew him though knew that he was a standup guy. He might as well have been a made guy. He would never talk against the families, never flip.

The crew that he was part of was completely destroyed. Mike was dead. Enzo was in jail and looking at a long prison sentence. Anthony was facing his own legal issues. The hammer that Anthony was waiting to drop already had.

Depression started to set in as he sat there and thought of all his troubles when Cristina and Lourdes walked into his room. They quickly turned his depression around when he saw them, but he didn't know they were about to unwillingly deliver more bad news to him.

He brightened up and smiled as the two sisters came into the room. "Hi!" said Cristina as she flashed her beautiful smile at him. He greeted the two sisters with hugs and kisses.

The doctor followed them into the room with information regarding Anthony's discharge. He ran over all the information that Anthony would need regarding care of his wound and follow up appointments. Everyone listened intently and then the doctor left the three of them in the room.

Anthony stared at the door wondering when Debbie was going to come in. Cristina pulled two chairs over next to Anthony and her and her sister sat with him. Anthony smiled at them and asked, "Uh oh, what's going on?"

Cristina looked at Lourdes for a brief second and then back to Anthony. She took a deep breath and then said, "Lourdes and I were thinking, what do you think about coming and staying with us for a while? You know, until you felt well enough to be on your own."

Anthony looked at Cristina and then back to Lourdes. "What's wrong with my house? Isn't it a little tight for four of us to stay at your place?"

Lourdes thought about it for a second and then said, "That's the thing Anthony, it wouldn't be four of us. It would just be the three of us."

Anthony thought about that and put his head down for a minute and then asked, "I guess Debbie is back to her stance about not wanting me in the house, like she did before I went on the deal?"

"Well," started Cristina, "it's not exactly like that."

Anthony shifted his gaze towards her and asked, "Well, what is it then?"

Cristina swallowed hard and decided to let Anthony know everything. "Sweetheart, Debbie left the house and moved out."

"What?" asked Anthony shocked. "Where did she go?"

"We don't know."

Anthony laughed for a second, not willing to believe what Cristina just told him. He continued laughing for another few seconds and then said, "Come on, let's be for real."

Lourdes reached out and held Anthony's hand and Cristina did the same. Now it was Lourdes's turn to try and explain it. "She really left Anthony. The other night when she came home from here and you were talking with Mickey about your legal issues. She came into the house in a mood that neither of us have ever seen her in. She went on this rant of how she couldn't do this anymore and she needed to leave."

Anthony couldn't believe what he was hearing. "I knew she left here annoyed, but I didn't think she was going to go to that kind of extreme."

Cristina continued, "She went on about something that Mariana told her."

Anthony quickly looked over at Cristina and asked, "Mariana? What did she tell her? When?"

Lourdes answered "Mariana came here to see you a week or so ago and she ran into Debbie in the hallway. She started telling her about some of the things she told us in the safe house. You, the future, you running things."

"Fucking Mariana! Why the hell would she tell her those bullshit stories?"

Lourdes frowned and said, "She did more than tell her."

"What do you mean?" asked Anthony.

"Apparently, she showed her."

"What?" asked Anthony unwilling to believe anything he was hearing.

Cristina added, "Debbie said Mariana held her hands and showed her things. You, in the future, in power, killing people and ordering people to be killed."

Anthony closed his eyes and shook his head in frustration. He couldn't understand why Mariana would have done such a thing. It was as if Lourdes could read his mind when she said, "Debbie asked her about the future. Mariana didn't do it on her own." Not understanding herself why Lourdes would say that, Cristina looked at her sister in confusion. Lourdes never looked back at her.

"Where did she go?" asked Anthony.

Cristina swallowed hard as she answered, "We don't know Sweetheart."

"Oh come on, you two have to know where she went. You're her sisters. What did she do, go to stay with your mom?"

Cristina pleaded, "Anthony, you have to understand, we wouldn't lie to you. There was a terrible argument in your house the night that she left. She pretty much gave us an ultimatum, her or you."

Anthony asked, "And you two chose me?"

After a minute of silence Lourdes laughed and said, "It wasn't a hard choice."

Cristina laughed and playfully slapped her sister's arm. "Lourdes!"

Anthony smiled for a second and then said, "There is no way I am going to allow myself to come between you and your family."

Cristina reached out and held Anthony's hand again, this time much tighter. "Sweetheart, listen to me. You are too important to both of us for us to turn our back on you. You were there for both of us when no one else was. You were there for me at my darkest time with Carlos. No one, and I mean no one will ever come between you and us!"

Anthony tried to hold his emotion in. Lourdes reached over and took his other hand again and squeezed it. "Family, over time, will repair itself. Don't you worry about that right now. What you need to do is concentrate on getting better and worry about your legal issues. Do you understand?" asked Lourdes.

After a second Anthony reluctantly agreed. Cristina and Lourdes both reached over and hugged him at the same time. "You let us worry about helping you get better, okay?" asked Cristina.

Anthony smiled and replied, "Okay."

"Good!" said Lourdes as she stood up and moved behind his wheelchair. "So, do you want to go and stay at that house or do you want to come and stay with us?"

Anthony smiled at her, "I'll come and stay with you two. We have to stop there though so I can get something's out of there."

Lourdes bent down close to Anthony's left ear and said, "We figured that and we already packed your stuff for you. It's waiting to be picked up at the house." Looking at him from the corner of her eye she reached over and kissed him gently on his left cheek. "Whatever you don't have we can go shopping!"

Cristina stood up and watched her sister and Anthony acting playfully with each other and said, "Oh no, shopping! You don't want to go shopping with her!"

"Hey!" said Lourdes. "What's wrong with my shopping?"

The three left the hospital room laughing with each other.

The car ride home was quiet. Cristina was driving the GNX and it didn't even bother Anthony that anyone other than him was driving his car. They pulled into the driveway and Anthony looked up at the house. Slowly the three of them got out of the car and made their way into the empty house. Anthony looked around the living room and he could feel Debbie's presence even though she wasn't in the house. He could smell the scent of her perfume. He looked around again and tried to keep his emotions in check. Sensing what was going on in his mind Cristina rubbed his arm and said, "Lourdes and I will take the bags out to the car. If we missed anything else just grab it."

Anthony said, "Okay," and started walking up the stairs as the girls took his bags out to the car. He looked at pictures on the stairs as he made his way up to the second floor. He walked into the bedroom and grabbed some bracelets of his that were in a jewelry box, then he grabbed his chain and cross that were laying on the dresser. He paused and looked at a picture of Debbie and himself. Tears welled up in his eyes as he stepped backwards and threw himself onto the bed, back first, clutching the gold chain. Crying and in emotional pain he screamed out, "DEBBIE, WHY!?!"

Twenty five hundred miles away in Colombia, a tattered and beaten Mariana laid in a small stone cell that only contained a twin size cot and a toilet. She shuddered and pulled at her red stripped hair as she began to cry. She curled herself up into a fetal position and quietly said to herself, "Antonio, you're in pain. Your first pain!"

To Be Continued

Cast of Characters
In Alphabetical Order

Joan Amaya	La Reina
Jennifer Castellanos	Lourdes
Jessica Castro	Ana Maria
Lizette Coronado	Cristina
Vincent Cueva	Enzo Crescenti
Vincent Diaz	Anthony Farrell
Frank Fata	Mike Maffasio
Marcos Antonio Gonzalez	Roberto (Bodyguard 1)
Jesus Hernandez	Carlos
Charles Medenilla	Bodyguard 2
Haley O'Berrigan	Debbie
Linda O'Berrigan	Brenda
Ceazar Reyes	Luis
Diana Romero	Mariana
Sara Rosenberg	Teresa

The Sixth Family

Photo Credits

Photography done by Javier Larenas and Ñero
Hair and makeup done by Lisette Valentin
Cover design by Jeffrey McGovern
Interior photos edited by Tyme Girtain

Seeds Of Power

La Gerencia Publications, LLC

Coming soon:

The Sixth Family
Rise To Power

www.lagerenciapublications.com

lagerenciapublications@gmail.com

Find us on:

Facebook: La Gerencia Publications, LLC

Twitter: @LaGerenciaPubli

Google+: Anthony Felicette